The Daughter of the Veil

BRITTANY JOHNSTON

A Conquest Publishing Original

Conquest Publishing

https://conquest-publishing.com

Copyright © 2024 Brittany Johnston

Cover Design: Abigail Baia

Edited by: Siri Mossblad & Brittany McMunn

Map illustration: Victoria Diaz

All rights reserved. No part of this publication may be reproduced, distributed, or transmitted in any form or by any means, including photocopying, recording, or other electronic or mechanical methods, without the prior written permission of the publisher, except in the case of brief quotations embodied in critical reviews and certain other noncommercial uses permitted by copyright law.

Any references to historical events, real people, or real places are used fictitiously. Names, characters, and places are products of the author's imagination.

For the little girl who found a home in reading books and the woman who found a home in writing them.

Pronunciation Guide

Erissa Nierling: eh-RISS-uh NEER-ling
Rhazien Merrick: RAY-zee-in MAIR-ick
Novus Sapphirus: NOH-vuss suh-FEER-uss
Barrett: BEAR-it
Faldeyr: FALL-deer
Vilotta: VYE-lot-uh
Tyrmar: TEAR-mar
Susreene: SUS-reen
Mirielis: MAIR-ee-el-is
Vynoel: VYE-no-el
Esaleia: ES-uh-LAY-uh
Nerivae: NAIR-ih-vay
Kysriene: KISS-ih-REE-neh
Iselica: IS-eh-LEE-suh
Reeva: REE-vuh
Virion: VEER-ee-un
Drurrah: DRUH-er-uh
Draven: DRUH-ay-ven
Yorrith: YOUR-ith
Nephinae: NEH-fih-nay
Tiovriss: TEE-oh-vr-iss
Castian: CAS-tee-in

Berthina: BUR-thee-nuh
Kaellam: KAY-lum
Islone: ISS-lone
Micmus: MICK-mus
Meired: MAY-red
Towin: TOE-win
Thomrynn: TOM-rin
Ysalila: YUH-suh-LEE-luh
Orbas: OR-bass
Tiordan: TEE-or-dan
Imryll: IM-rill
Kyrenic: KYE-ren-ik
Thonalan: THON-uh-lan
Alrithia: al-RITH-ee-uh
Wilidon: WILL-ih-don
Genstine: GEN-steen
Selsula: SELL-soo-luh
Cosasria: KOSS-uh-SREE-uh
Thitelat: THIGH-te-lat
Relreina: REL-ray-nuh
Mr. & Mrs. Abrahms: AB-rahms
Rhynstone: RYN-stone
Carizzea: kuh-RIZ-ee-uh
Higcreas: HIG-kree-us
Cobrias: KO-bree-assMicmus
Dameknaar: DOM-ick-near
Rihpaidir: REE-per-deer
Nayanam: N-EYE-uh-nam
Maharigra: ma-HAY-ree-gruh

The Creator
Seelie: SEE-lee
Unseelie: un-SEE-lee
Zorathi: zor-RAH-thee
The Fefnirion: FEF-neer-ee-un
The Keeper- The God of Darkness: Malcufyre- MAL-kew-FEER
The Goddess of Water- Ezaheira: EH-zuh-HY-ruh
The Goddess of Spirits- Sylbane: SIL-bane
The God of Light- Pierthral: PEER-thrall
The God of Stone- Belfyndar: BEL-fin-dar
The Goddess of Air- Ismenilena: IS-men-ih-LEE-nuh
The God of Time- Reiynfarin: RAIN-fair-in
The Goddess of the Void- Morthyra: MOR-theer-uh

Emberhold: EM-ber-hold

Theanelis: thee-AH-NAY-liss
Eshirene's Wood: eh-SHY-reen's Wood
Orina: oh-REE-nuh
Gailme: GAYL-me
The Violent Wilds: the VYE-oh-lent Wilds
The Crying Grove: the CRY-ing Grove
The Veil: the VAYL
Cropari: crow-PAR-ee
The Waning Tribes: the WAYN-ing Tribes
The Restless Steppes: the REST-less STEPS
Freyborn: FRAY-born
Fate's Pass: FAYT's Pass
Avrenia: ah-VREN-ee-uh
Trilux: TRY-lux
Umirian: oo-MAIR-ee-un
Etelyra's Pass: eh-TEH-lye-ruh's Pass
The Mists: the MISTS
The Remnant of Whispers: the REM-nant of WHIS-pers
Zestiraen: zeh-STEER-ain
The Court of the Thundering Sun: the Court of the THUN-der-ing Sun
Alyneas: ah-LIN-ee-uhs
Agridelon's Pass: AG-ree-de-lon's Pass
The Court of the Flowering Sun: the Court of the FLOW-er-ing Sun
Asyhtheas: ah-SITH-ee-us
Neliladon: neh-LIL-uh-don
The Court of the Hunter's Moon: the Court of the HUN-ter's Moon
Nyllaserin: NILL-ah-SAY-rin
The Court of the Frosted Moon: the Court of the FROST-ed Moon
Niwyth: N-EYE-with

The Deities of Kaidreth

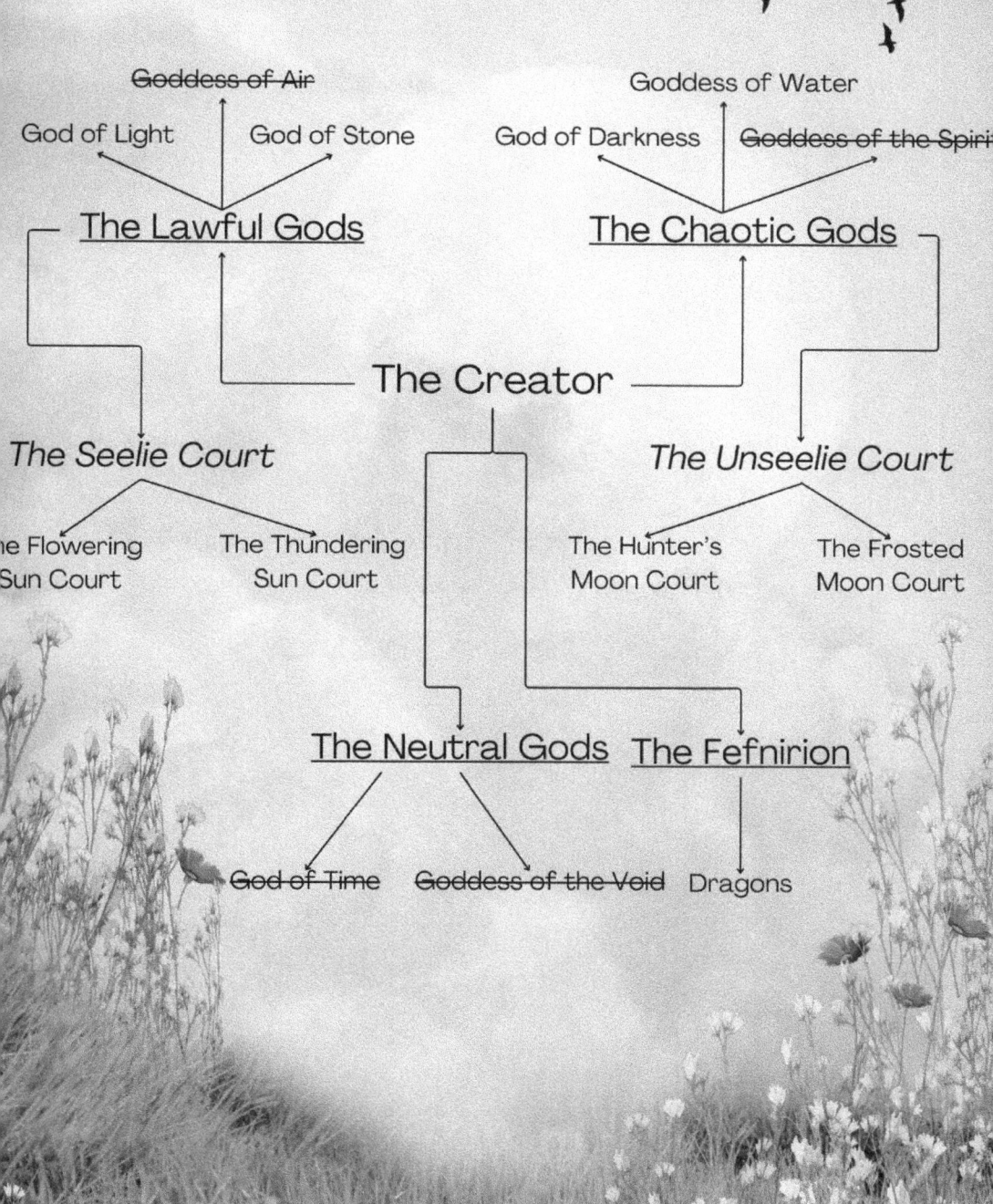

CHAPTER ONE

Erissa hated the voice that lived inside her head almost as much as the room acting as her prison.

It stretched against her consciousness with a lazy squirm. *"Who summons you?"*

She stood by the open window, trying to track the floral, woody scent snaring her attention from the people milling about the streets below. The wind shifted, ruffling the curtains with a frigid gust, and the aroma intensified.

"He calls to you." The voice became insistent. *"We must find him."*

Erissa ignored the low, silvery voice. No one called to her. She remained alone, locked in her room, and forgotten by all those within Emberhold's high walls.

The voice tried again. *"We need to find him. He can help free us."*

How did the voice expect her to leave with the door bolted from the outside and the light of day brightening the room? Even the hidden passageway she stumbled across in her rooms offered no hope of escape during waking hours, with its stone walls connected to the servant hallways. Only the full moon feasts her mother hosted allowed Erissa the opportunity to sneak supplies with all the servants gathered in the main areas of the manor during their duration, and another one would not be held for several weeks. She stood no hope of sneaking about during the day with the keep bustling with the sober activities of life.

The heavy tread of boots echoed down the hall, interrupting her thoughts. Only one man walked with such a singular purpose. Erissa's skin crawled at the sound of her father's steps.

What in the Creator did he need from her? She called for her mother, not him. Moons had passed since he had last come to her chambers, and nothing good ever came from his visits.

The voice hushed her thoughts with a snapped order. *"Hide the passageway."*

Erissa's eyes widened. She grabbed a dress from the dirty pile on the floor as she ran toward the hearth. If her father found the tracks in front of it, all her planning and the weeks of sneaking through the stronghold in the dead of night would be for naught.

She used the fabric to smooth the ash and dirt surrounding the cold stones, hiding the drag marks and footprints from before the grate. It took forever to disturb the dust as the footsteps neared, her heart racing all the while until her stomach threatened to empty.

His boots came closer, the sound almost upon her.

As she finished, Erissa stood, throwing herself into the chair closest to her as the bolt on her door slid free.

"Hide the dress," the voice shouted again when she did not move fast enough. *"Hurry."*

She tightened her hold on the destroyed dress, her breath hitching. Erissa scanned the room with desperate eyes, hunting for somewhere to hide it, finally shoving it behind the decorative pillow at her side.

Her father entered the room, brows drawn with irritation and malice coating his voice. "What have I told you about calling for your mother?"

Erissa fought the desire to flinch from his gaze. She should have known better than to believe her mother would come, but she dared not waste the opportunity to try. Her father already stood by the door with radiating anger. She might as well try to reason with him one last time before executing her plan.

"Try for what reason?" the voice asked. *"Nothing has changed, nor will it. So long as you remain here, they will keep you locked away. You will die in this room."*

Erissa squared her shoulders, ignoring the voice. "My naming day is approaching. I wanted to ask for leave of my ro—"

"No." A snarl darkened her father's ruddy, unforgiving features.

Her shoulders slumped, the desire to stand up to him fading. "You didn't let me finish."

"The answer is always going to be no. You will never leave this room." Her father marched to where she sat, leaning down until his hands rested on either arm of the chair, caging her in. Spittle flew from his clenched teeth, hitting her in the face. "If you haven't learned your lesson by now, I'm more than happy to give you a refresher."

Erissa swallowed the lump rising in her throat. She struggled to draw a deep breath as panic made her vision swim, revulsion souring her stomach. "I didn't mean—"

"Faldeyr, what are you doing?"

Erissa sucked in air as her father shifted from the chair to reveal her uncle standing in the doorway. Barrett had perfect timing. She hoped it would be enough to distract her father from his ire.

She hated when her father surrounded her like that, but more than anything, she hated *him*. Her panic faded into a rage as her father moved away.

Leaning back in the chair, Erissa crossed her arms, a mulish set to her mouth. The scent from earlier lingered in the air. She turned her focus to it as it intensified. She found solace in it, breathing in fresh air as she tried to relax.

"Brother, why are you here?" Faldeyr narrowed his eyes, leaning against the side of the chair. "Shouldn't you be in the courtyard? The blacksmith is due to arrive with the weapons I ordered."

Barrett shrugged as he stood in the door frame. "I'm escorting the maid with her lunch. Your decree doesn't allow for anyone else to let a maid in the room, and I didn't think you were here to deliver Erissa's meal." He stepped inside the room, revealing the girl behind him holding a tray.

A maid, younger than the last, walked with careful steps toward Erissa and balanced the heavy wooden tray. All the calm Erissa had found vanished as quickly as a diaphanous, faceless soul appeared over the girl's shoulder, an echo of her life. It hovered a few inches above the ground, devoid of color, as it stood in shades of gray. Its honeyed tone called out to her, a temptation she struggled to ignore when it came so close.

"No..." Erissa breathed the word on a silent prayer. She closed her eyes, hoping when she opened them again, the soul would be gone from her sight. But she did not have such luck.

"It's time, it's time, it's time." The soul moved around as if eager. Its sightless attention fixed on Erissa. *"Come with me, come with me, come with me."*

Barrett spoke, reaching for her. But Erissa did not hear the words over the pleading of the soul before her. It wrenched at something inside her, and pain blossomed in her chest at the distance between her and it. She wanted to answer its call, wanted to see what lay beyond its words, for the magic within her promised more. It cajoled, promising the pain would end with her acceptance.

"Follow it." The voice pulsed against her mind. *"Follow the soul."*

Erissa clenched her teeth to fight against the soul's pull. She would not follow, would not give in to the dulcet tones and their temptation when nothing but death would follow. If only ignoring it would change the fate its presence promised the poor maid. At least she could warn her.

Erissa stared behind the girl, pointing over her shoulder with a shaking arm. "It's her time. Her soul is there."

The girl's eyes grew fearful. She threw down the tray, food flying all over the entryway, and let out a piercing scream.

When she ran from the room, the soul sagged. It faced Erissa before following the maid with reluctant steps, still beckoning with its incessant call. *"He wakes, he wakes, he wakes."*

She tried to look away, unable to pull her eyes away, fearful of her father's reaction to the magic.

"You will never know your power unless you answer their call." The voice kept trying to entice her. *"What awaits you on the other side of the Veil will free you from your captivity. You need only touch the soul."*

Erissa fought against both voices and pressed her hands over her ears, shaking her head. "Stop. Stop talking to me."

"The gods be damned." Faldeyr turned on her. He looked between his daughter and the corner of the room where metal glinted in the midday sun. "If you can't control that blasted magic, we'll resort to other means."

"I have no hope of controlling something I don't understand." Erissa stood, refusing to cave to the threat or pleas—or anything else. Desperation made her voice quake, but her resolve hardened, her wrists itching as she refused to look at what awaited her in the corner. "If you would but let me leave my rooms, none of the maids would need to cater to me. I could take care of myself."

"And let your abominable magic wreak havoc throughout the city? It's bad enough we can't get a maid to enter your rooms without you declaring they will die. I had to hire this one as an indentured servant off one of the ships from Umirian," Faldeyr snorted, his cruel words poised to inflict more harm. "Besides, you know even less about caring for yourself than you do about controlling your urges."

"Then let me leave. What does it serve keeping me here when no one wants to enter my rooms? I'm not killing them, and still, I carry the blame for their deaths." Erissa stomped her foot against the stone floor. The defiance would cost her dearly, but she did not care. She was tired of this game with her father. "I can go. I could leave Emberhold and never darken your door again."

Faldeyr lunged, wrapping a hand around Erissa's neck and squeezing until she coughed. The panic returned. "Let us get one thing straight, girl. You will never leave this room."

Barrett advanced on them. "Brother—"

"Don't move." Faldeyr shook Erissa's neck like it were nothing more than one of the rag dolls the little girls carried below her window, his eyes never leaving hers. He bent until their noses brushed, spit flicking against her face once more. "I am Lord and Master of Emberhold, and you will obey. She does not leave this room." Faldeyr cut his eyes to his brother, ensuring the message was received. "Is that understood?"

"Yes," Barrett spoke through clenched teeth, his chest heaving with anger at his brother's command. "Now, let her go."

Erissa clawed at her father's hands as they held her firm. White dots blurred her vision, her lungs burning with lack of oxygen, and the concern her father would follow through and kill her this time.

Faldeyr sneered, waiting until Erissa hovered on the precipice of unconsciousness before throwing her to the floor. "Do not make me enter these rooms again."

Erissa coughed, dragging air back into her deprived lungs while her father stormed from the room. Her head ached where it cracked against the floor, but the pain in her chest receded as her breathing evened.

Barrett rushed forward, but Erissa shoved him away from her despite the hurt flashing across his face and deepening the wrinkles fanning out from his sad brown eyes. He did nothing while her father strangled her, and Erissa would not accept his help now that she no longer needed it.

"My star, wait here. I'll fetch some ice from the cellars." He turned to race from the room.

"Don't bother." Erissa's words brought him to a halt. She stood, brushing her fingertips across the bruises already forming around her lithe neck. "I'd no more accept it from you than I would from Father."

Barrett tried to reach for her. "My star—"

Erissa slapped his hand away, anger flushing through her cheeks to spread down her chest and arms. "Don't call me that. I haven't been your star in a long time, Uncle. Why do you still try to keep up the pretense? You're no better than my parents, but at least they no longer pretend to care."

An uncomfortable silence sat between them. Erissa wanted Barrett to contradict her words—to fight for her. He did neither. His shoulders slumped as he turned for the door, appearing as defeated as Erissa had become after being locked away for so long.

He stopped before reaching the doorway, turning to look at her one last time. "Things will be different someday, my star. I'm trying to find a way to make it so. Don't give up hope."

Erissa rolled her eyes as he left the room. They were easy words for him to say with his ability to live freely. She rubbed at the scars across her wrists, the tight skin itching beneath her flush of irritation.

No freedom existed for her, but her uncle remained right about one thing. It would be different soon. She needed to use the passageway once more on the morrow. Getting into her father's study would see her caught, but someone in the lower market had to sell maps with the docks being so close to its stalls. And once she had a map, Erissa could leave once and for all. But she would not wait for the next moon day feast. The voice spoke reason. Her father would kill her if she remained in this room.

CHAPTER TWO

Two souls whispered.

"Guide us, guide us, guide us."
"It's time, it's time, it's time."

The lingering, soft caress of the words cut across the pandemonium of the morning market. They were unexpected among the boisterous sounds of people hawking wares.

Erissa faltered when the voices reached her. Almost dropping the basket she carried, her breath misted in the cold air as she uttered a curse. She lost track of the warm, spiced scent she had followed. The enticing aroma of cedar and jasmine had drawn her into the middle of the market, distracting her from finding a stall selling maps to those fresh off the incoming ships.

"Answer the call." The voice clawed at her mind, begging her to listen. *"Destiny awaits us in the Veil."*

Erissa tried to ignore the voice as it blended with her own thoughts. Only moments before, it begged her to follow the scent and look where that got her. Not only did Erissa not have the map she needed to flee the confines of her prison, but now she had lingered long enough to find two unfortunate souls bound for death.

A familiar dread circled within her breast. It was a ravenous, unyielding pull as her eyes searched across the vast market for the souls only visible to her.

The souls were faceless but not without names as they hovered behind their corporeal forms. Echoes of the man and woman they stood behind, their forms translucent, containing featureless faces distorted against the light of day.

Whispered words from the souls continued to reach her.

"He wakes, he wakes, he wakes."

"You are needed. You are needed. You are needed."

Tears threatened to overwhelm Erissa as she stared at the couple, a queasiness settling in her stomach.

A merchant's wife stood behind a stall with several bolts of cloth draped across her arm. Mrs. Abrahms, a handsome woman with strong, angular features and graying hair, had the height of a giant next to her squat, balding husband as he haggled with a potential customer, pointing to the wares his wife held. Nothing about her appearance spoke of illness or old age. She should have had time. But Erissa knew Mrs. Abrahms's life would reach its limit.

When Mrs. Abrahms caught Erissa's stricken gaze, her pained expression had the woman glancing over her shoulder, trying to see what held the girl's attention. Her brow arched at finding nothing behind her.

The early light would have been sure to catch the distinct glow of Erissa's violet eyes, making her identity unmistakable. She made the mistake of coming to the market at the busiest time, thinking the deep hood of her cloak would protect her. She permitted the event with her father to provoke her into acting without thought, and now she paid for the mistake.

Erissa winced as realization turned Mrs. Abrahm's face white. A shudder went through her, the bolts tumbling into the mud as she dropped to her knees, wailing in despair and drawing the curiosity of a growing crowd.

Mr. Abrahms reached for his wife, startled by her behavior. He followed his wife's finger as her arm outstretched and pointed to Erissa. His knees buckled under the weight of her gaze. The corners of his mouth dipped in resignation. "It's time then."

Silence blanketed the market, all eyes darting between the cloaked Erissa, the cloth merchant, and his wife.

Erissa nodded once, struggling not to choke on the words she needed to say. It never came easier. "For both of you."

Gusts of wind grew about the streets, their icy chill hinting at the rain to come. The wind plastered Erissa's cloak against her legs, whipping the blue wool and streaming it behind her, the hood dislodging with the movement. She shifted her basket and tried to tug her cloak around her face, failing as another strong spurt of cold air tunneled through the marketplace.

An audible gasp came from the gathered townspeople, the sound ricocheting around the vast market when they spotted her incandescent eyes framed by delicate features and soft midnight curls. A stone pendant dangled from a silver choker, the amethyst stone enhancing the matching color of her eyes. Several people ran from the market, terrified cries following in their wake.

Mr. Abrahms cooed to his wife, trying in vain to soothe her anguish as the crowd murmured around them.

Erissa tightened her grip on the basket as the townspeople backed away from her. She flinched as most gaped in fear. Some eyed her with sorrow, their down-turned faces a copy of hers as they backed away. Others condemned her with hatred in their eyes.

Erissa understood why they blamed her for the inevitable deaths that had followed her from a tender age. She blamed herself, too. But even with their anger, they were wary of approaching. The people removed themselves from her path as if it might save them from her sight.

The blacksmith's son pushed to the front of the crowd. Drenched with sweat, the stained fabric of his apron clung to his chest. He looked around the square for what ensnared the agitated crowd's attention and found a woman standing off to the side. She looked lost, her features tight with pain.

"What's happening, Rhazien?" Tyrmar followed his son, wiping an arm across his forehead to remove the beads of moisture from his brow.

Rhazien grimaced at the feel of grime across his golden skin. Even in the dead of winter, the temperature of the forge burned the crisp air from inside the stone walls.

People exchanged glances, holding their tongues, and Rhazien thought it an odd reaction to the raven-haired beauty. Nothing about her screamed intimidation. In fact, he thought she might collapse as fear radiated from her so strongly he could taste it.

"You're new here, are you not?" An older man had pity on them, seeing the confusion mar his face. "She's cursed. It's best not to draw her attention. You never know what she might see."

An elderly woman appeared next to Rhazien. She gripped his arm to steady herself, and he cringed as if her hands were made of ice. The sensation reached deep, colder still than the surrounding wind.

Her words carried on the wind when she spoke. "That's the lord's girl. Death isn't far behind once she sees something over your shoulder."

"A witch?" Tyrmar paled, turning worried eyes to the old woman.

Rhazien understood his father's worry. The girl's eyes glowed violet with magic as she stared toward the merchant and his wife. It was magic his parents thought they would not find in the Southern half of Kaidreth with their superstitions and bigotry toward anyone with powers.

The old woman shook her head. "As good as, but not quite. The girl is something more. Something older. Wilder. Darker. The girl sees the souls of those fated to pass. They call to her." She turned her scarred, milky eyes to Rhazien and smiled in amusement. Her stare disturbed him—like she sensed how he recoiled when he took in the webbed damage across her face and delighted in his reaction. "Lord Faldeyr had her locked away. It's been years now, but the staff talk, and many a maid has died working in the lord's manor. Fear guides his actions. He fears what she will see next and the actions of the damned who follow her. Those who crave her power from beyond the Veil."

Rhazien tracked the younger woman's movements. The aroma of honeysuckle and tea assailed him the closer she came, making him feel drunk on the heady fragrance.

His arm rose, reaching for her as she passed in a rush. The unmistakable desire to follow her hit him. It only grew stronger as her emotions flooded through him, the intense feeling of her fear weakened his knees. But even through her fear, her undeniable presence carried the familiarity of an old friend and the intoxication of a new love.

"Pretty thing, isn't she?" The old woman's question brought his arm to a halt, his embarrassment darkening the warm quartz skin.

The girl hesitated before reaching the husband and wife. He contemplated the pain flashing across her features, wariness dimming her eyes, even as a resilient strength radiated while she kept walking. Her cloak fell around the graceful lines of her fuller figure. The wind caught the ends and twisted them around her feet. A lock of hair slipped free, tumbling over her shoulder and falling to her waist.

He battled the urge to walk to her and tuck the strand behind her ear. "What's her name?"

"Erissa." The old woman's smile faded into a raspy melody as she sang. Her voice unnerved the uneasy crowd.

Only Rhazien remained unaffected, ignoring the way the townspeople reacted like children clutching at wet nurses. He wanted no part of it, lost in his desire to follow the beauty and comfort her.

"Beware what lies behind the patterned wall,
—the forewarner of death.
For there is no way for one to stall,
—'til only bones are left.
Her violet eyes are in their thrall,
—even she cannot escape,
The destiny that dooms us all,
—and the world she will reshape..."

The raven-haired woman fled with the old woman's words. Rhazien tracked her movements, staring after her with curiosity rather than pity or fear. His feet shifted in her direction.

"Back to work, son." Tyrmar clapped a hand on his shoulder.

While Rhazien's father worried about their workload and wanted to make significant headway in the forge today, Rhazien did not care. The girl possessed his every thought. The desire to follow her became stronger, and he made to follow after her.

His father grabbed his arm, impatience coloring his tone. "We have orders waiting."

With slow, reluctant steps, Rhazien turned toward the forge and tried to shake the feeling he made a grave mistake by not following her.

Mud squelched and splashed against the hem of Erissa's cloak and dress, her shoes a hopeless mess. She hurried to leave the market. The noise echoed in the tense quiet, broken only by the hopelessness of Mrs. Abrahms's sobs.

With no choice but to go past them to leave the square, she turned her head, at a loss to meet the distraught gaze of Mr. Abrahms as he failed to comfort his wife.

The faceless souls reached for her when she passed, her steps slowing. Their words fought to consume her with their siren song.

"Take us, take us, take us."

"Hold us, hold us, hold us."

The voice rose inside of her, tracing along her thoughts. *"Give in. You cannot imagine what awaits you when you do. Give in, Erissa."*

Erissa ground her teeth against the desire to sink into the seductive words. They feathered across her skin and reached inside to grip her own soul, blending with the call. Both touched her. Their feelings were warm and comforting rather than cold or restrained. Their peacefulness called to her innermost parts, terrifying her and making her fear what lay beyond.

"Find us, find us, find us."

"Free us, free us, free us."

Hoping to out-pace the tones and the thoughts that lay alongside her own, Erissa ignored them and quickened her pace to leave the square. All thoughts of finding a map at one of the many stalls were forgotten as she moved into the city's heart. Desperation drove her on as she lost sight of her surroundings and grew closer to the walled keep.

Guards came running, two of the fleeing townspeople trying to keep pace behind them. They caught sight of Erissa and ran straight toward her.

One guard separated from the group, circling behind her as the three others closed in on every side. "We don't want to hurt you, m'lady. Come back with us. We want no trouble from the lord."

Tears flooded Erissa's eyes. She had failed. All her planning over the last year, and she had failed because of those gods' forsaken souls. Her head hung, and she allowed the guard behind her to grab her upper arm and lead her back toward the keep.

Walking toward the ornately bejeweled inner gate, her focus lay caught between what had happened in the market, what awaited her in the prison of her room, and the sight before her as the breathtaking gates came into view.

The imposing structures were encrusted with gems of all sizes; blue, purple, and orange hues sparkled like the deepest of sunsets. The stone structure behind the gate towered over the town as it rose by several floors. It appeared more castle than keep, with large stones carved in swirling, intricate patterns and pieces of amethyst twinkling like stars among the designs. The detailed lines demanded attention, moving against the rock and coming alive as they twisted and turned, flowering vines climbing across walls and over windows. The dancing elements called to her as profoundly as the souls. She barely remembered the gates from her youth, and what she did remember resembled nothing of what lay in front of her.

Erissa stopped, the guard halting with her. She looked at him and the others surrounding them to see if anyone else noticed the movement across the stones. Everyone else moved about their business, oblivious to the dancing lines. She turned her attention back to the walls as the guard dragged her along. How did no one notice the stones?

As Erissa approached the manor gates, her hood sagged down her back. The guards stiffened upon seeing her flanked by two of their own.

The taller of the two addressed her with familiarity. "Erissa! What have you done? You can't be beyond your room. Do you have no care for what your father will do when he finds out about this?"

Erissa tore her gaze from the pulsing walls, realizing her uncle stood with the other soldier. "Uncle Barrett." Defiance radiated from her. He would expect an apology, but she refused to give him one.

Her uncle waved them away. "Let her go. I'll see to her."

The guards on either side dropped her arms and left, leaving her in her uncle's care.

Barrett rubbed a hand over his weary eyes at her silence. "Come. I'll take you back to your room, and you can tell me how you snuck out."

Erissa hesitated, not wanting to surrender her only chance at freedom despite what had happened earlier. Guilt echoed inside her head. She needed an excuse for sneaking out. If they learned she had no plans to return, it would make things worse. While Barrett always tried to shield her from the worst of her father's reactions, it never worked.

"I only wanted to walk through the market. Seeing it through the window every day… it's torture. It's been so long since I've left the manor. Father acts like I'm a curse against his people. He can't keep me locked away forever."

No matter what she told herself, it never stopped feeling like all the fault lay with her—like she somehow caused the deaths herself—and her father did not help matters. She tried to remind herself she held no responsibility for the Abrahms' inevitable deaths.

But more than that, she hoped her uncle would believe her lie. If he were to learn her true purpose in being at the market, her father's wrath would make the gods' vengeance appear as nothing more than child's play.

"I needed to get out. Father is growing worse. I want to be free, not hidden behind stone walls, haunted by what might happen."

Barrett lifted an armored hand to her shoulder and squeezed, trying to steer his niece forward. His kind face softened with sympathy, belying the growing panic in his voice. "I've known your father my entire life. It comes with being his older brother." He winked as if trying to defuse the tension and elicit a smile but had no such luck. "If I can tell him how you snuck out and fix it, he'll go easier on you. Maybe even give you a little more freedom. But we need to head inside. Quickly."

The voice slithered into her mind once more. *"If you would only give into the call, you will find freedom from your sorrows. Don't you want to be free?"*

"We both know that isn't true. You've never stayed Father's hand. Why should I believe you would now?" Erissa pushed his hand from her shoulder, shoving him hard enough the older man tripped over his own feet and walked away. Better to get it over with. No matter her father's reaction, it would only give her more time to devise another plan. "I can't live like this anymore. I'll be one and twenty years in a matter of weeks. If he won't release me from these walls, I'll find my own way to do it."

"Erissa!"

She ignored Barrett as he called after her.

"My star, come back. Let's go through the servant's entrance in the back so we don't run into your father." Barrett tried again. He regained his balance and made to follow her but stumbled back in alarm.

As Erissa walked through the gates, the stones flared, smoldering against the gold metal that outlined them. Flames bled outward from the patterns covering the stones to lick along the filigree of the gates.

"Erissa!" Barrett shouted.

The second guard tripped as he retreated in crippling fear, falling hard to his backside while still trying to scoot away.

It ended as quickly as it had begun, with the outline of the gate ringed in soot. Barrett gazed after his niece in horror. "The spell... it's broken. Gods save us all. He'll come for her now."

The voice inside of her head laughed.

"What utter rubbish. You're trying to scare me, nothing more. I won't believe anything you say." Erissa straightened her spin, holding her head with a stubborn refusal to concede to anyone. She ignored her uncle and marched toward the manor entrance, her eyes fixed ahead. Any delay would only worsen what was to come.

She jumped as someone grabbed her arm and whipped her around. She had little time to recognize her uncle's face before he knocked the basket from her arms and flipped her over his shoulder.

Shock took over for a moment, and she allowed him to carry her, but it did not last long as Erissa kicked and flailed against the older man, still fit despite his age. "What are you—Uncle Barrett! Put me down!"

"I'm sorry, Erissa. I really am, but I have no choice." His arms tightened around her like steel as she kicked and twisted. All work stopped in the courtyard as Barrett carried his niece to the guarded double-door entrance. No patterns were on the stones, the thick, lined planks decorated with an intricate iron moon and sun, two halves creating a whole. The design glowed as Barrett approached with Erissa. "Open the door."

The guards shifted, hesitating to do as Barrett demanded with their young lady struggling against his shoulder. He growled at the delay, tightening his grip and hoisting Erissa higher. "Open the damn door. Now!"

"Put. Me. Down!" Erissa screamed against his back as the door opened, her hands beating against his bronze armor.

Barrett turned to the soldier on his left, authority dripping from his person. "Go find her father." He strode to the spiral staircase centered in the foyer and tossed the words to the remaining soldier, shifting his grip as she tried to kick him. "You! Get three other guards and come to her room."

Erissa clung to his waist as he took the stairs two at a time. Her movements stilled, the fast pace threatening to overwhelm her stomach. Tears gathered in her eyes. "You can't do this. It makes you no better than Father."

Barrett hurried down the corridor to the room at the end. Once inside, he eased Erissa from his shoulder and placed her on the bed. "I'm not doing this lightly. It's for your protection."

"Protection from what? What's so bad that I'm to be locked in this room night and day?"

"You'll have to ask your father. It's not my place." He walked to the door, giving instructions to the guards who came running. "I want four guards on this door at all—" The door closed against his retreating as Barrett left the room.

Erissa considered the room that had become her prison. Large enough for two, the bed held a confection of creams and pinks. The decor around the space reflected the bed, childish colors repeating in the chairs before the stone fireplace, the wardrobe, the rugs, and the tapestries. Everything was pink or cream. She hated it all.

Erissa climbed off the bed and paced. The size of the room fed her anger as she met a wall on each side. She avoided the far corner between the bed frame and the fireplace. But with each step that brought her closer to what lay in the darkened area, the sweat along her brow thickened.

The corner's contents mocked her as her chest flamed against the visceral goading of her emotions. Erissa moved her gaze anywhere but to that space, darting from furnishing to furnishing and color to color as her wrists itched. The sickly sweet combination of colors grated on her nerves, her temper building as she passed the chairs flanking the hearth.

Grabbing the pillows from them, she marched to the open window and threw them out. She grabbed the tapestries from the wall, rolled the rugs up, and ripped the linens on the bed. Each went out the window, littering the courtyard below.

Studying the work of her tantrum, she screamed with frustration. "I am not a child!"

Work stopped in the courtyard, all eyes turning to the sound as they watched the furnishings fly from the tower. Erissa's breath came in ragged bursts, masking the unmistakable steps of someone entering the room.

CHAPTER THREE

"Then stop acting like a child." Faldeyr opened Erissa's door, the wood cracking against the stone wall. He stomped forward with jerky movements, a scowl darkening his features.

Erissa's eyebrows drew together in irritation as her father entered the room, her mother a step behind. "The only person being childish is you, Father."

"This is only for your safety." He wiped a hand across his face, the motion reminiscent of his brother, but it lacked the weariness of Barrett's actions, with only his anger standing out against his set mouth.

"From what?" Erissa asked, hating how he kept up pretenses in front of her mother. Safety had nothing to do with locking her away when he challenged it with his every action against her. "What is there to say that justifies all you've done?"

"Faldeyr, it's time she learns. At least some of it." Vilotta tugged on her husband's tunic sleeve, drawing him to the chair before the fire.

Erissa stood before them, arms crossed and her foot tapping a fast rhythm.

"There are things we must tell you. Things about the power you hold, about who you are. Your power is..." Vilotta's brow wrinkled while she searched for the right word. "Coveted. There are those who seek it for themselves. Not only among the humans but among the magical realm as well."

"Your powers grew too fast when you were little, too noticeable. We didn't know how to protect you." Faldeyr rested his forearms against his knees, head hanging. "We went to the witches for help."

"There was one I trusted more than anyone," Vilotta said. "She cast spells on the outer walls and gate to hide you from those who sought your magic."

Faldeyr sighed, lifting his head, his eyes locked on the chains bolted to the room's far corner wall. "You're so stubborn and wouldn't listen. You kept trying to sneak out. We did what we had to by locking you in here."

"You chained me!" Erissa gestured to the chains lying in the corner of the room.

His cold eyes turned to his daughter. "And I would do it again." His rage carried through the room, but Faldeyr's gaze flicked quickly in his wife's direction as if remembering her presence and the role he needed to play. "You forced my hand," he added, "and you needed to be protected."

Erissa's anger grew with each word her parents spoke, her ears flushing under the heat of her ire. She longed to slap the words from his mouth every time he declared her responsible for his actions.

Ignoring her father, she turned to address her mother. "What powers? I see the souls of those fated soon to die, and they talk to me. That's it. My gift is no more than a curse."

Vilotta shifted to stand before her daughter. Her fingers moved to graze Erissa's throat, where a choker lay intertwined with an amethyst stone. She stopped short of touching it when Erissa flinched back. The distance her daughter placed between them pained her mother, the emotion easy for Erissa to see as it hollowed her face. But Erissa steeled herself against it. Her mother earned a lack of consideration.

Vilotta's fingertips ran through the air parallel to the dark stone. "Do you remember when we gifted you this?"

Erissa took another step away from her mother's hand. "What does my necklace have to do with anything?"

"We gave it to you on your seventh year," Vilotta said.

Erissa narrowed her eyes. "I remember vividly. It was the day you locked me inside."

"We had no choice." Faldeyr's words were gruff, lacking in emotion. They rang hollow. "You don't remember all the events of that day. We had the witch block most of them to keep you from repeating what happened."

"A witch?" Erissa's arms dropped to her side. "I don't understand."

"The year you turned seven, the wasting fever hit our borders. It was confined to the outer villages and hadn't yet made its way here. We believed ourselves safe behind our walls. We held a grand celebration for your naming year." Faldeyr hung his head, his eyes downcast and heavy, shame radiating off him as he played the part of a loving father in front of Erissa's mother. "It was foolish of us."

Erissa snorted at his display, catching sight of his eyes narrowing with the noise. What did it matter if she displeased him now? Hell would be paid for sneaking out, no matter her disrespect.

Vilotta, constantly lapping at the false humility of her husband, hurried to Faldeyr's side and leaned to wrap an arm around him. He indulged the gesture, patting her arm before she continued where Faldeyr left off.

"The entire town was there, from the oldest to the youngest, but you didn't pay them any attention. Instead, you went up behind dozens of townspeople and talked like someone else was standing there. It was funny at first, almost as if you were having a laugh. Then you started dancing."

Her parents shared a glance of remembrance. Vilotta moved to the window, talking over her shoulder. "You grabbed hands with thin air and twirled around in a wide circle like you were dancing with a crowd. The wind picked up speed around you, the current visible as it spun faster and faster. Flowering vines erupted from the ground and grew until they twisted into a canopy above where you spun. They spread around you, snaking through the village and climbing walls and houses until everything lay covered."

"You were laughing. Singing. The people were terrified. Everyone panicked and tried to flee but couldn't because of the plants covering everything." Faldeyr flexed his fingers, a frown tugging at his mouth. "The cleanup was a nightmare."

"Your father and I... you hid behind the vines, scaring us to no end." Vilotta used her sleeve to wipe at dry eyes. "We screamed your name. Tried in vain to get your attention. It took half the guard to break through the vines. By the time we reached you, the dancing had stopped. You were sitting on the ground, talking to no one like nothing strange happened."

Erissa's eyes narrowed. "You locked me away for most of my life. Everything you did to me... it was all because I spun air and made flowers?"

"Every one of those people *died*, Erissa." Her mother placed her hands on her hips, her eyes begging Erissa to understand. "Dozens of men, women, and children. No one you talked to that day survived. Not even an hour after that, the wasting—"

"I already know this. The people died. Everyone dies after I see their soul. But I'm not killing anyone, and you know that. The fever stole their lives, not my magic." What little remained of Erissa's patience thinned with every word, her breath growing labored. "And nothing you've said warrants the treatment I received from you."

"The townspeople became terrified of you. It didn't matter that each of those who died was already showing symptoms and didn't know it; they were still scared they would be next." Vilotta wrung her hands. "But there was more to what guided our actions. You were vulnerable. We had no choice. It's better to have everyone fear you than coveting your magic. If they fear you because they think you're responsible for the deaths, you're safer, and we can keep you sheltered within these walls."

Erissa stamped her foot on the ground, fisting her hands as she spun to face her mother. "You keep saying that. You had no choice. But you had every choice. You chose to lock me away, chose to treat me as you did, to allow others to treat me as they did. All because I made people afraid? You chose them over your own daughter and made sure no one would help me when you locked me away." She flung her hand, gesturing at her father. "You did nothing to stop what he did to me, allowing him to chain me to the wall and worse!"

"It was never about choosing them," said Faldeyr. "You wouldn't stay within the manor walls. No matter what we tried, you were always sneaking out. For your mother's sake, I did everything possible to keep you safe. We had to use the chains when everything else failed." Faldeyr's words dripped with sincerity, but steel hovered behind the honey-covered placation, making his words ring false.

Vilotta took a step toward her daughter. "There was no protecting you with that kind of power. The people became so afraid of you, and we didn't know what they would try to do to you, Erissa. There was little else for us to do between their reaction and others desiring to take your power for themselves. We had to seek the Fae witch's help. No one else was powerful enough to hide you or your magic. She placed spells on the manor and the gate, connecting it to the stone of your pendant. Your power makes you a target, not only to him but also to others...." Vilotta paled with her words, realizing what she had given away. Faldeyr ran to her as she swayed, catching her before she fell.

Erissa didn't miss her mother's slip. Ignoring the rest, she focused on a single word. "Him? Who are you talking about?"

"You broke the spell when you snuck out. The spells embedded in the stones were connected to the gate. So long as the pendant stayed behind the gate, you were safe. I don't know how you found a crack in the magic, but I'll make sure you can never use it again." Vilotta's eyes went wild, hysteria taking over as the words tumbled from her. "He thinks you died that day, Erissa. I convinced him you died of the fever along with everyone else, but now that the spells are broken, he can find you through your power. If you had stayed in the manor, the spells would have held. You should never have been unchained—you should never have left."

Faldeyr ushered a distressed Vilotta to the door. His face crinkled with worry about the toll the conversation took on her.

"Who are you talking about?" Erissa attempted to remove the anger from her voice, her hands reaching out with her pleading words. "Mother, I'm begging you. Tell me who he is. Tell me where these powers come from. I promise to stay inside the manor. Please. I'm your daughter. Don't do this to me. Don't stand by and pretend I'm protected here. I'm dying behind these walls, Mother. Please, don't leave me here."

Barrett stood waiting at the door as they approached. Faldeyr pressed his wife into his brother's arms. Vilotta relied on his support, but Erissa's uncle hesitated, his gaze locking on hers. A frown darkened his features.

"Take my wife to her chambers, brother." Faldeyr's voice cracked like a whip when the other man hesitated. "Now."

Erissa thought her mother a weak person as Barrett escorted her down the hall. She crumbled when confronted with the reality of Erissa's turmoil, leaving her to deal with the fallout from her father. And her uncle? She had never understood his role in all this.

A storm brewed beneath Faldeyr's features when he faced her, turning them cruel. A different man stood before Erissa with her mother gone from the room. "I won't have you upsetting your mother further. I don't know how you made it past the gates with every door but the main entrance sealed off. You can rest assured I will find out. You'll stay within these walls."

Erissa rolled her eyes despite the consequences. A soul-weary tiredness gripped her, and she struggled to maintain any semblance of respect. "Until what? I'm one and thirty years? One and forty?"

"Don't test me again on this, girl." Faldeyr spat at Erissa's feet. "I've stayed my hand a long time for your mother's sake. I don't want to use the chains again or do anything else that might upset her, but I will if you push me to it."

"I won't tolerate being locked in this room anymore. Father—" The brutal impact from the back of his hand against her face silenced the rest of Erissa's words. She staggered from the blow, bringing a hand to cup her stinging cheek.

"You will call me no such thing. I may pretend for your mother's sake, but it stops there. The day I agreed to your mother's scheme to have you is one I will always regret." Faldeyr circled her, his voice low and full of malice. "Know this, girl. You are nothing to me beyond a thorn I wish to rid myself of, and accidents can happen at any moment. The love I have for your mother extends only so far. I've protected you all these years only because of her, but I will not allow you to take over our lives and ruin them any more than you already have. If you leave these rooms, you will not come back alive."

With Faldeyr's threat hanging between them, he stalked from the room, slamming the door behind him. The sound of a key grating against the lock's metal reverberated through the quiet.

Her father's muffled voice instructed the soldiers. "No one is allowed in or out of this room unless accompanied by myself or my brother. This includes my wife and any maid."

Erissa fell to the ground, too stunned to cry. Her father had not always been this way. A time existed when she believed he loved her, the old memories stinging as harshly as his slap had, but that love had changed over the years until he no longer wished to hear her call him by any term of endearment.

Erissa had been at his mercy for longer than she had known his love. She remained unaware whether her mother understood the full extent of what passed between father and daughter, but the rest of the manor knew. The maids were forced to take care of her after one of Faldeyr's fits of anger. Erissa had never spoken of the violence she received from his hand, unsure if her mother would even believe such a thing of her beloved husband.

None of that mattered now, with Erissa doubled over against the stone floor. She remained there for the rest of the day, replaying the conversation, trying to find answers to what both parents had revealed—to find some glimmer of hope.

Erissa lay unaware of the passing time, only realizing the late hour when her door opened and revealed her uncle holding a tray of food.

Barrett placed the tray on a table between the chairs before crouching in front of her. "Erissa, come. You need to eat."

She did not move, refusing to make eye contact. Her violet eyes focused on the door. He tried again. "It won't be forever. I'll make sure of it. I won't stop searching until we can keep you safe beyond these walls. Safe from your father." He stood when she did not respond. "Eat something. Your mother will worry if you don't. I'll light the fire before I leave."

"No—leave it unlit. I'll light it when I get cold."

He paused at her tone. "Erissa, making yourself miserable won't change anything. Your father gave permission for fire and food. It's freezing in here, and you're still wearing your cloak. A little heat and food will do you good."

"That's not what I'm doing." She scrambled to come up with something to say. "I... I want it cold. It helps me sleep better. With the warmer under the sheets and the cold air on my face." She finally stood. Shaking her legs, she dispelled the cramps that had taken hold. She moved to stand before the hearth, blocking it from his view. "Uncle, please. I promise I'll eat, but I need to be alone."

He eyed the welt across her cheek. "My little star...."

"I want you to leave." Erissa's words snapped with anger.

Barrett relented, walking to the door. "We'll find another way. I promise you this."

She refused to speak, nodding her answer. When the door closed, she exhaled, a plan forming.

With her uncle gone, she went and grabbed the empty bag hidden at the back of her wardrobe under a pile of old clothing and added several plain dresses and toiletries. That done, Erissa sat down to devour the steaming soup. She wrapped the bread, cheese, and fruit in a torn cloth and placed it in her bag. With her preparations completed, she turned to face the cold hearth.

Resignation straightened her spine. "They can't leave me locked in this room for the rest of my life. I won't stand for it anymore."

"None of this will matter if you answer the song of the Veil." The voice returned to her head.

Ignoring it, Erissa took hold of the steel fire rod. She hooked it into the grate and pulled with all her strength. It groaned as she moved it inch by inch with painstaking care to avoid making any noise that might alert the guards outside her door.

When enough space opened between the pit and the back wall, she slipped through them. A push against the wall revealed a door hiding a darkened stairwell. Using the rod, she dragged the pit back into place, leaned over it to replace the rod, and grabbed the bag from the floor.

Facing the stairs, Erissa faltered momentarily before resolve hardened her will. She refused to die in this room. And she harbored no doubt that is what her future held if she remained.

After taking in the room for the last time, Erissa walked through the doorway and into the awaiting darkness.

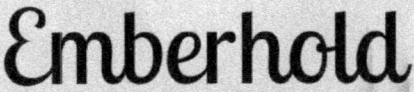

Emberhold

Barrett
Brother to Faldeyr

Faldeyr
Lord of Emberhold

Vilotta
Lady of Emberhold

Erissa

CHAPTER FOUR

Barrett placed a steadying hand against the dark wood of his niece's door, his fingers brushing the cold metal of the bolt. He commissioned it after the third time Erissa picked the original lock, using it to seal her fate all those years ago. The pain of that day ripped a hole in his heart, and try as he might to summon something—anything—to fill the hollow ache; nothing came close.

A shudder crept its way up his spine as another piece of him died when he slid the bolt home with ease. Part of him savored the sensation. He deserved every moment that haunted his soul for the role he played in her imprisonment. They all did—his brother and Vilotta included.

The desire to linger at Erissa's door tempted him. His second in command had proven himself reliable in the past when he struggled to leave her door. The guard would pass a productive night under his second's order. Besides, if Barrett stayed, his shadow interrupting the light spilling from the lamps on either side of her door, Erissa might not feel so alone.

With his mind made up, Barrett turned to the soldier stationed by the stairway, intending to call for his second. The words failed to leave his tongue as the soft tapping of leather soles echoed down the hallway.

Vilotta rounded the corner, breaking into a run, her gaze catching his. A delighted smile dimpled her rosy cheeks, bringing a youthful glow that reminded him of the young woman his brother had brought home so many years ago. "I hoped to find you here."

Barrett wanted nothing more than to slap the sparkle from her face.

His heart lay in tatters, his conscience shredding what little remained. Yet, there stood his sister-in-law, the girl's own mother, full of life while her child suffocated under their extreme restrictions.

His face must have given away more than he thought, for Vilotta stopped short of touching him, clutching her hands against her chest. "Are you well, brother?"

Barrett's hand twitched with another urge for violence. He settled for rubbing at the frown, deepening the years, wrinkling his brow. "How can I be?"

"Come." Vilotta linked their arms. "Let's take tea in my sitting room. Erissa needs her privacy, and a warm drink will soothe you."

She tugged at his arm when he did not move.

Barrett forced himself to take a step at the bequest of her guiding touch. He swallowed the hard lump of guilt, making his every breath labored with each step he took away from the door. "Shouldn't you be more concerned with soothing your daughter?"

Vilotta dropped his arm as they entered her sitting room. "Do we need to do this every time Erissa is disobedient?"

Three young girls prepared a pot of tea, setting out a tiered tray of petite sugary cakes and other delicacies on the gilded table surrounding the elegant furniture.

Vilotta walked over to the settee next to the servants and perched on its edge, her hands outstretched and waiting. "We can't let Erissa continue to dictate our lives. I'm tired of fighting about her."

He watched the girls cater to their mistress, giving her a porcelain plate. They were the same ones who prepared Erissa's thin soup and small piece of bread. The fruit and cheese had come from his own meal. Barrett's stomach turned as he compared it to the cake her mother nibbled. "The cost of the imported sugar used to make those cakes would feed a family of six for several months, Vi, and it certainly would cover adding meat to Erissa's meal. She needs a hearty stew on a cold night, not a thin broth with a few wilted vegetables."

"Must you ruin my appetite?" Vilotta sighed, placing her half-eaten cake on the table. "A lesser meal will help lower her weight. She's growing thicker about the waist with her idle lifestyle. Besides, she's lucky Faldeyr is allowing food at all."

"Idle lifestyle? Is that what we're calling it?" The thought of Erissa eating like a peasant while her mother feasted on costly desserts pushed Barrett's temper to its limit. He stormed forward and slapped the plate from her hands. "Who are you, Vilotta? Are you really the same woman who journeyed through the Mists and begged the Fae King to give you the child you treat like shit?"

Vilotta's smile faltered, her nostrils flaring as she breathed deeply. She gave a curt nod at the girls, and only once they left the room did she address him with measured patience that left his skin crawling.

"You're overstepping, brother. The older Erissa gets, the more she reminds me of you." Vilotta smoothed her hands across her skirts, her mouth pinched. "You're both filled with righteous vinegar, but while she lacks understanding, you know why Faldeyr and I have taken such drastic actions to keep her safe."

"Nothing Faldeyr has done brings that child's safety. You know it as well as I do." Barrett seethed, his teeth clenched. "At least I have the excuse of my vow's magic. What I cannot understand is why you support him in his abuse of that child—of your child!"

"Gods be damned, you were there, Barrett. You were there when the Fae witch said Erissa was the child of the prophecy. I won't hand her over, not when she can be used to change so much for our station. Erissa must be kept from the Unseelie at all costs." Vilotta stood, pacing the room. A wild look entered her eyes with her patience gone. "No matter what those costs are. That is the oath you swore."

"And what did I swear it for, Vi?" Barrett clenched his fists. "No one has come for the girl. What validity does the witch's prophecy have when season after season passes with nothing? How long are we going to torture Erissa this way?"

"You know how this all pains me. I can't even visit with her because seeing her suffering leaves me unable to sleep at night." Vilotta stopped her pacing, a pout overtaking her face as she placed her hands on her hips and whined. "Why, it took four glasses of wine to stop feeling guilty the last time I entered her room. Can you try to sympathize with me for a moment?"

"Sympathize..." Barrett choked on a strangled grunt. He never liked his brother's wife. Her selfishness made her a deplorable Lady of Emberhold, but the callous disregard Vilotta had for her child broke any lingering doubts she would eventually see reason. She had treated Erissa like a doll from the moment of her birth, playing with her when the mood caught Vilotta before she shoved her away, forgotten on a shelf.

"Erissa will manage. After all, she's made the most of things so far. And if she doesn't, she will bear the consequences without complaint, even if I have to sew her mouth shut." Vilotta walked back to the tray of cakes, taking another one. "I will never hand her over to the Fae."

Shock rippled through Barrett. "Vilotta, I beg of you..."

"Enough, Barrett. My mind will not change. I will kill her before I let him claim her." Vilotta sat once more, her eyes hardened by her brittle smile. "I won't hear anything more on the subject. Leave me. If you press me further, I'll call for Faldeyr."

Barrett turned, keeping silent as he marched to the door. His hand twitched again, but this time, it would find no relief. For if any harm came to his wife, Faldeyr would not hesitate to turn his ire toward Erissa, and Barrett's hand held murderous intent.

He had to free Erissa without triggering the consequences of his vow. Vilotta's cold declaration bothered him more than anything his brother threatened. Erissa grew ever closer to death with each passing day, and he would stop at nothing to see her freed from that damned prophecy and her delusional parents.

CHAPTER FIVE

No light offered a respite from the pitch-black passageway. Erissa used her free hand to palm along the slimy wall until she reached a narrow stone staircase. She eased down the spiral stairs, mindful of her footing and the slick steps in the dark. Her nose wrinkled with the sour, wet smell of the air, trying not to think about what coated her hands.

The sun had set when she reached the ending door at the lowest level. The door remained a solid, dark mass with nothing illuminating the cracks in the wood.

Concealed by flowering vines, the tunnel led her northwest of the manor. Erissa peered around the heavy door as she opened it. She shrank back into the depths of the passageway as the old hinges squealed in the night. When she was sure the sound had drawn no one's attention, she slipped out, arranging the vines to cover the secret escape.

Clouds hid most of the moonlight, their shadows allowing her cloaked figure to walk through the town without anyone observing her. Erissa had no specific direction in mind without knowing her destination or the surrounding area. She faced danger walking alone outside the city walls at night. She needed a plan and a place to hide until morning.

The inn and its stables were too obvious, making the tavern also off-limits. Erissa debated her options, standing shadowed between two buildings across from the tavern.

A crowd burst out of the tavern doors. Most of them were long into their cups, ignoring her while singing along to a bawdy tune. There were five of them, their tread graceless as they moved closer. She slipped deeper between the buildings to avoid the singing bunch.

She crouched behind a well-used wagon. Splinters snagged her cloak when she pressed herself against the wood.

When the singing grew fainter, Erissa approached the back of the building with hurried steps. Rounding the structure, she ran into a hard chest.

Hands grabbed her arms, their fingertips leaving bruises underneath their iron grip. "What do we have here? A thief among the shadows?"

The man shook her, causing the cloak's hood to fall. The unmistakable glow of her purple eyes revealed her identity.

"My Lady." The man released her, pushing her away in shock. She fell to the ground, a squeal escaping her while mud flew in each direction.

Someone found her—all her care and for nothing. No one would risk the consequences of not returning her to the manor. She had the Keeper's very luck.

"Stop being dramatic." The voice moved beneath her skin, the warm feel of it quelling some of her fears. *"You are not as helpless as you believe yourself to be."*

"I'm sorry. I didn't mean to shove you like that." Strong hands reached for her again, gentle this time, as the man cupped her elbows, drawing her to her feet. "My lady, are you hurt?" He tried to brush the mud from her gown. "Why are you slinking among the shadows this late? I mistook you for a thief."

"Don't call me that." It reminded Erissa too much of her mother.

"A great honor awaits you when you answer the call of the Veil. How do you propose to accept it when you cannot bear a meager title?" the voice snickered.

Erissa shook her head to clear it of the voice and stared at the man's chest while she regained her balance. His arms came to wrap around her when she swayed, holding her steady.

She tingled everywhere he touched her. His thigh pressed between her legs. Her breasts crushed against his chest. Firm muscles lay beneath her fingers; his own had spread across her lower back. Something knotted within her chest, the unfamiliar sensation unfurling, pooling as his warmth drew her in, a fragrance of wood, jasmine, and something more tickling her nose. It was intoxicating, reminding her of the scent that had drawn her into the lower market that morning. She breathed deeply, inhaling the warm, savory scent wafting from his shirt as she clung to him.

She lifted her eyes, the soft glow of the moonlight allowing enough light to see the tanned column of his throat. It led to a strong jawline, thin lips, and a sharply angled nose that sat slightly crooked as if someone had broken it at some point. Her eyes continued to climb until she stared into warm, honey-colored irises filled with worry.

Erissa had never seen him before, despite watching the townspeople from her window countless times. His rugged, handsome features were prominent and would not have escaped her attention. "How do you know who I am?"

He shuffled his feet, seeming to hesitate for the span of a heartbeat. "The market. I saw what happened with the merchant and his wife earlier in the day."

She paled. "Then you know." She jerked away from his hold and put distance between them. The frigid night hit her without his warmth. His soft, wooded smell was stuck to her clothes, permeating her senses and leaving a strange desire to move back into his arms.

The clouds shifted. Moonlight filtered between the buildings, filling the shadows with light.

"Tell me your name." He stepped into the light, his hands raised like he was trying to soothe a frightened animal. "Please, it's only a name."

Erissa took in his wavy brown hair reaching past broad shoulders. He had half of it tied back, highlighting his angular cheekbones and framing the golden cuffs he had over each ear with the matching rings on either side of his nose. He must be a few years older.

The voice purred in her head. *"He smells divine."*

Her eyes flew to his, color heating her face as he smiled. He flicked his tongue out against his lips, smoothing the fleeting smile, and for the first time, Erissa thanked the Creator, the voice spoke to her alone.

She judged him to be taller than most men in the town, with a well-built physique that left her wondering what kind of work built a man like that. While simply garbed, his clothes were well made, the warm layers padded and protecting him from the bitter cold even without a cloak. The man did not come from Emberhold with the style of his clothing and jewelry he wore.

His cheeks warmed under her perusal, her consideration making him shift his feet. "My name is Rhazien. Why don't I help you back to the manor? It's not safe for a Lady to wander alone this late."

Her eyes became guarded as he spoke. The violet depths burned with desperation, her stance wary as she sized him up, wondering how to get rid of him. No matter how sincere he came across, he was a stranger to her and a complication she did not need when she might be found missing at any moment. She had to focus on running.

"You can trust him," the voice nudged.

Erissa ignored it.

"Let me show you," the voice pleaded.

Rhazien's studying gaze met hers, a frown marring his handsome features. With each passing moment, an odd connection grew between them. It lay every feeling bare as Rhazien's concern overtook her. The depth of the connection startled her as his emotions flooded into her like water soaking from one end of a cord to another. She felt his sincerity, genuine and innocent, the heat of attraction he tried to push from his thoughts. As the moonlight spilled over them, revealing the deepening bruise across her face, Erissa felt his rage.

She tipped her head back, her face full of weariness.

Rhazien's expression hardened. "You don't want to go back there, do you?"

"No." The single word spoken with such conviction changed his expression. Erissa stepped backward as a sweep of anger overtook his features.

He swallowed and smothered the emotion. Rhazien gentled his features as he approached her until he was mere inches away. "Please, tell me your name. I only want to help you."

The plea reverberated through her, soothing her ragged thinking with the soft words. She sensed their truth and felt Rhazien's worry and desire to help. But something more lingered with it, a longing that matched her own strange feelings, making her wonder if he felt her as profoundly as she did him.

"You can trust him," the voice said again. *"Tell him."*

"My name's Erissa." She paused, weighing how much to reveal. She embraced the plea in the voices' words, even as she felt mad for doing so, allowing her shoulders to slump in relief. "I can't go back. I have to find somewhere to hide until I can gather supplies and figure out what to do. Somewhere they wouldn't think to find me."

"I have an idea." Rhazien took her hand.

Erissa regarded the casual touch with wonder. The feel of his calloused palm against hers raised the hair along her arms. How long had it been since someone had done something as simple as holding her hand? The gesture reached into the recesses of her heart, soothing the hollow ache that had been living with her for as long as she could remember.

Rhazien turned to leave, tugging her along as they moved through the shadowed buildings behind the market to the southern edge of the walled-in city. They occasionally stopped, sticking to the shadows while others passed.

He slowed their pace when they came near the outer walls, the city's gate looming ahead. He headed down a narrow, cobbled path, leading her in the forge's direction. The sound of metal striking metal hissed through the night, the stone building bright with activity despite the late hour.

"This way." Navigating the shadows with ease, Rhazien took Erissa to the back of the forge, avoiding his working father. "My family sleeps there." He pointed to a small home attached to the rear of the structure. "And I sleep there." He turned to a stable that sat a few yards away from the home. It housed four draft horses, their height towering over Rhazien's.

"You sleep out in the cold?" Erissa's eyes widened in surprise.

Still holding her hand, he led her into the stable and to a ladder against the back wall. "There are seven of us children with me as the only boy. At least out here, I get my own bed until I build a house. It's not much, but the furs'll keep you warm, giving you a safe place to hide tonight while the city gates are closed."

She stared at the ladder, gripping his hand tighter. "You're sure this will work?"

"We've only been here a few weeks, and no one knows we've met." Rhazien let go of her hand and placed his against her back, pushing her until she grabbed the ladder rungs. "Trust me. There's a bed in the corner. I'll sleep down here."

Her head whipped around in alarm. "You can't stay down here. It'll be odd for you to be found sleeping with the horses. Your family might comment on it."

"I can make up something about needing to be closer to them. It's not the first time I've had to do it, and it won't be the last."

"You don't know my uncle. He's the head of the guard and the one my father will send for me. Barrett is smart. He picks up the smaller details. If they realize I'm gone tonight, he'll sweep through the city until he finds me. He'll question why you're sleeping with the horses and check them over, and if he can't find anything wrong with them...." Erissa studied the wood in front of her. "You have to come up here too."

"Erissa—"

"I trust you, Rhazien." Erissa sighed. The voice, though annoying, had never steered her wrong. And Rhazien had shown himself to be a man of character this night. "You've helped me when no one else would after this morning's events. Helped when you didn't even have to. And you did it with no hesitation or worry about what my father would do if he found out. Besides, you've had plenty of opportunities to do your worst and haven't."

Erissa's words were anything but light, heating his face. He nudged her up the ladder. "You shouldn't give people such trust when you hardly know them. I only wish to help you and be worthy of something so freely given. I would never take advantage of you, but someone else might."

Her own face heated at his kind admonishment. "Someone will do worse if I get caught." She turned her back to him, her mind racing with everything she was not saying.

His presence provided a sense of safety. She had an instinctual feeling he would never cause her harm. The belief would undoubtedly sound insane if spoken aloud, given all that she had suffered at the hands of those who claimed to love her. She should know better than to place herself in such a vulnerable position, but she did not worry for her safety with Rhazien standing behind her. She stayed quiet and ascended the ladder, smiling at hearing Rhazien climbing behind her.

As she climbed over the last rung, she was unprepared for the sight in front of her.

A hay-stuffed mattress sat tucked in the corner and covered with a thick layer of furs. Another fur hung from a glassless window above the bed, stretched to block most of the freezing night air. A rickety wardrobe stood across from the bed, a washing station beside it. Her eyes traveled to the makeshift shelving where baskets held various produce, and a single chair sat beside a table that would struggle to accommodate Rhazien's size.

But the rafted beams caught her attention more than anything else.

Decorative pieces of metal dangled from them every few feet. Each stringed structure was unique; the material twisted around in circles or bent into shapes around differing widths of pipe and rods with a smaller round, flattened disk in the middle. The light metal held intricate, stamped designs.

Erissa walked to the bed where the largest of them hung from the rafters. While the others were beautiful, this one took her breath away with its elegance.

The metal curled around shards of glass woven between pieces of piping. Moonlight came through gaps between the wooden planks of the wall. The light reflected against the glass, throwing itself across the walls and into the shadows.

She sighed at their peacefulness. "They're like stars twinkling in the night sky."

Beneath each strand of glass hung thin pipes. Suspended between them were small metal disks shaped like clouds. They moved as a slight breeze worked its way around the fur-covered window.

They were unlike anything Erissa had ever seen. The swaying pipes flirted with the light wind, tiny slivers of light dancing upon the glass. She gasped as a tinkering resonance filled the air when the metal disks clinked against the pipes. Her fingers reached out, brushing against one of them, knocking the pieces into each other. Erissa giggled when the noise intensified, bringing her hand up to smother the unexpected sound.

Rhazien moved behind her, his breath tickling her hair. "Do you like the wind chime?"

"I love it." She relaxed into the graceful melody, the day's tension leaving her. "Did you make these?"

"Yes." His voice swelled with pride and something sweeter as her fingers brushed across the smooth metal while she stared with awe. "My father finds them a foolish waste of time."

"Nothing so beautiful could ever be foolish. Rhaz—" She stepped forward as she turned and found herself pressed against his chest once more. She tried to suppress a shiver at the feel of him, but her body betrayed her as the warm, earthy fragrance she was beginning to associate with him filled the surrounding air. The voice was right. He smelled divine.

Erissa thanked the Creator for the heavy cloak across her shoulders, shielding him from feeling the physical effect he had on her.

A rustling noise startled the pair apart, Erissa's face draining of all color. Rhazien pushed her behind him as they turned to the ladder. She brought her hands to his back, slender fingers fisting in the layers of his clothing as they both waited for the noise to repeat. They stayed silent, their quick, shallow breaths puffing out in the cold air.

When several minutes passed with nothing further, Rhazien's shoulders relaxed. "It must have been the horses. I think we're safe for tonight." He turned to face Erissa, her hands falling from his cloak. "Take the bed. I'll sleep on the floor."

"Rhazien, you've done so much for me already. I can't take your bed from you, especially on this cold night." She made to step around him, stopping short at the hands he placed on her shoulders.

"A Lady shouldn't be sleeping on the floor. I insist you take the bed." His eyes dropped to Erissa's lips as she bit the lower one. "I'll be fine. There are enough furs for the two of us. Neither of us will lack warmth tonight if that's what you're worried about."

Still, she hesitated. "I don't want to put you out any more than I already have."

"Then don't make me worry about you sleeping on the floor. Take the bed."

He pushed her backward until her knees hit the edge of the bed. He unclasped the clasp at the throat of her cloak, and she allowed him to pull the garment from her shoulders. Erissa's breath caught as his fingers brushed against her throat, a movement that made her feel warm despite the chill of the evening.

Rhazien draped the cloak across her bag. Erissa studied him while he walked across the room and placed the cloak and bag on two hooks.

As he moved back to the bed, their eyes met, and Erissa's face heated at being caught staring. She cleared her throat and spun around where she sat, grabbing several furs. She left two for herself but took the others and made a makeshift pallet beside the bed. "You really should take the bed. I'm used to the floor after years of pallets by the hearth. I'm sure you have a long day of work ahead of you tomorrow, and I'd hate to see you tired before the day breaks. The cold has a way of seeping into the bones."

Erissa missed what she had given way, focusing on the furs rather than Rhazien's perplexed expression.

"Why would you be used to sleeping on the floor?"

She straightened, turning away from Rhazien. By the gods, how would she explain that slip of the tongue away? Erissa climbed into the bed without further protest, and without further explanation.

The clouds shifted, casting the room in darkness as the moon disappeared behind the gray masses. Erissa was grateful for the lack of light, even as it made her feel like a coward. She wished to take the words back, not knowing how to explain them away.

Rhazien stayed silent. He slid beneath the furs she had arranged on the floor, and Erissa was sure he felt every bit of the cold, the spaces between the old wood providing plenty of room for the night breeze to whistle through.

The silence lengthened.

Erissa settled into the bed, wiggling her shoulders back and forth as she felt Rhazien's gaze bore into her. She sighed as she stilled, knowing the question was coming.

"Erissa, why did you sleep on the floor?" Rhazien asked. "Surely the wealth of the manor afforded you a bed."

She fiddled with the ends of the fur in her nervousness as the clouds moved again and moonlight cast its glow into the room.

The inner voice sighed. *"How many times must I tell you he is trustworthy?"*

Rhazien stretched to his full length, bringing his arms up to clasp behind the back of his neck. "You don't have to answer."

Erissa took a deep breath, her hands smoothing out the furs as if trying to smooth her nerves. She had never spoken to anyone about this. Never had anyone to tell. "Because my parents had me chained to the wall, and the chains didn't reach all the way to the bed."

Erissa glanced at him and struggling to make out his expression in the trickling moonlight. His mouth fell open with the shock of her words, his eyebrows drawing up.

She studied the emotions behind his eyes, feeling how his mind raced in disbelief as if half-convinced he had misunderstood her until Erissa continued speaking. "I've only been out of the chains for several moons. After what happened in the market this morning... I had planned to gather supplies to run away, but then my father threatened to put me back in them. He threatened to do more. I had to leave. I can't... I can't bear it."

Erissa was afraid to stare at him, but their connection pulsed as his horror grew at each word, the feeling rising until it threatened to bury them both. What madness was it to feel his emotions as if they were her own?

Rhazien interrupted the questions, beckoning to her. "How could a parent ever do such a thing?"

"It's a long story, Rhazien. And one I don't like to remember."

Erissa rolled away from him, burying herself in the furs until only her hair remained visible with the light from the tinkling glass overhead, dancing among the black tresses.

Rhazien's mind reeled with all Erissa had said. He stayed silent, not knowing what to think. The furs were moving in time to her breathing. He was sure she was crying, the movement of the coverings catching with every other breath.

As much as Rhazien wanted to press Erissa, she would tell her secrets in her own time, but he would not force her with any more of his prodding. "Erissa, I'd like to think we're friends after tonight. And being a friend means you don't have to tell me anything you don't want to."

She nodded her agreement. Her words were hushed as she spoke again. "Thank you. And thank you for helping me." She rolled toward him, her body tense.

"I would do anything to help you." Rhazien said nothing more. After a while, he watched as her body relaxed and her breathing evened out.

Long after Erissa had fallen asleep, Rhazien remained awake. A deep anger stirred within him, startling him with its intensity. That anger burned brighter as he pictured her chained to the wall like a beaten-down dog. The beginning of a colorful bruise on her cheek was telling enough, but to know they had placed her in chains ignited something deep within. He guessed at the horrors she must have gone through, comparing it to his childhood, where he'd spent roaming freely through the forests around the town where his family had made their home.

Rhazien and his siblings had been spoiled with affection, not only from his parents but from the Lord, his family, and his father's closest friend. The Lord had always treated Rhazien like a son. And the friend? Micmus would not hesitate to remove his own hand instead of laying it on another. Never mind the thought of them placing him in chains or allowing the other to do so. He would not chain a dog like that, let alone a child.

As his mind whirled, one thing remained certain before a restless sleep claimed him. He would do anything to keep Erissa from the manacles awaiting her.

CHAPTER SIX

Every creak of the wind against the wooden walls carried Erissa's imagination to whatever torment awaited if her father found her.

Rhazien thwarted her plan to leave at first light when he brought in their morning fare before heading to the forge. Extra guards were stationed around the gates, he had told her, making it impossible for her to pass through. But the longer she waited, the more anxious she became, left with nothing but her own worries as company.

Most of the day had passed since she had last seen Rhazien, the revelations of yesterday evening dampening their conversation as he readied himself to leave for the day. The sun descended, its golden rays bouncing between the shards of glass hanging over the bed. The sparse loft was huge without Rhazien's large frame dominating the space.

Since that morning, she had only left the bed once, attending to her needs after Rhazien had gone, terrified the sounds of her movement would alert her presence to anyone who passed.

The city pulsed with tension as though the buildings and their inhabitants disapproved of her running away. She spied on them through the narrow cracks between the wood and fur stretched across the window. Citizens kept to themselves, walking the streets with fretful expressions.

Guards roamed the streets in groups, methodically searching through every property without explanation. The commotion filled the air as the townspeople protested the rough treatment of their possessions. Her nerves became more frayed with every passing hour.

Erissa stared with longing at the bowl of fruit, cheese, and bread Rhazien had left sitting out on the other side of the room. Her stomach churned with hunger, the pains growing as the sun continued to set. The noise echoed against the room's silence.

The desire for food finally won, the scent of various evening meals taunting Erissa from the window. She crept from the bed, a fur draped across her shoulders to protect her from the cold, testing each foot against the old floor while making her way to the bowl. But all her care was for naught as the noise of boots scraping against the ladder filled the air.

She whirled around, hastening to find what protection the table and chair offered, flinging the fur over the back of the chair before crouching behind it. Seconds later, the heavy tread of boots moved across the floor.

"Erissa?"

She released the held breath at hearing Rhazien's voice. Erissa shot up from behind the furs. "Rhazien! By the gods, you scared me."

He let out a yelp, her sudden appearance startling him and sending him back a step. The stew he carried sloshed over the side of the clay pot he held, burning his hand as it soaked through the cloth wrapped around it. Curses followed his surprised cry.

Erissa gripped the back of the chair, matting the fur beneath her fingers. "I—I'm sorry. I didn't mean—"

Rhazien's words were a gentle chuckle. "It's not your fault, little doe. That'll teach me not to leave the lid off. My mother warned me." He walked with purpose to place the steaming pot on the table before moving to the window.

The cloth slid from his hand, and his burned skin flashed in Erissa's direction. The red tissue was inflamed with raised, glassy lines in the shape of a shield. The skin glittered in the light, looking unlike any burn Erissa had ever seen. It almost looked like scales covered his hand, but it had to be a trick of the fading light against his heated skin.

Rhazien untied the fur covering and stuck his hand into the freezing rain that started falling with the setting sun. He sighed as the water cooled the pain.

Erissa busied herself, hoping to make up for her blunder. She stepped from behind the chair, reaching once again for the bowl. She took the bread and cheese and, finding a wooden cutting board and knife, sliced them each a serving before setting the board in the middle of the table alongside the stew.

After a few minutes of cooling the heat from his fingers, Rhazien tied the fur in place over the window. He walked to where Erissa stood. She would not turn to him as he took her hand. "Look at me, little doe."

The inner voice stirred at Rhazien's touch. It made a pleased little sound, squirming through Erissa's body. *"Little doe has a nice ring to it. You should tell him we like it."*

She tipped her head to the side and met his gaze. "Little doe. Why do you keep calling me that?"

"Because that's what you looked like when you popped out from behind the chair. Like a little doe startled by a hunter in the woods."

Erissa scoffed, but it did nothing to remove the grin from her face. No one called her by a pet name. Not since before her parents locked her away. Well, technically, her uncle did when he called her his little star, but the name felt tainted with his involvement in the abuse hanging between them. She dipped her head, unsure of herself in this playful moment, her eyes falling to the red welts across the backs of Rhazien's fingers.

"Do you wish for it to be undone?" the voice asked.

More than anything, Erissa traced her fingers across his in the barest of touches, her heart heavy at all the ways her presence would cause him more harm if her father discovered her hiding here. "Oh, Rhazien. I'm sorry. I've caused such a mess in your life."

"Erissa, you're not—" His words cut off abruptly, his gaze moving to his hands. The blisters faded as Erissa slid her hand across the burn. Her gasp of surprise echoed his, his eyes locked on the healed skin as he marveled at it. "How did you...."

"I don't know." Erissa was at a loss for her actions, her eyes wide and tinged with fear. "I was thinking only of how much I wished to heal the damage I caused."

"And I answered your wish," the voice crooned. *"Our desires are one and the same."*

Erissa pushed at the voice and tried to focus on Rhazien as he kept talking.

"This wasn't your fault." He twisted their hands, catching hold of hers and bringing one to his lips. He placed a tender kiss on the back of her fingers, lingering for a moment. "Let's eat. I'm not much of a cook, but at least it'll warm us."

"You made this?" She blushed furiously as he ushered her into the chair, her skin tingling where his lips had pressed.

Rhazien laughed at Erissa's incredulous expression, making his way over to the cupboard. "You sound as surprised as my mother was when I asked her how to make it. I wanted you to have something warm tonight. The weather is only supposed to get worse." His humorous expression faded as he opened the cupboard. Finding nothing, he pulled two spoons from the lower drawer. "I should have asked for bowls. Nothing for it but to eat from the pot." Placing the spoons on the table, he picked up a wooden stool long forgotten in the corner behind the ladder, bringing it over to sit across from Erissa.

Erissa's mouth twisted in confusion, her head tipping to the side. Her eyes moved from the pot to the ladder. "How did you ever get that pot up the ladder?"

"With great difficulty and little grace. It was harder to get the stew past my mother than it was to get it up the ladder. I had to convince her the entire pot was for me. Luckily, it's cold enough to need a meal hearty enough to stick to the ribs, and I'm a glutton after a long day in the forge." He took a heaping bite of the meal and, at the dubious frown on Erissa's face, snorted around the spoonful of stew he had shoved in his mouth. His lips puffed out, blowing around the heat of the food.

Erissa laughed, watching him dance the hot food around.

He lifted an eyebrow at her amusement, waiting for the food to cool enough to swallow.

"You're going to burn your mouth." She pressed her lips together, trying to dampen her amusement.

When he could speak, he threw a wink in her direction. "You can always come over here, little doe, and heal it for me, but I think you'd have to use your lips."

A blush spread across Erissa's face as the voice within her laughed. *"He is more than you bargained for, but I like him."*

Rhazien gave a wide grin at her pink face. "You're ever more the little doe when your nose is all rosy like that."

She rolled her eyes, ignoring his teasing, and ate with relish, blowing on each bite before savoring the warmly spiced fare. Her brows rose as Rhazien frowned at her appetite.

He stared at the bowl of food he had stocked before heading to the forge that morning and found everything either still in it or sitting on the table before them. "You didn't eat today."

Erissa fidgeted against his statement. "I was too anxious to leave the bed. The soldiers have been working closer to us all day. Everyone who passed complained about it. I was afraid I would make too much noise."

"I'm sorry I didn't come back earlier. We've only been here a few weeks, and it's apparent the city was in dire straits with their smithing needs. There wasn't a break to be had all day."

"I didn't expect you to come back until this evening. You have responsibilities and that doesn't change because I'm here." Erissa took the remaining piece of bread Rhazien held out to her. "Besides, I'm used to waiting between meals. It wasn't a hardship."

Rhazien sat back in his chair, appraising Erissa. "You say the strangest things for one meant to be living in comfort. The manor boasts everything one would wish for."

"Tell him," the voice coaxed.

"It does, for some." Erissa chewed slowly, creating extra time to weigh how much to tell him. "I wasn't always one of them."

"I would never press for details you don't wish to give, little doe."

Little doe. The name had a nice ring to it coming from his lips. She hummed inside, feeling the sincerity behind his words. It would be all too easy to become addicted to him calling her that.

"You have trusted him so far," the voice encouraged.

Erissa swallowed her last piece of bread and, with it, her resolve. "When Father wasn't bullying me into acquiescence by denying me comforts, the maids refused them. Some were afraid of me, while some were afraid of my father. Others wouldn't come out of hate for what they think I am—what they think I do. There were days without food, a fire, or water to wash with."

"And your mother allowed this?"

"My father ordered it most of the time." Erissa's heart swelled against the wave of emotions fighting to crest within Rhazien. His anger made her uncomfortable and unsure of how to react to someone caring about what happened to her. It was weird to have a stranger care when the people who had witnessed her imprisonment turned a blind eye. She had a hard time believing he would have done the same. No, Rhazien would never stand idly by. "As for my mother—I can't say. To my knowledge, she did nothing to stop it and never came to visit with anything I might need."

Rhazien's shock clashed with a tidal wave of deep-seated anger he struggled to contain as the emotions played across his face.

He stood, pacing back and forth, his hands fisting at his sides. "You speak so calmly of this. At best, your parents were neglectful and, at worst, abusive. And you sit there and speak of it as if we're talking about the weather."

Erissa set her spoon down, her features pinching together. Now his anger started to annoy her. She had no clue what to do with it, and she did not welcome it in this moment when all she wanted to do was continue with her meal and drop this conversation. These were not memories she wanted to revisit. "What would you have me do, Rhazien? Rage and cry against what they did to me? I did my years of that, earning me nothing more than being chained to the wall. The punishments became worse with every plan of escape I made."

Rhazien saw her eyes dim, the color as flat as her voice.

Erissa pushed away from the table and came to stand before him. "When the tutors tried to help, they sent them away. Whenever I found a confidant in a maid—which was rare since most wouldn't speak with me—they were severely punished. And when Father grew tired of my escape attempts—he turned violent."

She turned her back to him, finding it easier to speak without looking into his eyes that saw too much. Easier to voice what she had never dared to say before this moment. When she spoke again, the words were hollow, almost broken, as she built a wall between her voice and her memories. "Do you want to hear the details of the beatings? Of how they ached worse than anything I had ever endured, each growing worse than the last? Of the bruises and the broken bones? Or do you want to hear how the taste of copper lingered for days? Am I supposed to leave here and return to that nightmare?"

Erissa was grateful Rhazien said nothing. She needed space at the moment, or she would never give voice to what had happened behind the stone walls. "When his whip and fists didn't break my desire for freedom, Father chained me to the wall. Even then, after everything he put me through, I never stopped trying to escape. So, they took away my comforts. Days without meals. A blanket by the fire instead of a bed. Moons without contact from my parents or uncle as they left me alone to consider my actions."

Her pain rippled through the air, cold as the wind blowing through the old wood of the stable. "Silence has a way of driving you mad, Rhazien. In ways that beatings and chains can't. The neglect of my needs only made the silence more isolating, heightening the way the chamber echoed with my slightest movement."

"Do you think I'm a figment of this madness?"

Ignoring the patient curiosity of the voice, Erissa focused on the sound of Rhazien as he stepped closer.

His heat radiated behind her, but he made no move to touch her. "Erissa, you don't need—"

Erissa continued as if she had not heard him. "But I fought to hold on to myself, grounding my madness in the city's symphony of noises floating through the cracks around my window. I didn't understand how to fight back when I was younger, but I'm older now. I learned to find anything to hold on to. Anything that kept the isolation at bay. I learned to play my father's game so well in the last few years, earning back pieces of his trust while acting as the compliant daughter." Erissa pulled her sleeves up, revealing the scars circling her wrists. "I kept playing that role until he finally freed me from the chains I bore for years."

Silence reigned for a moment before Rhazien cleared his throat. "How old were you, Erissa?"

She was glad he didn't use his special name for her, glad he didn't sully it with the worst of her memories. She swallowed hard against the tears. "Seven. They locked me away on the day of my seventh year. I was in chains a few years after."

"And how old are you now?"

She listened to the pitter-patter of rain against the roof for a long time before she turned around and answered. "Twenty."

Rhazien closed his eyes, visibly forcing down a lump that formed in his throat and the tears that threatened with each breath. The visceral response threw Erissa.

She forgot sometimes. Forgot how bad things were compared to the way she should have lived. The worst days had become normal when they were anything but. Thirteen years. The number was staggering, even for her as the person who had gone through it. She had endured the abuse of her father for thirteen years. Friendless. Alone. She shrunk away from the memories, grabbing onto the lifeline that was Rhazien's voice as he spoke again.

"Why didn't you run away instead of going to the market that day?"

"Where would I go without a plan? I have no other family. No ability to earn coin. I was trying to find supplies that would be easy to hide in my room while I figured out what to do." Erissa's shoulders slumped, and her eyes became guarded as the fight left her. "It's why I can't go back."

The tether binding them pulsed. Erissa sensed the agony and loneliness of her pain rip through him, an invisible connection that neither held the power to separate themselves from.

Rhazien took her hand. The presence within her brightened at the feel of his skin against hers, settling into a peaceful balm that soothed every bit as much as Rhazien's touch.

In her room, it had been too much to feel another person. It had been unbearable to even think of letting her mother's hand touch her pendant, but Rhazien's touch was unlike anything else. It called to her more seductively than even the whispered calls of the Veil-bound souls.

"Erissa, you can stay with me for however long you want. We'll figure the rest out day by day. We can work on a plan to get you beyond the walls, but it doesn't have to be decided tonight. The guards are on high alert. They're expecting you to slip away with the protection of nightfall. We'll come up with something, something they won't expect. For tonight, though, you're safe here."

"Safe?" The question hung heavily between them. She tightened her fingers around his. "I'm not even sure I know what that means anymore. The only safety I've ever known I found between the pages of the books they sometimes let me have. They were my entire world locked away in that room. I'd rip my favorite pages from the spines, hiding them in the folds of my dresses when they came to take the books away. Gods, the only reason I looked for an escape was because of those stories. So many of them with their stone keeps and secret passageways."

She glanced away from their hands to find his face solemn, an expression that did not fit with the laugh lines highlighting his features. His expression held an unending, burning rage. Not a rage directed at her; no, this was a rage burning for her. "I'm not sure I would survive it again, Rhazien—that empty, cold existence. Not when I've had this and been here with you in such warmth. It's unlike anything I've ever known. *You're* unlike anything I've ever known."

She swayed into Rhazien as he leaned down, but before they gave into their intense desire to kiss her pain away, voices carried from below.

Erissa paled at the first voice, her eyes going wide with fear.

"And you've seen no one, Tyrmar? They would have been short, wearing a blue cloak of quality fabric."

Rhazien froze as the second voice answered.

"You're welcome to check the stalls. My son beds down in the loft as of late. It's not much, but it should hold him over until he builds himself something. M'lord has been generous in allowing him to pick a plot outside the city, but the weather hasn't allowed for many viewings of the land." Tyrmar's voice became louder as he entered the stable.

Erissa's hand tightened around Rhazien's, her breath coming in shallow bursts. He placed a hand over her mouth, quieting the noise before it gave them away.

"This is the last area left to search. Come now, you must have seen something." Barrett's impatience bled through his clipped words.

"No, Sir Barrett. But I've been in the forge almost every hour these last few days. Even today, I only left to take my sup," Tyrmar said.

Rhazien took advantage of the noise as his father talked while soldiers searched the stable below. He pushed Erissa in the bed's direction, the echoes from the search hiding the sound of their movements. Lifting the furs, he motioned for her to climb under them. She hesitated before doing as he bid. After shoving her bag and cloak beneath the bed, he grabbed the furs from where they lay on the floor. He tossed them onto the edge of the bed before joining her. Rhazien tugged the furs until they covered their heads, hiding the glow of Erissa's eyes. Her head rested in the crook of his neck, his back turned to the open side of the loft. The position of his larger frame disguised where she lay against him.

"If anyone comes up here," Rhazien's words tickled in the barest of whispers, his lips brushing against Erissa's ear, "all they'll see is me."

She nodded, fisting her hands in his shirt. Her hair teased his lips where it brushed against them. The scent of him curled around her. Rounded curves molded to his harder length like they were born to fit together. She shuddered as Rhazien tenderly kissed her temple.

Erissa's eyes closed, losing herself in the feel of him for a moment. There was a connection there. One that she found herself powerless to resist, with his scent invading her senses and quelling the fears inside.

Finding themselves lost in the other, they missed the sound of someone climbing the ladder.

"Rhazien," his father softly called across the loft. "Rhazien?"

Feigned slumber with light snores came from Rhazien. Erissa bit her lip, smothering the building laughter that threatened to overwhelm her. The gesture almost cost them their charade when Rhazien's eyes focused on the movement. His snoring slipped, a low growl breaking through.

A chuckle escaped his father. "Boy sleeps like the dead. But as you can see, there's nowhere for someone to hide up here." Tyrmar's voice faded as he turned to the ladder. "Whomever you're searching for is long gone if they passed through."

Panic made Erissa grip Rhazien tighter when the sound of boots on the uneven floors moved closer to the bed. Her uncle's voice rang out. "Tell me, Sir Blacksmith, why would your son have two places at his table if no one has been here?"

All the breath disappeared from her lungs with her uncle's observation. Rhazien tensed against her.

A burst of nervous laughter filled the small room. "I've told you, sir, I've seen no one matching the description you gave."

The sound of Barrett's sword hilt being cleared of the scabbard froze Erissa's blood. Rhazien's hold on her tightened, preventing her from revealing herself.

Tyrmar's voice changed, the nervousness gone with the threat before him, anger taking its place at the insinuation against himself and his son. "Now, that's no way to be treating people, sir. I understand you have a job to do, what with you being head of the guard, but I'm a man of my word. I've seen no one matching your description, and I'm unaware that a father supping with his son is a crime."

After a moment, Barrett accepted this explanation, re-sheathing the hilt. "Curse the gods. When I get my hands on her.... My apologies, sir blacksmith. The job requires a suspicious nature, and we've been searching nonstop since daybreak. I thank you for your time."

The pair listened from the bed as the men descended the ladder. Guilt overcame Erissa at hearing her uncle's frustrated sigh at quitting the stables, an unwanted feeling she shoved to the side and refused to acknowledge. He did not deserve such an emotion, not when he was complicit in everything that had happened to her. She stayed silent until the two voices faded into the night. "Do you think they'll come back?"

"Not tonight. We can figure out a plan in the morning. For now, it's best to keep quiet."

"But Rhazien, I don't understand. Why would your father lie?"

"Like he said, my father's a man of his word. He didn't lie about seeing you. The dinner may be, but I helped my mother make the same meal for the family. I think that one can slide since it was our saving grace."

"He said...."

"That he had seen no one and then questioned an assumption." Rhazien moved the hair from across her cheek, draping it behind her ear. "We best get some rest tonight. We have an early morning."

The hands gripping his shirt let go and tried to smooth the fabric back into place, the evening events finally taking their toll. "Do you... mind staying here with me?"

"Little doe, you don't have to feel pressured—"

"That's not what this is about. Tomorrow, I'll leave. I can't stay here. And I'll be alone. I know I shouldn't ask. You've done so much for me already, and...." Erissa's words trailed off.

"And?" Rhazien moved slightly away, trying to see her face in the darkened room.

"I don't want to feel alone tonight." The words came out on a whine pulled from the deepest part of her like they had cost her something to speak them out loud. Like she had given him a piece of her soul with their utterance.

Rhazien tightened his arms around her. In answer, he pressed a lingering kiss against her temple as words failed him. Erissa marveled as their connection flared, coming to life as his thoughts flowed into her. Thoughts that made her question her sanity as his desire and protectiveness mixed with an overwhelming feeling of peace, feelings that echoed in her.

What did she make of this if she considered the voice madness? Did it even matter? The same peace echoed in her this night as she found safety in his arms, something she had not known for so long.

"Lean into it," the voice encouraged. *"At some point, you must trust what your eyes see and what you feel in the deepest parts of your heart. So, what are they telling you now? Can't you feel him calling to you—and something deeper calling to me?"*

Leaving her was the last thing he wanted to do, a feeling which matched her own desires. She had no explanation for the pull between them. Only yesterday, he found her hiding across from the tavern. Each minute with him passed as if they had been together for a dozen years. It did not matter that they had only just met. With his arms wrapped around her, she finally found a home.

A smile spread across her lips with his kiss. Lying curled in his arms, she knew she was safe. She breathed deeply, basking in the scent that made her take leave of her senses. What madness was this, finding such comfort in the arms of a man she did not know? Regardless of the circumstances, if only for tonight, she desired to feel a sense of belonging.

"Goodnight, Rhazien."

Only when her breathing had evened out did he reply. "Goodnight, little doe."

The rain grew heavier as the night wore on. The steady tread of Tyrmar's boots against the ladder rungs went unheard against the noise raging outside. He adjusted the candle in his hand, careful of his movements.

His brow creased against the racing revelation that refused to be quieted. Something was not right.

As he crested the last rung of the ladder, his eyes once again took in the table and the two seats reflected in the candle's soft light. His conversation with Sir Barrett did not sit well with him. He misled the man, testing his sense of honor.

Tyrmar crept to the bed and stilled when Rhazien shifted. The furs fell from his shoulder to rest against the lower half of his chest, revealing thick locks of ebony hair.

The ruse might not have worked against Barrett had the moon shone unhindered. With more light in the room, it would have been clear that even Rhazien's fur-covered form was too big for one person.

Tyrmar moved closer. He stared at the striking woman wrapped in his son's arms. Her identity was unmistakable, with Tyrmar having seen her in the market only yesterday morning. The soldiers were out in full force, leaving no doubt about who they were targeting.

Rhazien stirred again, curling the woman more fully against his side. A content sigh left him. "*Nayanam.*"

His son's words left Tyrmar frozen in place. If the girl were a *nayanam*, this changed everything. He reached for the furs at the foot of the bed, pulling them over the couple, a warding against the chilled air.

Turning, he padded to the ladder, scrubbing a hand against the wrinkles on his brow.

His son would not go to such lengths without reason, especially for a *nayanam*. Whatever lay behind Rhazien's decision to hide the woman would be discovered in the morning.

CHAPTER SEVEN

Tyrmar wasted no time after leaving the stables. He walked across the small yard and entered his home, uncaring of the water pouring from his clothes or the mud coating his boots as he burst through the door.

"Stop right there." His wife studied her sewing from the large cushioned chair she had dragged in front of the hearth. "Boots off. There will be hell to pay if you drag mud across my floors, Fefnirion."

"Louder, Susreene. I don't think those next to us heard you call me that, let alone the guard." Tyrmar's dry remark ignored her threat. He strode into the room until he reached the large table with its round, simple rug underneath. He pushed the table against the wall and kneeled next to the carpet. "We have to leave. Tomorrow evening. If we disappear any earlier, it will alert Emberhold's captain, and Rhazien will need the head start."

Susreene's hand paused. She breathed deeply three times, placing her sewing to the side and rising to move to her husband's side. "And what has he done this time?"

Tyrmar sat back on his heels. "The girl the soldiers are looking for... he's... hiding her."

"Of course. Rhazien is consistent. I'll give him that." Susreene chuckled. She crouched beside her husband, disgust flashing across her face at the water on the floor as it dampened her skirt. She pulled the rug backward, revealing a locked cellar door. "Remember the time he hid the butcher's daughter when she didn't want to marry? Or what about the time he stole the neighboring farmer's youngest from her bed in the middle of the night after she knocked out her teeth, tripping over the milk pail? It took hours to convince him her parents weren't abusing her. That boy's protective streak has landed him in endless troubles."

A snort left him, his lip curling in a wonder-filled smile as Tyrmar revealed the rest. "It's more complicated than that. She's his *nayanam*."

Susreene slapped his shoulder, all mirth gone. "Tyrmar Merrick, I'll skin every scale from your hide. You should have told me that first."

She pushed him aside and pulled a key from underneath the folds of her dress, loosening the piece of leather strip securing it. "You'll give him the gold. Tell our son it's proof of my blessing, and they'll need it to start over."

"You haven't even met the girl. We know nothing about her or her family." Tyrmar had no objections. He wanted to rile his wife. He liked her like that. Her eyes glowed with passion, and the emotion did wonderful things to her chest when it heaved with indignation.

"And our story was any different? We abandoned our people during a war to be together, defying the Creator's laws." Susreene whipped her head to look at him, the same glow he loved, lightening the color of her amber gaze. "If those beyond the Mists find out I'm still alive, there will be hell to pay, but your actions held no hesitation. Our boy is simply taking after his father."

"All right, dear. All right. They have my full support." Tyrmar kissed her temple, and she settled, nuzzling her head under his chin. "He'll head for Micmus. I'll make sure of it."

Her head snapped up at that, a smile revealing the youthful beauty she still held. "We'll have to circle around to Cropari once we get the captain off Rhazien's trail. Islone will ensure a hunt occurs, and I don't want to miss it."

"Worry about the packing first. Most women would be more concerned about running. *Again*." Tyrmar's tone grew more serious. "You know what this means, Susreene. If Rhazien has found his *nayanam*, prophecy is at play. We won't be able to protect him anymore. The war will reignite."

"Shush your foolishness. We've been running since the Remaking. What's one more time, one more war?" Susreene cupped her husband's face, brushing his mouth with a quick kiss.

Tyrmar took the key from her and opened the hidden door. "Store everything in the cellar until I tell you. I'm certain the captain will return tomorrow."

"Don't worry, husband." Susreene pulled their traveling bags from the shallow hole. "I've been waiting decades for Rhazien's hunt. I'm not about to ruin that with a few misplaced bags and fears of tomorrow. We survived the first two wars. Who's to say the same won't happen again?"

"Your oath is all that stands between you and death, brother." Faldeyr paced back and forth across his chamber, Vilotta perched on the edge of the bed. "How did the little bitch make it past the guards this time?"

If the oath allowed it, Barrett would have strangled Faldeyr long ago. He would not consider it a challenge. Faldeyr stood a head shorter than him with a spindly neck. It would be easy to ring the life from it.

"Faldeyr, please. There's no need for such names..." Vilotta reached her hands for him but let them fall as his head snapped to her with a glare.

"Go over it again." Faldeyr stopped his pacing and dropped his weight into a chair by the hearth.

"How many times tonight do I have to do this?" Barrett sat opposite his brother, running a hand through his hair. "We searched the upper and lower city, concentrating on the areas around the market and tavern, as well as the areas in the lower city nearest the gates. I found no tracks with the rain obscuring things, and no one has seen a woman matching her description."

"Maybe she stayed closer to the manor this time?" Vilotta twisted her hands, her voice shaking. "Where would she be able to go in this weather without anyone seeing her?"

"She wouldn't." Faldeyr drummed his fingers against the arm of the chair. They stilled, his eyes narrowing on Barrett. He knew what his brother would ask, and Barrett sent out a desperate prayer to the Creator to keep the secret dancing across the back of his tongue.

"You're sure you didn't see the girl?" Faldeyr leaned toward him, his hands grasping at the arms of the chair tight enough to tear the fabric from one side.

Barrett waited for the magic's compulsion, praying harder it would not come, and struggled to believe it when his tongue continued to lie still. "No. I haven't seen Erissa."

He thanked the Creator for listening to his intuition and leaving the stable without pressing the matter. The blacksmith lied. And anyone with good eyes and even the smallest amount of intelligence guessed at who lay tucked against the blacksmith's son. Barrett knew his niece lay shielded by the man's form. But he told the truth. He did not lay eyes on her.

Faldeyr gave him a considering look. "I have ways of making you tell the truth, brother."

Barrett held firm. "Then do so. Test my oath. I am telling no lie. I haven't seen Erissa."

"Enough, Faldeyr." Vilotta came to stand behind her husband and began rubbing his shoulders. She sighed when he leaned back into her touch. "We need to plan what to do next, not question your brother further. You know he would never risk the consequences of breaking his oath."

Some of the tension left the room as Faldeyr relaxed, allowing Barrett to sit back in his chair and do the same. His body melted into the soft cushion.

The worst of the night had passed, and he had not found his niece. But what would tomorrow bring? Would the blacksmith's son be able to keep her from her father's reach? There had to be a way for Barrett to help them escape the city.

"We need assistance." Faldeyr stood, pulling a knife from his belt. He passed it to Vilotta. "It's time to contact Thonalan."

Emberhold

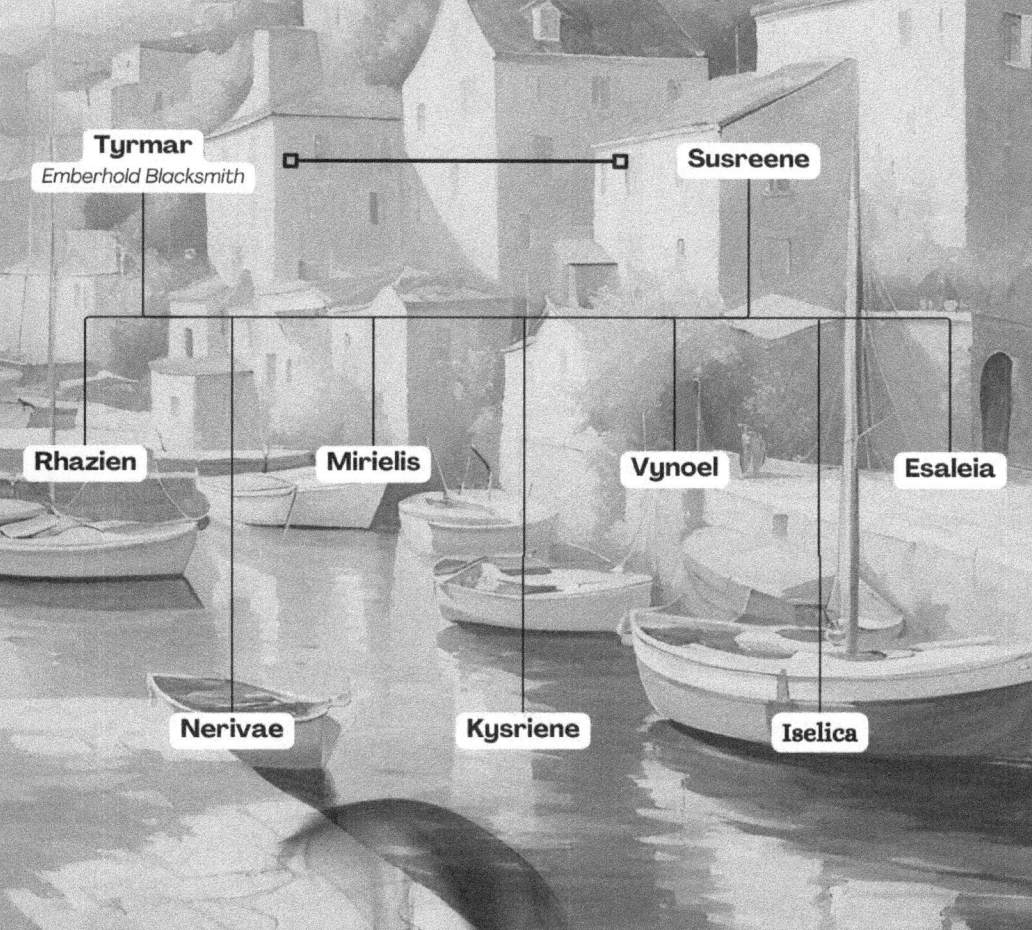

- **Tyrmar** — *Emberhold Blacksmith*
- **Susreene**
- **Rhazien**
- **Mirielis**
- **Vynoel**
- **Esaleia**
- **Nerivae**
- **Kysriene**
- **Iselica**

CHAPTER EIGHT

The following day dawned cold and wet. Peals of thunder drowned out the rain. A bitter wind whistled through cracks between the weathered planks of the loft. Rhazien's invention swayed overhead, its tinkling symphony contrasting with the violent roar of the storm. The others moved, adding their delicate songs to the languorous combination.

Erissa shivered against the cold and pulled the furs tighter around her, burrowing closer into the warmth. She savored the comfort of the moment, listening to the sounds of the storm alongside Rhazien's light snoring.

All too soon, he would rise and join his father in the forge. Leaving ahead of him waking was cowardly.

"Then don't," the voice snapped.

Erissa's anger flared at the voice. She wanted it to leave her in peace, but she had no choice. She had to go before he rose. Before he did something to change her mind. The tether between them grew stronger with every moment they spent together. It had become hard to tell where his desires began, and hers ended, making it difficult to know her own mind. She felt attached to Rhazien's very soul, and she was afraid the longer she stayed, the more she would grow used to the feeling. And that scared her most of all. The thought of not having it nearly brought her to her knees, and she never wanted to let someone have such power over her. No matter their connection or how much she wished to explore what it meant, she had no hope of staying.

"He is worth trusting," the voice pleaded, but Erissa ignored it.

If she had to leave, she wanted a moment to drink him in.

Even the gray light filtering in through the window did nothing to dim the bronzed glow of his skin so different from her own. The gold piercings on his ears and nose deepened his coloring. Erissa traced the air above them and his other features, as she memorized every line and angle.

She liked his nose and nearly giggled at the thought. Its strong slope gave character to his face and deepened the grooves running parallel on either side of his mouth. Laugh lines softened the angle of his lips as they relaxed in his sleep. Little crinkles around his eyes matched them, showing proof of how much he smiled, and Erissa was struck with the desire to wake him and see that smile one more time before she left.

Her hand traced a lock of his long brown hair, moving up the strand to hover over one of Rhazien's earcuffs. Each was a mirror of the other with gold shaped into the body of a dragon. The metal twisted together with small pieces of silver to create its scales. The tail wrapped its way down the length of his ear, coming to rest against the lobe with red stones dangling from where it pierced through the skin, while the head stretched over the ear to rest against his hairline. One wing hooked over the top of the ear from behind, covering it from view, the other raised as if the dragon was about to take flight. They would glitter during the day. Erissa wished with all her heart to see Rhazien's golden eyes framed by their light against his skin.

As the minutes counted down, every sound, every sensation of him pressed against her took on a heightened significance. She moved her head and placed it against his chest. The gentle thud of his heartbeat was soothing against her frayed nerves.

She inched away, careful not to disturb him. Only the threat of being locked away again—of being chained to the wall once more—had the power to pull her from his arms. Tears gathered in her eyes. Erissa swallowed the emotion, refusing to let them fall.

"You don't have to do this. Trust yourself. Trust me. He can help you."

Ignoring the voice, she slipped from his embrace, trying not to wake him. But her efforts were in vain when she crouched to retrieve her satchel. The planks, having become swollen with moisture from the night's rainfall, groaned under her shifting weight. The sound echoed across the room, standing out in the quiet between the clangors of the rumbling thunder.

Erissa panicked as Rhazien's eyes opened, their caramel depths thick with sleep. An arm stretched across the bed. He shook the slumbering fog from his eyes at finding nothing beside him. "Erissa?"

Urgency filled her voice. "I must go. I don't dare stay here much longer."

"So, you decided to sneak away while I slept?"

Her heart broke at the hurt in his voice. The sound of it shredded her conscience. "I have to go. And the sooner, the better. Daylight won't allow us to get away with last night's ruse. Barrett might come back to speak with you."

Rhazien rose from the bed and walked across the room. Erissa's curious eyes tracked his movements while he found a large sack and added a flint, clothing, and food to it. "We need to hurry."

"What are you doing?"

He ignored the question, placing a pot and utensils in the straining sack before turning his attention to the wardrobe once more.

Hanging on the doors were several knives and a hand axe. He slid the smaller blades into each of his boots, another hidden in the waist of his pants. A third larger one hooked into a loop on his belt. The hand axe joined it before he threw a heavy fur cloak over his shoulders.

"My bow is in the house, but I can grab a new one when we reach the next city. I have some money saved, and I doubt I would get a lie past my mother for needing it when I'm supposed to be in the forge all day." Rhazien moved to the bed and rolled the furs.

Erissa placed her hands over his, halting their movements. "Stop. Talk to me."

He gripped her hands. "I'm going with you."

The voice squealed, racing beneath her skin in its excitement.

Erissa tried to quell the hope his words caused for both of them. "You can't leave. You have a family here. Responsibilities. We don't even know each other. Why would you come with me?"

Rhazien's hold on her hands tightened. He brought her hands up one at a time and kissed her knuckles. "I can't imagine being here without you now."

She swallowed at the honesty in his eyes. His words wrapped around her heart, reaching the depths of her desperation and loneliness. The feeling scared her, leaving her trembling as if she were a newborn foal trying to walk for the first time.

Rhazien cupped her face, wiping the tears that had fallen, tears Erissa did not even know she was shedding as longing twisted her features. "I can't explain it to you any more than I can explain it to myself. But I can't walk away. I don't want to walk away."

"Do you know how crazy that sounds?" The words rushed out in a single breath.

"Are you telling me you don't feel the same?" Panic overtook his tone. "Erissa..."

Every emotion fought for dominance while she struggled to accept Rhazien's companionship, something her parents had denied her for so long. Her chest rose and fell with quick gasps as she trembled. "I'm afraid."

"Of me?" The question hung between them. For a moment, the room stilled, each waiting for her answer.

"No. Rhazien, I'm not afraid of you. I'm afraid you want to stay." The fear eased once Erissa voiced it, the words tumbling out of her. "No one stays. They're always afraid of what I might see. Even my parents. It was easier to leave me there alone rather than confront my power." She shrugged, the dismissive gesture outweighed by the pain in her eyes.

"I won't leave you the way they did." Rhazien's rage flowed into her as her pain became his.

When he said no more, Erissa held a hand against where he still cupped her face. "We don't have time for this, Rhazien."

"No, we don't." Rhazien pulled Erissa closer. With his arms wrapped around her, he kissed her brow, nuzzling against her. "But we have time enough for this."

Erissa brought her arms around him, her grip desperate. "Are you really coming?"

"It doesn't make any sense—running away with a girl I've known for two nights. I can't explain it or rationalize it away. I didn't know you in the market, but even then, an intense desire to follow you overcame me. It's more than attraction, more than thinking you're beautiful. There's a bond between us so strong I swear I can almost see the strands connecting us. I've felt nothing like it before. You feel like coming home. My heart can feel it even as my mind tells me I'm insane, and all I know is there's nothing that will keep me away."

Her heart lurched, the sensation so strong Erissa was sure he perceived the shift. Whatever doubts she had fled with the hope he offered her. He tightened his arms like he feared her running away from the weight of his words if his hold loosened.

"My mother told me some people are lucky because their souls recognize each other. Maybe that's what this is. The speed of this connection scares me, but I'm willing to follow it—and you—wherever it takes me. I can't let you go alone."

She pulled back, a brilliant smile unfurling as she whispered the words. "You're a very surprising person, Rhazien."

The voice laughed, leaving Erissa questioning its sanity. *"Don't worry. You will find out what is so amusing soon enough."*

With his food stores and possessions packed, the pair descended from the loft. The morning was alive with the sounds of the forge, the sharp pounding in time with the cursing coming from within as it competed against the growing ferocity of the rain.

Rhazien saddled the largest of the three horses before tying their bags on either side and adding the rolled-up furs from the bed. Next, he tied several bags of oats on the pommel before adding several large, tanned hides across the horse's back, covering the meager supplies. "It's not much, but these should help keep our stuff reasonably dry."

"What's his name?" Erissa leaned to pet the horse, hesitating from her lack of experience with such an animal. The horse sensed her fear as it whickered at her outstretched fingers.

Rhazien stroked his hand down the horse's neck. "Rhynstone."

The horse's ears twitched at the sound of his name. Rhynstone leaned in to nuzzle against Rhazien before nipping at his trouser pocket.

"He wants a sugar cube." Rhazien laughed. The rich baritone echoed along Erissa's spine, the sound tantalizing. She laughed along with him. He reached into his pocket, retrieved a sugar cube, and held it out to her. "Here, you feed it to him."

Her hand trembled as she took the cube.

"Now hold your hand out flat with the sugar in the middle, and Rhyn will do the rest."

Erissa did as he told her, holding the cube out for the horse to take. She grinned as Rhynstone nibbled the sugar from her hand, delighted as the horse nuzzled against her hair. "It tickles."

"Rhyn might be imposing, but he's a tenderhearted beast." Rhazien adjusted the hides once more. "We need to get going before my father comes for me. It's not that far off from when I'm supposed to be in the forge."

"It's a little too late for that, son." Tyrmar stepped through the doorway, shaking the rain from his hair and cloak, two large sacks in either hand. "Did you really think I'd be fooled by last night?"

Rhazien grabbed Erissa's arm, moving her behind him.

"You would put us through this again, boy? For a woman you don't know?" The question was more curious than anything, with Tyrmar's head tipped to the side. "We've barely settled in Emberhold, and you would turn this into another Freyborn?"

Heated color suffused Rhazien's cheeks. "It's not the same. You don't know what you speak of."

"Then enlighten me." Tyrmar sat the bags down and leaned against the door frame, locking one ankle over the other.

"Erissa's in danger. The Lord… he chains her in her room and worse. He'll end up killing her if she stays. She can't go back. I won't let her go back, and I won't let her go alone," Rhazien said.

Tyrmar spread a hand out before him, gesturing to Erissa, who peered at him from around his son's arm. "Whose word am I supposed to take on this? To level such accusations against the Lord is a grave matter. You don't know her word is trustworthy."

Erissa tried to push around Rhazien, but he blocked her once again. "I know enough." He spoke with conviction, his shoulders straightening. "You didn't trust me in Freyborn. I'm asking you to trust me now. Trust in the man you raised me to be. I wouldn't help her without cause. She... it's my *nayanam*."

Tyrmar considered his son's words. His mouth puffed to the side like he was chewing the side of his cheek. She gripped Rhazien's arm, her hold tightening when his father's gaze moved to where her hands rested, moving to see the same arm wrapped around her waist. Whatever *nayanam* meant, it impacted Rhazien's father.

"I'll buy as much time as I can." He straightened and took a large pouch from beneath his cloak with a deep sigh. "Take this. It's the gold your Ma has been hiding away. She said it's to bless your *nayanam*."

Rhazien caught the coin bag as his father tossed it to him. He pushed his cloak out of the way, securing it on his belt. "Father...."

"You have little time. I've no doubt the captain will be back this morn with questions. You must leave Emberhold now."

Erissa knocked Rhazien's arm out of the way, stepping past him. She ran up to Tyrmar and threw her arms around him. She pressed a kiss to his cheek, his skin still warm from the forge. "Thank you."

Tyrmar smiled, his cheeks ruddy. Rhazien came to hug his father, reaching around Erissa to wrap them both in his arms.

Before Rhazien let go, Tyrmar cleared his throat. "Rhazien?" Tyrmar's voice hung heavy with regret. "I'm sorry. For Freyborn. I should have trusted you."

Rhazien said nothing, his arms tightening for a moment.

"If you get in trouble, find Micmus. He won't turn you away." Tyrmar stepped out of the couple's arms. He bent to pick up the straining sacks and passed them to Rhazien. "Warm clothing for the girl and what's left of the food. Take Carizzea with you. You won't get far in this weather with only one horse." Tyrmar brushed a hand through his hair, his face clouding with uncertainty. "Be well, son."

Tyrmar left while Rhazien readied the second horse. Erissa stepped into an empty stall to change. Tyrmar had packed several sets of fur-lined clothing and boots. Grateful for the warm clothes, Erissa put on the trousers and a long-sleeved shirt. Both were snug against her body, but they chased the chill from her skin.

When she had finished stepping into the boots, Erissa came out of the stall. Rhazien had the second horse saddled. She passed him the bag of clothes, and he added them to Carizzea's lighter load.

With the horses ready, Rhazien turned his attention to Erissa. He walked across the stable to grab a fur cloak that matched his own. He placed it around her shoulders and pulled the hood up. Rhazien tucked Erissa's hair into the folds, covering the dark strands. "It's a good thing Esaleia left her cloak in the stall. My sister is fond of piling her hair into the most elaborate of monstrosities, so Mother always alters her cloaks to accommodate. This depth of the hood should hide your glow."

Rhazien and Erissa left the stables, Rhynstone and Carizzea following behind. They turned west, heading in the direction of the main gate. Rhazien hurried, the horses tailing along obediently while Erissa struggled to keep pace with their long legs.

"Wait... Rhazien..."

Rhazien slowed with Erissa's words, holding out his arm for her.

"What's *naya... nayanam*?"

"It's..." Rhazien coughed, turning to look behind them. "It's something my sister made up. A word for when someone is in trouble."

Laughter echoed through Erissa's mind, but the voice stayed silent, offering no comment on its strange show of mirth.

Erissa took the arm he offered again, dismissing the voice. "What happened in Freyborn?"

Rhazien missed a step with her question, causing the horses to chafe when their reins tugged with the movement. "My sister. She died." He said no more.

Pain overtook his features. Her curiosity died at causing Rhazien discomfort. She never intended to evoke painful memories, and as she imagined what having a sibling to miss would feel like, her own memories took over. She thanked the Creator—for all it was worth—that he denied her a sibling. Erissa did not want to know what her parents would have done to another child or how differently they might have treated them.

Terror gnawed at her when they came walking to the city gates. The townspeople filled the road, most walking opposite the pair, pulling carts or carrying baskets as they made their way into the market.

The guard subjected those who came through the gate to searches, soldiers checking their wares for the safety of all. Rhazien and Erissa lost themselves in the groups of workers heading beyond the gilded walls of the city.

Erissa reached for her hood and pulled it further over her face until it became almost impossible to see what lay in front of her. Gratitude filled her for the bitter bite of the rain; it provided a reason to hide her undeniable identity. The once pristine hem of her trousers became splattered in mud, and her cloak became saturated from the downpour. With her hood casting a shadow over her features, no one would guess the drowned woman was a Lady.

She worried for more than herself. With the family having already lost a child, she considered how it would feel for them with Rhazien leaving.

"Are you sure you want to do this?" Erissa's hand tightened across his arm, the knuckles white. "I'll be fine on my own. You have a family here and are starting a new life. You shouldn't throw that away on someone you don't know."

He steered her to the side of the throng where a carriage sat waiting, using its size to keep them out of the soldiers' view.

"Erissa, look at me." He waited until her eyes met his, the amethyst depths mesmerizing with their intensity. "There's nothing you can say to change my mind. I'm going with you because I want to, and I don't want to hear another protest."

Rhazien adjusted the cloak across her shoulders, pulling the material tight to fight against the aching chill of the morning and the rain reaching to her skin below. "I promise you; this is where I want to be, and I meant what I told my father. There is no way I would ever leave you to face any of this alone. Now, enough of your doubts. We have a lot of ground to cover today, and most of it will be by foot until we reach the outer limits of the farmland. If we put you on a horse now, your eyes will be visible to everyone on the ground."

Erissa smiled as he tucked her under his arm, and they rejoined the line of people. No matter her protesting, his willingness to go with her touched something she had long ago buried in her heart.

As they neared the gates, the guards were searching all those coming and going from the city. Erissa stressed against her lower lip while she searched those gathered around the townspeople.

She spied a figure through the rain that resembled her uncle. The soldiers were searching everyone in his direction. They examined carts, barrels, and wagons before removing the hoods of cloaks from those appearing to be of smaller stature.

Dread spread through her breast, the clammy feeling making Erissa sick. "My uncle is here for me." Hysteria threatened to overwhelm her with living nightmares of being dragged back into the manor and subjected to her father's threat. "What do we do?"

Erissa waited for the voice to speak up. It never came, worsening Erissa's fears. Had she offended it this morning, or did it foretell some dreadful event waiting for them at the gates?

Rhazien did not answer her question as her panic grew. He steered them to the gates, reaching under the hides to pull something out of his pack. It was a curled piece of metal, not unlike those hanging from the stable's musical pipes, but it had a discernible diamond-shaped head at one end and a tail at the other.

Rhazien slowed their pace until they had fallen back alongside an older couple steering a cart with two draft horses that rivaled Rhynstone's height. They had filled the cart with goods, enough to see them through the winter. The stacked wares created a cover for Rhazien and Erissa, and he slowed to match their pace, waiting for an open opportunity to use his crafted snake.

It came as the husband turned to answer a question from his wife as she pointed to the line of soldiers, her brow wrinkling. Rhazien took advantage of the momentary distraction and tossed the metal onto the ground before the horses.

Their eyes went wild with fear. The horses bucked against their harnesses to get away from the harmless twist of metal.

The man held onto the reins with a death grip, trying in vain to calm the frightened animals while the gateway exploded into pandemonium. Other horses fought against their handlers, the fear of the panicking pair palpable to them even through the heavy rain. People dove away from the beasts and their flailing hooves.

With chaos rivaling the rain for attention. Barrett directed the soldiers into the crowd to help control the people and frightened animals. Rhazien took advantage of the upheaval, rushing Erissa and their horses to the gates before the soldiers noticed them as they dodged through the squealing animals and screaming people.

Erissa's fingers dug into the palms of her hand, the sharp, hot pain contrasting with the cold rainwater pelting her, convinced they would be caught any moment. She struggled to breathe as they walked through the gates, half expecting them to come crashing down upon her.

The rain and chaos hid her between the horse and the man on either side. They passed through the gates with quick steps, Erissa almost running to keep up with Rhazien's fast pace. She looked behind her as they cleared the space, holding her breath. It flowed freely with no one following them.

Rhazien did not stop once they had crossed the threshold. He continued at a brutal pace, testing Erissa's endurance as her shorter frame struggled to keep up with him and the horse. Only the arm around her shoulders kept her moving alongside him, a buffer against the rain and her own nerves.

He stopped them as the houses became smaller and further apart. They were cleaned and well-kept while their owners stayed tucked away from the torrent of rain, its icy droplets growing fatter as they picked up speed and ferocity. It would be a frosty night, a night for fires made of oak logs with their fragrant smoke, but first, they had to get out of the city and head for the next town.

He let go of her shoulder and moved to adjust the straps on Carizzea's saddle. "Erissa, can you ride a horse?"

Erissa chewed against her bottom lip. "I'm not sure I remember how. It's been so long, but I'm sure I'll manage fine." Erissa hesitated as she went to stand beside Carizzea. While not as tall as Rhynstone, Carizzea was still an intimidating beast, her gray-speckled, white coat highlighting her powerful muscles. Erissa stared at the stirrups in fear and defeat, struggling to mount the horse and maintain her dignity without help.

"Here, little doe. Let me."

Rhazien's fingers grazed her waist, and he paused. When Erissa said nothing, he continued to move them, wrapping his fingers around the curves of her hips. Warmth spread through her at his nearness. Even with all the layers between their skin, the touch of his hand burned the chill away. A shiver built up her lower spine.

"You have to put your boot in the stirrup." Rhazien's words tickled against her ear as he stepped close, pressing his chest into her back.

A smile was in his voice, the gentle humor firing the blush ever at the ready when he touched her. Grateful for the deep hood hiding her face, Erissa placed her boot in the stirrup, hoping the blush would fade as she hoisted herself into the saddle with Rhazien's help.

No such luck graced her. Rhazien's hands lingered, one resting on her lower back while the other moved to the top of her thigh. Erissa twisted in the saddle, trying to make herself more at ease on the tall horse. The movement tugged at the hood of her cloak, revealing the side of her face. Rhazien grinned at her. He waited a moment more until she settled before he readied to mount Rhynstone.

Erissa panicked when his horse walked forward. The warmth from Rhazien's touch faded, leaving her cold as she contemplated the reins she held. "What do I do?"

A whistle cut through the air. Carizzea's ears twitched at the noise, her hooves shuffling her weight from one side to the other, splashing mud onto Erissa's already mud-caked boots and trousers. Erissa grabbed onto the pommel for dear life, convinced the horse would throw her from the saddle at any moment.

The horse shifted more, tossing her head against the reins, and Erissa slid against the wet saddle, her gaze locked onto the ground. Panic about what would happen if she fell from the horse grew uncontrolled. The image of

Carizzea trampling her underneath large hooves and breaking her bones left Erissa's breathing labored and her chest tight. Flashes of memories of past times when her bones had broken harassed her, each one more painful than the last as she relived the torment of her father's fists.

Her bones ached in the cold beneath her skin, worsening the onslaught as a particularly vile memory of when her father first strung her up for his whip. Her collar bones had broken from the force of her body weight, the healing made slower by the whipping she received. She hoped the memory did not pass through the tether binding her to Rhazien.

As the details sharpened into excruciating clarity, she called out for help. "Rhazien!"

Rhazien halted Rhynstone and turned his attention to Erissa. Another whistle pierced through the rain. Carizzea's stirring halted, and she started walking at the sharp command. He waited patiently for the pair to reach him. "Carizzea can sense your fear, little doe. Take a deep breath and think about relaxing your body while you breathe out slowly."

It took effort for Erissa to do what Rhazien instructed. With each breath, Rhazien breathed along with her. She melted into the sensation of being one and mimicked the feel of what he was doing. Even as the tension drained from her shoulders, her white knuckles remained clenched on the pommel.

"Take another one, little doe." Rhazien's tone was firm but cajoling as it wound itself along the fibers of the strange bond they shared.

Clinging to his words, Erissa breathed in and out once more. On the exhale, she loosened one finger at a time until both hands no longer touched the pommel.

"Take another one and then look up." Rhazien was painstakingly gentle.

Erissa inhaled slowly and raised her eyes to meet his on the exhale. What she found in his gaze left her feeling raw and exposed. His jaw was tense, highlighting the angles of his face and the compassion and fury that battled for dominance within his darkened gaze.

"You saw my memories, didn't you?" Erissa's shoulders sagged with guilt and shame, the question hanging between them.

"All of them." Softly spoken, rage dripped from the words. When she flinched against them, Rhazien cleared the emotion from his voice before speaking again. "Carizzea will follow Rhyn now that you're calmer. Hold the reins like this. You want to pull on the reins slightly and grip the horse with your legs as you lean forward to make them walk. To go left or right, pull back with gentle pressure using the hand on either side."

"And to stop?" Erissa tried to keep the panic from her words, overcome with anxiety about the idea of controlling such an animal, but paid rapt attention to Rhazien as he quickly showed her how to move and halt the horse using the reins and her legs. As he finished, the weather worsened.

"Let's get going." Rhazien guided Rhyn down the earthen road, taking note of Erissa to see if she was doing the same.

It took little prodding to get Carizzea to follow them. She appreciated Rhazien as he talked to her about the horses. Erissa needed the instruction, but she wanted the noise more than anything. The worst of her memories waited for her in the silence.

They moved quickly despite the drowned road. Eventually, the tidy houses changed to greater expanses of land with animals roaming behind fences, their well-worn homes sitting back some distance from the road. Unlike the citizens with the neat rows of houses sitting in the shadows of the walled city, these owners were outside, tending to the chores required of such homesteads despite the torrential onslaught.

For all the stress and worry, Erissa's elation slowly built at the newfound sense of freedom growing with each clop of the horse's hooves. She tried to hold on to that feeling as the rain continued, her long saturated cloak laying heavy as if a stone sat upon her shoulders.

Erissa directed a longing stare at the tendrils of smoke trailing upward from the chimneys of the homes they passed, wanting nothing more than a bed and warm bath. She doubted she would see either anytime soon. "Rhazien, where are we going?"

"We need to find somewhere to shelter until the storm passes." He stopped for a moment, uselessly trying to wipe the water from his eyes. He had to raise his voice over the rain, the droplets turning into sleet as the temperature dropped. "The rain's getting worse. If we're out here much longer, we'll both catch more than a chill." He surveyed the surrounding land through gray sheets of rain, trying to think of places to pass the night. His face twisted in frustration, and Erissa imagined he was thinking much the same as her.

Requesting a space to sleep in the barn of one of the houses dotting the road would be the best choice, but that needed to be avoided at all costs. Her appearance was striking, even partially hidden, and it would spell disaster if anyone caught her eye. Continuing to an inn with the current weather was unrealistic. The sleet thickened as quickly as her mind raced.

With nothing else available to them, Rhazien tugged on Rhynstone's reins and turned the horse north toward the dense forest. "We'll go into Eshirene's Wood and follow the forest up to the Wilds and go the long way to Gailme. No one will think you would dare to brave the Wilds alone."

"The Violent Wilds are a place of nightmares. I've heard the stories about the sinister things that live there."

"You shouldn't believe everything you hear."

"But the creatures—"

Rhazien cut her off. "Erissa, we have no choice. We'll catch sick if we continue in this weather."

She had no way to refute what he said. Staying quiet, she followed alongside Rhazien.

Erissa's heart pounded with each step Carizzea took, her hooves sounding like a drum pounding in her ears. The Wilds were legendary enough that even a girl chained to the wall had listened to the tales or, at the very least, read of them. Whatever fate awaited them in the chaos of the Violent Wilds was nothing compared to what lay behind her in Emberhold.

Shaking off her worries with a deep breath, Erissa squared her shoulders against the weight of her sodden cloak and reminded herself what was at stake should her uncle find them. She readied to ride into the wood as if heading to the depths of the Veil to face the Keeper himself.

CHAPTER NINE

Rhazien and Erissa shivered as they rode beneath the canopy of pine boughs, the temperature dropping drastically.

The scraggly foliage of the evergreen trees provided little shelter. Ice stuck against the damp needles littering the ground, the horses' hooves crunching against them. Matted brown needles blended with the hibernating brush with deadwood cradled among what few ferns remained. Their feathery swaths gathered icicles on their tips while darker patches of the quickly freezing water settled in the grooves of the uneven ground.

A long-suffering hope filled Rhazien's voice as they trudged on. "We need to keep going. The further we get, the thicker the trees will be."

Erissa nodded, too cold to do anything else.

They slogged through the forest, going deeper and deeper until the trees became closer together. Erissa grew more concerned about finding shelter to wait out the storm.

"Over to the left." Rhazien pointed toward a darkened area of the wood. "It looks like some kind of shelter."

She squinted, the promise of something overhead sheltering them from the rain, pulling her from her sorry state. She tried to see through the falling droplets. The harder she studied the area, the more it appeared like a shadow standing in the distance. It was difficult to see with the fading light of the passing day casting its gloominess against every tree and bush.

Rhazien steered them in the shadow's direction.

Towering oaks wove throughout the pine trees, with sycamores and firs peppered between them. The thick trunks spoke to the age of the wood. Many of the tree trunks intertwined with one another, creating an almost impenetrable covering with their bulky crowns braided together, leaving parts of the ground dry as they continued.

With each step, the shadow grew closer and took the shape of a building. Soon, they made out the walls of an old hunting lodge not much larger than the blacksmith's stable in Emberhold. Erissa groaned in relief, the sound locking in her throat as a shiver wracked her body.

It was in a state of advanced disrepair, the roof having collapsed over most of the threshold. The windows were without glass or a hide, and barren frames allowed the wind to whistle through. The sound rivaled that of the squeaking half-hanging door swaying back and forth. Brown, spindly vines covered the walls, their leaves having long fallen to the winter air.

Rhazien brought his horse to a stop. Carizzea responded to the gentle pressure on the reins as Erissa leaned back, and the horse came to a standstill next to Rhynstone. Rhazien dismounted. He was quick to help Erissa dismount, focused solely on getting her in front of a fire and into dry clothing.

"Wait here." Rhazien handed Rhynstone's reins to Erissa. He approached the swinging door, taking the knife from his belt and holding it out before him. Carefully, he pushed the door open, listening for any sound of disturbance that would signal someone else was making use of the dilapidated lodge.

Hearing nothing more than the sound of rain misting through the foliage, Rhazien stepped into the building. In the last of the remaining light, he found a large open area empty of all furnishings. A low wall cut across most of the remaining interior, the broken wood hinting at its former structure.

Finding nothing, Rhazien sheathed the knife once more and went back outside. "We can stay here for the night. Light a fire and warm up while we hide the smoke in this storm."

Erissa made to hand both sets of reins to him. "You make Rhyn and Carizzea comfortable. I can get wood for the fire."

He pushed her hand away. "You take them. You're in no condition to find firewood."

"Rhazien, take the horses." Erissa placed the reins into his hand. "Locked in a room for endless years, remember? I don't know the first thing about taking care of a horse, but I can pick wood off the ground. Besides, I'm cold. Maybe moving around will help until we get a fire started."

"Do you even know which wood to gather?" Rhazien smiled as her nose wrinkled in confusion.

"Does it matter?"

Rhazien's tone gentled, "Only if we want the fire to last without having to feed it constantly."

"This is pointless." Erissa huffed out a cloud of frigid air. "I can barely ride a horse and can't take care of one either. I can't pick wood, and I don't know the first thing about starting a fire or anything else about spending the night in the woods. I know nothing about taking care of myself. We both know I wouldn't have made it this far without you, and even if I had, I would freeze before long."

"Someone else locked you in that room, little doe. You didn't stay there by choice."

"That doesn't make me any less useless." Erissa's voice wobbled on the last word. It was a familiar refrain plowing through the cold to bury itself deeper into her heart. Feeling inept at the hands of another had been one thing, but it hurt more to deal with her own ignorance.

Rhazien reached for her hands. "There were many times I failed to light a fire when I first learned. Give yourself time. You learn by doing. And succeed by continuing to try after you fail." He brought the hand to his lips and pressed a quick kiss against her cold fingers. "Most Ladies wouldn't know how to collect wood or light a fire, not when they have maids caring for the rooms."

He laughed as Erissa swatted his arm.

"That's not the point, Rhazien."

"But it's the truth. You're the daughter of a wealthy high Lord, not a minor Lady in some river town. I have no doubt your mother also lacks the skill to light a fire."

"You have a point. Mother would sooner faint than dirty her hands."

He smiled, catching sight of the grin she tried to hide. "You want the driest of the fallen oak limbs. It's easy to tell them apart from the pine. Both kinds of wood have rings inside, but the oak differs from the pine with lines running outward from the center."

"We need to keep him," the voice purred. *"I adore his gentle patience."*

"Rings with lines." Erissa smoothed her hands down the front of her cloak, anything to keep Rhazien from noticing the blush spreading across her cheeks. She grimaced at the soaked material. "I'll be quick. The sooner we have a fire, the better."

Rhazien moved the horses to the nearest tree and tied the reins to a low-hanging branch. "Start with the smaller limbs. I'll come help when I've finished with Rhyn and Crezzi."

He tended to the horses' needs, covering their thick hair with the oiled hides to protect from the worsening cold as Erissa walked around the area.

She moved from tree to tree, collecting the smaller branches from the forest floor. The thick canopy overhead proved to be great protection from the worst of the rain. She was determined to show herself capable, inspecting each one before nodding to herself and adding it to the growing pile in her arms.

The movement helped return a sliver of warmth to her limbs, but it mattered little in such weather. She moved faster, craving the heat of a fire.

Erissa turned as Rhazien approached. "Is this enough?"

"More than enough to get us started." Unhooking the axe from his belt, Rhazien moved to a fallen oak. "Take them to the hearth. It was in decent enough shape for all that it's abandoned. I'll be along shortly. We need some larger pieces of wood and kindling."

Erissa sought their belongings while Rhazien gathered what they needed. He had placed them in the only corner where the roof remained intact, right beside the empty hearth. She was standing beside them, twining a long dead vine around her fingers when Rhazien returned.

"You should change into dry clothes while I start the fire." Rhazien placed his burden in front of the hearth and waited for her to respond.

Erissa stood lost in thought, the vine taunting her with her mother's revelation about the elemental part of her magic as the shivers finally caught up to her, causing her body to quake.

"Erissa?"

The sound of her name drew her attention. "Hmm?"

Rhazien moved to her side. "Are you alright?"

"Yes, I was only thinking."

"Of what?"

"Magic." Erissa sighed, the sound weighing heavily against the quiet rustling of evergreen needles beneath the rain. She ran her fingers along the length of the vine. "Having it is something many would die for, and yet, I can't make myself see it as anything but a curse."

The voice snorted. *"I will show you a curse."*

A smile twitched against Erissa's lips. She almost wished the voice would carry out its threat. Maybe then she might understand its purpose.

Another snort came from within. Erissa imagined the voice rolling its eyes with that one.

"If you haven't figured out who I am by now, there is no hope for you."

Rhazien cupped his hands around hers, halting their movement and bringing her attention back to him. "Change your clothes, little doe. I'll keep my back turned. You're shaking with the cold."

Rhazien was true to his word despite her desire for him to turn around. But at the same time, she did not want him to. She tugged at her sleeves, pulling them down over the scars on her wrists. They were bad enough, but the ones on her back and chest? They shamed her.

Another shiver made her teeth chatter, dislodging her thoughts, and Erissa changed as her face flamed at his nearness, the blush adding an extra layer of warmth across her body. He had the fire going by the time she finished peeling the wet garments from her form. Heat stirred against her skin, and she stood for a moment, letting the warmth build and her skin dry as the fire grew in size.

Freshly clothed, Erissa pulled down the thickest vines hanging on the wall. She tied the pieces together to create a rope. Knotting the ends around the two remaining posts, she was careful not to disturb their balance as they leaned precariously and gently hung the wet clothing to dry, leaving space for Rhazien.

"You can turn around now, Rhazien." Erissa beamed at him when he did, gesturing to her hanging clothes. "There isn't much coverage from the rain, but this should allow them to dry more. We can put the cloaks on the floor before the fire."

"And you thought you knew nothing that would be of use."

Rhazien's teasing brought forth a dark chuckle as she fought against the poisonous twist her mindset tried to take. "When I was little, I would hide among the hanging sheets and wait for my nurse to find me. I tripped once, pulling the line down with me. The housekeeper would have had my hide if she had seen. I had to drag an empty barrel across the rear courtyard to tie the line back in place before someone found out. That was only days before...." she trailed off, her face darkening in remembrance. Breathing deeply, Erissa shook her head, clearing her mind of such sadness with forced cheerfulness. "The maids braided the lines using the fibers from the trees that grew along the sea, and I thought it might work the same way using the vines. There's plenty of room for your clothing. I'll turn my back while you change."

Once Rhazien had swapped his wet clothes for dry ones, they sat before the hearth wrapped in the remaining furs, feasting on some of the fruit, bread, and dried meat he had packed. The warmth of the fire chased away some of the cold, but it did little to reach their bones.

Rhazien wedged Erissa tight against him. Neither talked for some time, simply sitting close and sharing the heat of their bodies. Rhazien's skin burned through his clothing. Stray pieces of her hair touched the side of his face as the wind stirred around them. Rhazien's chest rose in time with hers as she leaned into his embrace to savor his warmth. The hilt of his knife dug into her side, but she said nothing for fear he would move away.

The last light of day faded, the clouds darkening above them as nightfall overtook the forest. They were grateful for the warmth of the fire against the worsening chill of the air. The rain had slowed, with scattered drops breaking through the thickly limbed trees.

"My sister loved nights like these. They were few and far between." Rhazien's words were quiet and filled with longing as the weight of grief settled in his chest. "She would go to the tavern and sit before its fire and soak in its warmth, swapping stories and drinking ale while the rain fell outside. She loved the sound of the rain against the clay tiles of the inn's roof, and she'd come late, smelling of smoke and half-drunk with some new tale of adventure for the younger ones."

Rhazien's muscles tightened against the grief in his voice. He cleared his throat, breaking up the emotion that lay thick within it. "I loved her very much. She was as wild and untamed as the wind, but she had a kind heart that laughed easily. I miss the sound. It hasn't been long since we lost her. 'Twas only several moons ago, but it still feels like yesterday."

"What happened?" Rhazien stiffened beside her and shame-filled Erissa for intruding on his grief with her question. "I'm sorry, Rhazien. I shouldn't have asked."

"It's not a story I'm proud of. I..." Rhazien's grief clogged his words. He swallowed hard to dislodge the pain thick in the back of his throat. "I failed her, Erissa. If I had only done more, she'd still be with us."

Erissa hushed him and wiped away the lone tear, creating a path against his stubbled jaw. "You don't have to tell me."

She did not think Rhazien had heard her as he closed his eyes and leaned into her touch. She wanted nothing more than to ground him and pull him back from the edge of grief's abyss as he had done for her when she told him of her father's violence.

Rhazien surprised her when he spoke again. "There's a town a week's ride from here, out in the desert lands where the sand meets the forest, leading to the Mists with a river and the Violent Wilds on the other side. It's called Freyborn. It's where my sisters called home before my parents claimed them. Our fathers were friends. They sent word when their parents caught the wasting. By the time we reached the city, they were already gone, and the girls became orphans. We settled there, and my parents raised them as their own."

"Those poor girls." Erissa sniffled on the verge of tears. "The wasting ruined so much for everyone."

"They were strong for ones so young. It helped that we kept them in their home. To leave Freyborn after such a loss would have been too much." Rhazien rubbed at his temples. "It's a small town, rarely seeing any travelers, with the Mists separating it from the Fae on one side and the stories of the Wilds on the other. When people do come, it's mostly traders from Cropari. For those living there, there's no such thing as a stranger. My father and Lord Ernald were as close as brothers. Ernald treated us like his own, helping to raise the girls alongside his son and his tutors. He only had one son, Gabrien."

He spat the name.

Erissa tried not to flinch at the malice in his tone, so at odds with the man she had come to know. Her hand dropped to her lap, but she stayed silent, letting Rhazien speak as he desired.

"Gabrien was a different person when our parents weren't around. Cruel. Manipulative. Intelligent enough to hide his true nature from most. But men have a way of letting their guard down when they're in their cups. I got to see exactly the kind of man Gabrien was on several occasions." Rhazien paused, frowning. "My sister was beautiful. Wild. Carefree. She didn't want to be confined to society's rules for women. She was fiercely independent and drew people in like a moth to the flame. She wanted nothing more than to be one of the men. But the older she got, the harder it became for the men of the village to see her as anything but the striking beauty she was." Rhazien's voice turned wistful, a small smile playing about his lips. "Her eyes were the deepest shade of green." The smile disappeared with his next words, his face hardening to stone. "Gabrien became obsessed with her."

Erissa swallowed the bile that rose with Rhazien's words as she guessed at the rest of his story.

"He made a show of courting her. I tried to warn my parents against the match. I tried to warn her too, but Gabrien had them all fooled, and my words did nothing more than drive a wedge between us all." Rhazien stared into the fire. He didn't speak for a minute, lost in replaying the events.

Bits and pieces of memories reached Erissa through their connection, flashes of a beautiful woman with eyes that shined brightly when she smiled. The smile dimmed as one scene faded into the next, her expression wearing down until a completely different woman occupied Rhazien's mind.

When he spoke again, his voice had a desolate sound to it. "She loved him, but I don't know what he did to cause such a change in her. Whatever he did was subtle, little suggestions here and there, so she didn't notice how much she had changed to suit him. Her eyes stopped smiling. She rarely laughed. She stopped running about the town or going to the tavern. She used to help our father in the forge, but Gabrien wanted her to be more ladylike, and ladies didn't have calloused hands from hours spent hammering steel. She even stopped telling stories to our siblings. Slowly, everything about her faded against the person he wanted her to be."

A tear fell as she hurt for the girl Rhazien described. Erissa hurt for the person his sister lost when she changed herself to suit Gabrien's taste, the part of herself she must have grieved. Losing your identity was a pain Erissa knew all too well. It was pain that left you trapped without hope and frantic for any way to escape.

Rhazien turned to Erissa, his eyes wet and voice cracking. "She disappeared right in front of me, Erissa, but even then, it wasn't enough for him. When she didn't measure up to his expectations, he turned his temper against her."

Rhazien's story brought Erissa back to the days when she had only known her father's fists. She was afraid to hear Rhazien continue with his story, but Erissa knew he needed to give voice to the memories haunting him. "What happened, Rhazien?"

"I found her, broken and bleeding, in the Lord's barn. He just left in a bloodied heap on the floor." Rhazien stood, pacing away from her to stand in the darkened corner of the lodge where the light of the fire struggled to reach, almost as if he were trying to hide his pain and guilt in the night's darkness. "I almost killed him when I found him. If the other men had not been there to pull me back, I would have without hesitation. I wish I had. Maybe then my sister..."

Rhazien's breathing was uneven, his puff of breath visible in the fire's light as he paced back and forth in the small space. "She lied for him. To protect him or to protect me, I'll never know. And then he blamed her. Claimed she got drunk at the tavern and got on the wrong side of a man passing through Freyborn. No matter what I said, she insisted on the truth of his story, and our parents believed her. It was my word against hers, and everyone knew of my dislike for Gabrien.

"Months later, Ernald died, leaving his estate to his son with Ernald's brother acting as an adviser. Gabrien's demands of her worsened as he expected her to take on the role of Ladyship." Rhazien's words faded, almost as if he were afraid to give voice to the rest of the story.

Erissa imagined what it cost him to tell her. It mirrored the pain that consumed her when she told Rhazien some of what befell her, the bite of it so clear beneath her breast as it hammered at her heart. Telling such a monstrosity was like recounting a nightmare, and saying it aloud turned the nightmare into a waking hell.

When he spoke again, the words were hollow, sounding to Erissa like the grief was gone, a void of darkness taking its place. "She took her own life. Some of the townspeople found her hanging with a note pinned to her gown. The note... it told of how Gabrien had attacked her again, and she believed there was no other escape after lying for so long."

Erissa's heart broke for Rhazien but more so for his sister. She considered what the note must have said and how the young woman's feelings echoed Erissa's own when her father chained her to the wall. To feel so desperate for relief from something you believed you would never escape. Something others would never believe happened.

In Erissa's own anguish, she had endured the same. Something cold gripped her. Something much colder than the winter air surrounding them. It took her back to those moments when all hope was absent as the emotional toll of the darkest of her days dug further into the open wounds which plagued her. Why did she stay her own hand when Rhazien's sister had not done the same?

Rhazien's words interrupted Erissa's bleak reflection. "She died thinking no one would believe her—that I would be angry with her deceit. I went to find him after. To kill him. But he was gone, sent away by his uncle as soon as word of what happened reached the Lord's household. They didn't even have the decency to cut her down before having him run."

A storm of grief raged within him, and Rhazien broke against it.

Erissa rushed to him and wrapped him in her arms as sobs wracked his frame. There were no words of comfort, only the warmth of her body against his as she poured all of herself into the embrace.

"If my parents had believed me—if I had killed him when I had the chance—she would still be alive." When he ran out of tears and his throat was raw, Rhazien pulled away. "That's why I helped hide you the first night. I couldn't let something like that happen again, not when I knew something was wrong and did nothing."

Erissa watched as a shiver made its way through his body, both of them feeling the cold without the other's warmth. The sharp air removed the heat from the tear-stained face of the defeated man. She would serve the Keeper himself if it meant easing Rhazien's pain.

The trust Rhazien had given in telling his story humbled her. It warmed something in the recesses of her heart even as its edges frayed against his pain, adding to hers. Erissa knew the depth of pain and grief. Nothing but time would soften his loss, just as nothing but time would soften the pain of her life.

To address the situation with pretty words felt cheap. The maids tried to do the same at first, but such false platitudes were quickly worn out when no one tried to interfere. Erissa wished with every part of her being she had a brother such as him. Rhazien loved fully, and the deepest part of her held a spark of hope that maybe love was blooming between them now. She offered him no judgment, only understanding as she took his hands in hers and led him back to the fire.

When he seated himself again, she sat beside him and gathered the furs around their shoulders before asking the one remaining question. "What was her name?"

"Mirielis. Her name was Mirielis." A ghost of a smile touched his lips. "That's the first time I've said her name in moons. It's the first time I've spoken about what happened since her death. My family—no one will say her name anymore."

Erissa laid her head on his shoulder and wrapped one of her arms around his waist, feeling Rhazien accept the comfort of her embrace. His body slowly relaxed alongside hers.

Rhazien's story made Erissa question her family's reaction to her escape. Faldeyr made it clear he did not consider her a daughter anymore, but what about her mother? Would she grieve for her as profoundly as Rhazien grieved Mirielis?

She wanted to believe her mother loved her, but things were more complicated than her foolish wish. Her mother had never grieved for her while she turned a blind eye to her captivity. To expect her to do so now... Erissa should know better.

It was troubling knowing Faldeyr looked for her. It made no sense when compared to his words and actions. He should be happy she ran away.

Erissa pushed her questions aside, focusing on the problem at hand. With Barrett searching those leaving the city, her father must believe she hid within its walls. How long until they moved the search beyond them?

The dark surrounding them became less of a comfort as she sat in the light of the fire. It concealed everything around them, hiding her path to freedom on one side and the path to her doom on the other.

Erissa was on borrowed time, and it grew shorter with every passing hour.

They stayed like that for some time, each taking comfort from the other before Rhazien turned to press a kiss into Erissa's hairline, murmuring into her hair. "Thank you, little doe, for listening. For asking her name. I've missed the sound of it."

CHAPTER TEN

The embers had burned low by the time Rhazien stirred against Erissa, moving to add wood to the fire. His back blocked her view of his actions as he crouched next to the coals, but by the time he moved away, flames licked against the split logs and broken tree limbs he had piled together.

Erissa spread the furs over them again as he sat down beside her with a long sigh. He smelled of smoke, cedar, jasmine, and something sweet and crisp she could not name. She bumped her shoulder against his. "Is there anything I can do?"

Rhazien shook his head. "Listening to me was more than enough. My thoughts are wandering now, is all. All this talk of my sister makes me wish she were more than a mere human."

That surprised Erissa. "What does being human have to do with it?"

"If she were Fae or mated to a Fae, the mate bond would have protected her." The furs slipped from Rhazien's shoulder, bringing a burst of cold air against Erissa's side as he rubbed his knuckles. "It's not fair for humans to have been given so little from the gods when those with magic were given so much."

Erissa cupped her hands over his, stilling the agitated movement as a flash of his pain overtook her thoughts. "What do you mean? What is this about mate bonds and the gods?"

He flipped their hands, the chilled tips of his fingers causing dots to rise across the skin of her arms. "You don't know what mate bonds are?"

Erissa stared at him blankly. "Should I?"

"I thought everyone knew what mate bonds were." Rhazien's grip tightened. "Does the South not tell stories of the Fae and their bonds?"

There was a hard line to Rhazien's words. Desperation coated them with a double meaning, but one Erissa did not know and would not push for after the pain he relived tonight. She focused on what she did know. "They tell stories of deals made with the Fae and how they should never be done since a life is pledged in exchange, but I've never heard of mate bonds. Can you tell me about them?"

The fire crackled next to them, its heat building and warding off the freezing air as Rhazien wrapped the furs tightly around them. "Mate bonds were given by the Creator during the Remaking War. A mate is your magical equal in every way, but it's more than that. They're the other half of your soul, the piece that completes you. Neither you nor your magic is whole without your mate."

Erissa sighed with longing. "It sounds romantic."

"It isn't." Rhazien curled her closer into his side. "It was meant to be a failsafe, but the gods weaponized them, using mates to force the other into horrible acts during the fighting. They killed one of the mates from the pairs who resisted. Losing a mate drives the other to insanity. They never recover from the loss."

She tried to imagine loving someone so much she would do anything to protect them, but all that came to mind was Rhazien and the strange connection. She would do anything to see him safe, even if it meant harming another. "Why would the Creator allow them to do such a thing?"

"I don't know. The Creator has allowed things I will never understand. My father told me it was for the sake of balance in the world, but it never felt right. How can atrocities bring balance?" Rhazien stared into the fire. "The Fae must have felt the same. They turned on the gods during the Remaking, fighting back against their demands, so the gods took the children born of mates and threatened to torture them as a way to force their parents' compliance. It was the final straw for the Creator, and he intervened in the war, creating the Fefnirion."

Erissa leaned her head on his shoulder. "I *have* heard of them. Those are the dragons, right? The Wardens meant to protect us from the gods' games? Whatever happened to them? Do they have mates?" Rhazien gave a rueful chuckle, and Erissa raised her head, staring at him in confusion. "What's so funny about my questions?"

"Nothing," Rhazien assured her. He pulled Erissa's head back into place on his shoulder. "The Fefnirion have mates too. The Creator forbade relations between them and the Fae, worried about how powerful a child their union could produce. So, the Fefnirion are all men, their mates humans, and their children can't inherit their father's magic."

Rhazien paused, and Erissa tipped her head to look up at him. He stared intently at the fire, and she felt indecision flood their connection as if he carefully weighed what he would say next.

"There are rumors," he continued, "rumors of a Fae who ran off with one of the Fefnirion following the Remaking. They were never heard from again, and it was assumed they had died. But what if they didn't?"

Erissa's brow scrunched. "You think there's a half-Fae half-Fefnirion running around in the world?"

"I think anything is possible." Rhazien looked at her then, his eyes serious and mouth set. "The people of the desert lands pass down stories of the Fefnirion, of how only one is left after they gave up their powers to live with their mates. Their bonds are sacred, more so than the Fae. They gave up their calling to protect their *nayanam*."

"*Nayanam*? That's the word you used in Emberhold." Erissa sat up, pushing away from Rhazien. "I thought you said that word meant someone was in trouble."

Rhazien hesitated to say anything, and Erissa's heart thudded painfully against her ribs as she waited for him to speak. He collected himself with a deep breath and reached for her hands, rubbing his thumbs over their backs as he spoke.

"It's a word from the tongue of Creation given to the Fefnirion, though the desert lands have adopted it as their own. The Fefnirion lived among their numbers for centuries. We're used to their tongue. We use the word to explain an intense connection to someone, a connection like you and I have."

"Do humans have mate bonds with one another?" Erissa hated the hope that lifted her words.

Rhazien shook his head. "No, but they have soul ties."

Erissa cocked her head to the side. "What's the difference?"

"Soul ties can be completely broken and aren't as all-consuming as the mate bond. Mate bonds must be accepted. It's rare for one of the Fae to reject them. The bond never truly breaks, and your soul can never settle. It will long for your mate with the same intensity for the rest of your days."

"Why would someone throw away such a gift? To be loved unconditionally…" Erissa swallowed. It sounded magical, like everything she had always been denied but desperately wanted.

"Because not all mates get along." Rhazien shrugged. "Personalities clash. Being a magical equal doesn't mean you will like your mate."

"That sounds terrible." Erissa's heart hurt for those who were left in that position. To be so consumed by someone you did not even like sounded like its own sort of prison. "What about humans?"

"With soul ties, the connection is muted. The Fae can have human mates, but the human will have nothing but a soul tie. Mate bonds drive you to care for your mate and place their well-being and happiness above everything else. To harm your mate is to harm yourself. Those bound by soul ties don't offer their mates the same protection. They can act against them, and though it will bother them, it won't harm them."

Trepidation carried through her connection to Rhazien like he was waiting for something. Erissa mulled over his words, biting her tongue to ask the one question that burned within her heart. "Do you think we have a soul tie?"

"I believe there's a bond between us. One so strong it defies everything I thought I knew about them." Rhazien held her gaze as he paused. The wind whistled through the trees, the needles of the pines whispering against one another as the air grew thicker with anticipation. "You're my *nayanam*, my little doe. I will do anything to protect you."

The thudding of Erissa's heart picked up pace. His *nayanam*. His little doe. She liked that more than she thought possible and wanted him to be hers but was too afraid to say it. She stayed quiet, a pleased smile spreading across her face.

Her thoughts traveled through their bond, and Rhazien's words were gentle with understanding as he stood, pulling Erissa with him. "Help me spread the furs. We'll share them as we did last night. It's too cold for anything else."

As they settled for the night, Rhazien wrapped around her for warmth. Erissa allowed herself to dream of a future filled with soul ties, love, and the promise of a happier life.

CHAPTER ELEVEN

The handkerchief Faldeyr held did little to block the metallic odor of blood. He detested the practice of blood magic, only agreeing to use it because no other way existed to communicate with the Fae beyond the Mists.

Faldeyr reached the end of his patience. "Hurry and complete the spell. We would have finished this mess last night if you had not pitched a fit like a child."

Vilotta lifted the knife and pressed it to the wrist of a young maid. "My blood was not enough to open the portal to Thonalan, or did you plan on bleeding me dry?"

"You're one to talk, Vilotta." Barrett sat in the corner, bandaging the girls she had already bled.

His brother wore displeasure like a second skin, but Faldeyr did not care so long as the man did as instructed and kept the girls quiet. He had no intention of listening to them whine from a minor cut.

Confusion knitted along Vilotta's brow when she looked at her brother-in-law. "Whatever do you mean by that?"

Barrett rolled his eyes. "Only one of us is bleeding the maids, and not a single one is here by choice."

Vilotta scoffed, turning the knife to the next maid's wrist. "I'm only taking a little from each girl. They will be perfectly fine in a week when the cut heals. Blood portals require so much blood, and it's not like one person can supply enough and remain alive. This is better than killing one of them." She smiled at the trembling girl before drawing the blade through her flesh. "After all, we must all share in the household burdens."

Not for the first time, Faldeyr questioned whether his wife had lost her mind as she kept smiling at the whimpering girl. She worked through the line of maids, offering each one a word of encouragement, lingering over the youngest of the lot as she sought to comfort them. She failed to notice the way none would meet her gaze.

Faldeyr had heard the whispers. Even the lowest of their household thought their madam insane. As she stood in the center of the room, collecting jars of blood to draw the magical runes, he had to agree she fit the description.

When she reached the last of the maids, and Barrett had bandaged their wounds, they sent them from the room.

Faldeyr cursed their slowness. "The hour is waning. If we don't cast the spell now, the blood will be useless."

"Worry not, husband. You will speak with Thonalan soon enough. Have patience." Vilotta dipped each hand into the jars of blood. She drew a complex pattern of swirls on the stone with letters of an ancient language long forgotten to most of those on the human side of the Mists.

As she worked, the blood soured, more sticking to her fingers and less to the stone as it grew cold. She poured the contents of the last jar into her hand, wincing as it squelched in between her fingers. "I hate having to do this."

"You're the only one who can," Faldeyr pointed out. "We're human, Vilotta."

With the remaining blood, she connected the last lines, and Faldeyr leaned forward, unable to contain his excitement. He hated the mess, but the magic itself had a mesmerizing quality. What he would not give to hold such power.

The blood sizzled against the stone, bubbling until it turned a sickly green, and from it, a ghostly mist rose into the air. It shimmered and waved, forming a circular mirror until its sides became solid, and a male Fae appeared in the middle of its depth, peering at them with shrewd green eyes.

"Thonalan." Vilotta stood, wiping her hands on one another. It only made a greater mess of her appearance. "I sincerely apologize for the delay. The maids were not keen on giving their blood."

The Fae sat back in his chair, pushing his long curtain of braids over his shoulder and exposing the tipped length of his ears. He still carried the same smug air as when Faldeyr last met him. How Faldeyr wished to use the braids to strangle him.

Thonalan's smile did not reach his eyes. "Vi. To what do I owe this pleasure?"

"There has been a development, Thonalan." Vilotta rubbed at the dried blood on her palm. "I'm afraid Erissa has escaped her room."

He sprung forward as if tempted to throw himself through the portal. The Fae stopped in time, careful not to touch the ghostly power of the Veil. He eyed it warily, his lips thinning in anger. "The time grows near. Virion and Draven are readying to make their move. If we do not have the girl in time to circumvent their plan—"

"We're searching the entire city for her." Faldeyr stepped into view of the portal. "She has no money and no outside knowledge of the world. Before too long, she will surface to eat or sleep, and when she does, we will drag her back in chains."

"Why have you contacted me when your plan is foolproof?" Thonalan smirked, his eyes cold as the winter wind blowing in from the harbor. "Is it to announce your failings? Who proves incapable of handling one girl?"

"She's not a girl." Barrett's stormed forward. "That *girl* is an adult. She has rights by the laws of the humans and the Fae."

Faldeyr bared his teeth. "Watch yourself, brother. Her rights begin and end with her Lord, which I happen to be. She will have whatever freedoms I grant and nothing more."

"We have no time for petty squabbles." Thonalan pinched the bridge of his nose. "The Veil stands between all of life and death. Whoever harnesses its power will be untouchable—a god in their own right."

Faldeyr fumed as Thonalan enunciated each word as if educating a small child. "We are aware of this already."

"Apparently, you're not, or you would have taken better care to not lose the girl." Thonalan's voice cracked like a whip. "We need her to control the power and influence of the Veil. Without her, we are a gnat to the Keeper, and all our planning will be pointless if he breaks free from his prison within the Veil."

Faldeyr waved away the Fae's concern. "The Keeper is nothing more than a fallen god without influence or power. All he does is guide the souls who move on into the afterlife and watch over the ones who don't. He poses no threat."

"If you believe that, you're more hopeless than I thought." Thonalan's lip curled as he looked Faldeyr up and down. "If Virion gets the girl first and Draven is released from the Veil, he will kill the girl and free the Keeper, and neither of us will gain a throne. I can't overthrow the Seelie King without the powers of the Veil, and without a Fae army, you will never conquer the human lands. The girl is the only one with enough magic to overthrow Yorrith, and I will bleed it from her or end your sorry excuse for a life."

"Help us, Thonalan." Vilotta dropped to her knees, smiling up at the Fae like a lost lamb.

Faldeyr wanted to beat the look from her face. It was bad enough he needed help from the Fae, the gods' monstrosities, but did she have to beg in such a manner? It would not do, not when he would stand as Thonalan's equal once the Fae king lost his throne and Faldeyr rose as the king of the human realm. His queen would need to be made of sterner stuff than this.

Vilotta put her hands on her knees, leaning forward. "The Court of the Flowering Sun has the best trackers beyond the Mists."

"I will send men. Be ready when they arrive. And do not contact me again unless you have better news." Thonalan sniffed, looking at Faldeyr down his nose. "I have no time for the failings of a human."

The Fae broke the spell, and the portal wavered before collapsing into the same mist it arose from, sinking into the now-dried blood on the floor.

His wife turned to him. "What do we do now?"

"We're not waiting for his men." Faldeyr crossed his arms, considering what his next move would be. "There has to be someone who helped her. If we can't find her, we will find whoever they are, and gods have mercy on them, for they will not escape my wrath."

CHAPTER TWELVE

The sky remained dark and cloudy, even as the rain held off in the stillness of the early morning. A silence fell across the woods, one that had not been there the night before. Erissa startled awake against the lack of sound. Rhazien lay beside her, mouth open with the sounds of deep slumber.

Erissa eased herself from under the furs, unsure of what had awoken her in the quiet. Something changed in the air, like the moment before someone's soul called out to her, reminding her of how time stopped with their haunting pleas. She froze, reeling as her heart dropped at its implication. She eyed Rhazien with a kind of desperation she had never known. But his form remained unshadowed where it lay sleeping, no soul hovering next to his frame.

The voice refused to speak to her at all last night, making the silence more pronounced this morning as she traced its presence and found nothing. It wanted her to apologize for believing magic a curse. Erissa refused, and it only made the silence more ominous.

Still unsettled, she tried to shrug off the feeling and left the remains of the lodge, searching for more wood to add to the smoldering embers.

Rhynstone's soft neighing called to her as she stepped outside. He was no worse for the weather, tossing his head at her approach. Carizzea was more subdued but pushed her head into Erissa's shoulder. Erissa smoothed a hand across her braided mane. "You two couldn't sleep either?"

Rhynstone pawed against the ground impatiently and dipped his head to nip at the thick layers of her clothes.

Erissa chuckled at his antics. "I'm afraid I don't have a sugar cube, Rhyn." She swore the animal understood her. His cheeks puffed out against a long sigh. "Someone is spoiled. Be patient. Rhazien will be awake before too long, and I'm sure he will have something for you."

Rhynstone nuzzled against her shoulder. With one last pat against his nose and another for Carizzea, she moved from them, going deeper into the forest.

The quiet intensified the further Erissa traveled from the broken lodge, unnerving her, but turning back felt wrong. With each step, something lured her along, almost as if someone were calling her name.

Before too long, a sound broke the unnatural calm, the soft burbling of water catching her attention. Following the noise, she found herself in a clearing where a large creek fed into an even bigger pond. The flowing water sparkled against gray sheets of ice that spread across the surface in patches.

A woman stood before the pond, her back to Erissa. She was tall, with ebony hair cropped closely above her shoulders. She wore the thinnest of gowns, the cerulean gossamer at odds with the temperature. The tip of pointed ears poking through her hair marked her as Fae, but on closer inspection, it was the translucence of her appearance that stole Erissa's breath.

"Do not be afraid, child. I was once called Reeva. Although, I do not come to you with a soul's siren call. I am of the Veil, and I have come to give you a warning."

Whatever breath Erissa had regained left again with the woman's words, leaving her rattled, especially with the woman still oddly turned away from her. The souls never spoke to her this way, yet she was no doubt one of them with her pellucid appearance.

Reeva heaved a sigh with a slight shake of her head and turned around, a small chuckle sounding. "I have stayed within the Veil for hundreds of years, and the first time I venture out, the one I seek stands as if mute."

"You... your face!" The words came out in a shocked yelp as Erissa took several steps back. "You have a *face*!"

"Yes, most creatures tend to have one." Reeva spoke with humor, the hint of a smile highlighting full lips framed by a straight nose and large, curved eyes the same gray-blue as the frozen water behind her. Her face was strangely youthful, the delicacy of her pale skin heightening a sharp hardness behind her eyes that bellied her smile.

Erissa's cheeks heated as her self-consciousness grew with the woman's humor. "The souls I see never have clear faces."

"Ah, that explains much of your reaction."

Erissa stared at the woman, her head tipping slightly to the side as she studied her with wary eyes. "How do you know the souls call out to me? And how do you have a face when the others do not?"

"There is much that being bound to the Veil will tell you about those it tethers." Reeva turned and stepped onto the water, only her weight did not break its surface. "I am not about to pass into the Veil like the others you have encountered. Those souls have one foot in the grave and the other in the Veil, but I am tethered to the Veil and the land of the living. My body lies buried in the Crying Grove, allowing me to pass through the Veil and into this realm. A bond keeps my soul tied to the Veil, so I must return to it, one so strong the gods cannot touch it. But there is still hope. The Creator can undo what he binds."

Mesmerized, Erissa stared as Reeva walked across the mirrored reflection of the water. Not even a ripple followed her footsteps, the surface remaining pristine in its movements as the creek gently fed it. "What do you mean you're bound to the Veil?"

"'Tis an old story and one you will hear, but not from my lips. I have come to speak of something else. To warn you."

"Warn me?" Erissa moved closer to the water's edge. "You speak around me, revealing nothing, and I'm supposed to trust your warning?"

Reeva laughed with a pinched expression, the hollow sound echoing across the water. "The Veil is not the only one who binds me, and my words cannot betray, no matter how I wish they might. But even the magic of the gods has... allowances. While my intentions can never be completely pure, so long as my bond holds, there are ways around it." She came to stand before Erissa, reaching her hand out. "Come, child."

"You can't think for a moment I would wade into such freezing water."

"You can easily walk upon the water."

"Walk? On the water?" Erissa laughed, the sound an indelicate grunt.

"Do you know nothing of your own power?"

The chiding tone grated against Erissa's nerves. "No. Beyond being a parody of the reaper, no one has seen fit to tell me much of anything outside of the one time I made flowers and created wind. And given this... *informative*... conversation, I take it you'll also be keeping secrets."

"To think, you know nothing of your magic. This does not bode well for what is to come. Events must unfold as foretold. I can only interfere so far." Reeva crossed her arms below her breasts, considering Erissa, as the Fae spoke more to herself than the younger woman. "I do not think revealing some of your powers will cross any lines, and the magic has not blocked my thoughts of doing so...."

Erissa's eyes widened as an untamed longing replaced the annoyance. "You can tell me about this plague of magic?" She hated the way her voice picked up with hope.

"Plague?" Reeva snorted. "The gods will not take kindly to such a description of their gift."

Erissa waved her hand. "The gods can hang for all I care. They've added nothing to my life but misery."

Reeva's brows drew together, her face losing all mirth as her jaw tightened and her arms fell to rest by her side. "You walk a fine line, child. The gods hear all, even when they choose not to intervene. There will come a time when even you must call on them. What will the Creator have them do when one of his children maligns them so?"

Erissa ignored the question. She ran her gaze over Reeva, her tone of voice matching the sharpness that entered her eyes. "Are you going to tell me about my magic or prattle on about the choices of gods?"

"Such impatience is unbecoming." Humor changed the lines on Reeva's face and smoothed the concern from her brow. "But it is also understood. I cannot tell you what—*who*—you are, but I can tell a little of what your power is capable of. The Keeping binds me from telling you the rest."

Erissa tipped her head to the side. "The Keeping?"

An exasperated snort left Reeva. "Do not tell me you have no knowledge of the Keeping bond either?"

Erissa shook her head, embarrassed by her lack of knowledge about the world.

"The Keeping Bonds were created during the Remaking War. They are what turned the humans into Fae. It is blood magic that enslaves those it is used on, removing their free will." Reeva lowered herself with ease to sit upon the water and gestured to Erissa to do the same, waiting until the younger woman had arranged herself on the ground before continuing. "Your power is far greater than your ability to see souls beginning their journey into the Veil. It is of the Veil itself, creating a deep connection between you and the magic that holds it within this world, magic which straddles the line between life and death. Your magic possesses this same balance."

"I'm not sure I understand what you mean." Erissa's voice was small. She twisted her hands in her lap, giving her nervous energy an outlet.

Reeva smiled, her voice kind and soothing. "In its simplest explanation, you have the power of Creation. Anything touched by the spark of Creation is yours to command. This includes the elements of nature. I have no doubt you did a little more than create flowers and direct the wind."

"Supposedly, it was an impressive display of power that scared the gods out of everyone. I only know what I've been told."

"Supposedly?" The word hovered between the women, Reeva's gaze questioning as Erissa's dropped to stare at the water.

Erissa shrugged, the dismissive gesture at odds with the flat expression her eyes held. "My parents used a witch's spell to hide the memories, so there's little more I can say about what happened that day."

"Have you never tested your magic?" No judgment hovered in Reeva's question, only curiosity.

"How would I with no memories of what happened?" But with Erissa's words came other memories of how she'd spent her time locked away after that fateful day. Her eyes became haunted by the past, her jaw tightening against the emotions her memories evoked.

The change in Erissa's demeanor was not overlooked by Reeva. "People do foolish things out of fear, and the power of Creation inspires much of it."

Erissa weighed Reeva's words. "I don't understand how something that brings life can bring such negativity."

"Creation requires balance, and it is this balance that becomes unnerving."

"You're speaking in riddles again. Can you not speak plainly?" Erissa's brow pinched together, her hand rubbing against the creasing. "I beg of you—all I want is the truth."

"Think, child. You cannot expect everyone to hand the answers to you." Reeva's tone was sharp. "Creation is a two-sided coin. What is the balance of life?"

Erissa slowed her breath as the answer came to her, hardly daring to believe where her mind was headed. "You mean death. The balance of life is death."

"Yes." Reeva was pleased as she spoke. "In all things, there must be balance. Your gift is life itself, but it does not come alone. Death is also your gift."

"Death is my gift?" The air left her lungs with Reeva's words. She sputtered, drawing in desperate breaths as she fought her rising panic. "How can death be my gift when I only see the souls of those the Creator chooses? I have no power over their actual deaths."

"You misunderstand. No matter the side, the coin remains the same. As does your power. With the touch of Creation comes the touch of death, for you cannot have one without the other." Reeva gestured at the lightning sky. "Think of the sun. Its light brings life and death during each season. Even as it gives life, it holds the power to take it away and grant rebirth as the seasons change. What is scorched by the summer sun can find life again as its power wanes in autumn, and what is once dead, come winter, can grow again with the warming of spring. No matter the season, life and death find balance and live in harmony. Your magic comes with this balance, for even death is touched by the spark of Creation."

Erissa rolled her eyes. "That doesn't make any sense. How can I be the balance of life when I'm not killing anyone?"

"Because your magic can kill." Reeva's tone softened until it hovered above a whisper. "The call of the souls works both ways. They call to you with their foot in the grave, but you can call them from someone, severing their connection to their life. You can even call them from beyond the Veil."

Erissa paled. "I am death."

Reeva nodded.

"What—" Erissa's words broke off at the sound of a snapping twig echoing through the clearing.

Rhazien's voice followed the noise, calling her name. "Erissa..."

"I must go." Reeva stood. "I have already spent too much time here, and I have yet to issue my warning."

Erissa sprung to her feet, her arm stretched out with a dismissive wave at Reeva. "You can't go. Not now. I need to know—"

"I will return when I am able, but you must listen." Reeva's words cut Erissa off, coming fast as Rhazien's voice grew closer. "War is coming, and there are those who seek to find you to change its outcome. Those who, even now, are searching for you. You must hide from them at all costs. Your companion must hide, too. If they were to find either of you, all would be lost. You are our only hope to survive what wakes in the Veil. Do you understand?"

Reeva did not wait for a response.

Rhazien was almost upon them, his voice growing stronger with each call of Erissa's name. "Erissa, where are you?"

"Wait! Please, stay." Erissa's pleas went unanswered.

The Fae turned. Her words floated behind her, echoing against the light-kissed surface. The reflective waters remained still against each step. "I will come to you again. Until then, heed my warning."

The edges around Reeva's body blurred as she began fading into the background, becoming fainter and fainter until nothing remained but the sound of the bubbling water and Rhazien's continued calling.

"Erissa!" Rhazien burst into the clearing. He grabbed her arms, running his hands up and down the limbs like he was searching for injuries. "Are you alright? When I woke up and didn't find you...."

She cupped his face. "I'm sorry, Rhazien. I didn't mean to worry you. I needed a moment of privacy." Erissa was unsure why she hid Reeva's appearance, but something instinctual told her to keep the encounter to herself for now. Her heart pounded against the guilt building in her chest. She tried her best to swallow it down. "I should have woken you before wandering off like that.

"You had me worried."

Erissa lowered her hands and closed her arms around him, pressing her cheek against his chest. His heart was pounding. The fast rhythm matched the deceitful pace of her own. "I'm all right. I promise I'll wake you next time."

Rhazien held her to him, resting his chin against her hair for a moment before stepping away and taking one of her hands in his. Erissa made no protest as he led her away from the water. "Come, let's head back. We need to eat and move on. There's something about these woods that unsettles me."

And Reeva's words unsettled Erissa, for if death was her gift, who knew what lurked beyond the shadows of the woods.

CHAPTER THIRTEEN

No matter how many times Novus tortured someone, he never got used to it. The blood did not bother him anymore, not after his own had stained the very floor more times than he could remember, but the screams were different. They had a way of haunting the soul, even when he took great pleasure in ringing them from the mouths of his prisoners.

The Unseelie Fae Lord reclined leisurely upon his throne while he magically filleted a female with the entire Frosted Moon court bearing witness. There would be hell to pay when Drurrah, the other lesser Unseelie Lord, learned of the punishment. Genstine was technically a member of the Hunter's Moon court, but Novus would not delay his actions for Drurrah's arrival, not when the crime warranted the barbarity. She committed the crime on Novus's lands, and Novus would decide her fate, Drurrah be damned.

Black magic poured from him in thick waves of shadows. It ran down the throne, slithering against the floor to climb up the limbs of the Fae holding his attention.

A chain hung from the cathedral ceiling. Novus's eyes flicked to the monstrosity of his prison hanging overhead. It would be easier to place the Fae's head up there, but a point needed to be made, and her public punishment would make it well.

The hands of the chained Fae were bound and stretched high enough to keep her feet from reaching the floor. Her shoulders had dislocated some time ago.

Sweat beaded against her brow as the black magic reared back. It separated itself into thin strands, the edges sharpening into deadly blades. Novus commanded them from his throne with a flick of his hand. He directed the blades to slice her skin into thin strips of flesh. The scent of blood intensified, and a wailing scream left the woman. Her skin fell to the floor with a sickening plop. He repeated the process until the Fae choked on her screams, head dropping to her chest like a rag doll. Cuts covered her from head to toe—or at least what was left of her toes.

The screaming should have stopped by now. It grated on his nerves. Even Novus had not screamed this much when he hung in the same spot while his father carved into his back. Novus sighed, bored with the spectacle. "Have you been suitably punished, Genstine?"

When the woman did not answer, he cocked his head to the side, a vindictive curl lifting his lips. The churning, dark cloud swelled in the echoing silence. Its presence filled the room, power radiating from it and the Lord who wielded such a force with lethal precision.

No one escaped the impact of the magic as Novus let go of his restraint. It filled the room, a concussion without sound, forcing the gathered crowd to bend to its will.

"Are we not past this, Genstine?" Novus stood. He recalled the magic, a predatory smile deepening the curl across his lips as the woman cried in relief. Everyone else remained silent, holding their composure for fear of the consequences.

Genstine's tears were short-lived, realizing her mistake too late.

Novus moved in front of her. He gripped her chin, his nails digging into the skin until it bled. "Do not believe this is the end. I have more plans for you. Who knows... I might add you to my collection. After all, it does exist for occasions such as this."

Genstine's eyes glistened with unshed tears. She trembled as she fought against crying again. His hand clenched her jaw harder, his smile twisting into something sick that delighted in the pain he caused the woman by testing her endurance.

When no tears fell after several torturous seconds, he released her jaw with a harshness that jerked her entire body. The mutilated tips of her feet scraped the ground as she swayed. Genstine bit her tongue to keep from screaming, clamping her teeth on it so hard she tore through the flesh. Blood leaked from her lips.

"What do you think, Genstine? Your father's head hangs in my prison for the same crime. Selling child slaves deserves far worse punishment than a few missing toes." Novus pushed her when the movement slowed, her body swaying once more as a scream finally tore from her lips.

"Perhaps I can find another use for you. I am always in need of another pet. Is that not what you deserve after your crimes?" Novus grabbed her by the throat, leaning in to purr the words against her ear. "To be paraded in front of everyone as nothing more than an untitled slave for me to torture and starve at will? 'Tis fitting your punishment shall mirror all you have done."

His eyes cut to the old witch who entered and stood by the door before returning to Genstine, staring her up and down. "Each pet has its uses, and Berthina is awfully lonely. I might even be generous and leave your eyes intact if you behave. Berthina struggled with her training and paid the consequence for it, but fortunately for her, being a seer gave her a reprieve. Magic replaces her gaze, but you would not be so lucky."

The old witch's cheeks burned with humiliation at the Lord using her pain as a warning.

"Can you behave, Genstine?" The bleeding female nodded, her eyes filling with hope as he lifted a hand to her face and cupped it with a gentleness that mocked instead of comforted. "We shall see how well when I make you beg to sit at my feet. You will feel the pain of every child you harmed and everyone you sold, knowing what fate awaited them. I will make you beg for death before the night is through."

Novus turned away from the woman. He snapped his fingers in Berthina's direction and returned to sit on his throne. "Is it your turn to beg? Have you come to plead for more time, pet, or have you finally proved yourself useful and broken the spells you hid the girl with? You have pissed away your years waiting in Emberhold. I grow tired of your excuses."

Berthina did not keep him waiting. "M'Lord, you know a Fae deal was struck. I couldn't break the spells or speak of her until the girl broke the spells herself, and she did."

He leaned back, crossing one leg over the other. "Yorrith will be pleased now that I have proof the girl lives."

"There's more, m'Lord." Berthina bowed her head. "A man helped her escape Emberhold, and they ran off together. But he isn't just any man. I saw something when I touched his arm..."

Novus's patience thinned when she said no more. "Out with it, pet."

Berthina straightened. "He... he's a Warden... the last powered Fefnirion."

"So, the events of the prophecy are finally happening. The girl has found her mate." He leaned forward, power radiating from him once again. "Nephinae?"

A striking Fae stirred from the shadows behind the throne, the high slits of her dress flowing around her as she walked to stand beside the throne. The deep tunnels of scarring carved ruins into her flesh, marking her as a Zorathi, a Fae warrior feared for their ability to harness the magic of another against its wielder. But it was her white eyes that revealed her as the Zorathi leader.

"You have need of me?"

"Find the Seelie King, Yorrith. Tell him the time has come to honor our bargain. The Veiled One lives." Novus's gaze returned to the chained Fae. "Now, where were we, Genstine?"

CHAPTER FOURTEEN

Nothing prepared Erissa for the pain burning from her back to her legs as Rhazien pushed them along like a man possessed. Her chest burned against the exertion, her ragged breaths puffing in the air. She massaged her chest, kneading the tight skin.

They had doubled back after packing their supplies, taking advantage of the freshwater flowing from the creek and following an old deer trail along the winding path of the bank.

The five days passed quickly. Rhazien refused to rest while light still illuminated the path before them. He told her stories from his childhood to distract her from the brutal pace.

The one-sided conversations were appreciated. Years had passed without constant companionship, and Erissa found herself at a loss for how to contribute when her own stories held such a bleak reality. But there was more to it than that.

Rhazien filled in the quiet moments, which helped the time pass faster, but spending over a decade alone had her nerves on edge. Even if she did want to share her stories, the thought left her exhausted.

When they did stop for the night, she barely kept her eyes open as Rhazien set up camp, having fallen asleep the previous night before the fire had even been lit. She believed traveling would get easier as she became more accustomed to its physicality after years of confinement, but the horses bellied the misconception. Each horse chafed against the brutal pace. It prompted their riders to walk rather than sit astride.

Something about the woods had changed since the morning Erissa spoke with Reeva, turning the haven into something less trustworthy. The palpable difference must have fanned the flames of Rhazien's unease as he searched for threats around every tree.

Even Rhyn and Crezzi sensed something was different. She expected them to be more relaxed with the break from carrying her and Rhazien. The horses grated against their bits, remaining quiet and tense, with Rhazien leading them both as he stomped ahead.

Erissa's attention turned from the uncertain wood as her breath came in ragged gasps. "Rhazien... I can't... keep going."

"That's what you've been saying." Rhazien glanced over his shoulder, his pinched face golden in the evening light. "If we stopped every time you complained, we'd still be at the abandoned lodge."

She had been right about the stones in his earcuffs. They did glitter in the sunlight, the sparkling cuffs accentuating his chestnut skin as the light haloed around him. But she cared naught for how handsome he was when her body ached as it did. She would sooner slap him for the unforgiving pace than moon over him.

"I can moon for the both of us."

Erissa caught herself before she screamed at the voice echoing in her head. It had avoided her for days after she called it a curse, and she did not expect it to make a return so soon.

"I didn't return for you. Someone has to keep you in line where Rhazien is concerned," the voice snapped.

Rhazien's throat bobbed while his eyes scanned her person. She hoped he would swallow whatever sharp retort sat poised to leave his mouth.

It was bad enough she must endure the waspish mood of the voice. She would rather not deal with Rhazien's foul mood, too.

When he held his ire, she was grateful for his self-control. Her nerves were already frayed. Taking a verbal lashing might push her over the edge, and she had enough memories of those to last a lifetime. She did not want to add Rhazien's mood among those of her father's.

Erissa knew she appeared a fright with her face red under exertion against the freezing air, and the last thing she wanted to deal with was Rhazien's grumpiness. She had plenty of that on her own, unable to disguise her stiff walk while she winced against every hurried step.

Erissa came close to weeping in relief as Rhazien sighed and rubbed the back of his head. "We can stop here for the night and leave at dawn. It won't be more than another day before we reach Gailme. From there, we can find passage up the river. The further we get from Emberhold, the better."

She groaned against the trembling exhaustion as they stopped in a grove of wildling willows. The creek had widened into the full breadth of a river the further they went, feeding the towering willows and overtaking the embankment. The sandbar was dotted and stretched from one end of the bank's shallows to the next. Each tree was enormous as the width of their canopies overtook the grove, and their height blocked much of the gray light of the late afternoon sun as it began to set. The growing number of wildlings signaled how close the pair came to the Violent Wilds.

Erissa was unsure which she feared more, the Wilds or the Mists boarding the river at Gailme.

On the other side of the river lay a mountain range, its steep slopes rising dramatically from the ground. The Mists lay beyond, marking the boundary between the Fae and human lands. No matter their direction, she quaked against the stories of both. Those who entered the Mists vanished beyond the mountain passes, while those who entered the Wilds rarely returned sane, or so the stories told.

The cloak he had placed around her shoulders this morning lay balled beneath an arm before too long during their trek. While still cold, the air became bearable with the sun peaking between the trees and their fast pace, heating her blood and providing some warmth.

Walking over to one of the larger trees, Erissa placed her cloak on the bank and climbed onto the thick roots protruding from the river. She cupped her hands, reached into the rushing depths to fill them with frigid water, and drank her fill. Its temperature raised bumps along her arms, but nothing had ever felt as good against her skin. Erissa splashed water onto her heated face. She breathed a sigh of relief at washing away the grime of several days.

A twig snapped, and Erissa glared over her shoulder at Rhazien as he moved the horses forward to stand behind her on the bank. "Gods, but you will be the death of me."

"There's something about these woods." Rhazien tied both reins to one of the roots. The trunks of the trees were too wide for the ropes to wrap around. After removing the saddles and their burdens from the horses, he knelt beside Erissa. "Don't you feel it? It shouldn't be this quiet, not with the rain gone and the morning well underway."

Erissa fought to ignore the pulse of electricity that rushed through her from where Rhazien's arm brushed against her own. She took in the silence of the surrounding woods. No wind stirred the leaves, nor were animals rustling the brambles littering the brush-covered ground. Only the water moved, and even it splashed in a subdued manner against the roots of the willows. The frozen air hit her as a shiver tingled along her spine. "Maybe it's nothing more than being close to the Wilds."

"I don't think so. It's more than that. Besides, I grew up roaming the Wilds. Even in the depths of them, it's never this quiet."

"You've been in the Wilds?"

Rhazien smiled as horror and surprise fought for dominance over Erissa's features. "The Wilds border Freyborn across the river. They're nothing like the stories portray them... or almost nothing. They *are* called the Wilds for a reason." Rhazien shrugged, a mischievous light entering his eyes before he winked at her.

Erissa shivered, unsure if the creeping sensation along her spine came from the worsening cold as the sun set or Rhazien speaking of the Wilds like they were not the stuff of nightmares.

"It feels like snow." Rhazien glanced at the sky, taking in the fading light against the whitewashed clouds. "We won't make it to Gailme before it falls, and I doubt we'll be lucky enough to find another abandoned building."

"How long before we reach the town if the snow falls?"

"Another two days, at least, but I'm betting on longer with the weather not holding." Rhazien stood as Erissa shivered once more. "I'll cut some wood. We should get a fire going before the snowfall. Stay here with the horses. I'm going to see if I can find anything to forage. It's still early enough in the year to find some mushrooms and nuts. Maybe the gods will favor us, and I'll find some wild garlic."

"Are you sure you want me to wait? I can help."

"Stay here, little doe. You know how Rhyn can get testy when he's left completely alone. I don't want to find him if he breaks loose."

Erissa chewed her lip, watching Rhazien walk away. In all the days they had traveled, not once had he asked for her to stay with Rhynstone. Rhyn had been anything but testy as they traveled, and Rhazien's refusal of her help weighed on her.

Pressing her hand to her chest, she massaged the tight skin. Her heart beat out of rhythm beneath her hand. She waited for Rhazien to move further into the trees where he would find dryer wood.

When he disappeared from view, Erissa stared across the water in anticipation, sure that it would give way to the translucent steps of the mysterious female Fae at any moment.

With every day that passed, Erissa's desperation grew. She had dozens of questions to ask, but more than anything, she wanted to know more about what her powers were capable of.

Using them terrified her. Whether the fear came from her father or something deeper within herself, Erissa wanted to find out. Reeva had piqued Erissa's curiosity in a way nothing ever had before. A war waged within her as she debated whether her magic had the ability to bring anything but heartache and fear. To be intertwined with life overwhelmed her in unexplainable ways. But to be linked to death? Inconceivable.

Even as the quiet of the willow thicket lengthened, nothing appeared across the water, and no call whispered within. Her shoulders slumped in defeat at another day spent no closer to finding answers.

"It's hopeless." Erissa tossed the words to the horses as she stood, arms outstretched to keep her balance. She hopped from one thick root to the next until she reached the widest of the roots where it protruded from the base of the willow.

She groaned at the pain of each movement as she lowered herself to lean against the trunk. "I'm questioning if she's even real. And the voice. The souls. Minds can break all too easily in the dark, and maybe part of mine never made it out of that room."

Rhynstone tossed his head to the side, flapping his lips in answer. Carizzea nickered in agreement.

Erissa shook her head at Rhynstone's apparent agreement. "Of course, you both think I'm mad. You're probably the sanest ones here."

"Are you really so daft, child?"

Erissa jerked violently. The unexpected words threatened to unseat her, but she caught herself against the root and avoided plunging into the depths below. "Reeva!"

"Hush. There is no need to wake the dead." The sting of Reeva's words faded with the quick grin that spread across her mouth. "I told you I would come once more."

"Yes, but you didn't say when." Erissa winced as she ran her fingers down the scrape that formed across her palm with the harsh movement. "You like to take great pleasure in startling me."

"There is little reason for laughter within the Veil." Reeva lifted a shoulder before lowering herself upon a root across from Erissa. "You cannot begrudge an old soul such a simple pleasure." The smile faded, her expression turning somber as the mirth disappeared. "You tarry too long here. Those who hunt you draw ever closer. It would be wise to move on."

"We've only just stopped for the night. How do you even know they draw closer? Do you know where they are?"

"My tongue is still bound. I cannot say how I know or where they are. I can only say they will be upon you within a day. You should keep going. You're too exposed here."

"Exposed?" Erissa snorted. "Like we're going to run across anyone. We're too close to the Wilds. Rhazien said even the deer trails have been long neglected. And speaking of being exposed..." Erissa ran her eyes up and down Reeva's attire. The cut and color differed from their first meeting, but the style remained similarly thin.

Reeva fought the mirth threatening her face once more. "Souls do not feel the cold, and my former court has a dress code of sorts. I am used to this attire." The laughter faded from her eyes. "You misplace your trust in your location. The ones who seek you will not pause because of stories told to keep your young ones in line. Your proximity to the Wilds will not be a deterrent."

"But you won't tell me anything else about them."

Neither woman spoke for a moment, the statement hanging like a challenge between them.

Erissa finally broke the silence, a weary sigh lowering her shoulders. "I don't know what you would have me do. I can't go back, and apparently, I can't go forward. Something hunts me from either end, and I do not know which is worse."

"You speak in your own riddles, child."

"I must be learning from the best, then." A soft quirk of Erissa's lips softened the bite of the words.

"There is much I wish I could tell you, but I'm afraid being Fae changes the rules. There are agreements made that cannot be broken, and I have made so many to save the one I love above all others."

Frustration grew within Erissa's chest, the emotion choking her contemplations as surely as it did her breath. "I am tired of being confined to the words of other people."

"A sentiment I share as well." Reeva leaned forward and lowered a hand to trail upon the softly lapping water. A sigh left her, and with it came tension as Reeva straightened. "We do not have long, child. Your human will only leave your side tonight for as long as it takes him to gather supplies. Even I can see the affection he holds for you. An affection you appear to return. But, I did not come to speak of that either."

"Then why did you come? If it was only to issue another warning, you've already done so. Why stay longer?"

Erissa's blunt words shocked the Fae as she opened her mouth to answer but closed it when no words came. Reeva turned her attention back to the water in silence.

Guilt struck Erissa, and she lowered her gaze, too ashamed by her outburst to face Reeva. She regretted the harshness of her tone. For she did not know of the Fae who sat beside her, Reeva came close to feeling like a friend. But friendship required trust, and Erissa remained unsure of Reeva being worthy of such trust to be freely given with all that remained unsaid between them. Erissa recognized the Fae had more to her appearance in Erissa's life, but while something shrouded Reeva in mystery, Erissa enjoyed her coming. And not only because she wished to know more about her powers. Before Rhazien, it had been a long time since Erissa had spoken to anyone as a friend.

"You are right to question my motives, child."

Erissa's eyes snapped up to find Reeva staring at her.

"You hide little of your emotions. Or maybe it is nothing more than seeing pieces of my younger self in you." Reeva stood, brushing imaginary wrinkles from the slip of fabric she wore. "Already, I can hear your human returning."

Something occurred to Erissa as Reeva made to leave, the words stopping the Fae as she turned to walk away. "There are other ways you're different from the fated souls. Rhazien can see you, can't he? That's why you leave whenever you hear him returning."

"Clever, child. There will come a time when he knows of my presence. That time is not now."

"You wish me to continue lying to him?"

"I never asked you to lie. You did so on your own, the same way you lied to him about your magic. Does he know you can do more than see souls? Does he know what you are?"

Erissa's silence said everything she did not want to say. She did not even know what she was. Not really.

"No, I did not think so. How can you explain it to him when you know so little of it yourself? You cannot expect to know yourself if you make no effort to know your power." Reeva closed her eyes. "You are curious about me, child, when you should be curious about yourself, about your magic."

Reeva was right. She had no hope of knowing herself when she ran from everything she was. But she did not know how to fix that. All the anger left Erissa, and she sunk into herself, brooding.

The two settled into silence for a moment before something tugged at Erissa's curiosity as Reeva's hand waved in time to the current. "Why is it you only appear near water?"

"It reminds me of home and the one I love, especially as the weather turns." Light spilled across Reeva's face as she turned inward, a small smile softening the harsh lines of her features. "It is a beautiful land where a grand mountain feeds the clearest lake known to this realm. When it freezes over, the people come together as one for a festival of thankfulness to celebrate the rest of winter grants the lands. There is no rebirth without winter's rest."

Erissa brought her knees to her chest, draping her cloak around them to fight off the building cold of the air. "It sounds beautiful, your home."

"It is." Reeva's hand stilled against the water. "Maybe you will get to see it someday."

Erissa smiled, fiddling with the stone on her necklace. "I would like that."

Reeva pulled her hand from the water, gesturing toward Erissa's necklace. "Where did you get the stone? I've never seen an amethyst with shades of blue swirling when the light catches it."

She dropped the stone as if burned by the memory. "My mother gave it to me on my seventh naming day."

"It's beautiful."

Erissa hugged her knees tighter and tried not to think about what had happened after she had received the necklace. "I wish the memories were."

Reeva nodded as if she understood. "When is your next naming day?"

"Soon." Erissa lifted her head, staring over the water. She tried to find solace in the gentle sway of the current as it lapped against the bank. "Although I have no wish to celebrate its passing."

"Why not?"

Erissa shrugged. She picked at a tiny thread poking from the seam on the side of her trousers. "Because naming days have not been kind to me."

"I am sure your friend would go out of his way to make them kind."

The way Reeva watched Erissa made her squirm. She knew Rhazien would find a way to make it special, but that was part of the problem, so she whispered the truth. "I don't know what I would do with that kindness."

Reeva nodded again, returning her hand to the water. "It is hard to confront something good when you have lived so long without it. The one who controls my tongue does not offer kindness. But you, child, give it so freely to me. It is weird for me, too. It has been centuries since I experienced it. In truth, I do not know what to do with it either."

Erissa offered her a smile. "So, we are both struggling."

Reeva returned the smile with one of her own. "We are, but we can struggle along together for now. I would very much like to be your friend."

"I would like that." Erissa's smile widened.

The Fae cleared her throat as she stood, stepping back from Erissa. "I cannot stay longer. I am not supposed to be here, and if I linger, my missing will be noticed. Look for me. I will come again when I can sneak away."

She did not wait for a response and quickly faded from view. Erissa lay her head back against her knees. She had not asked a single question about her magic, but she hardly cared, for she found something sweeter in the conversation. She'd found a friend.

CHAPTER FIFTEEN

Exhaustion threatened to send Barrett tumbling down the stairs. The steep climb to his brother's den tested his fortitude after almost no sleep in the five days since his niece's disappearance.

The search for Erissa pushed the soldiers to their limits, with the weather hiding her trail. Their only clue was the missing son of the blacksmith. Barrett did not believe in coincidences. The man went missing less than two days after Erissa fled the manor. His father covered for them before packing his entire family and leaving in the middle of the night. Trying to find both groups took a toll on each soldier searching for them.

He swiped a hand down his face as he reached the tower's landing, his rough fingers catching on his unkempt beard. A sigh left him, his shoulders drooping, and he contemplated returning to his quarters to bathe and tend his appearance. The thought of climbing the stairs once more halted that idea.

Faldeyr found fault in the slightest of things. He would no doubt complain about his appearance no matter what Barrett did. Better to get the confrontation over with. Faldeyr had no doubt heard the commotion from Barrett's arrival through the open window. Things never ended well when anyone kept him waiting.

Barrett did not grant his brother the courtesy of knocking. He barged into the room, regretting his impatience as he slapped a hand over his eyes and tried to forget what greeted him.

His brother's latest mistress lay on her stomach across the desk, boredom clear in the way she studied her hand where it gripped the dark wood, letting out an occasional fake moan of pleasure. Faldeyr pumped himself into her, grunting like a pig.

Barrett sighed, not bothering to close the door as he leaned against the frame. He closed his eyes and crossed his hands over his chest. In a matter of seconds, Faldeyr yelled his release, and Barrett thanked the gods for their mercy. He opened his eyes to find the woman straightening her skirts.

"Enjoy the show?" Faldeyr pulled his trousers up, tucking his shirt into them, and righting himself. He stared at the woman, his lip curling. "Why are you still here?"

Her Lord's rude dismissal struck home. The woman's face flamed. She muttered an apology and raced from the room, leaving her shoes behind.

Barrett sighed again, the sound drawn out. He tired of his brother's actions. Picking up the shoes, he placed them outside the door and closed it. "You're not even bothering to lock the door anymore?"

"What's the point? The woman's not the first to be here, and she won't be the last." Faldeyr found his seat, motioning for Barrett to do the same.

Barrett dropped into the offered chair. "And Vilotta?"

"Refuses to sully herself, as she calls it." Faldeyr's mouth twitched. "She knows her place. Don't forget yours."

Barrett bristled at the implied threat. The familiar feeling of not being in control of his own actions weighed on Barrett. He should have been used to it by now with the vow hanging over him, and yet, it never became easier. "Do what you want to me, brother, but your wife should garner more respect."

"Respect?" Faldeyr laughed and looked at Barrett with pity. "You've always had a soft spot for Vilotta. One she doesn't deserve. She's well aware there are others and grateful for it. Sex is beneath her. It's too messy and inconvenient for one who rarely dirties her hands."

Barrett swallowed the lump of embarrassment that formed at his brother's words. He did not need to hear what his brother's wife thought of sex. But more than that, anger simmered deep in his gut. All his years of listening to Vilotta complain about Faldeyr's mistresses, and she encouraged them the entire time. He did not have time to deal with such nonsense.

Faldeyr reached for the pitcher on his desk. He poured himself a drink, offering nothing to Barrett. "Did you find the girl in Theanelis?"

"No, there were no traces of her or the blacksmith's son. Though, I found something else..."

Barrett hesitated in revealing what happened, but Faldeyr pounced, taking advantage of the power he held over his brother. "Tell me what happened, and leave nothing out."

"We found the blacksmith and the rest of his family." Frustration tried to drown him as Barrett followed orders. "You were right. Traveling with five young girls slowed them down. They were on the road to Trilux."

"Always so obedient." A twisted delight twinkled in Faldeyr's eyes. "I could make you do anything, and you would have no choice but to obey."

"Don't test me, Faldeyr." Barrett's teeth ground together. "I'm tired, and I don't want to deal with this."

"Is that a challenge, brother?" Faldeyr sneered. "You are mine to control, but maybe you need a reminder."

"Faldeyr, don't—"

"Drag the knife along the vein, brother." Faldeyr's voice deepened as he issued the command, holding out a sharpened blade he picked up off the desk.

Barrett's feet moved forward even as he protested, his hand roughly jerking up his sleeve, exposing his forearm. "You can't be serious."

"Now," barked Faldeyr.

Barrett's legs only stopped when he stood before Faldeyr. His hand rose, gripping the knife. Sweat beaded around the metal as his mind fought what his body was forced to do. His hand shook as he brought the tip of the blade to his wrist, vomit souring the back of his throat as he pressed it into his skin and drew the length up his arm. He bit his tongue to keep from screaming. Blood welled around the blade, pouring over Barrett's arm to make a puddle on the floor.

"Stop." Faldeyr's command halted the blade's path. He moved around his desk leisurely and rifled through one of the drawers until he withdrew an embroidered handkerchief. He threw it at Barrett. "Press it into the mess before you ruin the floor."

Barrett snarled as he used the white fabric to apply pressure to the wound. "The floor wouldn't be in danger of staining if not for you."

"If not for your insolence, you mean," Faldeyr snapped, "or do you need another lesson?"

Barrett closed his mouth, seething.

"Where have you placed the blacksmith and his family?"

Barrett's fists clenched, and he cursed the bargain he made with his brother for the thousandth time. "The blacksmith is in the dungeon awaiting your command."

"And the women?"

"With Vilotta." Barrett scratched his beard, using the action to hide the satisfied smile hovering. "She intercepted us in the courtyard and insisted."

Faldeyr's face hardened. "Did you plan this?"

Barrett remained silent, regretting nothing. Vilotta proved herself to be a useless mother. He was Erissa's saving grace, even if the girl never knew.

But right now, Faldeyr had a role to play for his wife, and she remained the only one capable of protecting the blacksmith's children from the horrors Faldeyr would have in store for them. She might be a useless mother to Erissa, but Vilotta, always the face of perfect motherhood in the eyes of Emberhold, would protect the blacksmith's children to maintain her reputation.

His brother contemplated him for a long moment. "There will be consequences for this."

Barrett snorted. If Faldeyr's rage awaited him, he might as well make it worth it. "I expect nothing less from my benevolent Lord."

"I will deal with you later." Faldeyr sat back in his chair, drumming his fingers against the oiled wood. "For now, see to stitching up that mess and begin interrogating the blacksmith. I don't need to remind you what I will do to the man if you fail."

The threat hit as intended. Barrett turned on his heel and quit the room before he did something stupid. Like launching himself across the desk to strangle the man who he stopped recognizing as a good man thirteen years ago.

CHAPTER SIXTEEN

Rhazien reappeared minutes after Reeva faded from the grove, his arms full of firewood with a small dead rabbit lying on top. Its blood dripped onto the wood from where it had already been gutted, the steady flow tightening Erissa's stomach. Steam rose from the animal in the cold air. A bulging satchel swayed with his long stride from where it hung at his belt.

"The gods were kind tonight." He set the wood and rabbit on the ground before removing the satchel. "I found a trove of mushrooms, wild garlic, and onions. The rabbit wasn't too hard to catch either. We can make a pot of stone soup."

"You can hunt?" Erissa found the notion surprising despite how the pastime remained common enough among men. She also imagined a blacksmith would need to be well-versed in the different ways their forged weapons functioned. Even her uncle hunted, but she had little experience with the world outside of her chambers, and she did not know the first thing about finding any food in the depths of the woods.

"Hunt, fish…" Rhazien shrugged, his brow furrowed. "Both were Ernald's favorite pastime. My father and I often joined him. My mother wasn't fond of either. She's softhearted in taking an animal's life, but the meat on our table had to come from somewhere."

Erissa stared at the animal, drawn to its dark eyes, glassy with death as guilt overtook her expression. "I can well understand how she must have felt at taking the life of something so innocent." Erissa moved from the roots to the embankment, stepping gingerly to keep her stiff legs from collapsing underneath her and sending her into the freezing water. "How can I help?"

Rhazien unsheathed the smallest knife he carried and handed it to her. "Can you cut the food while I build the fire and skin the hare?"

Erissa nodded, taking the knife. Their fingers brushed, and Rhazien snapped his hand away, clearing his throat and stepping away. Her shoulders sagged at the rejection. She averted her gaze, leaning down to pick up the satchel. "That I can do. Can't be any different from cutting my own food, right?"

"That's right. You cut them the same way but leave them in larger pieces."

She moved to a large, flat boulder along the riverbank, placing the sack and knife upon it before returning to Rhazien's bag for the cooking pot. By the time she had everything rinsed and cut, the fire burned, growing in height while Rhazien busied himself with skinning their fare.

When he finished cutting the meat off the bones, he went to the river's edge and knelt along the embankment. Erissa stared with shameless abandon as Rhazien rolled back his sleeves and dipped his forearms into the cold water, washing the blood, travel, and exhaustion from his limbs before turning his attention to his neck and face.

Erissa ached to fill the silence between them. "Why do you call it stone soup?"

Rhazien moved from the water and scouted the area. Bending low, he picked up a rock and held it triumphantly, a pleased smile replacing the crooked cockiness from before and softening the tired lines across his face. "Because a stone is the secret ingredient."

"A stone?" Erissa arched a brow in disbelief.

Rhazien shook his head with a chuckle. "You don't need to stare at me like that. I haven't taken leave of my senses."

"I don't know." Erissa pursed her lips to hide the smile threatening to break free. "You are talking about eating rocks…"

"Only if we want to crack a tooth." Rhazien came and took the pot from her and placed the stone into the pocket of his trousers.

Erissa followed him as he knelt and used his knife to spear the meat and add it to the pot. He placed it against the burning logs. "Are you going to tell me what the stone is for?"

"So impatient, little doe."

Rhazien's tone was light, teasing her with the words and bringing a small smile to her lips. It had only been a week since he found her hiding behind the cart, but moons might have passed for all she felt closer to him. She had spent more time speaking with Rhazien than anyone else in the whole of her life. She enjoyed it, but it also terrified her.

Erissa hesitated to put too much hope into what his being with her meant. A distance lay between them as if they were nothing more than friends. He had barely touched her since their first night entering Eshirene's Wood. And it bothered her when it should not.

She wanted the Rhazien from the stable loft. She wanted the man who nearly kissed her, not the man who had yet to really touch her since their night in the abandoned lodge. She glanced at him, brooding. Did he know she kept something from him?

After unsheathing two of his longer knives, he took the stone from his pocket and pinched it between the blades. He used the knives to keep from burning his fingers, placing the stone in the middle of the fire. "My father would make us stone soup when we went on hunting trips. A rock heats faster than a pot filled with freezing water. Once it's nice and hot, you place it in your stew, which boils it quicker. But you have to be careful and make sure the rock is dry. Placing a wet one in the fire will cause it to burst into pieces. Trust me when I say we don't want that to happen."

"I take it you learned this from experience." Erissa sat beside him. "It must have been wonderful... having a father who wanted to teach you such things."

"He's a good man and an even better father. He's taught me many things, but not all came without consequences." Rhazien's expression changed. His lips thinned as he turned from the fire to consider her. "There's a lot I've learned from experience."

A shiver crept down her spine, but not from the cold. Rhazien's words were flat, his eyes dull, and Erissa found the words telling when coupled with her deceit. What if Reeva had been wrong in hearing Rhazien's return, and he had observed them? What if his words went beyond anything he might have seen or heard? His voice might have been flat, but it held pain.

Erissa opened her mouth to speak and snapped it closed as words failed her.

A snort filled the air, the sound jolting both of them as their focus moved to the horses. Rhazien rose and went to check on them. Rhynstone's ploy became obvious as he nipped at Rhazien's pockets. "I have nothing to give you, Rhyn. Settle down and stop begging."

When he returned, he carried Erissa's cloak and placed it around her shoulders. He lowered himself next to her with a tired sigh. Using the knives, Rhazien picked up the rock and plopped it into the waiting pot. "It will still take time for the meat to boil, but at least this will shorten the wait."

It was coming on evening by the time the soup was ready. Neither one of them did anything to break the silence. Erissa tried to ignore it as they ate. She turned her attention to the fire, savoring its heat on her front while the soup warmed the rest of her.

When they finished, she gathered their bowls and washed them in the river. She took her time returning and placing the items back into Rhazien's bag, uncertain if he wished for her company. Her steps faltered as she returned to the fire, leaving a space between herself and Rhazien when she sat. The fire turned to embers and ash as the night wore on, the smoldering pile losing its heat with every moment.

Rhazien finally broke the silence. "I'm going to collect more fuel for the fire."

"No!" Erissa lowered her voice as her shout echoed across the water. She winced. She did not mean to shout, but Reeva's warning swirled in her mind. Maybe she should tell Rhazien about it? But then, how would she explain her magic? "We should put it out."

"Why?" Rhazien's features hardened, his brow falling into a tight line as he challenged Erissa. "We might have snow before too long."

Erissa worried her lower lip. He was right to question her, but she had no answer to give him. Whether she fully trusted Reeva remained to be seen, but it would be foolish not to heed her warning. "Rhazien, please. Let's put the fire out for tonight."

He stood, staring at her with a raised brow, and she cringed away from the accusation it held. After a moment, he took the pot and stalked over to the river, filling it to the brim. His gaze set her on edge as he walked back and dumped water over the embers.

Rhazien tossed the pot beside the fire and put distance between them as he sat down, his palms on his knees. Erissa tracked his movement. Her shoulders slumped, the space between them and the frown that marred his features spoke of a cold night of discomfort for both of them. His brow scrunched into a frown as he let out an irritated sigh.

She flinched against the sound. He had to regret coming with her. She was sure of it. Not only did he leave the comforts of home for her, but she now denied him what few comforts he could find in the forest.

Tears built.

It was on the tip of her tongue to tell him about Reeva, her warning, and all Erissa had learned of her powers. She wanted to tell him. But the longer she waited, the quicker her courage faltered.

She did not want to change the way Rhazien looked at her, and it would change things, especially with her powers steeped in death. When he looked at her now, he saw *her*. Not as a burden, not as a means to an end with her magic, he saw only her and had said he wanted to be there with her. But what did that matter against what she was?

She swallowed hard, trying to force the tears back, but failed.

It made sense against Reeva's words. If life is the balance of death, taking life is the balance of giving it. Erissa did not need to confirm the notion through Reeva to know it as true. And he would hate her for it. For her powers. For what she was. Just like her parents and the townspeople. No one had ever accepted them, accepted *her*. But more than that, he would hate her for the lies she told as he threw his life away to save someone not worth saving.

"Why are you crying, little doe?"

The quiet question made the tears fall harder. Erissa curled into herself, trying to hide her body as she shook with the force of her guilt and shame. She stiffened when an arm wrapped around her waist and another tucked beneath her legs.

Rhazien drew her into his lap with great care. She tried to wrench herself from his grasp, but he held her tightly, his arm a steel band around her. A hand reached to cup her face. The calloused fingers pressed into her skin, turning her face to his. He used his thumb to wipe away her tears, his tender gaze settling on her panicked eyes. "I imaged myself immune to tears after having so many sisters, and you have proved me wrong."

Erissa ached at the indulgence in his expression. It offered comfort, and she did not deserve it. "There are things I can't say. Things I'm hiding from you. Things I'm not even sure I understand. And I can tell you know something. That I'm lying to you. But even in seeing your anger, I keep hesitating, to be honest. You'll hate me once you learn of it." He would hate, hate her magic as she hated it for all the pain it brought into her life. It was why she would not talk to it, why she wanted it to leave her alone. She faulted it for everything. Without it, her life would have been normal.

"You cannot seriously continue to blame me for everything that has befallen you." The voice stirred. *"I am a victim as much as you are, and one day you will have to see that."*

Erissa did not want to hear it. The tears worsened, blurring her vision and leaving her gasping for air.

"I will never hate you, little doe. Never." Rhazien pulled her closer and kissed the tears below her tightly closed eyes. "The way you are made is no accident. No matter what you tell me, it makes no difference. My days will unfold with yours."

"But you will hate me. Everyone does in the end." Erissa turned her head away.

The voice stirred, coming to life at Erissa's pain. *"Things are different. You have Rhazien, and you have me. You only need to open yourself to us. We are waiting for you."*

Erissa hiccupped, trying to control the rising emotions threatening to swallow her whole. "Losing out on so much for so long and having everyone walk away... the pain is unbearable. But losing you?" The words stuck to the roof of her mouth as she struggled to get them out. "It's unlivable. I don't know what to do. I'll lose you if I'm honest and lose you if I'm not."

He drew her head to his shoulder, holding it there while saying nothing. The pain of his silence reached its icy fingers into her, the feeling colder than the snow that now fell around them.

She listened to the steady beat of his heart against the soft noises of the river and the horses standing by it. His arms tightened around her, and she buried her face against his chest while her tears slowed.

"I've been a right ass, haven't I?"

The rueful words were unexpected. Erissa tipped her head back to see his face.

"I heard you that morning. Talking to someone. At first, I thought you were speaking to yourself, but another voice joined yours. When I found you alone, I thought I had to be mistaken." He shook his head as if he was trying to shake away his suspicions and failing. "But I hung back the next day when I went to find wood for the fire. You waited for someone, and they never came. The next time we stopped, you did the same. Each evening followed the same pattern."

Erissa gripped the front of his shirt, wrinkling the fabric as she held onto it. "Why didn't you say anything?"

"I meant what I said in the loft. I will never make you tell me something you don't want to." Rhazien's gaze softened with his voice. "I want you to tell me. Even if it hurts me. But only when you're ready."

Erissa tried not to nurture the spark of hope that flared warmly beneath her breast. His actions conflicted with his words. "You still pulled away."

"Trust him, Erissa," the voice whispered. *"For yourself. For me. I have never led you astray."*

Rhazien's bronzed cheeks deepened with color. "I didn't expect it to hurt so much. When you didn't trust me enough to tell me who you were talking to..." His laugh was nervous when he spoke again, the sound catching as it carried over to Erissa. "Which is crazy. To expect you to give everything of yourself over when it's only been seven days..." He trailed off with a shrug.

"I *do* trust you. You expect as much because you've given the same to me. I *want* to tell you. But I'm afraid. Losing you because of what I have to say is..." Erissa sat straighter in his lap and took his face in her hands. Her fingers tingled with the contact, the tips brushing against the spikey, dark stubble left to grow. "Rhazien, look at me."

When their eyes connected, she sucked in a breath at the raw emotion she found in his. She traced her fingers along his face, a sweet caress that had him tightening his arms around her, bringing their faces mere inches apart. They shared one breath, their chests heaving. The quick heat of it rose like smoke between them in the freezing air.

Erissa smiled when the voice purred, and she gave into its pleas. "You broke the silence, Rhazien. I'm becoming whole. If, for only a moment, you have made time start again."

"I don't want to lose you, little doe."

A small sound escaped her lips, and his eyes dropped to her mouth. Erissa bit into the full bottom curve of her lip as if the motion would take the sound back. Her world narrowed to nothing but the feel of him, his hardness against her softness. She pressed herself into him, tipping her head and bringing their lips closer until only half a breath lay between them, and his scent enraptured her. Erissa slid her hands into his hair and tried to close the small space still between him.

"You can tell me to stop. I don't expect you to..." Rhazien resisted even as he moved her to sit astride his lap. "Tell me to stop, Erissa."

"No." The violet light of her eyes burned darker, the shade deepening with desire, and Erissa spoke from a combined voice, one where her magic blended with her soul. She wrapped her legs around his waist. "I want you to kiss me. I want... we want..." Erissa snapped her mouth shut, horrified she almost revealed the voice and its desires.

She traced a finger across his lips when he still hesitated, her eyes following the movement. She smiled when they parted on a low moan. Erissa pressed forward until her lips brushed against his as she whispered, "Please, Rhazien."

As the plea left Erissa, Rhazien slanted his lips across hers. His arms tightened around her when she leaned into the embrace, his firm hold molding their bodies together. Their mouths twisted together, clumsy at first with Erissa's innocence, but she soon caught his rhythm and returned each lingering caress as their tongues collided and their breath intertwined.

Rhazien groaned into her mouth, deepening the kiss. He devoured her, the force of his kiss making her cry out. He swallowed the sound.

The tether between them tightened with rising pleasure, and Erissa lost herself to it, her very existence narrowing until she knew nothing more than Rhazien's pleasure mixing with her own. She ground herself against him, trying to appease the ache flooding between her thighs.

The hand on her back moved until it was in her hair. It wound itself through the strands, taking a fistful as Rhazien broke the kiss and gently pulled her head away. His other arm tightened around her waist, halting her movements.

Erissa opened her hazy, lust-filled eyes. She tried to wiggle her hips but found only frustration as Rhazien's arm refused to give way. Her hand slid down his chest, reaching lower, but Rhazien tightened his grip on her hair, pulling only hard enough to gain her attention. "Erissa, stop."

"I don't..." Confusion muddled her desire as Rhazien's words registered. "Did I do something wrong?"

His lower hand pressed her down as he thrust himself against her. Her core throbbed in response, and she let out a strangled whimper. "Rhazien..."

Tightening the hand in her hair, he tipped her head back, exposing her throat. "There's nothing wrong with what you did, little doe." He leaned into her, pressing kisses up her neck to whisper in her ear. "You can feel how much I want to continue." His lips traced a path back down. He nosed the black ribbon of her choker out of the way and bit the skin at the base of her throat, murmuring the words through the small kisses he placed against the stinging mark. "But when I finally have you, it will be when there are no secrets between us."

Rhazien's words doused her desire. Erissa's cheeks flooded with embarrassment as the reality of her behavior sunk in. She had been so consumed with her feelings that she gave little consideration to how Rhazien must have perceived her loss of control. She made to scramble off his lap, as disgusted with herself as she guessed him to be, but he would not let go, his arm a vice that kept her spread across his arousal. "Let go of me."

"Tell him the truth," the voice begged.

Rhazien shook his head. "No."

The single word spoken with such arrogant authority infuriated her. "Let me go, Rhazien." She tried in vain to move once more and earned nothing more than a dark chuckle from him as his strength far outmatched her own.

"I rather like having you here."

"And I would rather move." Erissa shoved at his chest, turning her head away. "It's embarrassing enough to be rejected. I'd rather not draw out the humiliation."

"I'm not the one doing the rejecting right now, little doe." The words were blunt but not unkindly spoken. Rhazien released her hair and drew his hand back to cup her chin. He guided her face back to his. "I watched an entire city cower as you walked past them and considered them mad, for all I wanted to do was follow you and your honeysuckle perfume. My beautiful little doe with her haunted eyes filled with such loneliness. I'm here with you, Erissa, and I'm not going anywhere."

Erissa's nose wrinkled as her face scrunched together. "Honeysuckle perfume? I don't wear perfume."

"He likes us," the voice simpered. *"Tell him the truth."*

Erissa ignored it.

"Is that all you took in from that?" Rhazien laughed then, a deep, rich sound of such joy that Erissa was powerless not to return, the sound of it choking in her throat as Rhazien dropped his hand and rubbed his nose in the crook of her neck, breathing deeply. "You smell of honeysuckle and tea. I nearly lost my senses from it as you walked past me."

"Rhazien..." His name came out on a strangled moan.

"Yes?" He trailed small kisses up her throat, stopping to nibble against her ear. "Do you need to hear it again?" He grinned, his lips curling against her skin. "I'm here with you. Whatever you're hiding from me, whatever you think is so bad, we'll weather it together. We've come this far on trust alone. Can't you find a little more for me?"

Erissa batted a hand against his chest. "What happened to not forcing me to tell you?"

"I'm not forcing." He pressed another kiss below her ear, making her shiver and bow against him. "I'm convincing. There's a substantial difference between the two."

"Uh-huh." She hated to admit it, but as his teeth scraped lazily against her skin, his *convincing* had his intended effect.

He sensed it, too. His hand traced the path of his kisses, skimming down her throat and chest until it rested between the curves of her breasts, between the parted ends of her cloak. Dropping his hand down lower.

The callouses on his hands scraped against the fabric covering her stomach. Erissa wished he would lift the end of her shirt. She arched her chest forward, an invitation she hoped he would not ignore. She struggled to fully comprehend the desire she desperately wanted to give in to. Her skin hummed underneath his touch, the sound vibrating into the darkest parts of her, and she was helpless against the hypnotic pull.

His fingers traced lazy circles. She cried out as he skimmed the underside of her breasts with one of his circles, the sensation of the fabric rubbing against her skin intensifying things. Rhazien laughed, the sound of it reverberating against her skin where he still pressed his kisses, nipping each spot his lips touched. "Are you convinced yet?"

The question jerked her from his touch-induced haze. She pushed away from him in annoyance at his teasing, and he let her this time, a satisfied smile making him even more handsome and challenging to pull away from. The desire to storm away from him fought with her desire to sink her teeth into that cocky grin, but instead, she scrambled out of his lap and rushed to the river, needing distance to think clearly.

Rhazien chuckled. "I'll take that as a no."

If she had a rock in her hand, she would throw it to wipe the smug arrogance on his face. "You don't play fair."

"I never claimed I would." He stood, running a hand through his hair to dislodge the melting snow. "Know this, little doe. I won't stop trying to change your mind."

Without his body pressed to hers, Erissa fell victim to the temperature that had dropped with the sun's setting, but it was not the cold that sent a shiver coursing through her core. Rhazien disturbed her with the promise lingering behind his honeyed gaze.

The moon showed through the clouds, its light giving an ethereal glow as the snow stuck to the ground. The thickening layer offered them no chance of warmth for when they slept tonight. Her eyes moved to Rhazien, and a stone settled into the pit of her stomach as she made her decision.

CHAPTER SEVENTEEN

It surprised them both when Erissa started speaking. She almost smiled as Rhazien's mouth popped open, but the reality of what she needed to reveal smothered the sensation. "You did hear me talking to someone... to a soul. One different from the rest. She doesn't *call* to me like the others. There's no enticement or chanting. She *talks* to me the same as we are speaking now. She's Fae and not bound to my sight alone, even though she's fixed to the Veil. Others may see and speak with her as clearly as I do. She told me..."

The words trailed off, and she labeled herself a coward, one unworthy of the man standing before her. The man who had sacrificed so much for a runaway he had barely met.

"You've seen no other like her before now?"

The curious tone caught her off guard, his response differing from what she expected. Erissa shook her head, her heart picking up its pace as he stepped toward her.

"I don't care what this creature has to say." He took a second step. "If you told me she said you'd stab me in the heart with one of my daggers, I would choose to stay." And then he took a third. "Without any regret for what I left behind. No matter what she has said, I will still choose you."

Rhazien's words hardened her resolve. He had upended his world for her without a second of hesitation, asking for nothing in return until now. All he wanted was honesty between them.

Erissa swallowed her pride and her fears along with it, and with a steadying breath, she told him the truth. Not because she wanted to but because he deserved it. "I don't know where to start."

He waited in silence, allowing her to gather herself.

"I can do more than see souls fated for the Veil. I have elemental magic, and my mother said they were hiding me from someone, that they imprisoned me to keep me safe, but something about it wasn't right. If they were only hiding me from someone, why did my father do the things he did? It doesn't make sense." The words wouldn't stop after they started. Erissa found freedom in the rush of them tumbling out of her. With each reveal, the internal chains still weighing her down lost another link. "I knew nothing beyond this when you found me hiding. The soul, her name is Reeva. She knows everything about me. Who I am, what my powers are, and where they come from. But she hides more than she tells."

"And what has she told you?" He took another step as he spoke, moving beyond where the fire crackled.

"My power is connected to the Veil, to the power that holds it in this world. It's part of the reason I can see the fated souls. I have the power of Creation itself. Power over anything that its spark of life has touched, including the elements." Erissa linked her hands tight enough for the blood to drain from her fingers. "But such power must be balanced, or so Reeva says. And the balance of life is..." She did not say the word, no matter how many times she opened her mouth to speak it aloud.

Rhazien took another step, now standing an equal distance between her and the fire. She imagined how she must appear, drawn and broken and as pale as the snow falling thickly around her.

He met her halfway with another measured step, saying what she had failed to speak aloud. "Death, little doe. The balance of Creation is the Veil, and the balance of life, death."

Her face crumpled with the sound of her special name attached to such ugliness. "I can call the soul from a person and end their connection to life. Don't you see now why I wouldn't tell you? My magic can kill people."

One more step brought him within reach of her.

"There's more, Rhazien. I am not only hunted by my father. I'm hunted by the man my mother wished to protect me from. And according to Reeva, I'm hunted by another as well, although she can tell me nothing of it."

Erissa expected him to turn from her. She buried her face against her hands. "I have placed you in great danger in my selfishness to have you near when I should have told you all along about what awaits me. They will close in on us from every side, and Reeva has said this evening at least one of them draws near." Her voice broke with sorrow, but she forced the words out anyway, no matter how they tore at her heart. "Don't you understand, Rhazien? You must leave me here for your own safety. It's selfish for me to want you by my side. I'm putting you in danger, even if I don't want to admit it to myself."

Rough hands wrapped around her wrists, and she flinched against the contact. She tried to break away from Rhazien's hold, but he tugged her wrists down and around her back, capturing them in one hand as he used them to push her into his chest.

She stared at his chin, not wanting to witness the anger that must be written across his features. He used his other hand to take hold of her chin and forced her face up, his grip threatening to bruise her tender flesh as she fought against him. "Leave. Before they find us. If you go now—"

Rhazien's lips slammed against hers in a searing, devouring kiss that stole the breath from her lungs. When she tried to twist away, his hand drifted down to take hold of her throat, his fingers squeezing, pressing the pendant of her choker into her skin as he held her still against his kiss. It warmed under his touch, tingling against her skin.

The kiss demanded a response with a clash of tongues, and Erissa caved under the pressure. She would take the kiss if it was all she would have of him. Wanting more than what he already gave spoke of her selfishness. A part of her hated the greed that consumed her, even as another small part reveled in it. What did that make her? Erissa had no desire to use him. She wanted him safe and far away before anyone found her, but she did not pull away from what he freely offered. She wanted this moment more than anything, a moment of true happiness, and with each coaxing movement of his lips, she slipped further away from the right or fair thing.

Closing her eyes, she surrendered to him, dropping every wall. Something sweet settled deep within her, and she kissed him back.

A hum started within her as she offered herself to Rhazien's kiss. The warmth of it radiated as it ran in every direction through her being. The magic, unlike anything she had ever experienced before, coursed through her veins and connected her to everything. To every piece of Rhazien as he stood before her. To the ground beneath her feet and the river at her back. To the sky and the snow that fell. To the beasts that stood near them and the willows winding their way across the path of the river. And to the shadows that framed it all in the moon's soft light as it peaked through the snow-swollen clouds. Their life source pulsing against the wild beating of her own heart as it found the rhythm of Rhazien's and matched it.

He tried to break the kiss first. Rhazien's lungs burned with the hasty need for air, a need Erissa echoed.

The voice prodded against her thoughts. *"I can sustain both your desires. Surrender."*

Erissa did what she had never done before. She surrendered to the voice's desire.

Magic poured into Erissa, soaking her very soul in the depths of her power. Her hand found the back of Rhazien's neck, pulling him in tighter as she stood on her toes to deepen the kiss. The magic grew within her. It bled into the kiss, sustaining their lungs with a continuous breath of life until it overflowed.

Electricity charged the air as if lightning crackled all around them. The snow froze, suspended while the clouds parted, and Erissa drew the stars from the night sky. A black mist enveloped them where they stood. Light burst from her in shades of violet. It entwined itself with the star-kissed mist, the two twisting together until the colors blended so seamlessly they were one as the force flowed through them, around them, and into the fabric of the world.

The horses panicked as everything around them exploded with life. The river swelled against its banks, the dormant grass and shrubbery curled through the snow, and the naked limbs of trees thrived as leaves grew thick and lush. Willows groaned in delight as they earned their wild name. Their branches thickened, the spindly lengths braiding together until their trunks grew taller as their roots soaked up new life from the burgeoning river. Their canopies spread across the grove, creating hidden little worlds beneath the thickly hanging limbs.

As the horses called out in fright, Erissa's power reached out to them, drawing upon the earth as she found the spot where hooves danced in trepidation. The magic flowed into Rhynstone and Carizzea and touched upon their spark of life. She calmed their fears and settled the fast pace of their hearts, leaving them content beneath the willow covering them all.

Her back bowed with the force of the magic she channeled, forcing her to break the kiss as it whispered to her to let go. Someone called her name with a familiar voice, but it sounded far away. Another call joined it, one she had learned long ago on all those nights she had been chained. Both voices tempted her, and there was no untwining herself from their seductive calls, so she placed her focus on the sensations surrounding her body.

Something warm and hard pressed to her front. A content sigh left her as she held onto it tighter. With its warmth against her front and the twinkling mist caressing her from behind, Erissa finally knew freedom, as if she found her true home. A last sigh left her lips, and Erissa let go, surrendering to the seductive plea as the magic beckoned her.

CHAPTER EIGHTEEN

"The King is not to be disturbed."

Nephinae rolled her eyes and shoved past the frantic young Fae, trying to stop her from entering the king's chambers.

In the last five days, Yorrith found excuse after excuse when she tried to meet with him. He left her no other choice but to corner him in the dead of night. Let him try and hide from her now, she would not be deterred.

"You must stop, or I will call the guard." The boy flung his hands out, blocking the door. "The King left clear instructions that he didn't wish to be disturbed.

"Try your feeble attempts on someone else. I know well the King keeps no guard. The fool is too softhearted for the harsh realities of his position." She jerked the hood of her cloak off, exposing her white hair and matching eyes. Nephinae fed her power into her orbs, and they glowed brightly, the sight leaving the boy trembling. "Now, move out of my way, child."

He bowed his head and mumbled a protest but stepped aside.

She hated to threaten the boy with her position. All Fae feared the Zorathi, especially its leader. After all, she had made the rest of the Zorathi warriors with her blood during the Remaking War centuries ago. Each one she'd created removed a piece of her soul. Little of humanity remained in Nephinae, and if it were not for the purpose she found in the Court of the Frosted Moon, she would have left this world behind long ago. But all anyone would ever see was the monster the gods of light and darkness made her to be. This night, she would use that fear to her advantage.

"Do not interfere." Nephinae let the threat in her voice linger. "Should anyone disturb us, I will be most displeased."

The boy nodded, keeping his head down. "Yes, Zorathi."

Nephinae dropped her magic as she swept by him and let herself into the King's room, closing the door behind her.

Light peaked between the swaying curtains on the balcony, casting shadows everywhere she looked. She expected a level of opulence that matched the stories told of the Seelie palace of Zaestiraen, but she got nothing more than a halfway-furnished room and the sour smell of too much wine in the stifling warmth.

"Seelie?" Nephinae removed her cloak, flinging it over the changing screen as she moved further into the chamber, revealing her dress as a mix of chains and fabric interwoven across her body to mold against her breasts and drape down her front, leaving long slits clear to her hips. The balcony light flickered against the large gemstones inlaid on the screen. Her brow lifted as she appraised their worth. The room held more wealth than it first appeared. If the rest of the room held the same in its simple furnishings, the King's room alone would feed the entire Unseelie court for the year.

Nephinae hazard a guess at who had insisted on this ostentatious display. Yorrith, ever the simple man, would not have chosen such crass furniture. Only one person lived that would convince the King and the thought of the Fae who betrayed the King's heart to flee beyond the Mists left a rotten taste in Nephinae's mouth as her lips curled with disdain.

The closer she came to the balcony, the more light illuminated the surroundings. Wine bottles littered the floor, her feet connecting with the long necks as she stumbled over them. How many were from tonight?

Nephinae's heartbeat picked up pace. What madness drove the King to drink in excess?

"Yorrith?" Nephinae pushed aside one of the balcony curtains. She found him standing in the moonlight against the stone railing, another bottle dangling from his hands. "There you are. You have been avoiding me for days."

Her voice startled him, making the bottle fall over the edge of the balcony. No crashing sound would follow at their height. Zaestiraen stood as tall as the mountains behind it, but the King paid no attention to the height of the balcony as he stumbled forward a few steps.

Yorrith stared at her wide-eyed, swallowing hard as he took in her scandalous dress. His eyes lingered on the curves it revealed, his voice slurred with wine and huskiness. "By the Creator, my dreams haunt me. The Zorathi plagues me even here."

He dreamed about her? Nephinae ignored the way his admission and the desire in his gaze made her shiver. She should not have come this night. Their past lay between them, and he would never forgive her for the way she left things.

Letting the curtain fall behind her, Nephinae moved to stand beside the king, leaning her hip against the stone wall. "What has you drinking to excess, Seelie?"

"You ask me that every night." The King laughed, turning toward her and stumbling.

Her hands shot out, grabbing onto his arms to keep him from toppling from the balcony to his death. "The gods be damned, Seelie, will you take care?"

Yorrith fell against her. All his humor fled as their chests touched. His brow lifted. "You are really here?"

"I am flesh and bone, Yorrith. Same as you." Though she loathed to do it, Nephinae pushed the King back. She came here for a reason, and her Lord grew impatient. "Are you too far gone tonight? Novus sent me with clear instructions."

At the mention of her Lord, Yorrith snarled, moving closer until their chests touched once again. "To the devil with what he wants, Zorathi. I hate his name coming from your lips."

He swayed, and Nephinae looked at him closely. His face held more lines, a rarity for the Fae, and common sense deserted his tongue. "How often do you drink like this?"

"Often enough to sleep. It evades me night after night." Yorrith shifted his weight like a guilty child, his tone hollow.

Alarm slammed into her. Nephinae gaped at him, struggling to swallow her shock. His words halted her intention to call in the bargain. She had never heard Yorrith speak with such profound sadness and had never seen him drunk. What drove him to this state each night? "You do this every night?"

He sighed, dropping his head to her shoulder. "Even gods grow tired, Zorathi."

"Are we comparing ourselves to the gods now?" A smile softened Nephinae's gaze as she teased him. She ran a finger down his cheek and cupped his face.

"No." Yorrith shook his head, the smell of Fae wine wafting from him. "I'm not worthy of such a title. Not after the Remaking. Not after her…"

Nephinae stiffened, unsure of who he meant. Did he call for his first love, the mate who rejected him, or the lost love that cost him the most? One of the three would destroy her, so she steered his thoughts to other things to protect her own. She pushed him away. "You give too little credit to your charms. You are worthy of more than you think."

His eyes widened with shock, but she did not stop him when he wound his arms around her waist. "Says the one who didn't think so."

"You say far too much when in your cups. I never said such a thing." Nephinae sighed and stroked his hair as if he were a child.

"I'm tired, Nephinae." Yorrith nuzzled into her neck. "By the gods, I am tired."

Her heart broke with his admission, one the Fae King would never make in the light of day with a sober tongue, and she held no words to comfort him after all that lay between them. Nephinae did the only thing she would allow herself to do and led him inside, kicking the bottles out of their path. She lay him on the bed, and when he made to speak, she shushed him.

"Sleep, Seelie. Mayhap your dreams will treat you kinder than I."

She hummed a song well into the night and long after the King had fallen asleep. A song most had forgotten through the centuries, even among her people. One from the time of the Remaking when the Zorathi did not exist, making her dream of what life might have been if the Creator had intervened earlier in the war. A song that spoke of peace and love and everything becoming a Zorathi denied her.

The war cost each of them everything they held dear. Nephinae lost her chance for any true happiness and love with becoming a Zorathi, and Yorrith lost more than most when a spell meant to save them all had disastrous consequences that spread the fractured souls of his god and their court across time. None of it mattered, with her hand in his hair and a content smile softening the harsh lines of his face, making him appear far younger.

Yorrith stirred against her hand, murmuring something nonsensical, but his eyes remained closed and his breath even, and Nephinae found herself unreasonably jealous. For never had sleep treated her as warmly as it did the foolish drunkard before her. But more than that, it never treated her as warmly as the King sleeping beneath her touch. The time would come when she called in Novus's bargain, but for now, she would grant Yorrith peace before she gave him hope and ripped it away.

CHAPTER NINETEEN

The calling of Erissa's name came again, louder this time, more familiar, and she followed its sound through an endless sea of shimmering shadows and purple stars. It called to her again and again, each time stronger than the last.

"Erissa…"

The stars whispered their goodbyes.

"Please, Erissa…"

The violet lights receded.

"Open your eyes, I beg of you…"

And the mists faded with a last kiss against her skin.

"Little doe, please, come back…"

She quite liked the sound of that. Little doe. She savored the name. Only one person ever called her that.

"You have to open your eyes, little doe. Please, open them for me."

"Rhazien," Erissa whispered his name with longing. "I love being called that. Can you do it again?"

A bark of hysterical laughter brought her into the moment, her eyes flying open. She found herself lying on the ground with twin pools of amber staring down at her, visible only by the light of her eyes, their depths shadowed with worry. "Rhazien?"

"By the gods, I thought I lost you." He seized her arms, dragging her against him in a crushing embrace.

The last of the magic loosened its hold on her. Rhazien's embrace grounded her in the moment. Reason returned, as did the memory of the magic flowing through her. She placed her hands against his chest and pushed him away enough so that the cast of her glow illuminated him. "Are you alright? I didn't... I didn't hurt you, did I?"

"You would never hurt me." He took her hands and kissed each knuckle.

"This is why you must leave. I wasn't in control. What I did was—"

"Beautiful. I won't let you call it anything else." Rhazien stood, bringing Erissa with him to the wildling's curtain of swaying branches. A question filled her eyes, and he answered it with a sweep of a hand, moving the branches aside and leading her from beneath them.

The grove had been transformed into the full bloom of spring. Every color greeted her, framed by falling snow that disappeared before whitening the land. Blossoming foliage covered the ground, the trees lush and sparkling with life underneath the full moon and its starry sky. The wildling willows, tall before, now towered over the water, the abundant branches twisted intimately and reached to trail across the ground.

Erissa stared at it all in wonder. "I... did all of this?"

"We did all of this. Have you forgotten about me?" the voice asked, a laugh breaking through.

Horror spawned within Erissa's chest. How had they done this?

"We became one as we were always intended to be. This is the least of what we can do."

If that were true, it became even more urgent that Rhazien would leave her.

"By the gods, not this again," the voice swore.

"I can feel the worry coming off you in waves." Rhazien squeezed her hand. "What you did... Erissa, you joined spring and winter into something magical."

Rhazien was right; the renewed grove held great beauty, but it terrified her. The enormity of holding such power without understanding how it worked left her choking on everything unknown. Unchecked emotion spread beneath her skin, writhing in a way that left her tense and ready to flee from the testament to her power.

Rhazien spun her around until he drew her against his chest. The tension faded from her body when he wrapped his arms around her waist. A smile tugged at his lips, and he nuzzled her neck.

"Do you think me a monster because the weapons I forge are used to end the lives of others?"

"Where did that come from?" Erissa turned her head, giving him greater access. "You're not responsible for what another person does."

"What about my own actions?" His chin came to rest upon her shoulder, his breath tickling her ear. "If Gabrien hadn't run off, he'd be dead by my hand. Would you think me a monster then?"

"There's nothing of a monster in you, Rhazien."

"Then why do you think of yourself as one?"

The chiding tone brought color to her cheeks. She held onto hope, hope that part of her needed him to continue. Needed him to say the words.

Rhazien twirled her around once more, and Erissa fell further under his spell with his understanding of her needs. She needed to see his eyes, knew he spoke honestly and nothing more.

"How you decide to use your power is up to you. But I know you, little doe. There are times I can feel every emotion running behind those eyes, and when your power flowed through me..." Leaning down, he kissed her with the kind of kiss he might have given her if things were different and they had met under normal circumstances. The kind of kiss that spoke of courting, flowers, and dances at festivals. And when he pulled back, his eyes reflected the truth of his feelings, and her own mirrored the same.

"There will be no more talk of my leaving. You are mine, little doe, as surely as I am yours. And I intend to stay with you. Always. Now come, let us get some sleep while we still have time."

She smiled then, a small, simple smile filled with all the hope she had never allowed herself to fully feel. He answered it with a brilliant grin. One that transformed his face. And at that moment, she had never viewed anything more beautiful.

CHAPTER TWENTY

Erissa hovered between her nightmares and waking as a hand pressed against her mouth.

A cold sweat coated her, chilling her skin in the night air. Fear paralyzed her. Trembling followed, a physical betrayal she fought hard to suppress but failed as the memories of every time she had been dragged from her sleep and beaten flashed through her mind. It only took seconds for her to go through the catalog of violent memories haunting her.

Shouting voices came closer. Erissa's fingers dug into her sheets. She trembled harder from the angry-sounding voices, ready to fight against the onslaught she sensed coming but more terrified of the reaction awaiting her if she tried to protect herself. She hated the tears that leaked beneath her closed eyelids, another betrayal.

Only no fabric touched the tips of her fingers as her hand dug into phantom sheets. Soft blades met her touch. They tickled her palm as her fingers drifted through them. Their edges were surprisingly sharp against her delicate skin. She ran them over each blade, questioning if her father had truly broken her mind this time.

Voices traveled through the night air once more, and the hand tightened across her mouth. Something rough scratched against her lips. The sensation returned when the hand shifted slightly, allowing her more room to drag air into her petrified lungs.

The voices grew closer, and the hand shifted once more. Another catch against her lips.

A scent drifted to her, something familiar. It tickled the back of her mind, the fresh smell of wood mixed with something else. Jasmine, she mused. It intensified as someone moved closer, and she flinched despite herself when a breath puffed against her ear.

The hand went deathly still, and Erissa cursed herself for being so weak. She braced herself for the fist that came next. But then it didn't. She strained against the hold on her mouth as another hand slipped beneath and hauled her against a hard chest that smelled of wood, jasmine, and another fragrance. It stirred something inside her, confusing her as her body relaxed into the arm about her waist.

A breath tickled her ear again, but she did not flinch this time. She leaned into it as lips brushed against her ear, and a voice barely above a whisper spoke to her.

"Wake up, little doe." A kiss was pressed to her ear. "You're safe, but you must wake." Another kiss below her ear. The pressure across her mouth lessened, the calloused hand pulling back slowly.

Erissa's eyes opened, their brilliance illuminating the face in front of her even in the dark of night. "Rhazien?"

Again, he barely whispered. "I'm sorry I scared you, but you must be quiet. We are not alone."

Voices sounded in the air again, followed by the tread of multiple horses. They were much closer than before, the words easy to discern, as they made no effort to conceal themselves.

A female was speaking. "We should check under every tree. There might be some—"

"There'd be no point." The gruff voice of a man cut her off. "The girl might be worthless, but the boy? He wouldn't keep her in one place for long. Besides, the fire is cold."

"Like that matters with greenery all around. There are plenty of places for them to hide and signs of their tracks all over," she snorted. "Besides, this isn't normal. Look around us and tell me that magic didn't create this mess?"

"Who cares if it did? We tracked the girl here, and the boy wouldn't chance someone finding her through her magic if she made all this," the man said. "He would cross the river and head for Gailme. If we hurry, we might catch them on the road."

"You think they would risk being found in the city? Her violet eyes will draw nothing but attention. The boy is no fool. He will stick to the Wilds."

"The decision is made. We head for Gailme."

"Tiovriss, the girl is the Veiled One. You shouldn't underestimate her so easily. Virion told us to bring her to him as soon as possible. The spell needs to be done before the next month is upon us if we're to release Draven from the Veil so he can free the Keeper. There's no time to be wrong. I still think—"

"Enough," the man spat. "If I wanted your opinion, I would ask for it. Why Virion sent you with me... of course, I'd have his favor too if I warmed his bed."

"How dare you!" the woman screeched. "I've earned my place."

"Yeah," the man laughed unkindly. "On your knees."

"If you think—" the woman's voice cut off on a strangled grunt.

"I'm growing tired of your tantrums, Alrithia." The man's voice turned frigid, raising the hair along Erissa's arms as he spoke. "Virion's only instruction was to keep the girl alive. If one of us goes missing, it's of little consequence. I'd suggest you remember that and keep to your place."

The woman said nothing more. The seconds ticked by in a painfully slow silence before a decision was made. Rhazien and Erissa listened as they retreated across the water, the horses splashing through the shallows of the sandbar.

They waited a long time, keeping quiet as they made sure the pair had passed and were well on their way to the river town.

Rhazien spoke first, moving her from his lap. "We need to find the horses. We'll be lucky if we catch them."

Erissa's brow furrowed. "Where are they?"

"I sent them running in the direction of the Wilds as soon as I made out those two crashing through the trees." Rhazien scrubbed a hand across his brow. "I heard them shouting at each other several miles back. It's a wonder they didn't wake you."

"What are we to do now?" Erissa caught the ends of her cloak and picked at the travel-worn hem. "With those two heading to Gailme, we can't travel there."

"There's no other option but the Wilds, little doe. We can still reach Cropari before a week has passed if we find the horses." Rhazien picked up their bags, handing the lighter one to Erissa. The heavier ones he slung across his back. "We need to go now. Rhyn won't stay patient for long. He's too close to home and familiar with the trails, and Crezzi will follow his lead."

Erissa stood there, uncertain. "You're sure of this? It's the only way?"

Rhazien smiled, catching her off guard. "Are you afraid of the big, bad Wilds, little doe?"

Her arms crossed with a roll of her eyes as she stared up at him. "As afraid as any sane person would be."

"Don't worry about the Wilds." Rhazien swooped down and captured her lips with his. After a short tease of a kiss, he pulled back, nipping against her lower lip before lifting his head.

"That's not playing fair." Erissa swayed, drunk on the brief kiss, a pout forming.

"The faster we get through them, the better. There are plenty of things I'd like to do to you, little doe, but when I do them, it will be in a warm bed in Cropari where I can feast on you properly." He winked as he walked away, leaving Erissa staring after him, her mouth open and face ablaze.

Rhazien turned around when she didn't catch up with him. He called after her, his voice full of laughter, "Come, little doe. Cropari awaits."

CHAPTER TWENTY-ONE

They walked through the rest of the night and all the next day and a half as Rhazien tracked Rhynstone and Carizzea's path, determined to put as much distance between themselves and their trackers.

Rhazien filled the time by telling Erissa stories of his sisters, about the cities he had visited, the world she had never seen, and he told her more about the Fae. Now, as they walked, Rhazien told her how the Veil came to be.

"The Remaking was the first war." His steady voice kept her anchored as her legs burned at their brisk pace. "The god of darkness, Malcufyre, started the war in his quest for more power. He hoped to challenge the Creator once he overthrew the lawful gods, but all he earned was banishment into the Veil, forever sentenced to being the Keeper of Souls."

"Being the Keeper is a punishment?"

Rhazien nodded. "The Creator made him responsible for the lives he took during the war. He created the Veil, making it a resting place for those who could not move on and a transitionary place for those who could. The Veil is built over the Buried Court."

"What's the Buried Court?"

"It's the tomb of those who sacrificed themselves for the Veil's creation. The magic is made from their souls."

"Sacrificed?" Erissa's head whipped around to stare up at him. "The Veil was made from souls? The Creator killed people?"

Rhazien met her gaze and shrugged. "Something as powerful as the Veil requires blood magic, even for the Creator. Their freely given sacrifice binds all but the Creator and those touched by the Veil's magic from passing through its boundary."

"It seems a crime all on its own to place the one responsible for so much death in charge of helping the dead pass into the afterlife, especially when such a price was paid to make the Veil." Erissa panted slightly as she tried to keep up with Rhazien. His breath was too even for someone walking as fast as they were. He had barely worked up a sweat, and Erissa was sure she looked like an overworked horse as a droplet of sweat ran down the back of her neck.

Rhazien chuckled, offering her a hand as the ground rose and the terrain became sharper. "That's what I said when my parents first told me the stories."

"Why not kill him? Why leave the god of darkness alive?" Erissa asked, accepting the help as her thigh gave a vicious twinge.

"Balance." Rhazien pulled her against his side, taking some of her weight as he pulled her arm through his. "Killing one of the gods would change the ratio between the Lawful and Chaotic gods, especially with both the Neutral gods gone. Their numbers are even, each having lost one during the Remaking."

"What happened to the Neutral gods?" Erissa sighed as the pressure on her thigh eased. She wanted to ask Rhazien to slow down before her leg collapsed, but she stayed quiet.

"The goddess of the void died, but no one knows what happened to the god of time. Time magic is volatile, and a spell went wrong during the war when Reiynfarin tried using time magic to prevent the Keeper's actions. He disappeared, along with all the Fae he created. Everyone assumes they're dead."

Erissa braced a hand on her thigh as the pain built. "What happened to the rest of the Fae the other gods created?"

"The Fae were split into two major courts, the Seelie and Unseelie. Each major court has a King, and there are two lesser courts with a Lord for each." Rhazien eased their pace as she started favoring her leg. "There's the Seelie of the Lawful gods with the Flowering Sun and Thundering Sun lesser courts, and then there's the Unseelie of the Chaotic gods with the Hunter's Moon and Frosted Moon lesser courts. The two major courts don't get along."

"I can imagine not after the Remaking and everything the Fae were forced to do." Erissa smiled up at him, grateful for the slower walk. "Thank you for slowing."

Rhazien gave a playful pinch to her arm. "You could have asked me to slow down if your leg was hurting. Do we need to stop?"

Erissa shook her head. "Holding onto you helps, and I'm anxious to find Crezzi and Rhyn."

"Here, let's try something else." Rhazien stopped, pushing Erissa behind him as he crouched on the ground. "Climb on my back?'

"What?" Erissa stepped back. "I can't do that. I'll be too heavy."

Rhazien patted himself on the back. "C'mon, little doe. The longer you fight me on this, the further the horses will get."

She moved forward, placing her hands on his shoulders. "Are you sure?"

"Yes." Rhazien fanned his arms behind him, gesturing for her to listen. "Now, stop worrying and climb on. I've been carrying my sisters like this for years."

Erissa leaned against him and yelped as he stood, forcing her legs to wrap around his waist to keep from falling. "Rhazien!"

"If I waited for you to settle yourself, we'd never start walking again." His light, teasing tone removed any rebuke in his words. "Your leg needs a break. I can feel how much it's hurting you through the bond."

Erissa hoped that was all he could feel as a blush spread across her body at their closeness. His sides rubbed against her thighs with every step he took, heating her core and provoking sensations she had only read about. If he knew what she felt right now, she would perish on the spot.

Rhazien carried her like that until the cold eventually faded against warmer weather the further north they traveled. The heat became too much, and she insisted on walking as it tested her endurance.

She had removed her fur cloak and rolled the bottom of her trousers up to her knees but refused to push up the sleeves of her borrowed shirt and expose what lay underneath. "How can it be so cold this morning yet so warm right now? It's only been two days since we moved on."

"We're nearing the Wilds." Rhazien arched an expectant brow.

When he did not continue, Erissa shrugged. "And that's supposed to tell me, what exactly?"

"The swamps of the Wilds give way to the desert lands."

Erissa's nose crinkled, her head tipping to the side. "What does that mean?"

Rhazien's eyes bored into her when she stared blankly at him. "I don't understand what you're asking."

"Those names." Erissa's forehead creased. "I don't understand what you mean. What's a swamp and a desert?"

"You're asking me what a swamp and a desert are?"

She laughed at his cautious question, not understanding his issue. "Yes, Rhazien."

"Have you never learned the terms before?"

Erissa's eyes narrowed. "No."

"You don't know what a swamp and desert are," Rhazien muttered the words to himself, giving her an unreadable once-over. "Have you ever heard of Kaidreth?"

She shrugged. "No."

"You've never seen a book or a map with the name?"

"No." Erissa stared straight ahead as she barely said the words loud enough for him to hear. "I wasn't allowed any maps or books about the lands."

Rhazien reached for Erissa's arm, stopping her. "Erissa..."

"Rhazien, please." She tried to shake off his hand and keep walking, but his next words halted her movements.

"You don't know the name of the continent." The words came slowly as he connected their past and present conversations. "I'm guessing you don't know what a continent even is. It's why you didn't leave Emberhold at the first opportunity."

"Stop, Rhazien." Erissa lifted a hand to her pinched brow, rubbing at the headache forming.

But Rhazien's words came faster. "There was *literally* nowhere to go because you knew nothing of what lay beyond the city's walls."

"I said stop!" She ground her teeth against a flash of anger, ripping her arm from his grasp. "I am *not* stupid."

"That's not what I mean, little d—"

"Don't you dare call me that right now." Erissa marched away from him. She would be damned if he took something precious to her and sullied it as he made too much of her ignorance. The building heat of the air was forgotten as a fire raged within her.

"Erissa!"

She ignored him. Picking up speed, she lengthened her stride, desperate to out-pace him, but her efforts were futile as his long legs quickly caught up with her.

"Erissa, please wait." His fingers brushed her arm. "Talk to me."

"I don't want to talk to you." She jerked away from his touch. Her footing slipped with the harsh movement, pitching her forward and making her drop her pack.

Rhazien caught her as she fell. In one swift movement, he pulled her up and twirled her around until her back lay against a nearby tree, her hands trapped between them.

"Let go of me." Erissa fought against his hold.

"I think we already know I don't intend to fight fair." He smirked, the words an arrogant boast.

"Must we keep doing this, Rhazien?"

"Must you keep making me, *Erissa*?" The corner of her mouth twitched, and his eyes locked on the movement. "You think this is funny, don't you, *Erissa*?"

The corner of his own mouth lifted when her lips curled into a pout. "I liked it better when you called me your little doe."

"*I'm* not the one who told me to stop."

"And *I'm* not the one who made me feel *stupid* for asking a simple question."

Rhazien tucked a strand of hair behind her ear. "No one can make you feel anything. That power is all yours."

"Says the one who's only known the joy of a loving family." The sneered words did not stop. "People can make you feel all sorts of things after they strip everything from you."

"I'm not one of the people who hurt you then, Erissa." Pressing his forehead against hers, he sighed. "But I did hurt you today, and for that, I am sorry."

"You didn't have to act like I'd grown two heads. I told you the tutors stopped coming a long time ago. Beyond the basics of reading and writing, I learned little else from them. Everything I know comes from reading the books my mother kept." Erissa shrugged as Rhazien straightened. "She read little beyond love stories."

"Being told is one thing. Seeing the results of it is another."

Erissa worried her lower lip between her teeth, her temper fading. "My ignorance is not from a lack of trying."

"You're not ignorant, little doe. Far from it. There are some gaps, but it doesn't mean I see you differently. I know you're not stupid." Rhazien taunted her with kisses to make up for his blunder. He placed one on the tip of her nose and more across the corners of her mouth. When he finally opened his lips across hers, he groaned.

Erissa melted against him. She purred low in the back of her throat when he raked his teeth against her bottom lip and sucked it into his mouth. A mewling protest left her when he finally pulled away. "You won't always have the chance to kiss my anger away."

"Maybe not. But I can do other things to distract you from it, especially if it means you keep making that sound." Rhazien slid a hand between her legs, cupping her mound. "Maybe I should move lower and kiss these lips instead. I bet you'll forget all about your anger then, won't you?"

Erissa blushed furiously as she grew slick where his hand pressed into her trousers, a sensation she had only ever read about in romance novels and had no experience with. She wiggled against it. "You have quite the wicked mouth."

"And you don't mind it." He traced lazy circles around the spot that throbbed against the taut fabric. The material grew wetter with each pass of his fingers until her desire soaked through. "Besides, you're not angry anymore, are you?"

"Have you always been this arrogant?" Erissa dropped her head against his chest, shivering in response to his touch.

Rhazien laughed, and Erissa smiled as it rumbled through his chest. She enjoyed making him laugh.

"You can blame my sisters for that. They filled my head with all sorts of nonsense about being the best brother they had."

"What utter rot. You're their only brother." She lifted her head, giving him a dirty stare. "Can we stop talking about your sisters with you touching me *there*?"

He laughed and kissed the top of Erissa's head before stepping back. "Come here, little doe. There's something I want to show you."

Holding her hand, Rhazien picked up her forgotten pack.

"I'd rather continue what you started." Erissa dragged her feet as he led her further into the trees.

"You might like this better." Rhazien kept going until he came across a wide enough space free from vegetation. He knelt against the damp earth, dropping their bags, and cleared the leaves, sticks, and other such matter from the ground.

Placing her hands on his shoulders, she leaned over him. Erissa's curiosity grew as he traced a pattern into the dirt. "What are you doing?"

"Trying my hand at map-making."

"You're making me a map?" she asked with reverence, the tone causing Rhazien to peer over his shoulder. She dropped to her knees beside him. A hand covered her mouth. No one had dared to give her such knowledge before. She doubted Rhazien fully understood what the gesture meant. He offered her what she had always been denied, giving her a different sort of freedom that rivaled her elation after finally passing through the gates of Emberhold.

"I thought you might like to know where we are and where we're heading."

The words barely registered. Everything around Erissa slowed and blurred as tears sprang to her eyes. In her wildest dream, she had never imagined having someone like Rhazien in her life. He brought joy to her days, even when he vexed her, and she wanted more than anything to repay his kindness.

Rhazien drew mountains and forests, adding rivers and streams as they outlined cities. Something loosened inside her. It silenced every doubt that had been shouting at her in the wake of something so pure and sweet.

The threatening tears overflowed as Erissa trailed her fingers over the indented markings, careful not to disturb their lines. "You drew me a map."

Rhazien stood, bringing Erissa with him with an arm around her hips. "You'll feel better knowing where we are."

Warmth bloomed in her chest, curling tendrils of heat spreading through her. It lit her from the inside, violet light suffusing her skin, making her luminescent.

"I'll have to start being mean to you, little doe." Rhazien ran his finger down the bridge of her nose. Where his finger traveled, the light darkened a shade. "Can't have you lighting up like a beacon."

Erissa stretched her arms out to the side and marveled at the change in her skin. She laughed as she ran her fingers down one arm, watching the color deepen to a shade beyond her eyes. She stood on her toes and reached for Rhazien, drawing his head down to give him a feather-light kiss. "Thank you."

Her lips had darkened when she pulled away, her light burning brighter. Rhazien cleared his throat, his amber skin becoming ruddy, and pointed out their route across his map.

She listened with rapt attention, asking questions about the different locations he had marked until the sun rose high overhead, and their stomachs rumbled with hunger. Only then did Rhazien interrupt her. "Let's eat while we keep moving. We'll lose the horses if we tarry much longer."

"I suppose we must move on eventually." Erissa agreed with reluctance, the corner of her mouth turning down. "I only wish it was on paper so I could take it with me."

Rhazien laughed, letting go of her to use the toe of his boot to wipe the map away. "Don't worry, little doe. I have plenty more I can tell you. I will be your very own walking map."

With the map no longer visible in the dampened earth, they moved onward, trudging across long-forgotten animal paths for the rest of the day, heading away from the river as Rhazien told her everything he knew of the world she had been denied.

Night had overtaken the sky by the time they found the horses tearing at the scattered patches of thigh-high grass where the forest floor transitioned into the wetland of the swamp.

Rhazien whistled sharply, a command both horses recognized as they turned and trotted back to them. Rhynstone butted his head against Rhazien's before nipping at his shirt pocket. "I should have known I'd find you filling your stomach."

Rhynstone fluttered his lips in response, nudging the pocket once more. "You'll have to wait for the next town, you greedy beast." Rhazien pushed his head away. "I'm all out of sugar cubes."

Carizzea approached them more slowly. Erissa held her palm out when the horse stopped a couple of feet from them. "Hello, Crezzi."

The horse let out a low whicker, nodding her head up and down as she walked closer until Erissa stroked her fingers down her forehead. At the gentle touch, the horse settled, coming closer to sniff Erissa's shirt. "Not you, too. Oh, you two are ridiculously spoiled."

"It's really my sister Esaleia's fault. She's always sneaking into the stable to give them sweets." Rhazien tried to keep a straight face but failed as Rhynstone shoved his nose into his trouser pocket. He jumped back, flailing his arms at the horse, only to have Carizzea nibble at him from the other side. "Leave me alone, you beasts."

Erissa laughed at their antics, watching as Rhazien fought off their attempts to root around in his trousers. He eventually threw his hands up, letting the horses pick around his clothing to see his lack of sugar cubes for themselves. Erissa swallowed her laughter and attempted a serious tone. "I'm sure it was all Esaleia's fault, and her brother had nothing to do with it."

The horses finally settled, and Rhazien led them to a copse of trees near the high grasses, where they found them grazing. He tied their leads to a low-lying branch, leaving enough room for them to continue feeding.

When he returned, Erissa had already laid out their furs into one large pallet for two. Rhazien cocked a brow at seeing her kneeling in its center, smoothing her hands down the wrinkles in her trousers. "I thought... after... there was no need... for two." Erissa wished for a hole to appear and bury her in its depths.

The voice inside her cackled. *"Presumptuous, are we?"*

It had a mind of its own, the voice, and delighted in coming out when Erissa least expected it. She preferred it had stayed quiet this time and not point out her error. Erissa wanted the ground to swallow her whole.

Rhazien said nothing. He lay beside her, pulling her into his arms. She stiffened momentarily, unsure of where things might lead, but he did nothing more than tip her face up and quickly kissed her lips.

"Let's grab what sleep we can. We've a two-day ride to the Wilds and four more after that before Cropari. We both need a hot bath and comfortable bed, and I'm impatient for both."

CHAPTER TWENTY-TWO

The gods would damn Barrett for his actions.

He sat next to the blacksmith's wife for the evening meal covered in the man's blood. Two days of lashings had done nothing to break him, and Faldeyr grew increasingly angered by the smith's stubborn refusal to speak. When the lashings had not worked, Barrett resorted to harsher means, the amount of blood crusting his clothing testifying to the violence he inflicted upon the man's back.

He did not want to be there, but a command was a command, so Barrett sat with the scent of copper lingering over the garlic and herbs.

The wife flinched away from him as he offered her the dish of buttered potatoes. He wanted to apologize—needed to apologize—but with his brother at the table, his tongue lay quiet.

Faldeyr frowned as the line of food stopped moving. He directed his ire toward the woman as her gaze stayed fixed on the blood-soaking Barrett's shirt. His fist banged on the table, startling them all. "Take the damned potatoes."

"That is no way to treat our guests, husband." Vilotta smiled as the woman grabbed the bowl, lifting her glass of wine in a mock salute. "Susreene and I have been catching up. It must have been centuries since we last met."

"Centuries?" The oldest of the red-headed children lifted her head, staring at her mother in confusion. "Did you misspeak?"

Susreene's hand shook as she clamped it over her daughter's. "Hush, Vylnoel. You misheard, and it's impolite to question one's elders."

Vilotta laughed, a tinkling sound that grated on Barrett's nerves. "Susreene, you are being quite naughty. Have you been lying to your husband and children all this time? Do they know nothing of your heritage?"

"Lying about what?" Vylnoel looked between Vilotta and her mother. "What is she talking about?"

"Let me tell you a story, child, about a war called the Remaking. After its events, the Creator remade the order of the world, separating the human and Fae and creating an afterlife for all in the Veil." Vilotta stood, moving to take the chair next to the wary girl. "When the Creator made the world, he also made eight gods to sustain his creation and separated them into three groups to maintain balance."

"The Lawful, Chaotic, and Neutral gods. Everyone knows this." Vylnoel rolled her eyes at her sisters, and they each fought to smother their giggles. "And then he made the humans to keep them from being lonely."

"What a clever girl you have, Susreene. But let us see what else she knows." Vilotta smirked, reaching for the child's hand with a gentle touch at odds with the calculating look in her eyes. "During the war of the Remaking, the Chaotic gods tried to overthrow the Lawful and Neutral gods. When they realized their powers were limited against each other, the god of Darkness, Malcufyre, created the Keeping Bond, a magical spell that enslaves those it is used on."

"Vilotta..." Barrett's shoulders tensed. Whatever Vilotta had planned would bring nothing but ruin for the rest of the evening. "Can we do this another day? I am tired."

Vilotta ignored him. "When Malcufyre used the Keeping on the humans, it bound them to him, turning them into something more than human."

"I know, I know." The youngest bounded in her chair.

"What is your name, sweetheart?" Vilotta smiled at her.

"I'm Iselica." The little girl had the same red hair as her sisters. She puffed out her chest as she introduced herself, drawing a slight smile to Barrett's face despite his misgivings. She reminded him of Erissa at that age.

"What a pretty name." Vilotta ruffled her curly hair. "What do you know about the Malcufyre and the Keeping?"

"The Keeping turns humans into Fae." Pride filled Isleica's face, and she grinned.

"That's right, little love. The Fae of the Lawful are called the Seelie, and the Fae of the Chaotic are the Unseelie." Susreene motioned her over, her voice tight with worry. Some of it faded as the young girl climbed into her mother's lap, but much of it remained as she eyed Vilotta with suspicion.

Vilotta's eyes flashed with jealousy quickly enough that Susreene and Faldeyr missed it, but Barrett did not. He struggled not to roll his eyes at her self-inflicted jealousy. She had the blame for the distance between herself and her own daughter. Did she expect anything else after all that happened?

When she masked the reaction with another fake smile, Vilotta continued her story. "You're right, Iselica. The Keeping is how the gods created the Fae. The gods used the Fae to wage war against each other, with one of the Neutral joining the Lawful and two of the Neutral joining with the Chaotic. Morthyra, the god of the Void, fought alongside the Lawful gods."

At the mention of Morthyra, Susreene blanched. Barrett stared between the women, his unease growing.

Vilotta noticed, her eyes narrowing as she stared at Susreene's stricken expression. "Poor Morthyra was no match for the God of Darkness. Malcufyre ran through her court, wreaking havoc as he tore his way through the void-bound Fae she created to get to her. He made Morthyra suffer as he killed all but one of her people, a newly created Fae he planned to use for himself. Then, Malcufyre skinned the Goddess of the Void alive. He fed her flesh to one of his Fae to create the first Zorathi—an abomination of lightning and darkness bound to serve the Unseelie. The rest of the Zorathi warriors were created from having the Fae drink her blood."

The room had fallen silent. Even the servants did not dare to move as their mistress told the gruesome end of the Goddess of the Void. The children looked ready to bolt from the table.

"The female Void Fae that Malcufyre saved escaped as he created the Zorathi. Rumors followed her disappearance, especially when a Fefnirion disappeared on the same day. Some wonder—"

"Enough." Susreene stood, her arms wrapped around her youngest child, fury outlining her features. She came to her senses as Vilotta and Faldeyr both stood, backing down, her eyes darting to her girls. "You're scaring the children, Vilotta, and it is nearly their bedtime. Perhaps you can finish your story another time?"

Barrett stood as well. "Yes, the girls are clearly tired. We can't have them up all night with bad dreams. How will anyone else be able to sleep?"

Vilotta pouted. "How will they ever learn their mother's history without knowing its beginning?"

"Leave it, dearest." Faldeyr lowered himself to sit and began eating. "All this talk of death will sour my meal. Let the brats go to bed. I've grown tired of their company."

Susreene dipped her head in his direction. "I'll tend to them now. Thank you for your understanding. This has been a lovely meal." She nodded again, this time to Barrett, flinching at the blood staining his clothes, and ushered the children from the room.

"Must you always spoil my fun, Barrett?" Vilotta took her seat, picking at her plate.

"Must you needle the woman?" Barrett sat as well, loathing his role in her distress. "There was no need to tell the young ones about the war."

Faldeyr grunted and changed the subject. "How goes breaking the blacksmith?"

Barrett hesitated. "He is... stronger than we gave him credit for."

Anger filled Faldeyr's voice. He threw his napkin down on the table, standing again. "If he doesn't break within the week, I'll take matters into my own hands. I can promise you will not like my methods, brother."

Barrett watched as he stormed off. Vilotta chased after him, begging him to slow down. For the first time in two days, Barrett's shoulders dropped with despair. Whatever his brother had planned would not be good for any of them.

Something had to be done. Barrett's oath lay tied to Erissa's life, but there had to be a way around his brother's orders. He would not let another child fall victim to a madman's plans. Barrett had a week to break the man out of the cell and get him and his family out of Emberhold for good, and he held very little hope of its possibility.

CHAPTER TWENTY-THREE

The stories about the Violent Wilds told of gnarled, withered trees in a dark forest boasting brambles and thorns along its impassable grounds. It held the stuff of nightmares and legends with beasts that stalked the paths by day, and worse, hunted your soul by night. The reality ended up being quite different.

The Wilds were nothing like Erissa expected.

With the noon sun filtered through the trees, there were no signs of anything ominous that justified the feared name. The Wilds had a simple beauty, with thick willows weaving through the dense swamp trees.

Erissa's shoulders slumped. While grateful the stories were exaggerated, all the same, it did not stop a heaviness from settling within her.

Her mother told her stories of the Wilds at a young age. They were mainly to keep her behavior in line for fear of being sent to their depths, as all children were raised on the tales of the land that bordered the Veil, but she treasured the memories. She held onto them through her captivity, repeating them to herself, willing the lonely hours to pass more quickly. To have them be anything other than what she imagined let her down in ways she had not been prepared for.

As they traversed the difficult paths, Erissa considered how Rhazien hunted through the growth. The spongy ground had places barely wide enough for the horses to walk as it dipped in and out of the dark, muddied water that spread across the low-lying land. Droves of insects hovered around the wettest areas, making Erissa's skin itch in anticipation of their irritating bites. Hunting would be a messy pastime in the mucky atmosphere.

A persistent moisture blanketed everything it touched. The cloying feel stuck to Erissa's body, molding her shirt to her back and breasts and creating a second skin out of her trousers. Rhazien had made her unroll the legs of her trousers before they had even reached the boundary, marking the entrance to protect her from the many pests that favored the boggy water. His ears had to be melting underneath the dragon cuffs.

The little bugs never ended once they found their presence. One came right after another until Erissa stopped trying to swat them all. The sound had gotten to her, reminding her of days she would rather forget with beating wings of the swarming nuisances traveling like soul whispers down an imaginary wind.

She wished more than anything to talk with Rhazien, but he rode ahead, letting Rhynstone have free rein to find his footing along the uneven path as it narrowed the further they went. She mimicked his actions with Carizzea, knowing her horsemanship risked much on the unstable terrain.

They traveled while the sun was high, only stopping when Rhazien found a wide, raised area where the ground was dry enough to make camp for the night. Erissa helped Rhazien care for the horses. Her movements spoke of newfound confidence. She followed his instructions and removed the burdens from Carizzea's back, being sure to brush the horse down afterward.

Erissa found the rhythmic brushing motion soothing to her wandering mind as the whispers of little wings grew louder. She hummed to tune them out. Surprise left her stumbling over the tune once Rhazien quickly joined in on her song. His tone added a rich harmony that complimented the old song her mother used to sing to her before she locked her in that room.

Their combined notes left her curious. "How do you know the melody?"

Rhazien's hand stilled against Rhynstone's coat. He gave a slight cough. "My mother. She sang it when she tucked us in for bed."

"Is it a popular song in Kaidreth?"

There was hesitancy in how he answered her. "It's a Fae song, one they sing to their children."

Rhazien finished with his horse before her and set up the rest of the camp. He rolled the oiled cloth across the sodden ground but did not bother with the furs. Erissa thanked the Creator they did not need them as another bead of sweat rolled between her breasts.

She joined him on the cloth after she finished Carizzea's brushing, resting her head against his shoulder. Things had changed between them. The sweet emotion she had when he drew the map continued to flourish inside her long after the light faded from her skin.

She tipped her head, catching his gaze, and smiled. "Can I hear more about Kaidreth?"

"What do you want to know?" Rhazien asked, answering her smile with a sweet one of his own.

Erissa lowered her gaze, her eyes sweeping over the swamp as she thought about what she knew of the world and what she did not. "Well, you already told me of the Fae today. Can you tell me about the Fefnirion?"

Rhazien tensed and then relaxed so quickly Erissa would have thought she imagined it if not for the flash of anxiety that barreled from him.

She looked at him again. "Rhazien?"

"Sure, little doe." He smiled, but there was something brittle about it this time. "When the Creator intervened in the Remaking, he created the

Fefnirion from the eternal fire of Creation, breathing a spark of life into the flame and hatching the dragons from its embers. They are meant to be Wardens, shielding the world against retaliation from the gods. Their flames can burn through the gods' magic and kill them should they try to return to this world."

Rhazien settled the more he talked, and the anxiety between them eased. "But being a Warden is a lonely life. All Fefnirion are males. They lived in seclusion for centuries before it proved too much to handle."

Erissa loved the sound of his voice. It soothed her. She stayed quiet, letting him speak at his leisure as she basked in its comfort.

"The Fefnirion left their mountain caves in the Mists and ventured into the world, settling in the desert lands. They found their mates in the humans. The dragons slowly gave up their calling to live mortal lives with their mortal mates and the human children those pairings produced."

That piqued Erissa's interest. The dragons must have felt great heartache when they did not age. "It would be hellish to find your mate as an immortal creature only to lose them to a natural life span."

Rhazien nodded. "Fefnirion mates will live longer than a normal human lifespan after they're fully bonded, but they're still mortal. It was hard on the dragons. They abandoned their calling one by one and settled into human towns to live out their days with their mates. Those in the desert lands revere them, especially in Cropari. They're considered masters of the lands, and everyone defers to them."

Erissa pulled away from him as the air thickened. "Those in the South never speak of them."

"The South fears anything magical." Rhazien passed her a length of hardened jerky and a stale piece of bread with an apologetic grimace. "I'm afraid it's all we have, but it should last us to Cropari. I'd try sucking on it before you bite into the meat."

They ate in silence for a time, the whispering of the flitting bugs growing louder. It bothered Erissa, but Rhazien sat contentedly beside her, oblivious to the noise while finishing his meal.

Erissa tried to focus on eating, but the sound continued, so she tried to make a game of it as she quietly counted out the cadence. "Whisper, whisper, whisper, one. Whisper, whisper, whisper, two. Whisper, whisper, whisper three. Whisper, whisper, whisper—"

"What are you mumbling, little doe?"

Erissa tucked a strand of hair behind her ear as she turned to Rhazien. "I'm counting."

"All the ways you find me handsome?" Rhazien lifted a hand to his chest as if touched by the notion.

"Oh, yes." Erissa admired him with an exaggerated stare. "I had almost counted to two but ran out of handsome things." She laughed at his wounded pout. "No, I'm counting the sounds from the bugs. They're driving me mad. I don't know how you deal with it, but I guess you got used to it after all your time here."

Rhazien tilted his head. "The sound from the bugs?"

"Yes, it's been nonstop." Erissa pinched her nose as the noise grew. "I hope it fades as the night goes on."

"I don't hear anything." He leaned into her, pressing a hand to her forehead. "Are you feeling alright?"

"What?" Erissa pushed his hand away, her mouth twisting to the side. "How can you not hear them?"

"Erissa, there's no sound. If it were that loud, it would bother the horses." Rhazien gestured to where Rhynstone and Carizzea were tied. "They're content."

"You really don't hear it?" Erissa's eyes were wide, crinkling her brow.

"No." Rhazien shook his head. "I don't hear anything."

"Maybe I need to sleep." Erissa rubbed a hand down her face as she yawned. "We barely got any sleep after finding the horses."

"Maybe." Rhazien covered her as she lay down beside him.

"Daughter of the Veil. Daughter of the Veil. Daughter of the Veil."

The words rustled through the air, waking Erissa during the twilight hours. She sat up slowly, the whispered words calling her again.

"We need you. We need you. We need you."

Erissa swayed as if still sleeping, the whispers growing louder, like the soft, continuous fluttering of insect wings.

"You must come. You must come. You must come."

The words seduced her in the moment between slumber and wakefulness, reaching to the depths of her soul, a temptation that compelled an answer as she stood and walked away from the camp.

"Be with us. Be with us. Be with us."

She wove in and out of the trees, reckless in her footing. She walked directly through the swamp, straying from the old trail someone had long carved through the damp ground.

"Quickly. Quickly. Quickly."

"Erissa!" Reeva suddenly appeared at her side, her face frantic. She waved her arms to distract Erissa. "You cannot fall prey to the call of the Veil. You must stop. Do not listen to such madness."

Erissa walked on, following the ethereal murmurs.

"He stirs. He stirs. He stirs."

Reeva grew desperate as Erissa continued to ignore her. She contemplated the distance between Erissa and the camp, her face hardening before disappearing into nothing.

Erissa's stride did not break. Her steps grew faster, feeling the connection to the Veil growing stronger with everyone.

"Find us. Find us. Find us."

She nodded. "I'm coming."

CHAPTER TWENTY-FOUR

"I won't ask you again." Tiovriss crouched in front of the innkeeper, careful not to slip on the blood pooling atop the wood floor in front of the inn's hearth. He ran a thumb through the blood dripping down the man's chin. The way humans bled so easily fascinated him. "Where is the girl?"

The innkeeper flicked his tongue out, wincing as he used it to feel along his cut lip. "Please, believe me. The girl you're looking for hasn't stepped foot in Gailme."

Tiovriss licked his thumb, savoring the metallic taste. Very few things tasted as blood did.

"He knows nothing." Alrithia pursed her lips, an edge to her voice. "If you had but listened to me for a moment in the clearing..."

"Stop nagging if you want to keep your tongue, woman, and hand me the damned blade." Tiovriss held out a hand, never taking his eyes from the bound and bleeding man.

Alrithia slapped the curved knife in his blood-stained palm with more force than necessary.

"Now, we're going to play a little game." Tiovriss trailed the knife down the innkeeper's bruised cheek.

"Leave him alone!" A little girl's voice rang from the other side of the room where she sat bound by rope.

"Tell me the truth, girl, or you can watch as I slit your father from ear to ear. Where is the woman?" Tiovriss jerked the innkeeper up by his hair. He held the blade to the man's throat. A twisted leer overtook his face. Either way, the man would die.

"Don't hurt him." Tears streamed down the girl's face. "There's no lady with purple eyes. I swear it. I swear..."

Alrithia stepped between Tiovriss and the young girl. "We're wasting time here. If we leave now, we can be halfway to the Wilds by this time tomorrow."

The sick smile Tiovriss wore fell. He wanted to rid himself of Alrithia as eagerly as he did the innkeeper and his daughter. Her death would come in time. Right now, they had work to do.

He slammed the innkeeper's head down against the floor until the man's nose broke with a sickening crack. The daughter screamed, and Tiovriss ground his teeth. "Shut the brat's mouth."

Alrithia stood her ground, her fists clenched at her sides. "Enough with this. You've had your fun here. It's time to leave. Virion is losing patience with us, and I will not continue being taken to task because you're inept. I told you the girl wouldn't come this way."

"I don't answer to Virion, and the Unseelie shite knows it. Thonalan will not bow to him. Neither shall I." Tiovriss spun the blade with a twist of his wrist, and Alrithia eyed it warily, taking a step back.

Tiovriss roared and dove for her.

She fought him as they fell, the resounding crash shaking the floorboards. Tiovriss overpowered her with ease.

He pinned her beneath him, straddling her hips. Lifting the blade, he ran it across her trembling mouth, increasing the pressure of the sharp edge until it sliced through her bottom lip. She let out a garbled scream, and he savored the sweet sound of her pain, a smile twisting the lower half of his face.

Tiovriss pinched her mouth, pressing the knife against her throat. "Be a good girl, Alrithia, and keep your mouth shut. You've exhausted my patience."

Alrithia bucked her hips, trying to free herself. The knife slipped against her skin, drawing blood again, and Tiovriss laughed mercilessly.

His grip tightened, the brutal hold bruising her jaw and forcing her mouth wide. Tiovriss leaned over her.

She locked wide eyes on his, fear finally showing as she shivered against his hold. Good. She should be afraid. There were plenty of things to do to her in this position, and if she did not behave, she would find herself further at his mercy. The length in his pants hardened against her as his thoughts wandered. Alrithia twisted against his hold with a terrified squeal.

His pinch intensified, his hand like a vise as it forced her mouth open wider. He held her gaze, bending over her face.

Tiovriss licked along her bottom lip and groaned when her blood coated his tongue. He gathered it in the back of his mouth, mixing it with his saliva, and spit into her open mouth.

Alrithia fought harder, choking on the disgusting mess.

Her efforts did nothing but make Tiovriss laugh. "You should be used to such treatment. Are you not Virion's whore?"

The child sobbed hysterically behind them, twisting against her bindings as she fought to break free. Her crying increased as they held firm.

Tiovriss ignored her, focusing all his attention on Alrithia. She stared at him, her expression murderous, but she stopped fighting.

The lack of resistance bored him. Tiovriss shoved her head into the floor with a violent shake of his hand and stood.

He stalked over to the innkeeper, dragged his head up with a fist in his long hair, and slit the man's throat.

The daughter screamed until her voice broke from the effort. She slumped against the chair, all resistance leaving her.

Alrithia moved beside Tiovriss with obvious reluctance. She mimicked his actions as he dipped his hand into the pool of blood spreading around the dead man. Using their bloody hands, they traced runes onto the wall and stepped back as the blood dried into a sticky mess on their fingers, waiting.

Minutes passed before the wall disappeared behind a green haze. A man appeared. His lean features were accentuated by black hair tied back high on his head, revealing his pointed ears.

"Virion." Alrithia smiled, running a hand through her red hair, straightening the tangled locks. "I've missed you."

Virion ignored her, turning his head to address Tiovriss. "Have you found the girl?"

Tiovriss bent forward and used the dead innkeeper's apron to wipe the blood from his knife. "She isn't in Gailme."

"You have failed me. Again." Anger sharpened the angles on Virion's face. "What am I to do with you now?"

Alrithia moved in front of Tiovriss. "We won't do so again. I believe the girl is traveling through the Violent Wilds."

Tiovriss shoved the woman away with a snarl, making the girl behind them whimper. Virion eyed the young girl, a calculating gleam in his eyes. "I'm sending Castian and Kaellam."

"That won't be necessary." Tiovriss crossed his arms.

The look Virion gave him was thunderous. "I'm not asking. They will find you in the Wilds."

The girl whimpered again, drawing Virion's attention. "Take the child with you. She will make a fine gift for Castian."

"But we can't hand her over to such a monster. What he'll do to her is vile. See reason, Vir—" Alrithia stopped her protest as a hand collided with the back of her neck, squeezing against her fluttering pulse.

Tiovriss tightened his grip, forcing her to her knees, his tone mocking as he addressed Virion. He pressed a blade into her neck until blood welled against the sharp metal, and a malevolent smile spread across his face. He wished to do nothing more than slit the whore's throat, the thought growing more appealing with every moment. "We'll take the girl. Anything to keep Castian happy."

Virion's gaze lingered on him, but Tiovriss refused to bend, meeting his gaze unflinchingly. "See that you do."

Tiovriss released Alrithia as the green haze faded into nothing. "You heard him. Gather the girl. She'll ride with you."

He thanked the Keeper when Alrithia obeyed his order. If they hurried, they might catch the girl as she traveled through the Wilds. He told Virion what he needed to hear, but he would be damned before he let Castian find the girl first and collect his reward. Let the little girl distract him for a night or two. Tiovriss would continue the hunt on his own while Castian played.

And Alrithia? She would be the Keeper's whore once they reached the Wilds.

CHAPTER TWENTY-FIVE

"Wake up! We are running out of time!"

Rhazien shot up, wrenched from the depths of slumber by a shouting voice.

"Finally! You sleep like the dead, boy."

He stared at the translucent woman standing next to him, blinking hard. Rhazien swiped a hand across his face as if she would disappear if he removed the sleep from his eyes.

"Boy! I am not some apparition come to haunt your dreams." Reeva lost all patience with him. "You must come with me without delay. We have to stop her."

Rhazien scrambled to his feet, peering around the camp. "Erissa?"

"She is gone. Are you not listening to me?" Reeva stomped her foot. "You have strayed far too close to the Veil, and it has called her. If we do not hurry, it will claim her for—"

"For what?" Rhazien grabbed the axe from where it sat next to his bag and placed it on his belt. "You're the soul—Reeva—the one she's been talking to?"

Reeva focused on the blade, her features stark white. "Wherever did you find such a weapon?"

"I made it."

"Impossible." Reeva shook her head, her voice trembling. "Such weapons cannot be forged unless one is—"

"It's an axe, nothing more." Rhazien cut Reeva off, crossing his arms as she stared at him. "Where's Erissa gone?"

"She is walking to the Veil. I was powerless to sway her from its influence." Reeva let go of her worry for the axe with obvious reluctance. "We must get to her in time. All that is foretold will be lost if we cannot stop its call, and your weapon will have to be turned against her."

Rhazien stiffened. "What are you talking about?"

"You will have no choice but to kill her should the Veil claim her soul. If you do not, the world will perish."

"Never." Reeva stepped back at Rhazien's vehemence, his hand slicing through the air. "Make no mistake, if it comes to the rest of the world or Erissa, I will damn the world without hesitation."

"You are a complication I had not expected." Reeva's arm lifted to point out the direction. "We must hurry before you doom us all."

Rhazien set off, easily following Erissa's path through the disturbed ground in the early morning light. It led away from the safety of the marked trail. His long legs made quick work of the distance, jumping over vines, roots, and other vegetation as each footfall fought against the porous terrain. He did not care if Reeva followed. He only wanted to reach Erissa in time.

As he crossed the swamp floor, the trees converged. An unearthly green fog spread itself through their numbers, its cloudiness shifting between the muted appearance of the swamp and the rich vibrancy of fresh growth, the colors fighting against each other as they refused to blend.

The heavier the fog became, the more the trees curled away from it and into one another, finally caving to the pressure of the magic. The trees rose higher than those found in the rest of the Wilds to escape its glowing reach.

All sounds faded with the presence of the fog.

The quiet unnerved Rhazien. Even the waters lay still as if cowed into submission by whatever force pressed its silence. In its wake, Rhazien pushed himself to run faster. The fog parted where he passed, shrinking away from his interfering steps.

His pace quickly led him past the trees into a clearing. The fog had grown, its swirling mass rising into an otherworldly wall overtaking the sky as Rhazien stood before the Veil. But the woman standing between him and the afterlife concerned him more than the intimidating presence.

"Erissa?" Rhazien tried again when she did not respond. "Little doe?"

Erissa's arms stretched to either side of her body. Tendrils of the Veil trailed from its depths to wrap around the offered limbs. They undulated across her skin like a lover's caress. Erissa smiled, staring at the snake-like strands with a fondness that frightened him.

"You cannot let the Veil seduce her further." Reeva's voice carried to him from behind. "But do not touch her. Her magic protects her as its equal. The Veil cannot take what is not freely given from her, but you are not bound by the same laws of magic. There is no one left who can speak to what would happen should the tendrils draw against *your* soul."

"How do I get it to release her?" Rhazien removed the ax from his belt, his racing heart calming slightly with the familiar weight.

"My tongue is bound." Regret rang heavily on Reeva's words. "There is no more I can do to help her. The rest is for you to figure out. Only you may void its magic. You must hurry before her soul is called too far."

"Well, that was perfectly clear. I now know exactly what to do." Rhazien's shoulders tensed, his words snarling out in his feeling of helplessness. "I can well understand Erissa's frustration in speaking with you if you're always this helpful."

"Neither of you know what frustration truly is," Reeva muttered.

Rhazien ignored her sullen words, all his attention remaining on Erissa. She murmured soft words to the Veil as it slowly enveloped her.

Cautiously, Rhazien moved toward her, speaking with each deliberate step. "Little doe, can you hear me?"

Erissa turned her head to the side at his approach, but she remained silent, her eyes fixed on the Veil where it touched her skin. She acted as if the tendrils circling her arms were the smoothest of silks, but as Rhazien walked closer, his stomach dropped. The Veil left lesions that grew worse with each stroke against her skin.

"Little doe, I need you to listen to me." Rhazien tried again, coming to her side. He tried to keep from gagging on the acrid stench of decay coming from the Veil. "You're not safe here. Come with me."

He raised his hands, still holding the axe.

The Veil hissed when the axe came closer, and Erissa's eyes snapped to the weapon. "You're upsetting it. It doesn't like that you're here."

A shiver worked down his spine at her detached words. "Who doesn't like me?"

"You need to leave." She tipped her head but kept her eyes on his axe as she nodded like someone whispered in her ear. The eerie green light of the Veil reflected against her eyes, turning the deep lavender shade into something more sinister.

When she spoke again, the words were hollow, all sense of her identity erased by a cacophony of voices mimicking her own. "We will not tolerate your being here for much longer, blacksmith, and neither will he. When he comes for the Veiled One, he also comes for you."

The haunting words reached deep and ripped something free inside of him. Rhazien's fright became a breathless terror that stole the air from his lungs. The taste of that fear burned the back of his throat. There was no longer a connection to Erissa. With every false word that came from her voice, her presence faded as someone clawed it from his very soul until it left him with nothing but a hollow ache where her light should be.

Rhazien broke under the weight of the loss. The unbearable sensation drove him to madness. If he had awoken sooner or moved faster, or if he hadn't spent such precious time talking to Reeva instead of immediately heeding her warning... Nothing of Erissa remained, and he held the blame for not being there as he promised. "The gods have failed her. *I* have failed her. But I won't do so again".

With an enraged cry fueled by his desperate grief, he swung his axe in a wild arc.

"No, you stupid boy," Reeva shrieked.

Rhazien staggered as the blade met the strands of magic, the force of the blow nearly knocking him from his feet. The axe cut through the poisonous coils of the Veil. They shattered against the blade, the blow scattering the minuscule shards around the clearing and across his skin. They tore through his flesh, the magic grinding into the wounds as if made of sand. Rhazien grit his teeth against the searing pain.

The undulating strands that remained against Erissa's limbs melted into her skin. Without the Veil holding her upright, her body collapsed. He lunged for her, catching her with his free arm, and carefully lowered her to the sodden ground. It cushioned her with a soft, sucking sound that echoed in the quiet aftermath.

"Little doe..." Rhazien's voice caught against the quaking of his shoulders. Hot tears poured down his face, catching on his jaw before splashing onto Erissa's pale skin. He dropped the axe, and with his hand, he wiped the tears from her face with great tenderness, his thumb remaining to trace the angles of her cheekbones, watching as her chest rose and fell with shallow breaths. "I'm sorry. I'm here now. You're not alone. I'm here."

Rhazien drew her body against him, uncaring of the blood trickling from his cuts and hers. His heart broke all over again as she remained still and frozen in the Veil's magic with her soul trapped.

Reeva walked into the clearing, her jaw clenched. "No one has wielded a void blade in that manner."

"You have to help her." Rhazien would beg if he had to. "Please, we have to do something."

"I am sorry, Rhazien." Reeva shook her head. "She breathes, but her soul cannot remain interwoven with the tainted magic."

He swallowed his tears, refusing to accept Reeva's words. "There must be a way to save her."

"The Veil is not what it once was. The evil inside has changed its nature, and if Erissa cannot withstand it—as the Veiled One and its magical equal—there is no hope. For her or anyone else." Reeva shuddered. "We will all fall at the hands of the Keeper. He will find her soul soon and be freed upon this world."

Reeva's words reached into his grief, lighting it and stoking its flames until it burned into something more volatile. "Your concern is rooted in how to use her for your gain when she deserved so much more than this from the gods."

"I have spent a thousand years with something undeserved but born out of love." Reeva knelt beside them. "She is not the first to deserve more from life, and she will not be the last with what shall come now that we have lost her. The gods use whom they please, and there is naught we can do to change that."

"You speak in riddles once more." His teeth ground together, his tone growing louder with every word. "You assign her a role that makes no sense except to serve your twisted games while you stand over her body. Have you no shame?"

Reeva leaned into Rhazien's face, anger coating her words. "There is no shame in speaking the truth. She is more than you can see in your grief, more than either of you can imagine. The men who hunt her do not do so without purpose. If they find her, they will bleed the magic from her to unleash the evil locked within the Veil. She is the one—the only one—with the power to change what happens next. Without her to stand between them and the world, they will shape a future that seeks to destroy all that we know of life."

"I see her. More than you know. You want her only for your purpose." Rhazien stroked Erissa's face. "But I see her as she is and want nothing more than to give her all she never had, not use her for the benefit of everyone while at the price of herself."

"Think, boy! This goes beyond such frivolity." Reeva's sharp tone darkened Rhazien's eyes, but he did nothing to interrupt her as she continued. "You are more than what you are pretending, with a blade you should not have been able to make nor wield. I have not missed its significance nor misunderstood what drives your affection."

Rhazien shook his head in denial. For Reeva to know the truth changed everything, and he did not care, not when all he held dear lay unmoving in his arms. "Erissa is what matters, and all you have done since waking me is focus on that damned blade. You're more concerned about its existence than her life." Rhazien's mouth went dry, the rough feel of it only increasing his temper as he denied Reeva's accusation. "I'm a blacksmith. Making blades is my livelihood. There's nothing more to it."

"Do not think to dance around all I have said with such blatant lies. I know what you are, as surely as you must if what you say is true, and you made such a weapon. That blade should not exist. *You* should not exist. The child is not worldly enough to understand what you hide, but I have lived through more than a millennium. I have seen what such blades and their masters can do."

Doubt spread across Rhazien's face. "There's no way for you to have seen such a thing. Not unless you were at the—"

"The Remaking," Reeva interrupted. "I would not know unless I was there. I stood before the Creator himself on that day. Do not think your claim of being a simple blacksmith will fool me."

Rhazien snapped his jaw shut from where it had fallen open. "This isn't helpful. I don't care if you reveal what I am. Tell whomever you wish. I care naught for the consequences without her. If you were truly there, you surely know something to help Erissa."

"What do you think I am trying to do? I have told you both my tongue is bound in its answers, and if I wished to reveal your existence, I would do so without hesitation. If Erissa is what matters most, then think, boy! Even the mists of the Veil fled from your path. Use that knowledge of yourself to your advantage." Reeva's words remained unforgiving as she reprimanded him. "You should not be so willfully ignorant of who you are and what you are capable of."

"Use that knowledge..." Rhazien's brow furrowed as he regarded the axe and then Erissa. He raised his gaze to meet Reeva's calculated stare. "The blade...?"

Reeva said nothing, but there was no need; Rhazien made the connection. No one had ever made such an attempt before. The idea bordered on blasphemy and would reveal all to the gods. But his eyes widened, a wild hope overtaking him as his body shook. He would damn the consequences. "I made the blade. If I can imbue the metal, then surely there must be a way I can push the same into Erissa and force the Veil out..."

Reeva's eyes screamed their answer, the swirling slate-colored depths changing from anger to satisfaction.

Rhazien lay Erissa across the ground as far away from the Veil as he dared to take her. Smoothing the hair from her face, he breathed deeply, slowly exhaling as he placed both hands on her chest. "By the gods, this better work."

He tipped his head back, staring up at the dark sky. The expanse of darkness was small next to the irradiated wall of the Veil. Rhazien tried to imagine how the gods would measure up standing next to it. Would they tower over its endless height, or would the sheer force of its power and breadth dwarf them until they appeared as insignificant as Rhazien? Did it even matter? "Hear me now, for I know you're watching, listening. I will do anything to save her, even if it means binding her to me."

"You will do no such thing!" Reeva rose to her feet, all sense of refinement gone as her fists balled and she snarled. "Down that road lies only madness. 'Tis no living when bound to the Keeping. I would know."

Rhazien's eyes smoldered into a burning amber when he met Reeva's gaze. "Then you had best pray the gods heed my threat. For I will do anything to bring her back, even if it means binding her to such a fate and spending eternity in service to learning its undoing."

He offered her no chance to say more. He focused all his attention on Erissa and what he needed to do. With both hands still pressed to her chest, Rhazien let down the barrier he kept erected around himself.

A golden light built along his skin, growing until it burned like fire across the entirety of his being. It continued to build, shaping itself into wings of fire that stretched behind him. The golden flames fused with licks of ruby, the hue darkening until it left each tip blackened. He rolled his shoulders. The muscles relaxed as he broke down the carefully constructed control he always maintained.

Reeva stood gaping.

Rhazien gave her a wolfish smile, smoke curling from around his mouth. He willed the black tips of his fire to grow, feeling them burn darker as the stones across his earcuffs glowed, each adding to the cascade of power rolling off him.

The warmth of it against his skin reminded him of the hottest days in the desert lands of his home, where the sand would burn your feet for merely catching sight of it. He took that heat and fire, pouring the raging warmth through his hands and into Erissa.

She bucked as the power hit her, melting beneath her skin. The voices of the Veil screamed from a mouth-stained deep crimson as his fire bled through her parted lip. It choked the screams, strangling them until not even a whimper remained.

Rhazien's eyes moved across her body, tracing the invisible lines of the Veil where they lay beneath the surface. For each one of the sickly tendrils he found, a new lick of fire emerged. His flames wound around them, pulling them from the roots and through her skin, overtaking the wriggling rot. His fire ran along their lengths, devouring the Veil's putrid magic with greedy flickers of light.

Over and over again, Rhazien pulled the strands of the Veil from Erissa. With each one he removed, her breathing evened out, color returning to the rest of her face until only one remained, wrapped through her heart.

He slowed his movements as the thick rope tightened around her heart like the most sinister of snakes seeking to crush it.

The haunting mass of green spread, encasing the pulsing organ with a web made from the icy touch of the Veil's depths. Her breathing faltered as the power pulsated and spread through her veins, changing her lifeblood into something thick and murky as it started sucking her soul into the powerful magic.

Rhazien laughed, understanding what must be done. If the Veil wanted a soul, then a soul he would give.

His rich laughter rippled triumphantly against the boundary of the Veil. He nurtured the flames, giving it pieces of his own soul to feed on until they burned with an intensity that rivaled the sun. Rhazien held no care for the attention he attracted from the heavens, no care for what it cost himself. He knew nothing but Erissa as he taunted the magic of the Veil with his soul and its void-bound flames.

Rhazien reached around Erissa's heart and used the flames to burn away the cowering snake. When the last of the Veil disappeared against the obliterating light of his fire, Rhazien coaxed Erissa's frantically beating heart with it, soothing its pain until the pace slowed and her body relaxed. He stroked the flames across every part of her, bringing her magic forward as he cajoled it with the heat of his own, using it to warm the chill left behind by the Veil.

Her powers swelled as life returned to them. Rhazien found Erissa beneath the flowing magnitude. The hollow ache in his chest faded with her presence, the connection between them flaring to life and filling the dark crevice its absence had created.

She pushed further into him, adding her breath of life to his magical flames until the interlaced entities grew into an uncontrolled blaze that consumed them, engulfing their bodies with its healing spark, leaving no hint of who they were under the roaring flames.

They spread, rising to meet the wall as the flames raced after the tainted magic. It burned through it with such ferocity that the wall recoiled until all that illuminated the area was the righteous fervor of Rhazien's blazing fire as it scorched the outer reaches of the Veil.

CHAPTER TWENTY-SIX

The grim twist of Reeva's mouth only added to the heaviness plaguing her spirit, a heaviness at odds with a strange desire to laugh at all she'd witnessed. She pressed her fingers to her throat, massaging the length of it, swallowing the misplaced response. To say the boy had surprised her was the understatement of her existence.

She did not know who held more power: the girl foretold to be their savior or the boy who combined their powers to burn the Veil without so much as touching its wall? The implications of the answers changed everything.

Even for one of his kind, Rhazien's power rivaled anything Reeva had seen in thousands of years, giving her pause. If the night air held the ability to touch her skin, the warmth would have done little to chase the chill from her bones at watching him bend such power to his will.

The boy had done what no other of his kind had ever, which must have attracted the gods' attention with his exceedingly rare magic. Only one other outside of the Veil stood as Rhazien and Erissa's equal, and it would not be long before he crossed the Mists that separated the lands and found them. What would he make of this complication?

"*Her violet eyes are in their thrall, even she cannot escape...*" Reeva sang to herself, considering Rhazien as he waited for Erissa to wake.

She gazed upon the heavens and its multitude of stars. Reeva understood one thing above all others: the corruption of the Veil had thinned its safeguards, and the prophecy had started.

"*Three magics come that must attune, twice blessed before the gods....*" Reeva tapped a finger against her chin as she recited the words. She stared at the scar marring the boundary of the Veil from Erissa and Rhazien's combined magics, but her gaze remained clouded. "Would the Creator really give us such a simple hope? We're damned if he has. For I know the one who comes beyond the Mists, and he will never claim the blessing."

She traced a fingertip across her lips, still feeling as if she tasted the blood which sealed her fate. With the waning of the Veil's protection, it would not be long until Draven escaped the prison of the Buried Court. They were running out of time. The last words came from her with a ring of finality. "*The Keeper comes, a baited bore. And someone must be crowned...*"

Erissa had to admit that the Violent Wilds had more than lived up to their name. The smell of burning death suffocated her senses as she opened her eyes and stared directly into twin pools of molten amber. "Rhaz—"

Rhazien's lips crashed down against hers, cutting off the words. He wrapped his arms around Erissa and hauled her against his chest, murmuring the words against her mouth between kisses. "I lost you."

Erissa clung to him. "I heard you calling me, digging me out from under the voices."

"I've never been more scared in my life." Rhazien broke the embrace. He ran his hands up and down her arms while his eyes traced their way across every inch of her.

Erissa did the same for him, seeking any injuries her magic missed healing. It had burned even the blood away with no lingering evidence of what happened. She marveled at how the magic left them unmarked by the wounds.

Something bothered her about her patchy recollection of the event. Had she not been locked behind the souls? The flames came before Rhazien pulled her from the Veil's influence, didn't they? Or had they come after? Did he control them? Erissa bit her lip, her eyebrows squishing together while she tried to find the missing pieces.

Reeva's voice broke through her questions. "You need to leave this place. The Veil will soon recover, and it will not take kindly to being harmed this day."

"She's right." Rhazien stood, helping Erissa do the same. "We should pack our things and move on. It will take another four days to reach Cropari. We can rest during the day if we ride while it's dark. We're too vulnerable to make camp at nightfall."

"You mean I'm too vulnerable." Erissa's shoulders sagged. "I'm sorry, Rhazien. I don't remember much of what happened after leaving or beyond breaking free of the Veil's hold. I was so lost. How did I come back?"

Reeva snorted. "The morning's events went well past your magical abilities. Only one trained in the voided magics can do what the boy did and withstand the Veil long enough to take you from its grasp."

"Reeva..." Rhazien warned.

"I don't understand..." Erissa stared between them. Something eluded her, and it had everything to do with what happened after the Veil gained control.

The air grew taut with tension as Reeva's hands fisted at her sides while Rhazien radiated malice at the Fae with his stiff posture and grinding teeth.

Erissa shook her head "One trained in voided magics? I don't know what that means."

"It means the boy is lying to you." Reeva's lip curled, but she said no more.

Erissa frowned. "About what? Voided magic? You haven't even explained what that means, and Rhazien doesn't have magic. He's been nothing but honest with me about his intentions since we met."

"And you're not?" Rhazien snorted as if Erissa had not spoken. "Have you deigned to tell her anything about why you're here? Let me guess... that's something you've failed to mention in your little secret meetings."

"You insolent child!" Reeva's voice shook with the force of her anger.

Rhazien's face flushed as he glared, his own voice rising. "Better an insolent child than a monster who uses people for their own gain without telling them."

"And what about your lies?" Reeva laughed, an ugly sound that did not reach her eyes. "My tongue is bound, and I cannot break its binding, no matter how desperately I wish to. But you have no such excuse. You lie to her about everything you are. What do you think will happen when she finds out? There will be no gallivanting away with a happy ending. You will *crush* her!"

"Reeva!" Erissa stepped between their argument, hands on her hips. "I have listened to enough."

"The boy cannot be trusted!" Reeva's chest heaved with anger.

"Rhazien. His name is Rhazien." Erissa remained calm on the outside, her expression blank, but her heart raced on the inside. The conversation made no sense. Reeva threw around accusations while keeping her own secrets. And Rhazien? He denied nothing, which told her more than he probably wanted. She opened and closed her mouth, trying to find the right words as she regarded Reeva and Rhazien. "There are things you're both hiding from me."

"Little—"

Erissa held up a hand, silencing Rhazien. She closed her eyes, ignoring the whispering noise that had yet to fade. Too much had happened tonight. Her head ached, her stomach churned, and her chest burned whenever she breathed too deeply. She did not want to waste the rest of the evening unraveling their secrets. "You're *both* hiding something from me. But now is not the time. We need to leave. The Veil is still calling me."

She walked away, back to where their belongings waited, but stopped. Erissa scrutinized them over her shoulder—the only two people in her life who mattered—and set her jaw. "There will come a time for each of you to spill your secrets. Until then, you've earned my trust. Please. Don't make me regret giving it."

What Erissa would not give to hear the inner voice right now. It had always come intermittently without explanation, but she had heard it more often since the morning in the market. She missed it. Her world had begun crumbling, and eventually, she must start picking up the pieces. Maybe it knew how.

As Erissa walked away, Reeva considered the area where Rhazien had combined his and Erissa's magic to scar the boundary.

"Rhazien?" She said the name slowly as if testing to see how it rolled off the tongue.

She waited until he stopped following Erissa and faced her. "Remain vigilant. The further you travel, the weaker the Veil's call becomes, but be careful not to mistake it as a guarantee of safety. I must go. There are those within it who call me, and I am powerless to do anything but obey."

It did not take long to pack the few possessions lying around the campsite. They had taken little out when they retired for the night.

Erissa handed the bags to Rhazien, stepping to the side of Carizzea while he tied them to the back of her saddle. They remained silent throughout the exchange. Questions burned behind Rhazien's eyes, and her mood lacked the patience to entertain them.

When he finished the last knot, Erissa placed a foot in the stirrup and grabbed onto the pommel. It had grown easier over time to mount the horse with repeated practice, and she no longer needed Rhazien's help to take her seat.

She froze as he wrapped his hands around her waist.

Rhazien rested his chin against the crook of her neck. His slow breathing tickled the strands of hair against her skin. "Are you truly all right?"

Erissa leaned into his arms to remove her foot, her eyes rolling as she sighed. An unkind retort tested her tongue but failed to leave her lips as his body trembled against hers. She moved around to raise her arms and wrapped them around his neck. "I'm fine. A little upset with myself for being so easily led astray. And a little upset with you and Reeva for starting a shouting match."

"I'm sorry, little doe." Rhazien's color deepened, his face sheepish. "I didn't mean to lose control of my temper. It wasn't fair, especially because Reeva was right. You don't know everything about me."

"I won't pretend like you hiding something doesn't bother me. But I can understand I'm not going to know everything about you from the beginning. There are things I'm sure I haven't told you, and I kept my secrets." She cupped his face, and, rising on her toes, pressed a kiss against his lips. Her violet eyes sparkled as she drew away. "We've known each other for a fortnight. I don't expect you to have told me everything. There's a lifetime waiting for that..." Erissa cleared her throat, blushing at making such an assumption. "At least, I hope there is."

"There is. There's a lifetime waiting, little doe." Rhazien tightened his arms, tugging her close against his chest and burying his head into her neck.

"Maybe I'll try some of your *convincing* tactics on you." Rhazien's chest muffled Erissa's laughter-filled words.

"That sounds..." Rhazien's flirty tone disappeared as his whole body went tense against her. "Do you smell that?"

Erissa brought her hand up to pinch her nose, nearly retching at the foul, sour taste coating her tongue as she breathed. "What is that?"

A low growl had them turning to stare across the open space.

Erissa blinked in disbelief at what stood on their other side.

A naked woman's upper body protruded from a leonine form with powerful legs that ended in vicious black claws. The maimed body held marks as if the same claws had twisted around and shredded it, flesh carved away from the bone, the stench of death wafting from the gaping wounds. Its face held a worse horror.

The sickly green light of the Veil emanated from it, casting a sinister glow that raised bumps along Erissa's arms. It had no eyes, the sockets empty and filled with sludge from the swamp waters. Clumps were torn from her waterlogged hair. What remained of its framed lips mutilated with the malefic light. It weaved through the closed mouth, stitching the halves together.

It growled low in its throat, a strange sound that resembled a strangled scream as its sightless gaze locked on Erissa.

Rhazien shoved Erissa behind him, reaching for his axe. "Get on, Crezzi, now."

Erissa tried to summon the voice, and with it, magic. But nothing happened. It slumbered in her mind, exhausted from the events at the Veil.

"Erissa,' Rhazien shouted, "get on the horse."

She clutched Rhazien's arm in a blind panic. "I won't leave you."

"Don't argue." He jerked the arm from her grip and used it to push her into the horse, keeping his gaze locked on the beast. "It wants you. Get on the horse and ru—"

"Rhazien!" Erissa screamed as the Veil-twisted creature charged them.

Rhazien threw himself at the beast. He brought his axe above his head and swung with deadly precision. The axe connected with the macerated chest, tearing through the rotting tissue and embedding itself in the bone.

The beast let out a muffled roar, the surrounding light flickering, and it stumbled back a step. Black ooze flowed around the axe, staining the blade and coating Rhazien's hands. It teetered on its feet as the light surrounding it faded, draining through its body and into the axe. The more the light faded, the more its strength waned.

Rhazien abandoned his hold on the axe and reached for a blade on either leg, leaving himself exposed to the dark talons swinging through the air in a wild arc.

"Watch out!" Erissa screamed.

Rhazien jumped back, avoiding the maiming swipes.

The creature roared again, fighting the hold of the magical stitching. It swung its paws once more, but Rhazien was faster.

He stood and brought his arms up in a powerful arc, severing the clawed feet. Stepping close, he crossed the blades against the beast's neck and sliced in a deep crosscut against its throat until the head hung grotesquely to the back on a scrap of flesh. The foul black sludge sprayed over him. It poured down the length of the torso to pool beneath its feet as the corpse gave a violent sway and fell to the ground.

Bile rose in Erissa's throat at the rotten smell wafting from the beast. She covered her mouth with the sleeve of her shirt and stepped around the congealing blood to reach Rhazien. "Are you hurt? It didn't get you?"

"Stay there." Rhazien held his hands out, stopping her from approaching any further. "This reeks."

"What are you going to do?" Erissa pinched her nose, trying to block the smell, but instead of helping, she tasted its stench as she opened her mouth to breathe. "By the gods, what was that thing?"

Rhazien sighed. He tried to use the back of his hand to wipe the thick blood from his eyes. It only worsened the sticky coating, leaving it clumped against his lashes. "I'm going into the swamp. Its fetid waters have to be better than this."

Erissa gagged at the scent, blanketing her tongue. She stopped pinching her nose. "Anything is better than this."

"Follow me. Let's get upwind of this mess." Rhazien went to take Rhynstone's reins but stopped shy of touching them. "Can you lead them both?"

"Absolutely. We don't need to spread such nastiness to the leather." With great reluctance, Erissa lowered her arm and took a pair of reins in each hand. She walked upwind. "You can follow us, though. There's no way I'm walking downwind of you."

She led the horses and Rhazien away from the overpowering rot. The land rose the further they walked, leaving behind the gentle slopes that led into the boggy water. It cut off sharply, giving way to deep outcroppings that left Erissa nervous about her footing. "What do you think attacked us?"

"Something twisted by the Veil." Rhazien's voice carried from a distance. "Reeva said something about its power growing, but its magic is corrupted. You must not have been its only victim. Something so grotesque had to be touched by its taint."

They kept walking for some time. When her eyes no longer watered from the disgusting odor, she stopped. Erissa tied the reins to a nearby tree, leaving enough room for the horses to graze on the patchy greens littering the ground. "This should work. The water is deep enough to wade into, and at least we can breathe now."

"Speak for yourself, little doe." Rhazien lifted a shoulder and sniffed. He jerked his head away, his nose wrinkling as he shuddered. "What I wouldn't give for a piece of soap."

"I can help with that." Erissa went to Carizzea's saddle and searched through her bag. "I packed some of the soap from my room. You'll smell like a girl, but it should do the trick. I can turn around and tend to the horses while…" She trailed off as something splashed behind her. Erissa whipped around, staring at Rhazien in disbelief. "What are you doing?"

"Bathing?"

He had jumped into the water fully clothed except for his boots; they remained sitting on the steep bank. Even his jeweled earcuffs remained in place, the metal glistening in the light of the rising sun as its first rays filtered through the trees.

"Pass the soap. I'll take smelling like you any day." Rhazien held his hand out, standing waist-deep in the water. "Although it might prove too much of a distraction. All I'm going to end up doing is picturing everywhere you've trailed that soap down your—"

"Hush." Erissa interrupted him. She tried not to smile as she threw the chunk of sweet-smelling soap to him, her cheekbones stained with pink. "You take great pleasure in teasing me."

"Who said I'm teasing?" Rhazien tossed her a wink, taking the leather strip from his hair and dunking his head under the water.

Erissa held her breath as she waited for him to come back up. It would not surprise her if some terrifying animal lurked in its depths after all they had experienced since entering the Wilds.

When his head finally broke through the surface of the water, she breathed deeply, the pain in her chest relenting from bringing in the much-needed air.

He peered at her curiously, his eyes dropping to the hand that rested between her breasts as it moved against her heavy breathing. His eyebrow lifted in a silent question. Erissa waved it away, too busy quenching the need of her lungs to answer.

Rhazien turned his attention to the sticky black goop. He scrubbed against the stained fabric of his shirt until suds overtook the material. But despite the black bubbles, the fabric remained dark. He rinsed himself under the water and resurfaced to find little had changed. Again and again, he worked at cleaning the decayed blood from this clothing without success.

A frown tugged against his mouth, his nose wrinkling. "I'm afraid this is all for naught. All I've done is make the clothes smell like flower-covered refuse."

Erissa shook her head, laughing from where she perched on a moss-covered stump. "You would need to burn them to rid the fabric of the odor. It's strong enough to wake the dead. I can still smell it from here when the wind shifts."

"There's nothing for it. They'll have to go." Rhazien untied the laces on the front of his shirt. With the sides hanging up, he gestured to Rhynstone. "Can you remove the spare set from the larger bag?"

The blush, that had only moments ago faded, returned to heat Erissa's face as she stared at the expanse of tanned flesh. A sprinkling of dark hair trailed down his bronze chest, framed by the dark ink staining the skin. The pattern had scales, and Erissa's eyes traced the lines of the design, drinking in the way the richly colored lines highlighted the golden hue of his skin.

"Erissa?" There was laughter in Rhazien's voice.

"Hmm...?" The reds, yellows, and blacks on Rhazien's chest danced around one another, standing apart in vibrant bursts before fading into the next color. Her fingers itched to peel back the layers of the shirt to see how far it went to either side.

"You have a little drool hanging from your lips."

"What?" Erissa drew her sleeve across her mouth. "Where?"

"Caught you staring, little doe." Rhazien laughed. "You won't find those clothes under my shirt."

Erissa leaped to her feet, refusing to turn her face in his direction. "I wasn't staring at anything."

She stomped off to retrieve the clothing as Rhazien laughed. She fought to contain her smile at being caught, gathered the clothes, and placed them near his boots. Afterward, she sat on the stump again and faced the horses, giving Rhazien privacy.

"You can keep watching. I wouldn't mind."

She heard the smile still present in Rhazien's tone; only she guessed it would be full of the smug arrogance he wore so well. Erissa denied him the rise he sought with his teasing. "What's Cropari like?"

"It's a lot different from Emberhold and the Wilds. The heat here is wet and sticky, but Cropari is desert land. That kind of heat sucks the moisture out of the air. And sometimes, it's so hot in the summer, you can't walk outside for fear of melting the soles of your shoes."

Erissa tried to picture what it would be like to see nothing but sand on the horizon with air so hot you melted into the ground. Her imagination failed to picture it, not when she had never seen sand. Would it lay flat and white against the ground like it did in the Emberhold harbor?

She brought her feet to rest upon the wide stump, tucking her legs beneath her chin as Rhazien continued.

"The animals differ from anything you've seen. While they have horses, they're few and far between. Only the wealthiest families keep them. Everyone else travels by camel. They're about the size of a horse with two humps on their backs, although they can be larger and far stronger than horses. They can carry double the load and travel much greater distances, and camels can go long periods without eating or drinking."

Erissa found it harder to picture a bumpy horse than the endless expanse of sand. "They sound fascinating. Will we get to see one?"

"Yes. There's a beautiful oasis near the city. Micmus loves to take the children there. I'll show it to you, little doe. We ride camels to it and spend the day splashing around in the water."

Erissa smiled. She did not know what an oasis was, but the relaxed way Rhazien talked about it made her want to see it. "I would very much like for that to happen. "

"You can turn around."

Erissa turned around to see Rhazien out of the water and kneeling on the bank, the top of his boots gripped in one hand. His ruined clothing lay in a pile next to the water. He lathered the boots and scrubbed the blood from them using a handful of moss. When he had finished rinsing the soap from the leather, they were no worse for their ordeal, the blood having easily washed off the treated material.

Rhazien put the boots back on and came over to take her hand. He helped her rise from the stump and guided her to where Carizzea stood grazing. "Let's get moving. We have a long day of travel ahead of us, especially since we won't be stopping until the next sunrise."

CHAPTER TWENTY-SEVEN

"The change in the lands is worsening." The Seelie King's voice echoed loudly in the cavernous hall. "We cannot keep delaying our response. Every day, the taint of the Veil spreads."

Nephinae paused as she reached the door and placed a hand against the ornately carved panel. A smile hovered on her lips. She brightened at the thought of interrupting Yorrith's meeting. He would hate the interruption, and Nephinae relished any chance to get under the Seelie King's skin.

His voice cut through the quiet once more, penetrating the door. "The humans are reporting vraiths coming out of the Wilds. If this is true, then the barrier of the Veil grows weaker, and it is not alone, for the Mists were formed with the same magic and are now in danger as well."

Concerned murmurs met the announcement.

"We must bring the fight to Virion without delay. His influence is growing among the Unseelie, and you, Drurrah, have done little to quash it. Without intervention, there will be war, and I don't think I need to remind anyone what will happen if Draven is freed from the Veil. His imprisonment has already corrupted the Veil. If he escapes, the vraiths escape with him, and we can assume he has an army of them at his disposal. Already, Virion is aiding his cause. They will never get over Novus ruling the Unseelie. Virion will stop at nothing to gather supporters and unseat him."

Nephinae shook her head. The foolish King needed to consult with the witches to seal the room. Having the wrong person listen in on such a meeting would not do. Better to put a stop to his prattling before he ruined things for them all.

She brought her other palm to rest next to the first, allowing her power to build along the grooves carved into her skin. White light traveled down their lengths until the magic centered in her palms.

The corner of her mouth tipped up as she gathered the ferocity of her magic and burst through the doors with its blinding light.

Wood shattered, flying in every direction and raining down on the seven Fae seated around the table. Many of their arms lifted, covering their heads as the women shrieked and the men leaped from their chairs. Only Yorrith remained seated, a brow arched in Nephinae's direction, almost like he expected her arrival.

A pout twitched against her lips. She had no fun in making her grand entrance when the one she wished to rile most looked at her with amusement.

Nephinae continued drawing on her magic, cloaking herself in its power. It failed to reach the heights of her Lord's, but it remained impressive all the same. She waited until every eye turned in her direction before sauntering into the room.

The silence screamed. But then, it always did when a Zorathi paid a visit.

Her eyes never left Yorrith as she walked straight to the table. She did make for an impressive sight with her white hair and missing irises, the bright white of her eyes reflecting the brilliance of the light running through her scarred channels.

The two Seelie Lords, Thonalan of the Flowering Sun court and Cobrias of the Thundering Sun, stood with their mates and backed away from her approach. Drurrah, the Unseelie Lord of the Hunter's Moon court, inclined his head with a slight nod that bordered on disrespect.

"Missing someone, Yorrith?" Nephinae let her magic crackle along her skin. "My Lordship will be most displeased. You know how Novus likes to be included in these things. The Frosted Moon court should be apprised of these meetings."

Yorrith stood, and Nephinae had to admit he cut an imposing figure in the bright light of day with his broad shoulders, close-clipped chestnut hair, and sea-green eyes. Unlike most Lords, Yorrith kept himself in fighting condition, which showed in the powerful lines of his tall frame.

He leaned forward, placing his fists on the table, a bored tone to his voice as if he expected her arrival. "I don't answer to you, Zorathi, or your Lord."

Nephinae copied his stance, bending over the marble. The light-infused white magic filling the grooves in her skin bounced across the cold stone. "Get out."

Thonalan and Cobrias heeded her words. They ushered their mates from the room, only remembering to bow to their King at the last minute.

Yorrith sighed, sinking back down into his chair, a dismissal in the way he waved his hand at her. "What do you want, Nephinae?"

She ignored the question, cutting her eyes to the remaining Unseelie. "Are you in need of motivation, Drurrah, or will you remove yourself from my presence without interference?"

Anger heated Drurrah's face at being so easily dismissed. "Watch your tone."

"Or you will do what?" Nephinae rolled her eyes. She always got under Drurrah's skin with ease, and this time was no different.

"Careful, Zorathi." Drurrah's gaze narrowed, anger lacing every word. "Your Lord isn't here to protect you."

"The only thing keeping you breathing is an order from *our* Lord—excuse me—*our King*. The second Novus lifts his command to keep you alive is the second you die." Nephinae laughed, the rich sound condescending as she stared. She easily provoked him, the Fae ever ready to fight against Novus and those who counted him as a friend.

Yorrith scoffed, but she ignored him. He would not intervene in the conflict. Yorrith hated Drurrah almost as much as Nephinae did. Drurrah never should have received a pardon for his actions in the Keeping War, no matter how he changed sides at the last minute. If he had not fought with Draven in the first place, the war might not have happened, and her court would not have suffered the consequences of its aftermath.

Drurrah refused to back down. He summoned his own magic, and the air filled with moisture, surrounding them with water. He wrapped the flowing strands around her, attempting to bind Nephinae with them.

Nephinae held herself at ease, a cruel smile shaping her lips as lightning bled from the scarring and wound its way across her body to electrify the water. The waves binding her sizzled with the strength of the power Nephinae fed into it. "Oh, it's been so long since I have played."

But Drurrah calling on his magic proved too much for the King. Yorrith slammed a hand on the table, rising from his seat. "Stop this at once, Drurrah. To attack anyone using Unseelie magic on Seelie land is a declaration of war."

"Let him attack, Yorrith." Nephinae sat in one of the vacant chairs with a devious smirk, uncaring how the electrified water burned the seat's fabric. "My reputation is well earned, and it has been too long since someone issued a challenge. I have grown weary of the respite."

"What reputation?" Drurrah sneered. "Everyone knows your position was earned on your back. Tell me, Zorathi, is *your Lord* as sadistic in the bedroom as he is outside of it?"

Nephinae snarled. The last thing she needed was Drurrah putting that idea in Yorrith's head again. The two had barely survived their last argument where she denied a relationship existed between her and Novus. "Do not mistake my allegiance for weakness. I follow his orders out of courtesy. I am not bound to honor his vows the way the rest of his court is. Test me one more time, Drurrah, and you will see what earned my reputation and our Lord's respect."

"I will never bow to him," Drurrah seethed, spit flying from his mouth as he spat the words.

"The time will come, Drurrah. Make it easier on yourself when it does, and bow willingly. I promise you, the consequences are not worth your pride." Nephinae flipped her long hair over her shoulder. "If you test me on that day, I will break your pride in full view of your court without hesitation. Then we shall see which Lord they bow to."

The water fell with a splash around Nephinae's feet as Drurrah turned on his heel, quitting the room in a rageful silence, his mate scampering to keep up with his longer strides. Nephinae knew her words settled deep against the very pride she threatened. She made no idle threat.

Yorrith rubbed his temples. A muscle ticked beside his brow. "I see you continue to make friends wherever you go."

"Of course I do." Nephinae crossed one leg over the other, the high slit in the side of her dress falling to the side. She wrinkled her nose at the smell of the burned fabric. "After all, I am quite delightful."

A ghost of a smile tugged at Yorrith's lips. It disappeared as quickly as it had come as his eyes roved over the skimpy dress and all it revealed. He swallowed hard, his face turning to stone. Nephinae thought it a shame. He looked younger when he smiled.

Yorrith cleared his throat. "Why are you here, Nephinae? Surely, this is not a social call if you have gone to such trouble to empty the room."

"You never were one for small talk, Seelie." She shrugged. Now that the time had come, she struggled with how to tell him why she came. She would build his every hope only to devastate him with Novus's demand. "My Lord has sent me to deliver a message. I thought you might need a moment of privacy after hearing it."

His mouth hung open with a dramatic display of shock. "A Zorathi considering the needs of others?"

The words should not have stung, but they did. Nephinae looked away. His mockery cut her to the quick. She traced a finger along the lines decorating the marble.

As with everyone else, Yorrith knew her as nothing more than a ruthless warrior in service to a brutal Lord. Their notoriety, while well-earned, kept them both alive more times than she remembered. But if only for this moment, she wanted someone else to know the heart that beat beneath it all.

Nephinae rolled her shoulders, ridding herself of the ridiculous thoughts, and returned to the task at hand. "Things are as Novus suspected long ago. Spells were in place to hide the girl, but they are now broken. Berthina says the girl lives."

The color drained from Yorrith's face. He swayed before falling heavily onto the chair. She thought he might tip over the side, but he gathered himself. A wild hope shone from his eyes, and for the first time in thirteen years, Yorrith gave a genuine smile. "She... lives?"

Swallowing the emotion sitting at the back of her throat, Nephinae nodded. "The girl lives."

"This isn't a trick?" The hope on his face faded to panic. "He would never..."

"*I* would never." Nephinae leaned forward, letting him see the honesty in her gaze. "She lives, Yorrith."

"She lives…" Yorrith stared at her with wonder. Tears gathered against his lashes until they finally fell, and Nephinae looked away, the moment too raw for her to intrude on as his happiness called to her. Yorrith dropped his head, a hand pressed to his heart, as he cried his joy. "She lives, she lives, she lives."

Nephinae let him have this moment. After all these years of waiting, he deserved it, especially since her next words would kill the hope radiating from him.

Yorrith laughed, lifting his head. "Where is she?"

"She has run. Only you can sense her magic. We are to find the girl, and when we do…" Nephinae breathed deeply and forced the next words from her mouth. "He is calling in his bargain, Yorrith."

"No." The light around Yorrith died as he whispered the single word.

She watched him fall into a place beyond grief and anger as sorrow broke every hope he had carried all these years. An empty shell of a man remained. His heart cracked in half the first time he lost her, but losing her a second time? She did not think he would survive it. But what other choice did she have? All of life hung in the balance. "Ready yourself to leave in the morning. Imryll and Kyrenic will join us."

He stared at her, unblinking.

Nephinae smothered the guilt building within her breast and rose from the chair.

Yorrith spoke when she reached the battered door frame. "Will I get to see her? Will Novus at least allow that much?"

"For a time. How long that will be, I cannot say."

"She truly lives?"

"She lives." Nephinae hated the way his voice had cracked. She turned to look at him, her heart groaning at the hope and despair intermingling across his features. "I swear to you, Yorrith. The girl lives."

The weight of it all hit him, and with a wild laugh that stuttered into a wail, the Seelie King sobbed.

She would not go to him in the light of day. She had lost that right long ago with all that lay between them. As she squared her shoulders and left the room, Nephinae had never hated herself more.

CHAPTER TWENTY-EIGHT

Erissa relaxed the further west they traveled. Nothing more attacked them as they left the Veil behind, and the whispers faded against the wind.

After four days, the swamp slowly morphed from a waterlogged, humid terrain to the arid heat of the desert. The trees thinned out until only a scarce few made up the landscape. Even those changed, their limbs becoming scragglier. They bent against the ever-present hot wind as they flowered, their pungent and smokey perfume flavoring the surrounding air.

The ground became firmer, and the plants more sparse. The rich soil beneath them gave way to a dense, sandy ground rising with every step. Rolling hills developed, making the land resemble the churning water Erissa grew up viewing from her bedroom window. Rhazien called them dunes.

Unlike the waves that broke against the rocks surrounding the bay of Emberhold's port, the dunes sat frozen in undulation, forever halted from crashing down into the waiting sand below their height.

The thick foliage of the plants also changed. The ferns and thorny bushes were gone, replaced by brightly flowering vines and large plants with shiny, flat leaves that grew like blossoming flowers. Erissa did not expect to see such beauty in the plants of the desert. Rhazien had described it as a land full of endless sand. His descriptions did little to capture the magnificence of it all. It showed a different kind of beauty, but one Erissa found soothing in its simple vibrancy.

Tall, smooth trunks of another plant grew across the land, and they were unlike anything Erissa imagined, with limbs that branched out into various arms. Spiked protrusions covered the plants. Rhazien told her they were called cacti. Some were sacred, while the people of these lands regularly ate others. His favorite meal included strips of the waxy green cactus fire roasted alongside lamb and placed between the folds of a soft bread dipped in oil and herbs.

All different shapes and sizes of cacti spread across the land, but the more arms they had and the longer they grew, the older the plant was.

Rhazien gestured to one of the tallest plants. "It takes hundreds of years for each arm to develop."

Erissa regarded the plant he pointed out. "Stop teasing me. That plant would be thousands of years old if what you said is true."

"You doubt me?" Rhazien held a hand against his heart, a lopsided grin making him look younger. "I'm wounded, m'lady."

He told her more stories as they followed a visible road, its path stamped flat among the rolling dunes. Some stood taller than if she had climbed upon Rhazien's shoulders while he sat atop Rhynstone. Many would have dwarfed the gates of Emberhold.

Erissa enjoyed the stories. Rhazien had talked more to her over the last seventeen days than her parents in the last ten years. He used words to draw her another picture of the lands, and the stories became precious to her. He did not talk to her out of obligation, his excitement unmistakable in its enthusiasm.

Was this what love should feel like? Her heartwarming at each new story that expanded her remembrance of his dirt-drawn map? The question ran circles in their mind as they traveled.

Another two days had them nearing the decorative archway that marked the entrance to Cropari. Travelers abounded in every direction except the Veil side of the Wilds. Rhazien and Erissa approached the waiting throng of people seeking entrance into the city.

The sun-dried bricks composing the arch glittered in the high sun. Long ago, bleached specs of sand twinkled like sunlit glass against the colorful designs drawn with a delicate hand, a rich tapestry of blues, reds, yellows, and greens.

"It tells the story of Cropari's rise." Rhazien's voice was close, and she turned her head to find Rhynstone alongside Carizzea, its owner leaning over the saddle precariously to deliver the words to her alone. He pointed to each section as he spoke. "From the first settlers with their dirt floor huts to the building of the doorway after a long and bloody battle for freedom from the Waning Tribes, the paints tell the history of these people."

"It's beautiful." Erissa traced the tale with her eyes. "Are all the buildings decorated like this?"

"Not all, but most, especially the grander homes. It's a competition between the wealthier families to see who can have the most colorful and uniquely painted house. You'll like the outside of Micmus's home. Its paintings are more detailed than these. His wife, Islone, grinds gems into the paint. Once everything has dried to the wall, she takes handfuls of sand and rubs it against the bumpy areas to unearth their colors. The gems shine in the sunlight."

Erissa quieted as they moved closer to the gates. The crowd of people made her feel as if the space was closing in. It had been different when she was in Emberhold's marketplace. Those were the people she had grown up seeing from afar, while these people were strangers.

Cropari held more people than the city her father ruled over, if the gates and crowd of travelers were any indication.

Riding the horses through the gates overwhelmed her after everything that transpired in the Wilds and all the changes in the landscape. With the world much larger than she had believed, Erissa did not know what to expect. Panic rose thick in her throat, and she slowed her breathing, counting between exhales to keep it at bay.

Rhazien caught her attention. "We're in this together, little doe. In whatever comes next, we'll be fine if we're together."

She loved the way he looked at her. It made her feel less alone in such an impressive space. "How do you always know what to say? You soothe all my fears with an ease I envy."

He shrugged. "I've had—"

"A lot of practice? Let me guess," Erissa teased, "your sisters?"

"There are six of them and one of me. You learn quickly to keep up." Rhazien talked more about them as they rode through the city.

With the crowds thinning the further they went, Erissa relaxed, allowing Rhazien's voice to wash over her even as she studied the city's details.

Rhazien had been right about the homes. Even those without murals along their walls made up for it with brightly colored fabrics hanging from doorways and windows. Flowers of every color sat in baskets surrounding the homes, with some yards filled with cacti and others with floral and smoke-flavored trees with their bright yellow buds.

Unlike the homes found in Emberhold that boasted more than one floor of rooms stacked in neat rows along the city roads, Cropari homes held a single floor and peppered the land at differing distances from winding paths.

Cropari had a more carefree atmosphere than Emberhold. The chaotic groupings of houses created a messy pattern as the road weaved around them, but beauty abounded even in its lack of order. The city carved itself around the needs of the people, rather than everyone striving to match its obsessive order, something that challenged the rigidity of Emberhold. Erissa enjoyed the difference as she pictured what it would be like to live here.

Each home boasted a large garden, some of them in the front while others sat off to the side or behind. The people filled them with flowering plants that perfumed the air and tidied rows of crops. Many plots held the two-humped horses Rhazien had told her about, along with sheep, goats, and chickens. The homes boasted the same bricks that built the city's entrance, with little variations in color outside of the bright fabrics and paintings.

The people more than made up for their uniformly built homes as they gathered in groups around stalls and their gardens. Tables and chairs graced spaces with generations of families enjoying the midday meal together. If anything, they were more vibrantly colored than their homes. Their shirts, skirts, and trousers contrasted heavily against the hats and scarves they wore. Even so, it all blended well together, a prismatic abundance of hues enhanced by the many pieces of jewelry they wore. Many people held similar or more piercings than Rhazien, and nearly everyone had at least one ear covered with a cuff.

Rhazien might have called Freyborn home, but he resembled the Croparians with his gold rings and dragon ear cuffs. His father had not worn the same accessories in the stable. Erissa liked how the warm tones of the jewelry accentuated Rhazien's brown skin, the color having darkened as they rode under the desert sun. Erissa's own completion reddened beneath the harsh light, becoming dry and painful to the touch.

The changes from Emberhold were striking. The air held differences, fragrant with exotic flowers and spiced with the warm and savory aroma of foods that left her wishing for a bite of something more than hard, stale bread and tough jerky. Life revolved around these smells as everyone clustered around animals, gardens, and food.

Her eyes moved against the riot of colors, taking them in against the fragrance of the air. She did not want to find such vibrancy beautiful. It had a serene air about it that one could grow used to. She needed to be careful with that. Only heartache awaited her when they left, for Cropari would only be another place she did not call home.

Their progress slowed as people recognized Rhazien. Many waved in their direction, shouting greetings and invitations to share a meal. He waved back at them, calling out his salutations to some while smiling at others. He had a home among these people.

But for all the attention Rhazien received, they paid Erissa more. People called out after her, asking Rhazien questions about her presence at his side, suspicion darkening the brow of some while curiosity twinkled in the eyes of others.

An itch crept its way along Erissa's spine as people stared. Her eyes darted around the growing crowd, frantically searching for the sound of a wailing voice or a shadowed form behind the great number of people. Her nerves refused to settle even upon finding nothing out of place.

One of the bolder women walked alongside Rhazien's horse. "Bringing a girl home, Young Master?"

"There's a first time for everything, Primae." Rhazien winked.

The woman poked his leg. "Islone will have your head for not sending word."

"Islone will love her." A quizzical frown tugged at his mouth. "I'm more concerned with introducing her to the Elders."

"The Elders?" The woman sniffed. "That's the way of it?"

A breeze ruffled Rhazien's hair, sending the length flying into his mouth. He tucked the strands behind his ear. "Try to keep it to yourself for now. I'd hate for Islone to hear it before we have a chance to get there."

"I have never been a gossip." A scarf hung around the woman's neck, and she pulled it up, covering the lower half of her face as the sultry breeze picked up. She stepped to the side, putting distance between Rhazien and herself. "Is the girl daft or too besotted to ride upwind from your stink?"

Erissa giggled as Rhazien and the woman bickered, some of the tension leaving her. But the fear remained, gnawing away at the core of her being.

Soon enough, the woman said her goodbyes, leaving Erissa and Rhazien to continue winding their way through the city.

They were riding in the full light of day, and with it came the worst of the heat. It had been impossible for Erissa to remain cloaked, her identity hidden beneath the deep hood. Her eyes were easily noticeable, especially in a place where color reigned.

More people called out to Rhazien, but he refused their questions concerning Erissa's identity. Gratitude lay alongside her fear until the two blended together, leaving Erissa's stomach uneasy.

Rhazien held his hand out and waited for her to take it. She blushed, the heat darkening her sun-reddened cheeks, but answered his silent invitation and placed her hand in his with the horses riding close together.

Whispers broke out at their display of affection. The older generations gazed upon Erissa with interest while the younger children let out teasing remarks. A few younger women were uncaring of the gesture and became more flirtatious in their invitations. Rhazien left them dejected as he raised Erissa's hand and placed a kiss against the backs of her fingers.

Erissa felt an unfamiliar feeling of animosity against these women, and her voice came out snippier than she intended, hardened by jealousy and growing worried. "Do you not call Freyborn home?"

"I've always been more at home in Cropari. Freyborn lies two days' ride southwest of here. We came here often as children to visit with my father's friend, Micmus, and stayed for a little over a moon after my sister passed. Many of the older generations scolded me more than once as a child."

An image of Rhazien as a mischievous child had Erissa lifting a brow in mock disapproval. "I'm sure you deserved every one of those scoldings."

"And many a girl chased after me when we'd stay here." Rhazien cocked his head at Erissa and smiled with an arrogance she now expected and often wanted to slap from his face. "But not a one compares to you, little doe."

Erissa heard the sincerity in his words and his elation at being here, the connection echoing his heartbeat against her own as it moved in a content rhythm. Their connection had only grown stronger since their dangerous encounter with the Veil. She felt the peace he carried close to his heart. Rhazien had a home with these people, and there had been one in Freyborn as well, while Erissa had...she did not want to think about it. Where would she call home now that she had traveled so far from all she had known?

"Are you all right?"

"You're always asking me that." Erissa forced a smile, feeling the falsity of it stretching tightly across her mouth. "I'm fine, only tired. It's been a long... how long *has* it been? A few days past a fortnight?"

Rhazien wore his concern for her like a second skin, making her stomach drop at uttering such a falsehood. Maybe once they had rested, she would talk to him about where to go next. She wanted to stay with him, and he had said much of the same, but she wanted a home that went beyond his presence.

Far from convinced by her reassurance, hesitation colored his tone. "Micmus resides around the corner. I'm sure they won't mind seeing us to our room once we're there. It's a hard enough journey up here under normal circumstances, and we've had anything but that."

Erissa nodded. "A place to wash and a solid bed beneath me after all this time on the hard ground has me near tears."

"I think we'd both benefit from my having a bath more than anything. It's been days, and I still smell of that rotten gunk." Rhazien laughed with a shake of his head. "C'mon then, little doe. Let's get both of us a bath and a bed. You'll be begging to stay here forever once you see the size of the bathing chamber."

"Chamber?" Erissa's eyes widened in disbelief. "There's an entire room only for bathing?"

Rhazien smiled, leading them further down the road without another word until they rounded the corner. As they did, a grand, sprawling house came into view, rivaling all they had passed.

Rhazien stopped Rhynstone outside the courtyard of the stunning home. He dismounted and helped Erissa do the same. A young man came running from the back. He halted before them and held his hand out, saying nothing.

"Orbas! You must have grown three feet since I last laid eyes on you." Rhazien handed both reins to Orbas, who smiled a wide, toothless grin. He bowed his head repeatedly, his blonde curls flying everywhere, and led the horses away.

Erissa paid little attention to the exchange. Her eyes focused on the house. The entire façade was one large painting. It covered even the door, making it difficult to tell it apart from the walls.

The sand-colored bricks were invisible underneath the bursting color. Its pictures demanded attention. The walls shimmered against the sun's golden rays, creating a stunning array that rivaled the beauty of the gateway arch. While the story of Cropari was enchanting, the story depicted on this house took Erissa's breath away.

Beasts covered in gleaming gemstones decorated the bricks exactly as Rhazien had described them. Each painted being had a great span of wings attached to its back. The gems making up the wings lent the noble beasts depth, making them appear as if they were in mid-flight. They flew around one another in a timeless dance, their snouts raised to the heavens as fire poured from their mouths. They flew as sentries against the gods. Their fire created a brilliantly flamed barrier between them, the humans, and the Fae, crafted in painstaking detail below.

Two of the winged beasts stood apart from the others. The smaller was blue, its gem-encrusted scales reflecting the light like a sunset against the water of a bay. It flew above the others as if they answered to it, but the other flew above him. Erissa found herself drawn to this one and its magnificence.

The large red and gold body was three times the size of the blue. The red scales faded to golden wings of fire as the color faded into orange, the orange into the deepest of reds, and the reds into a black that was a darker shade of coal. No fire roared forth from its mouth. Curling smoke took its place, but it did not lack intimidation with the missing flames. The gods themselves cowered from the smoke as if one caress of it would be their doom.

It reminded her of Rhazien. She wanted to inspect the lines of ink outlining his body, wanted to see if she would find a tail at one and a head with curling smoke at the other.

"I see you like my wife's dragons. The blue one used to lead the Fefnirion clan. Now, there's only one. The red dragon."

Erissa jumped at the gravelly voice to her right, terror gripping her. She tripped over her feet as she tried to get away and sent herself careening into Rhazien. His arms wrapped around her while chuckles came from every direction.

"Gracious! Micmus, you'll be the death of the girl." A woman grabbed her shoulders and removed her from Rhazien's arms. She stood taller than Erissa, nearly the same height as Rhazien. Her features were quite plain with lines around her mouth and eyes, but her eyes shined like emeralds against straight, coppery hair that fell to the wide curves of her waist. She wore the same colorful garments as the other women, with a linen scarf around her neck the same shade of her eyes, which were full of questions she directed to Rhazien with an arch of her brow. "And who have you brought us, Rhaz?"

An older, short, portly man held an arm out to Rhazien. He wore navy robes accentuated with a belted sash the shade of watered-down wine. He appeared a plain man next to the vividly dressed woman.

"Micmus!" Rhazien took the man's arm and pulled him into a fierce hug.

"Did you roll in camel dung before coming here?" The man's lip curled against Rhazien's stink. "Never mind. I'm not sure I want to know. Whatever are you doing in Cropari, son? You've only been gone a little over three moons. Is the South not to your liking?"

Erissa squirmed. The woman let go of her and focused on Rhazien. "And *who* is this?" the woman asked once more.

Chewing the bottom of her lower lip, Erissa worried over what the couple would think of her eyes. A nervous hope brightened them. Although, this was not Emberhold, and no one outside of Rhazien had any knowledge of what she was capable of.

When the men finished embracing, Rhazien picked up the woman as if she weighed nothing and twirled her around. "Islone! Where are the children?"

Islone laughed, the sound a high-pitched squeal. "They are sitting for their lessons." She asked the same question when he placed her on her feet. "Who is your friend?"

Micmus and Islone shifted their attention to Erissa. The humor fled their faces as they took in her back-lit eyes. Islone swallowed hard, and Erissa's hope plummeted with it. Maybe Cropari and its people were more like Emberhold than she imagined.

Rhazien placed an arm about her waist, molding her side to his. "Micmus, Islone... I would like you to meet my wife, Erissa."

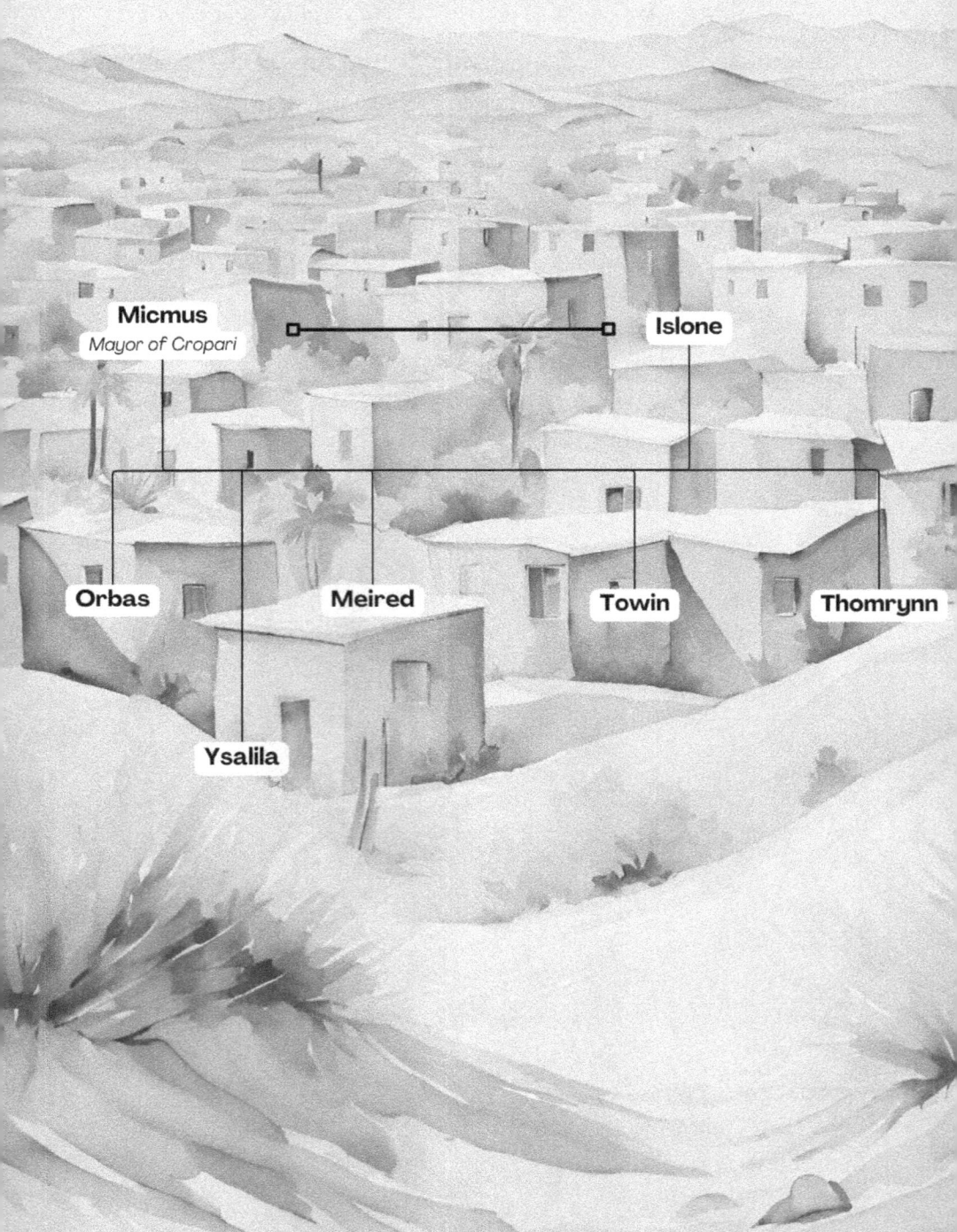

CHAPTER TWENTY-NINE

Erissa choked on a lump of emotion at Rhazien deceptively claiming her as his wife. It sent her into a coughing fit. Rhazien and Micmus both reached for her, patting their hands on the sides of her back, trying to break off the hacking that consumed her.

What game did Rhazien play, announcing her as his wife to people he cared for? She mercilessly trampled the wild pleasure that his calling her his wife had caused. It had to be a means to an end, not a sign of a future together, and she needed to remember the difference, especially after seeing the couple's reaction to her eyes.

As Erissa's fit subsided, Islone smiled kindly at her, the emotion falling short on her face even as a knowing twinkle came to her eye. "First time hearing it out loud?"

Erissa nodded.

"I remember tripping over my feet and falling face first into an undignified heap when Micmus introduced me as his wife for the first time." Islone then turned to Rhazien and slapped his shoulder. "And why were we not sent word of this? We had to find out with you showing up at our door unannounced?"

Rhazien shrugged, a sheepish, dimpled grin transforming his face. He was like a child trying to talk their way out of trouble when caught sneaking treats. "We've only known one another for a short time."

"How short?" Islone demanded.

"We met a little over a fortnight ago." Rhazien kissed Erissa's brow, the lies slipping easily from his charming lips. "We wed three days after meeting and have been traveling since, but we ran into some trouble with bandits in Eshirene's wood. We had to go through the Wilds to get them off our trail. It's been rough traveling."

"Was there a reason for such haste?" Micmus threw Rhazien a wink.

Seeing the exchange left Erissa sputtering in denial. "We're not... it's not what... Rhazien didn't mean..."

"Micmus!" Islone elbowed him. "Come, let's go inside. You poor dears must be exhausted after all the excitement of traveling."

Islone led the way into the house, gesturing for Erissa and Rhazien to follow her.

Cool air hit Erissa's face as she crossed over the threshold. She welcomed the respite from the heat outdoors.

A large main room dominated the space, with hallways branching off to the left and right. They had divided the space into separate areas with low walls which housed a variety of plants in pottery painted to match the dragons from outside. One part of the room housed a kitchen, another a low wooden table with rugs and cushions spread around it. The last of the areas held similarly styled larger cushions. Some were big enough to accommodate more than one person, while others lined the wall as a place to rest one's back. Paintings hung around the room while draperies interwoven shades of purple, red, and gold with green and were tied back above the low walls.

The deeper colors made the space calmer, creating a quieter atmosphere that was much needed after the spirited display outside. But it did little to soothe Erissa's frayed emotions. She was on the verge of collapse and longed for a moment to herself.

Rhazien spoke, reading her unvoiced desire. "Would you mind if we retired until the evening meal? We've had little sleep since entering the Wilds."

Islone nodded in understanding. "I think a bath is in order, too. We love you, Rhaz, but the smell coming off you is atrocious."

Rhazien laughed, the familiar sound of it comforting Erissa. "There's a story behind the stink."

"Which you can tell us later. Come, let me see you to your room." Islone turned to the right, leading them through a wide doorway, down the hall, and to the last of the rooms. She opened the door, gesturing inside.

Rhazien hesitated. "You needn't go to such trouble. My regular room is fine."

Islone waved away his words. "One so newlywed deserves some privacy. Besides, I believe your lovely bride might enjoy the sunken bath." Mischief twinkled in the woman's eye. "Something tells me you will use it quite often, though not simply for bathing."

Erissa did not understand her meaning. "What is a sunken bath?"

Islone laughed, but not unkindly. "You will see, and once you do, you might never wish to leave it nor bathe another way." The older woman hugged her. "Take your time. We won't expect you for dinner. I'll have one of the maids bring a tray in a few hours' time. The bed is freshly made, and extra linens are in the wardrobe." With those parting words, the woman left them alone.

"Come, little doe. Let's wash the days away and get some sleep." Rhazien took her hand, leading her into the room.

While not as large as the main room of the home, it came close. The widest bed Erissa had ever seen sat on one side of the wall. It had no frame, was covered in white linens, and was surrounded by pillows and cushions of every size, pattern, and color. Low tables sat next to the bed, and a wardrobe occupied the side of the half wall facing the bed. But the moisture in the room grabbed her attention the most.

The heat of the desert had been drying, the climate different from what she was used to. The room felt more like the water-laden breeze that blew in from Emberhold's bay. It was not unwelcome as her skin drank in the room's dampness. At least something remained familiar.

Her eyes moved to the other side of the room. Small squares covered the wall in a vivacious shade of blue. Each contained an etched white dragon with yellow eyes. Flowers boarded the edges of the squares.

"They're called tiles." Rhazien's arm wrapped around her waist from behind, and another stretched past her chest to point at the floor. "Look down."

A gasp of delight escaped her.

Cut into the floor lay the outline of a dragon wing made of stone and stained to match the tiles. Steaming water filled its depth as the surface moved in rolling ripples.

"The water comes from a hot spring in the ground. It never cools and always bubbles from the heat. There are ledges built into the bottom where you can sit and soak away your troubles for as long as you desire."

"Who knew such a thing existed?" Erissa placed her hand over Rhazien's, where it rested against the curve of her stomach.

"I was hoping you'd like it. Micmus and Islone have one in their room as well, but the other rooms share a much larger bathing chamber with another hot spring. We loved to splash around in it as children. It's where I learned to swim."

Erissa stared at the hot water with excitement. "You might never get me to leave such a bath."

"That's the plan." Rhazien's tone held a smirk as he spoke. "But I want you well rested on the day I hold you in its depths." He kissed the spot where her shirt left her shoulder exposed at the base of her neck, causing her skin to pebble. "See to your bath—alone, for now—while I grab our belongings and make sure the horses are settled in well. There should be soaps lying on a shelf against the other side of the wall. Towels, too."

Erissa did not need to be told twice. Before Rhazien had a chance to quit the room, she was already kicking off her boots. His laughter at her eagerness echoed as the door shut behind him.

When she removed all her clothes, Erissa walked around the wall. Steps led down into the water from one side of the wing. She sighed in rapture as she lowered herself into the water.

The water rose to cover her breasts in the deepest part when standing. Erissa relaxed into one of the seats carved into the ledge. The water lapped against her neck when seated.

The heat bordered on being too much as her skin reddened in the water. But for the first time in a long time, Erissa felt the stiffness in her chest fade in the heat. With the bubbling water around her, she closed her eyes and let go of all that happened, basking in the warmth.

"Comfortable? I had despaired of finding you alone after the last several days."

For a second time that day, Erissa flinched beyond reason as the words came from beside her, slipping below the water. Her nose stung as the water went up it, and she reemerged, rubbing it to take away the burn. "Reeva! Do you always have to sneak up on me like that?"

"One might assume you would have grown used to it by now. It is not like I can announce myself by knocking upon the door." Reeva shrugged, sitting with her legs dangling in the water.

"But you can sit on the ground." Erissa gestured to where the Fae sat.

"I don't claim to understand the magic confining me. The ground and other areas like it are solid, but I cannot interact with them beyond standing or sitting."

Erissa ignored all that Reeva said and addressed the Fae bluntly. "You want something, or else you wouldn't be here. Is this another of your warnings?"

"You are rather belligerent tonight." Reeva shifted her weight, bringing one leg to cross against the other.

Erissa scrunched her nose and sighed. "I'm tired. I do not intend to be rude."

Reeva dropped her gaze to her feet as she kicked them around. The water did not change with her movements. "You're not wrong. I do wish to speak to you. The boy—"

Erissa cut her off. "I will not remind you again he has a name."

Reeva leaned into Erissa's face with a hard gleam in her eyes. "And I will not remind you again he's lying to you."

Going through it once more sat low on her list of priorities after finally having a moment to herself. Rhazien was hiding something, but what did that matter when compared to every way he had been there for her since that first night? Erissa shook her head, defiance in every line of her face. "I won't listen to this."

Reeva refused to give up. "You cannot trust him, and you are too blinded by your heart to see it."

"Do not treat me as if I'm some ignorant child. Rhazien has proven he's worth trusting. I don't know if I can say the same for myself. His being with me has done nothing but put his life in danger."

"And if his secrets were worse than your own?" Reeva's patience snapped, all niceties gone. "What would you do then? What would you do if he harbored something so dangerous it might call down the wrath of the gods—of the Creator himself on all of us?"

"Reeva, I'm too tired for this." Erissa rubbed at her temples, her eyes closed. A pounding had begun beneath them, and she wanted nothing more than to relax with no worries about what would happen tomorrow. "Please, leave me in peace tonight. Everything has been so…"

"We are all tired, but it does not mean we should willingly walk around with our eyes covered. There is much about what happened at the Veil that defies all that humanity is capable of. One without magic would not have—"

"Reeva!" Despite her vehement interruption, Erissa struggled to find the right words. She dropped her hands, eyes opening and filled with unshed tears. "I have had a lifetime's worth of suffering at the hands of the people who were supposed to love and protect me. Rhazien is the only thing good to ever happen to me. He's a good man for all his arrogance and secrets. Can you not let me enjoy it for a little while longer? All I want is this bath and to lie undisturbed beside him this night and simply be at peace."

Reeva sighed, her shoulders drooping as she leaned back and rubbed her own temples. "The boy—"

Erissa breathed harshly, the lines of her face settling into murderous intent.

"*Rhazien…* is not what he seems," Reeva said the words like speaking with a mouth full of glass. She gestured to herself. "His kind are selfish, and it is because of them the Keeping War even happened. If they had retained their magic—"

"Reeva!" Erissa snapped. "Stop. I don't want to hear this."

"Fine." Reeva's voice turned hollow. "Ignore what I'm saying and continue living in ignorance."

No sooner had the words been uttered, Reeva disappeared, fading into nothing as the last of her voice echoed against the tiles.

CHAPTER THIRTY

Virion never understood his father's fascination with blood. He closed his mouth against the rancid taste of it permeating the air, exhaling through his nose.

Blood stained the marble floor, covering the patterned stones in a coagulated chaos of human viscera. There would be no getting all of it from the cracks between the tiles, but one made such sacrifices when dealing with blood magic.

The human's efforts to fight back almost impressed him, though they did not matter in the end when Virion's boot crushed through the man's skull. Humans were no match for the strength of the Fae. It was as easy as squishing a grape between his fingers, with no fun to be had in killing him so quickly. Virion would have drawn the process out had the man not become such a nuisance with his escape attempts.

Virion shifted against the high back of his chair. It looked right at home with the carnage around the room, the deep burgundy a match for gore across the floors. He drummed his fingers against the fabric on the armrest. The restless motion did little to temper his impatience.

"They're late." The words reverberated across the cavernous chamber of the temple. There was little in the way of furniture to muffle the sound against the stone. Virion sighed, his shoulders dropping as he closed his eyes.

A male voice interrupted his moment of peace. "There were complications."

"Tiovriss." Virion smirked, his eyes slowly opening as he drawled, "I've no time for such excuses. Did you find the girl?" He stared across the room to where a portal appeared above the human's remains. Its gaseous gray color faded into the swirling edges of an oval while the inner area sharpened until a large man appeared. He looked sickly as the drab color of the portal washed him out, his paleness stressed by the quickly darkening blood running down his tan leathers.

"We lost her trail heading into Gailme but picked it up again when we doubled back into the wood. I followed them into the Wilds, missing them by a day at the—"

"How did you lose her, Tiovriss?" Virion rested his arms against his knees, the malice glittering in his eyes rivaling the fury in his voice. "The spell is foolproof. I enchanted the compass myself."

Tiovriss snorted. "The spell is only as useful as the girl. There's nothing to track if she doesn't use her powers."

"She's not using them?" Virion sat back, pinching his chin between his fingers. Why would the girl break the spell and not use the powers she possessed? It made no sense. Power changed everything.

"The compass has only spiked a few times. It's making her difficult to find but not impossible."

"Interesting. I wonder…" Virion smiled, his eyes calculating. "The girl might not know how to use her powers. That would account for the gaps in her tracking."

"A weakness we can exploit." Tiovriss ran a hand through his hair, the dried blood flaking against the blonde strands. "There's more."

Virion's gaze sharpened. "I have little tolerance for any more mistakes."

"The girl not using her powers is no mistake of mine, but that's of little consequence."

Virion rolled his eyes. "If you can't handle a simple task, I will find someone who can. Perhaps it's time for Alrithia to lead."

"You'll find it hard to pass me over for your whore." Tiovriss bared his teeth, panting.

"And why is that?" An edge crept into Virion's words.

"There's a distinct lack of people in the Wilds." A wild gleam shone from Tiovriss's eyes as he held a blood-covered hand in front of his face, smiling at the coppery splashes across his skin. "Blood magic requires a sacrifice, but nothing about the magic says the blood need be human."

Virion stood with a roar, flinging his chair across the room.

"Will you miss your pet?" Tiovriss laughed. "Alrithia called out for you as I bled her, convinced you'd avenge her death."

Virion froze with the taunting words. "You think I care about her?" He laughed, the sound cold and ugly. "I care naught for her life, only the inconvenience of breaking another to suit my tastes. You have caused me a great hassle."

"Poor pet. Such confidence for someone so easily tossed away." Tiovriss flexed his fingers, moving the glowing light of the portal across the blood. His gaze dropped to the ground and narrowed. "Better to start over. Her shrill squawking was unbecoming."

Virion descended the raised platform to stand beside the splinted chair in front of the portal. "Castian and Kaellam will join you soon. I don't expect there to be any more failures between the three of you."

"Good." Tiovriss bent out of Virion's view, and a terrified squeal broke as he stood, holding the hair of a bound young girl in his fist. "I took this one in Gailme, as you suggested. She should keep Castian happy, which is necessary because, as I said, there's more. I need him to cooperate." Tiovriss stepped closer to the portal. "There's someone with her. One who might be a Warden."

"What?" Virion tensed. He swallowed hard to remove the shaking from his voice. A Warden held the potential to ruin everything. "Are you sure?"

"Her magic led me to the boundary. The Veil's side is burned as if lit on fire, and there's a dead vraith not too far from it. It's drained of all magic." Tiovriss pulled a cloth from his back pocket and tried to wipe his hands clean.

"This complicates things." Virion set his jaw with a curt nod. "Castian and Kaellam are more than needed if one of their kind is involved."

Tiovriss scratched at the dried blood on his neck. "What do you want us to do?"

"The plan hasn't changed. Bring me the girl, but kill her little friend." Virion's gaze darkened. "And I would be careful not to fail this time, Tiovriss. Draven is running out of patience."

CHAPTER THIRTY-ONE

Erissa's bath ended with Reeva's disappearance.

What she had said to the Fae rang true. She wished to be at peace for a short time, but Reeva's words left her unable to find that peace as she lingered in the water.

She gave up trying to relax and left the bath.

Erissa wrapped a silk robe around her and sat on the edge of the bed, waiting for Rhazien. Maybe she should have stayed in the water. He did promise things would happen in its warmth.

But as soon as she made the decision to return to its depths, Rhazien called out through the door. "Little doe, are you decent?"

Decent? He wanted her decent? Erissa stood and moved to open the door, confusion drawing across her brow.

He was smiling as the door opened, but the smile faded as his desire slammed into her, his eyes raking her form and lingering where the silk clung to her skin in wet patches.

A blush fired at his slow perusal, and Erissa fidgeted with the robe's belt. "Are you coming in?"

Her question made his eyes snap to hers, but they quickly dropped again, halting at her breasts. Her nipples pebbled as he kept staring.

"Rhazien?" Erissa tugged on his sleeve.

Rhazien cleared his throat, looking anywhere other than her, and entered the room.

Erissa shut the door behind him and stood there, unsure of what to do as Rhazien kept his back to her. "Is something wrong? I thought you were coming back quickly?"

Rhazien spoke over his shoulder, still refusing to look at her again, his voice stiff. "I thought I'd wait until you finished your bath."

"You didn't have to." Erissa did not know what to do. He acted strange, but maybe he needed her to come to him. Anxiety prickled at the thought, but his desire still came to her, and hers built alongside it. She moved forward with cautious steps and placed her palm on his back, rubbing small circles into the tense muscles. "You need to bathe, and I can—"

He pulled away, spinning on his heel to face her. Rhazien reached for her hands, holding them gently, his thumbs mirroring her touch as they rubbed the backs. "You don't have to do this, little doe."

"But I thought we were going to…." Erissa frowned. "Isn't this what you wanted?"

"I want you to be sure of how you feel." Rhazien stepped away from her, dropping his hand to fist at his side.

Erissa braced her hands against her hips, tapping her foot. Her head spun from the difference in the desire of Rhazien's emotions and the coldness of his words. "I'm telling you what I want. Why are you acting like this?"

Rhazien ran a hand through the length of his hair. "I want you to want this as much as I do. We're not going to have sex because I've pressured or teased you into it."

Erissa snorted, throwing an arm out in dismissal as her desire crumbled. "That's rich, considering you're trying to talk me out of this. How much more clearly can I tell you I want this?"

"Did you tell me in truth?" Rhazien stepped closer. He trailed a hand against her shoulder. "You've hardly made a declaration of wanting more—of wanting me the way I desire to have you."

"What happened to the cocky arrogance from the Eshirene's Wood?" Erissa stalked away from him and toward the bed. She snapped at Rhazien over her shoulder. "For all your promises of more, you've done little to fulfill such words. Even today, it's been some time since I entered the bath, and you're only now returning to argue with me about it."

Rhazien followed her, the arrogant humor returning to his voice. "You were waiting for me, little doe?"

Erissa spun around, eyes wide and cheeks defensively stained. "No."

"You *were* waiting for me." Rhazien rocked back on his heels with a self-satisfied gleam in his eyes that matched the smirk twitching over his lips.

"And if I was?" Erissa wanted to slap the pleased look off his handsome face.

Rhazien's face softened. He picked up a strand of Erissa's hair, running his fingers around the curl. "I would have told you another time as I tell you now. You are exhausted and overwhelmed. To push you would have only served my needs and not yours."

"You don't get to make that decision for me." Erissa crossed her arms, her eyes impaling him as if her glower were a knife.

"Why are you so angry with me? I'm trying to do the right thing... for you." Rhazien tucked the strand of hair behind her ear.

"Because you make me question everything!"

They were both surprised by Erissa's shouting. She smoothed a shaking hand through her hair, taking deep, calming breaths.

Rhazien's response threw her. It was kind, and she hated that having someone treat her well crawled beneath her skin. She preferred it when he teased and cajoled her responses, taking control and drawing them from her in measured pieces where she did not have to think. His arrogance and surety in her response to him made it less awkward for her to give in to her desires. It made it easier for her to have them in the first place.

"That's not what I'm trying to do. I want to care for you the right way." Rhazien's tone reminded Erissa of the night they first met when he tried to learn her name, and he meant his words to be soothing. "I know I pushed you in the wood, but then the Veil took you. The pain I felt when I thought I had lost you... You needed rest and time to heal after what happened, and I know you're overwhelmed with reaching Cropari. All the change is weighing on you against everything you've known of life. I can feel it. I wanted to give you time to adjust, not an expectation of sex the moment we got here."

"I don't want you to make that choice for me. People have been making all of them without my input for most of my life, and I don't need that from anyone, especially not from you. I don't need more time. I want this. I want you. The more time I spend with you, the more I know it's true. But now I'm worried you don't feel the same, that this is all one-sided. I'm so far out of my depth with you." Erissa looked to the floor, flexing her toes as she wiggled them into the rug beneath. "I would have said as much if you had come earlier. I've never had to talk about my feelings for another before or voice any desires. It's new, and I didn't know what to say when you were teasing the other times."

"That's why I wasn't pushing." Rhazien put a finger to her chin, lifting her face until their eyes met. "I want you to feel free to make any choice you desire. I never wish you to feel like I've trapped you into a life you don't want. If we take this step, you need to understand it's not one that can be taken back. You will be mine as surely as I'll be yours. We will be bound together as *nayanams*."

Erissa grabbed his wrist, holding it in place when he would have moved it away. She stepped closer until her breasts pressed against his chest. "You've given me a kind of freedom I've never known. My heart beats freely now, Rhazien. And I feel it beating in rhythm alongside yours. It's a rhythm I can't silence. One I don't want to."

"Little doe—"

Micmus's voice called through the door. "Rhazien?"

Rhazien groaned, leaning down to press his forehead to Erissa's. "What does he want?"

"I heard that," Micmus called out again. "Thitelar is here. He needs your help at the forge. Something about the metal not bending right and needing your help with the fire."

"Give me a minute." Rhazien raised his head with a sigh. He stared at Erissa, regret weighing on his features. "We're not done with this conversation."

"You promise?" Erissa fiddled with the belt, keeping the robe in place.

He swooped down, capturing her lips in a fiery kiss that warmed her more than the bath had. She swayed toward him, grateful for Rhazien's hands on her shoulders, for she would have melted into the floor without them holding her steady.

Rhazien smiled as he pulled away. "I promise."

CHAPTER THIRTY-TWO

Erissa sat on the bed, waiting for Rhazien. But her exhaustion won before he returned. She slept within minutes of her head resting against the feather pillows.

Her restless sleep gave way to nightmares, the details of her past and present mixing until Faldeyr became rooted in the Veil and its hunger for consuming her powers. She fought to get away from him. Her father commanded the Veil against her, using it to wrap around her wrists like ghostly chains.

Faldeyr reached for her, and Erissa flinched as he cupped her cheek. "Erissa, love..."

Erissa reared back from him. Love? Had he ever called her by an endearment?

He spoke again. "Erissa, it's time..."

His sweet voice cajoled, inspiring anything but fear.

"Wake up, love..." Her father's image flickered, brown eyes and red hair fading in and out of view.

A hand reached for her, and Erissa had a strange desire to meet it halfway. She grabbed onto it, holding on for dear life, and let it pull her from the clutches of the Veil.

Erissa balked as she woke to a hand pressed against her forehead. She scrambled to the side, away from whomever it belonged to, and fell off the bed.

"Erissa!" Islone crawled across the bed, peering over it.

The cushions on the floor broke Erissa's fall. She lay there, catching her breath as she became aware of her surroundings. "I'm in Cropari?"

"Of course, love." Islone reached for her but stopped when Erissa flinched at the quick movement.

Fear laced her words. She did not care if she exposed herself to Islone. Erissa needed the reassurance, needed to know she was somewhere safe. "I'm not in Ember—home. I'm not home?"

Climbing off the bed, Islone crouched by her side. She spoke with patience, guiding Erissa back into the moment. "No. You're in Cropari with Rhazien and staying at my home. We're the only two people in the room."

"Rhazien?" Erissa whipped her head around the room, looking for him.

"He's with the children." Islone arranged herself on one of the other cushions, careful not to touch her. "I'm afraid Micmus kept him from returning to your side after helping Thitelar. When that man starts talking, there's no way out of it. By the time he came back into the room with food, you were already asleep. He left you to recover from the journey while he bathed away that wretched smell in the other spring."

Bowing her head, Erissa closed her eyes, steadying her breathing to temper the panic trying to take over.

"That must have been some nightmare."

Erissa slowly felt more in control. "They've returned recently."

"It's the travel, love. Exhaustion does strange things to our minds." Islone rose to her knees and picked up the tray from the bed. She placed it between them. "Let's eat. Having something in your belly will help."

Islone beamed at her expectantly. Erissa picked up a mug of soup with reluctance, dimming her eyes. But as she ate, it warmed her from the inside, and the tension left her frame.

"See? All better." Islone took the empty dish, stacking it on the tray. She picked it up and moved to place it on the bed. "We need to hurry. Rhazien and Micmus are waiting for us outside."

Erissa let Islone help her stand. "Where are we going?"

"To the night market." Islone picked up a basket full of clothing lined with wool. She passed it to Erissa. "Put these on, love, and come join us. You're in for a treat."

Erissa stared at the velvety night sky. It glinted with stars as she walked alongside Rhazien, Micmus, and Islone. They were not the only ones heading to the western part of the city where the night market was located. People packed the twisting road, heading in the same direction.

Everyone dressed differently in the evening. They had traded the short sleeves and thinner fabrics for thicker garments that covered them head to toe. They were no less colorful for the change, many wore the same scarves from earlier around their heads.

Islone had bundled her and Rhazien in the same manner, which had thrown Erissa at the time, given how hot it had been, but she was grateful for the extra layers. The heat of the day had disappeared, ushering in a stiff wind. It left a chill against the skin, even with the warm clothes. Erissa shivered against it.

"Cold, little doe?" Rhazien's arm wrapped around her shoulder.

Erissa leaned into his embrace. "A little."

Islone tucked the ends of her scarf beneath the neckline of her shirt. "It will be warmer in the market. Each stall has a *dameknaar*."

Erissa's brow knitted. "What's a *dameknaar*?"

"It's a hollow hearth made from clay, usually in the shape of a teardrop." Micmus reached for Islone's hand. "Not all the desert lands have clay. Cropari trades in clay-produced goods, making everything from the *dameknaars* and water jugs to pottery and jewelry."

Islone patted Erissa's arm. "You'll see in the market, dear."

The foursome continued their trek to the market, stopping every few steps as the townspeople came up to Micmus and Islone. The younger couples mostly sought answers to their problems, but even some of the older residents presented their issues to the couple. Erissa observed the interactions with growing curiosity.

"Micmus is Cropari's head merchant and mayor." Erissa turned to Rhazien as he spoke. "Cropari is a more progressive city than Emberhold. There's no central Lord here, and succession isn't passed through families. The people vote on their leaders."

Erissa listened to how Micmus talked to his people. He gave them his full attention, often stopping to hear the troubles laid before him. The exchanges differed from what she could remember of her father's interactions with his people. Micmus was fair but willing to listen, turning to Islone more than once for her opinion on whatever matter he was addressing. He would smile when she finished speaking as he clapped his hands in appreciation for her sage advice. Islone sputtered at his praise, refusing to accept it while she swatted his arm. But for all their playfulness, it was clear he held his wife in the greatest of esteem, and the people did as well.

The difference in their interactions compared to her parents was palpable. Her father had always treated her mother as if she were made of the thinnest vellum and would tear under too much pressure. It had been years since they had walked among the people, let alone spoken so candidly with them, and Faldeyr would consider it a hit to his pride to ask for her mother's help. Her mother would be reluctant to give it even if he did. After all, she had done anything but speak up over his treatment of her daughter. If she would not speak reason for her own flesh and blood, Erissa imagined she never would for someone else.

Rhazien squeezed her shoulder; his face tipped down in concern. Erissa reached a hand to squeeze his where it lay. She gave him a tight smile that did not reach her eyes but kept walking when Micmus and Islone moved on.

The cold had seeped into Erissa's bones by the time they reached the market. She did not believe a chill worse than the sleet that had plagued them on fleeing Emberhold existed, but the desert night made for a powerful rival, even with Rhazien keeping her pressed tightly to his side as she trembled.

Islone broke away from Micmus. She took one of Erissa's hands in her own. "The temperature changes can be difficult to get used to. Micmus might be a while. The market is around the corner. We can have some tea and warm up. He'll find us, eventually."

"Tea sounds lovely." Erissa tightened her fingers around Islone's for a moment. The older woman gave her hand a light tug, and Erissa took the hint, allowing herself to be moved from under Rhazien's arm. She picked up her stride, matching Islone's eagerness to get to the warmth the market promised.

As they rounded the corner, Erissa cried in delight as the market came into view. Tents sat in a large circle outlining the market, each one more richly detailed than the last. She had seen nothing like it.

"Cropari is fascinating. It's like color is a living entity with the way it's woven through the culture." Erissa tried to take everything in at once. "My home is quite plain in comparison. Everything matches."

Islone patted Erissa on the back. "Every city has its own beauty."

"Ember... my home," Erissa caught herself, "is nothing like this. Cropari is bursting with life. I never want to leave."

The market shone with light from the strangely shaped hearths Micmus had described. *Dameknaars* sat inside wide tents, the smoke from the fires undeterred as it left through a wide hole in the tops of the tents. The tents were open on one side, facing into the market with merchants sitting on the ground atop cushions. They displayed their wares in the same manner, with more cushions spread in front. The light cast enough of a glow to see everything laid out, but it stayed subdued by the enormity of the tents, keeping the brightness from blotting out the stars in the sky.

They made tents of every color, creating a tumultuous blend illuminated by the fires found within. Stitching covered the fabrics in ornamented designs with gems inlaid, much like Islone had done with her home's painting. It should have been garish with the conflicting colors, but the vibrancy brought everything together.

Islone led the way to one of the larger tents, where a group of elders crowded the opening. A soft floral scent hovered in the air as they came closer.

One man called out at their approach. "Lady Islone! And Rhazien, too? What a surprise!" He rushed to meet them, taking Islone's arm and escorting her to a cushion one man had vacated. She dropped Erissa's arm, leaving her to follow with Rhazien. "Come, come, m'lady. The tea's fresh. It's the perfect time for a cup."

"Higcraes, how many times have I told you to stop referring to me as your Lady? It's Islone to you and everyone else. There are no Lords or Ladies here." Islone's gentle eyes softened her rebuke.

"Never, m'lady." Higcraes's laughter echoed through the other elders. Deep lines wrinkled around the dark skin around his eyes and mouth. "We would never offer you such disrespect."

Islone lowered herself to sit on the cushion, her high cheekbones darkening as she shook her head in denial of his words. "There is no disrespect in considering us friends."

All eyes turned from Islone with Erissa and Rhazien's approach. He stopped next to Islone and gave a mock bow. "M'lady." Rhazien's lips pressed together as he fought to keep from laughing with the other men at his teasing.

Islone's tone filled with mirth. "Gentlemen, have you met Erissa?" A devilish look came to her eye, promising Rhazien retribution for his teasing. She raised her voice. "Our little Rhazien is newly wed."

The laughter and chatter around the market died as Islone's voice carried.

Higcraes whipped his head between Erissa and Rhazien. "He's what?"

Micmus groaned. "Wife! You didn't!"

"Husband?" Islone shrugged, her voice louder. "Everyone would have found out eventually that Rhaz has found himself a wife." Her smile grew as the market burst into action.

Micmus yelled above the commotion. "I hope you're pleased! If you don't scare the poor girl away after this, Rhazien will surely never bring her here again."

"They came to our doorstep with a sack each." Islone waved a dismissive hand with a roll of her eyes. "They'll thank me when they head home with more than one loaded camel."

"You are married?" Higcraes addressed Rhazien, the other men waiting intently for his answer. "By Cropari's standards or those of another city?"

"By two nights and a declaration to Micmus." Rhazien inclined his head. "My apologies for not stating it sooner to the rest of the elders. I didn't wish to overwhelm my bride on her first day."

"You've only just arrived." Higcraes turned to glance at the other men, continuing only once each had nodded. "We accept the reasoning for the delay, and we'll begin shortly."

Erissa missed something with their conversation. Her eyes widened as they moved around the market. Many of the people ran around frantically grabbing baskets and piling them with goods, while others used knives or their bare hands to rip strips of fabric from their clothing or tent sides. "Rhazien, what's going on?"

"Best prepare yourself, little doe." Rhazien stepped behind Erissa and placed his hands on either shoulder, pushing her down into the comfort of a cushion a woman had rushed over to them and placed on the ground. He chuckled as the woman bowed repeatedly to Erissa while backing away. "Croparians have strict traditions for marriage. We're about to get the full force of it."

The woman was bowing to her like she gave Erissa a great honor, and all the while, they were both lying. Erissa did not want to deceive anyone more than they already had. Her words were frantic. "But Rhazien, we aren't—"

"Marriage is different in Cropari, too," Rhazien interrupted. "There are no bride prices, no negotiations, and everyone of age may love as they please without the constructs found in other areas of Kaidreth." He leaned down, whispering the next words for her ears alone. "The lovers run away together, making a game of it with the town. They sneak out late at night, meeting the other in the shadows, and they go hide somewhere around the city."

Erissa leaned into him, shivering again, but not from the cold. "What happens to them?"

"The couple hides for two nights as everyone searches for them. If they make it to the third sunrise without being found, they come out of hiding and declare themselves married to their elders. Sound familiar, little doe?" Rhazien moved closer, his lips brushing against Erissa's neck with the hint of a kiss. "In the eyes of Croparian law, we *are* married."

Erissa's breath hitched with his whispered revelation, her heart picking up speed. The heavy pace battled between excitement and disbelief. A pang accompanied the fast pace, a yearning for the truth in his words and for a place of home within his heart, for he already occupied that space in hers.

She stared at the sea of people as they crowded around her and Rhazien. There were so many, as if the entire population stood around them. The older men had moved into the throng. Each person carried something in their arms with a strip of fabric hanging across their shoulders.

Higcraes stood in front of the crowd. He carried his own scrap of fabric, a teapot clutched in his hands. Much to Erissa's surprise, the man dropped to his knees, his bones creaking against the ground.

He pushed the teapot until it sat an arm's length from him on the ground in front of Erissa and then cupped his hands over his heart and leaned until his forehead touched the ground. "In the name of the Creator, we share a piece of our homes and our hearts, meager as some of these gifts might appear. They are given with love along with a prayer, a blessing to grace your home in the hopes of giving it the same heart that beats within our own."

Micmus pushed his way to the front of the crowd and knelt before the other man. He removed the scarf from around his head, the deep gold fabric matching that of Rhazien's eyes. He addressed Higcraes, "Rise, brother."

Micmus held out an end of the scarf and waited to speak until Higcraes sat back on his heels. "I recognize you, Elder Higcraes, and come to you as Rhazien Merrick's claimant with his father unable to be here and hold such an honor. He will forevermore be the eldest son of my household."

"Do you accept, Rhazien?" Higcraes asked.

Rhazien reached for Erissa's hands, threading their fingers together. "I accept."

Islone copied her husband, removing her emerald scarf. "I recognize you, Elder Higcraes, and come to you as Erissa..." she trailed off, twisting at the waist to arch a brow at Erissa. "Your name, dear?"

"N-n-n-ierling." Erissa swallowed the stutter. "Erissa Nierling."

Islone nodded and turned to address the elder once more. "I come to you as Erissa Nierling's claimant, with her mother unable to be here for such an honor. She will forevermore be the eldest daughter of my household."

"Do you accept, Erissa?" Higcraes asked of her.

Erissa hesitated. Her thoughts returned to Rhazien's instance earlier that having sex would bind them as *nayanams*. Would this be any different? Did she want it to be? Doubts assailed her. But as she looked at Rhazien, they quieted. His eyes shined as he stared at her, red flecks flashing in the gold and warming the coldest parts of her. She knew what she wanted to do.

CHAPTER THIRTY-THREE

"He is late, Neph." The magic around the dark-haired Fae pulsed as he sat on his throne. His shadows played about the white and blue carvings on the midnight stone. He ran his fingers through the magical mist. "I have better things to do than wait for disrespectful kings."

"You haven't been on time for anything in centuries, Novus." Nephinae sounded bored with his complaints.

Novus smiled like he scented blood, and his magic laughed. "That is your soft spot for the Seelie coming through."

"A soft spot for Yorrith?" Shock brought Nephinae from the shadows. "What soft spot?"

He counted on his fingers, a smirk playing against his mouth as his magic weaved around him. "One, you called him by his name. Two, do you think I do not know about your midnight palace rendezvous? Three, you defended his honor not but a moment ago. Four—"

"Defended his honor?" Nephinae crossed her arms. "I did nothing of the sort."

"Are we ignoring the midnight rendezvous?" Novus's smile widened.

"Will you stop saying rendezvous?" Nephinae threw up her hands, stomping around his throne to stand in front of him. "There are none. The Seelie kept evading my attempts at an audience. I simply tracked him down when he had no other choice but to listen to me."

"You simply tracked him down in his rooms five times and spent the entire night there?" Novus leaned forward, looking her up and down in the scandalous dress that exposed way more than it hid, scraps of silk-lined lace covered only the most strategic places held together by delicate links of gold chain. "Why would I ever have the impression they were rendezvous?"

She balled her fists, looking away from him. "If you say rendezvous one more time..."

"You'll what, Neph?" He reached forward, gripping her chin and forcing her eyes to his. "Wear another sexy dress for the King?"

Nephinae smirked this time. "I'll—"

"Lovers really should flirt in private." Yorrith's voice broke through their bickering as he walked up behind them. Novus tensed as Nephinae flushed a brilliant shade of red.

She jerked against Novus's hold. "We are not lovers."

Novus let go of her chin, leaning back to lounge on his throne once more. "Seelie, do you take pleasure in abusing the time of others?"

"No more than you do, making others walk in on such vulgarity." Yorrith's chest heaved with thinly controlled anger.

Novus stared between the two Fae, noting their reactions. He had been teasing Nephinae, but he gave a second consideration to her actions. More lay between the two than he realized. Rendezvous might be the correct word for their late-night meetings.

Genstine hobbled into the room, breaking his train of thought and the uneasy silence between the three as she carried a trembling tray of wine in her hands. The length of the chains she wore rattled against the floor. Her mutilated toes and fresh wounds were visible in the bright light streaming in through the bank of frosted windows behind the throne.

Yorrith gaped in horror at her appearance. "By the gods, what did you do, Unseelie?"

Novus flicked his eyes at the battered Fae shaking in her chains before dismissing Yorrith with a bored wave of his hand. "Don't mind her."

"Don't mind her?" Yorrith's indignation grew as red as his face. "Her gods' forsaken toes are missing."

"A fitting punishment." Novus sighed, already tired of the Seelie's company. The King never stuck to his own affairs.

The King stared at him as if he had grown two heads, disgust curling his lip. "No crime justifies cutting off a female's toes."

"We are not here to discuss my pet." Novus would not give an inch to justify his actions. Let the Seelie believe what he wants. He earned his reputation, but no one ever stopped to ask why he drew such a harsh line. Perhaps if they knew Genstine's crime, others would not be so quick to judge. If the Seelie wished to remain in blissful ignorance, he would do nothing to change the King's mind. "May we get to the matter at hand?"

Yorrith took a menacing step forward. "If you think I'll ignore this—"

"You have no choice but to ignore it, Seelie." Novus let the aura of his power leak from his control, forcing Yorrith to bend at the waist. He would not be challenged while seated on the Unseelie throne. "I hold the power in this exchange, and you would do well to recognize it. Nothing in the bargain dictates how I will treat the Veiled One. Remember that before you try to intervene in my court."

Yorrith fought for control, his fists clenched. "Are you threatening my—"

"Who is having a lover's quarrel now?" Nephinae snapped her displeasure, interrupting their exchange. Despite her intentions, she overcame the tension, and both men calmed down.

Novus let his magic recede, gaining control of his temper as the mist faded. "Bickering changes nothing about the situation at hand. The girl will be brought to me. You are to leave in two days' time with Nephinae and whoever she chooses to accompany your journey."

"I want a new deal, Unseelie," Yorrith insisted.

"That's Unseelie King to you," Novus sneered.

Yorrith ground his teeth. "You are not King yet, not while Draven still draws breath."

Novus waved away Yorrith's words. "I am the true King, and you know it as well as I. The magic claimed me the moment I bested Draven in the Keeping War. Your insistence on belittling my position does nothing to help your cause, or do you want me to take it out on the girl?"

Yorrith shook with rage. "She will be treated with respect and safe from any harm. Without the deal, I won't help you."

Novus cocked his head to the side, staring at the king with bright eyes that honed in on the king's weaknesses. "Do you believe you're in a position to be making deals?"

Yorrith held firm. "I will break the original deal that binds her to you and suffer the consequences before I see her come to harm."

"The consequences are your death." Novus felt nothing at the King's demands. He shrugged. "If you break the deal, it changes nothing about what I must do, but it would complicate matters."

"Then so be it." Yorrith lifted his chin. "Make the deal, Unseelie, or I won't help you."

Nephinae intervened at the mention of breaking the Fae bargain. "If a deal keeps things civil, what is the harm?"

"The harm is a war looms, and someone is sure to betray us, for the Seelie and Unseelie never agree on anything. Many on both sides joined Draven in the Keeping War. We cannot predict if they will do so again, with Virion gaining influence in his quest to free Draven. I can no more guarantee the girl's safety than I can my own." Novus sat forward. "What you ask for speaks of emotion, not your position, Seelie King. I won't make the deal. You are bound either way. Your death cannot save the girl. At least by my side, she stands a chance of surviving the coming war."

Nephinae moved closer to the Seelie King, her doubts filling the air with her fear for the King's life. "Novus…"

"Enough, Neph. I won't entertain this discussion any longer. Gather your supplies and your companions. You leave in two days." Novus stood, calling for this magic. He stepped into the shadows as they wrapped around him, watching as Nephinae stepped toward the King, her face falling as he jerked away from her.

As he faded into the mist of power, Novus pitied her. Everyone thought him heartless. Maybe they were right after all he endured under his father's rule following the War of the Remaking. But another war loomed on the horizon, and someone had to remain impartial to the girl and her role, for he would not hesitate to sacrifice the Veiled One's life to save them all.

CHAPTER THIRTY-FOUR

Erissa stared between the people in front of her, the silence growing. Anxiety churned within her breast. She turned to Rhazien, her breathing picking up pace. She opened her mouth in a silent question. She wanted him to be happy with her decision, but the people of Cropari held her back.

"It's alright, little doe." Rhazien tucked a long, dark curl behind her ear. "They're honoring you as a bride of Cropari, but you don't have to accept. They will understand. I will understand."

Erissa exhaled, a helpless whine leaving her lips. They offered them a ceremony of sorts from what she gathered. But one steeped in a lie, no matter how much she wished it to be true. Looking around the market at the gathered people, she felt every protest shouting in her head. They gazed at her with an eager sort of kindness and excitement that pulled at the pieces of her heart. No one in Emberhold offered her such acceptance, and no one in Emberhold had cared for her the way Rhazien did. If this was a lie, she wanted it. "I accept."

Higcraes nodded, the motion repeated by the rest of the elders standing behind him. He took a knife and cut his scarf in two. "We split our offering, a boon to the Creator. May he bless you before the gods and offer the protection of the Fefnirion."

"To the bonds that tie." Micmus handed his scarf to the elder.

Islone did the same. "And the creation of one."

With quick hands, Higcraes knotted each strip together until his scarf combined the others, creating a circle.

When finished, he handed the scarves to Micmus and stood to face the crowd. "Approach, friends. We honor Rhazien and Erissa this night with our prayers and gifts of home and hearth." He quit the crowd after speaking, leaving room for the others.

One after another, the Croparians dropped to their knees, pushed their gifts into the growing pile surrounding the couple, and gave their strips of fabric to Islone. She tied them to the circle, the women's scraps on her side and the men's on the end with Micmus' scarf. When she judged them to be finished, Islone would move to the next open section on the circle. It reminded Erissa of the canopied tents with their mixed patterns.

Erissa went numb against the constant attention. She plastered a smile on her face and said all the right things while an ache grew inside of her. The number of people overwhelmed her, but something else nagged at her thoughts. Her skin crawled in the presence of such unconditional kindness. It had been a long time since anyone other than Rhazien had shown her kindness, the concept as foreign to her as the lands and people were. She chafed against the unexpectedness of it despite how right it resonated within her.

Emberhold and its people had stopped being her home the second they abandoned her to her father's mercy, and everyone turned a blind eye to it. But Cropari? These people welcomed her openly and warmly, so why would this reception leave her feeling even more disconnected?

The tracing of Rhazien's hand against her neck startled Erissa out of her melancholy place. He guided her closer, murmuring the words against her ear. "That ache in your chest is building inside of me. Are you overcome, little doe? It's been a long day."

Erissa twisted her fingers in her lap. "It's disconcerting."

"What is?" Rhazien grazed the back of her neck with his thumb. "The attention? It can be a little much, but everyone means well. They would never want to make you feel uncomfortable."

"It's not that, Rhazien. It's..." Erissa tipped her head down, her voice small. "The kindness... it's strange to receive it after living without any. You, Islone, Micmus, these people..." She looked up, her eyes filling with unshed tears. "I don't know how to act or what to do with it."

Rhazien cupped her face, brushing away the lone tear that traced her cheek. He kissed her, taking his time, much to the amusement of everyone around them who had not heard the pain behind Erissa's muted words.

She let herself relax, pouring all her confusing emotions into the press of his lips on hers. With little care for the opinion of those watching, Erissa lost herself to the kiss. Rhazien remained her only constant, the one who kept her safe and grounded at every turn.

As Rhazien broke the kiss, she hoped her ability to rely on herself would grow with time. She wanted to mirror his strength instead of always stealing it.

"We're almost at the end of the receiving, and then it won't be long until we head home for the evening." Rhazien smoothed a hand down her hair.

Erissa contemplated the dwindling line. Only a few more people remained, clutching their offerings for the couple. She nodded, pasting the smile back on her face as a hunched older woman approached. Rhazien had borne much for her. She owed it to him to last through the end of the line. She also owed it to those who welcomed her without qualms, distrust, or malice.

The woman carried a woven basket full of orange spheres. She bowed as everyone else had, pushing the offering to lie at Erissa's feet and handing Islone the strip of fabric.

Erissa peered at them with curiosity. "What are those?"

"Oranges, dear. They're a citrus fruit." Islone picked one up. "Do you want to try one?"

She hesitated, watching as Islone dug her fingernail into the soft flesh of the fruit and peeled the skin away, revealing a white texture on the outside.

Islone hooked her thumbs into the top part of the fruit and split it down the middle. As she did, a sweet, crisp fragrance permeated the surrounding air.

Erissa reached for a piece of fruit Islone held out for her. She lifted it to her nose, inhaled the fresh, sweet scent, and popped it into her mouth. As the flavor burst across her tongue, Erissa's smile grew genuine, and she wiggled where she sat, savoring the juicy flavor.

Islone laughed, handing Erissa more fruit, which she eagerly gobbled down with a moan. Nothing she had tasted in her lifetime compared to it. It smelled familiar to her, which surprised her. Emberhold's cold weather rarely grew more than berries and apples, and even those tended to be imported from the East.

"Delicious, are they not?" Islone peeled more of them.

Rhazien plucked a piece of the fruit from Erissa's hand and popped it into his mouth. She glared at him, her mouth too full to say anything, and Rhazien chuckled. "I think we've found your favorite food, little doe."

He leaned across her, reaching for another orange from the basket, and Rhazien's scent hit her. Her mouth dropped open as she recognized it as the same scent from the market, only this time, she could make out the other aroma.

The intoxicating blend made Erissa's mouth water. It brought her back to that moment around the fire in the woods, the scent permeating the air with something she did not recognize as they took comfort from one another. She moved closer to Rhazien, nuzzling against his neck and breathing deeply. "Rhazien, you smell like cedar, jasmine flowers, and oranges."

"Oranges, huh? They're most certainly your favorite now." Erissa felt his bark of laughter vibrate through the skin where her nose lay tucked against him. "If you keep doing that, you're going to get more than a single kiss."

At the sound of others laughing, Erissa jerked away, her cheeks flaming. She wished the ground would swallow her into its depths, embarrassed by her brazen reaction.

"Never be ashamed of showing your love for someone, Erissa." Islone finished tying the last fabric scraps to the circle and handed it to Micmus.

If only it were that easy for her. Erissa had loved her parents at one point. When did the chains kill the emotion? When her earlier attempts to break out of her room and find her mother were met with scolding—and later, fists from her father—rather than the loving embrace of a parent who wanted her around? Erissa felt hollow as the memories flashed through her mind. When love is attached to violence, there is nothing but shame until the feeling of love disappears altogether.

Islone rose and held her hands out to Erissa. "Let us stroll around the market. There's something you might enjoy seeing."

Erissa accepted Islone's help and rose from the cushion. She hooked their arms together and steered Erissa further into the market. They walked in silence until Islone led her to a pole in the middle of the area. It had lines coming from it, reaching to the ground in a makeshift tent. Each of the lines held thin strips of fabric knotted several layers deep.

Erissa reached for the clothes, stopping short of touching them. "They're beautiful."

Islone trailed her fingers across the fabrics. "We call each of them a *rihpaidir*. They're prayers. We tie them here to let the prayers carry on the wind to the heart of the Creator."

"Do you think the prayers actually make it to the Creator?" Erissa frowned.

Prayers had always been nothing more than wishful thinking. At least in her life anyway, but something about the day made her wish the Creator would answer.

"You tell me." Islone bent down to pick a scrap of fabric from the closest basket. She held it out to Erissa.

Taking the scrap of fabric, Erissa contemplated what she should pray for. She wanted freedom and a future that went beyond how others sought to fear or use her. Maybe the Creator would hear her prayer for freedom, but her thoughts turned to Rhazien. He had taken her hand in the middle of a crisis and brought her into the light. She feared what the future held, scared of what he hid, but she did not fear him. Erissa tied the *rihpaidir* to the line with shaking hands and closed her eyes as she offered a prayer into the wind.

Arms wrapped around her waist from behind, and Erissa relaxed into Rhazien's embrace. She had smelled him as he approached, savoring the sweet, crisp earthiness unique to him.

Rhazien kissed the top of her head. "What did you pray for?"

Erissa's cheeks, colored from the cold, deepened, grateful their position hid her face from his prying eyes.

A deep voice saved her from answering. "You know better than to ask after her prayers, boy."

Erissa twisted in Rhazien's arms to view who had spoken. One elder had walked over to them. Stooped with age, his skin wrinkled like old leather left in the sun for too long. She started to smile as Rhazien laughed, but the smile froze, half spread across her face.

A clammy feeling spread through her chest, clutching at her lungs and stealing the breath from them. Erissa tensed in Rhazien's arms, and he held her tighter with the change in her posture.

Behind the elder stood the blurred shape of his soul.

Erissa braced herself for what she knew would come next but failed as the seductive words washed over her.

"It's time. It's time. It's time."

"We need. We need. We need."

"Join us. Join us. Join us."

The words were strong, the soul's voice firm and insistent as if the Veil itself bled through its call to lure her in.

And it awoke the voice lying dormant within her. *"It's the sweetest of temptations, and you deny it every time. Answer the call."*

Erissa screwed her eyes shut, shaking her head. She would not listen, would not give in.

"You punish us with your foolishness." The voice sulked.

Anger and fear fought within her as her heart filled with dread. Why did this have to happen here, of all places, and on a night such as this? Her body shook. She would never be free from this power, not when a day did not pass in the city without her becoming the harbinger of someone's death.

Erissa sagged in Rhazien's arms, dropping her weight against his chest. His arms turned to steel, hoisting her up to keep her from falling to the ground. "Erissa?"

Islone turned worried eyes to her. "Are you alright, dear?"

She should say nothing to acknowledge she knew what would happen on the morrow. The thoughts died as she considered the sense of family the people of Cropari created around one another. The man had been one of those who offered her his heartfelt gift. She would not betray such kindness by not telling him what awaited him on the morrow.

"You need to spend the evening with your loved ones." Erissa did not mean to blurt the words at the man, but now that she had, the others did not stop coming. "It's important. You cannot leave their sides. This night is all you will have. Make it precious." Her voice broke on the last word, and she dropped her eyes, no longer able to keep looking at the man. "I'm sorry."

"M'lady?" asked the man, addressing Islone.

"Erissa? Are you well?" Islone reached a hand to Erissa's forehead.

Rhazien moved her out of reach before Islone's hand could touch her. He held Erissa aloft, supporting her dead weight. "You're sure?"

"It's there. Beyond his shoulder." Erissa buried her head into Rhazien's chest. "I wish it were not so. I would give anything to make it not so. This man does not have long left."

Erissa raised her head, her eyes full of unshed tears. She gazed upon the elder and watched the confusion change to understanding as her eyes burned brighter.

The man swallowed. "Are you a seer, child?"

Islone laughed uncomfortably. "The girl is no seer. I don't know what kind of game they're playing at—"

"Of sorts." Erissa cut Islone off, biting down hard on her lip. She eased the pressure as the metallic taste of blood hit her tongue. "You will have tonight at the least. I cannot guarantee tomorrow."

"The gods have blessed me this night with your presence." The man held his hand out for Erissa. She paused only for a moment. His hand lay feverish against hers, his fingers stiff. He smiled when she tightened her hold. "You have given me a gift in knowing it's my time. I can savor this night and prepare for what comes tomorrow. Thank you, child."

The man hurried off, and the soul trailed behind him reluctantly. It had not stopped calling out to her, repeating its phrase.

"Explain yourselves." Islone's eyes filled with fire, her tone demanding.

Erissa ignored her, lost in her grief as she watched the elder return to his family. His face filled with peace as he brought each person in for a hug. "I don't even know his name."

Rhazien answered her in a hushed tone. "Wilidon. The elder's name is Wilidon."

"Rhazien Merrick," Islone demanded. "You will tell me what this is about."

Rhazien sighed, loosening one of his arms to reach up and guide Erissa's head to his shoulder. "There is much we need to tell you, but it will wait until tomorrow.

"Can we retire for the night? It's all too much." The hollowness of her voice echoed loudly in her head. Erissa clung to Rhazien. Her fists bunched against his shirt.

"Alright, little doe." Rhazien kissed her nose, his eyes crinkling in concern. "Let's go tuck you in."

Erissa offered no resistance as Rhazien led her to the market entrance. Islone walked beside them, speaking angrily to Rhazien. Erissa tuned her out. Her eyes tracked the elder. He walked from person to person, embracing all he passed, spending a moment with each person, a peaceful light adding a youthful glow to his features.

As if he sensed her watching, he met her gaze and gave a slight nod, his smile kind and filled with gratitude. Erissa returned the nod, letting her words carry on the wind. "May the Creator be with you, Wilidon."

CHAPTER THIRTY-FIVE

Sweat, blood, and urine covered the dungeon floor.

Opening his mouth as he inhaled, Barrett tried ridding himself of the putrid stench coming from the depths of the cell-lined undercroft. His efforts were in vain. He gagged at the taste of the air and closed his mouth. Better lodged in his nose than coating his tongue.

The blacksmith held firm in his silence, refusing to betray his son no matter what torture Barrett unleashed.

"Your fortitude is admirable." Barrett's chest heaved in the frigid air. His shoulders and arms ached from his ministrations, his limbs heavy with regret. He longed to be anywhere else. "But this fortitude will also see you killed."

The man hung in the center of the chamber, his wrists bound by iron and suspended high into the air. His shirt lay in tatters, most of the back ripped away, with only the front hanging like an apron to protect him from the cold. A week's worth of cuts, blood, and bruises covered his frame, the man barely recognizable under the blood and grime.

Barrett crouched in front of Tyrmar. "Faldeyr's patience extends only as far as it benefits him. If I fail, he will send another more vicious in their interrogation. And I can guarantee it will be one of your girls chained here next."

The mention of his children caught Tyrmar's attention.

"Please." Barrett did not consider himself above begging. "Give me a name. Pick any town, and I will sell whatever tale you give me and see you and your family safely away from his reach."

Curiosity brightened Tyrmar's eyes, and Barrett nearly smiled. A lesser man would have broken long ago. Maybe Erissa would stand a real chance with a son raised by a man with such strength.

Tyrmar strained against the chains, the long lengths rattling. "Why?"

"I don't want to be here, but an unbreakable vow traps me." Barrett ran a bloodied hand through his beard, the tangled growth his one continued act of defiance toward his brother. "I cannot lie to his Lordship. You must give me a name. It doesn't matter if your son is there so long as a name falls from your lips."

The man considered his words, intelligence flashing behind his bloodshot eyes. "You would twist the truth and sacrifice your honor for an unknown man and his family?"

"I have seen you stretch the truth without hesitation for the benefit of your son, and you both saved her with no regard for your own safety."

Tyrmar coughed, wincing against the bruising on his chest. "And you know this for certain? That we helped the girl?"

Barrett stood and walked to the door where a satchel sat upon a wooden chair. Flipping it open, he pulled a twist of metal from its confines, holding it as he stood in front of the blacksmith.

The man's face paled beneath the bruises lining his cheeks and jawline. Tyrmar set his mouth, saying nothing, dissent and fear battling in his eyes.

"Your son's craftsmanship is remarkable, especially with his contraptions hanging from the stable rafters. Besides, did you really believe I wouldn't notice two people lying in that bed?" Barrett twisted the length of metal in his hands. "He's smart too. What better way to startle the horses than to throw a snake at their hooves?"

"He's a clever one," Tyrmar admitted. He shifted his weight, groaning in his attempt to right himself and relieve the pressure from his arms.

"I could say the same for Erissa. It took years of giving her the same book with the hidden staircase in the hearth, but she finally figured it out."

"You care for the girl." Surprise stressed Tyrmar's words.

A sad ghost of a smile flickered in the torchlight. "Is it so hard to believe?" The shock hurt, even if Barrett deserved it. No one would think he cared for his niece, no matter his question, with all he was forced to ignore of her treatment.

"Against your actions?" Tyrmar answered without hesitation. "Yes."

Barrett flinched at the man's reminder.

"I have no true knowledge of what happened to the girl, but Rhazien believed her life was on the line. He risked the safety of us all for that belief." Tyrmar paused, weighing his words. "It is you who hunts her. It is you who has hunted us all. And now it is you who tortures me in this dungeon. Surely, my doubts about your affection for the girl are warranted."

"I made a vow. One before her birth."

"What vow keeps a man trapped within inaction?"

Barrett took his time answering, unsure of how much to reveal. He stared at Tyrmar, taking the man's measure. The truth hovered across his tongue.

Tyrmar coughed again, interrupting his thoughts as the man twisted his body to hack over his shoulder. Barrett smothered a laugh at the absurdity of the man's ability to maintain proper etiquette when bound by chains. He choked down the desire as the remaining scraps of Tyrmar's shirt fell from his arms, exposing the dragon tattoo twisting across his shoulder and down his peck.

Barrett's blood ran cold at the inked design. "You're a Warden."

"No one has called me such a name in a long time." Tyrmar tilted his head. "How would you know of such a thing?"

"It explains why I haven't broken you after all this time. It would take more than a human to break a Fefnirion."

Tyrmar gave a slight nod. "You did better than most, I'll give you that. But you didn't answer my question. How do you know about the Wardens?"

Barrett nearly denied the man an answer, but what would the point of that denial be with so much already said between them? Barrett wiped a hand across his face. "Thonalan."

If Barrett thought the man white earlier, it had nothing on his ghostly appearance now, an impressive feat with his darker complexion.

"Thonalan?" Tyrmar's eyes widened. "What is the traitor's role in all of this?"

His surprise caught Barrett off guard. "He's a traitor?"

Tyrmar's gaze darkened. "He backed the mad Unseelie King, Draven, in the Keeping War, only switching sides at the last minute and helping to seal him in the Veil because he knew the last of the Fefnirion were getting involved. The bastard would have helped Draven to the end."

Barrett swore. "Faldeyr and Thonalan are well known to each other. His wife introduced them."

Tyrmar scoffed. "It's not possible. The wife of a human Lord never has dealings with the Fae."

"I can assure you this one does." Barrett gazed at the stone ceiling, picturing his sister-in-law lazing about her rooms. "Vilotta is quite proud of her connections beyond the Mists."

"Vilotta is here?"

"She's Faldeyr's wife and Lady of this manor."

Tyrmar's brow drew together. "How does the girl and your loyalty to your bastard brother factor into this?"

Barrett winced at the disgust in the blacksmith's voice at the mention of his so-called loyalty. "Faldeyr and Vilotta were unable to conceive and went to the Seelie Fae King to beg his aid for Vilotta's desire for a child. When he agreed to help them, a witch had a prophetic vision telling the King the child would be the Veiled One."

Tyrmar's mouth fell open. Words failed him as he stuttered.

"Vilotta nearly fainted with the news." Barrett wet his dry lips. "Word spread quickly. Thonalan and Cobrias, the Seelie High Lords, sought an audience with my brother and his wife. Faldeyr fell under the spell of Thonalan's grandeur, and the two hatched a plan. When the time came, they would use the child as a power play against the Seelie throne, installing Thonalan as the new Seelie king. In return for his help, Thonalan would join Faldeyr in a war against the humans, instilling Faldeyr as their King under one united sovereignty."

"And your part in this?" Tyrmar asked.

Barrett shook his head. "I knew nothing of their true ambitions. Faldeyr and Thonalan came to me with a plan to keep Erissa safe from those in the Unseelie court who would seek to gain her magic. The two of them argued for the need for a Fae bargain. I pledged my vow to serve Faldeyr in any way he demanded, believing he would wield that power for Erissa's safety, and Thonalan sealed the bargain for us. To break the bargain in any manner forfeits Erissa's life. That is the cost of the bargain." Barrett scratched at the dried blood on his arm. "But the magic doesn't work on you. I feel no compulsion to keep my secrets, though I don't understand why that is."

"It's the Warden powers. Fefnirions are protected from binding magic." Tyrmar sighed. "There is nothing more foolish than a human mixing with Fae deals."

"I know that now, but at the time?" Barrett shrugged. "I have loved the child since she rested in her mother's womb, and I was desperate to do anything to see her safe and happy. Now, I am only desperate to see her freed from her father."

Understanding softened Tyrmar's face, and he nodded, wincing at the strain in his neck. "Hindsight teaches a man many things."

Barrett tugged against the collar of his high-necked shirt, the fabric choking him against his many regrets. "It was easier in the beginning. Easier for Faldeyr to play the loving parent. Things changed after a time. Erissa's powers were more than we knew how to contain. His anger and resentment grew, and I was bound by the bargain to honor my vow no matter what violence he visited on his daughter."

"Did Vilotta never intervene?" Tyrmar shifted his weight from one shoulder to the other with a wince. "She's the girl's mother. It's hard to believe she damned her to the fate set before her."

Revulsion colored Barrett's words. "Vilotta is a vain creature concerned only with her personal needs. With Erissa locked away and out of sight, Vilotta kept her out of mind."

The two men fell silent for a few moments, each grappling with the information.

Tyrmar spoke first, his sympathy palpable. "I imagine it must carry unmeasurable pain to watch the girl suffer, knowing the only way you can save her is through death."

"Sometimes, I think it might have been better to break the vow. Even if it meant costing Erissa her life." Barrett did not recognize the sound of his voice as he said the words that haunted him any time he let his mind wander. "Pure selfishness guided my actions to keep her here. I will never have children of my own. It's why Faldeyr is Lord despite my being older.

By the Creator, all I hold dear in this world is that girl. She is mine in my heart."

"There is much I wish I could change with how I handled things with my family. My girls share no blood with my wife and I, but they are no less mine than Erissa is yours. My oldest daughter died because of my poor decisions and inaction." Tyrmar cleared his throat and spit a wad of blood-laced bile onto the floor. "You did what you believed to be right. There will come a time when Erissa understands this."

"You give me far too much grace for my role in all her tragedy."

"And you give yourself too little," Tyrmar said. "You made a fool's bargain, but you made it intending to keep the girl safe."

"I've been stalling the hunt in every way the bargain allows."

The two men eyed each other, a sense of respect growing between them.

"Avrenia," Tyrmar offered. "My boy will take the girl to Avrenia. I have a friend who lives there. One that can help hide Erissa's magic. Rhazien will seek the man's help."

Barrett nodded.

A smile cracked across Tyrmar's split lips, and Barrett offered one in return.

"If our prisoner can still smile like that, you're failing, brother."

Barrett stiffened at Faldeyr's voice as the Lord walked into the room behind him, sweat beading across his upper lip, paranoid his brother had heard their conversation. He wiped it away with the back of his hand, lest his brother believe it to be more than the exertion from his torture efforts. "So now you're lecturing me on the right way to torture someone?"

Tyrmar let out a feral snarl.

Confused by the man's action, Barrett arched a brow at the Warden. He turned, following his gaze to regard his brother. His breath died in his lungs.

Faldeyr gripped the arm of a red-headed young girl, her face so pale Barrett feared she might faint at any moment. "What is she doing here?"

"Leverage. If he won't break for himself, perhaps he will for his daughter." Faldeyr moved closer to his brother. "What will it be, blacksmith? Your son or your daughter?"

Panic filled Tyrmar's eyes. He glanced from his daughter to Barrett.

Barrett forced himself to breathe. Lifting a hand, he used it to tug at his beard and disguised a slight nod in the action, hoping the man picked up on it.

"Avrenia." Tyrmar's shoulders slumped as much as the tension in the chains allowed. "I sent him to an old friend in Avrenia."

"This friend's name?" Faldeyr demanded.

Tyrmar ground his teeth. "Cornaith."

"And the girl?" Faldeyr salivated in his eagerness.

"She is with him. I swear it." Tyrmar looked at his daughter. "Release her. Please. Nerivae had no part in any of this."

Barrett watched sadistic pleasure swirl behind his brother's all too observant eyes, his stomach dropping as a sick feeling settled in its depths. That feeling intensified when Faldeyr smiled.

"Why would I do that?" Faldeyr sneered. "There are consequences to be had for in aiding the girl's escape. You stepped too far, blacksmith."

"By the gods, Faldeyr." Barrett stared at his brother in horror. "She's a child."

Faldeyr waved a hand in dismissal. "And by the end of the night, she will be nothing more than another body on the pyre, along with her father."

At his callous words, the girl began sobbing and tried to twist from Faldeyr's hold.

Tyrmar let out a roar as he fought against his chains. "You bastard. She is innocent in this."

Barrett straightened to his full height. "I won't do it."

His eyes hardening, Faldeyr shoved the girl into Barrett's arms. "Do I need to command it of you, brother?"

The brothers stared at one another, neither willing to back down.

"It would be far too easy to order you to kill them." Faldeyr chuckled, a pitying look in his eyes. "Imagine it, brother. Imagine all the excruciating ways I can make you to torture the girl before you slit her father's throat in front of her and burn her alive."

"You would kill an entire family—a woman and her children—for the sins of the husband?" Barrett demanded.

Faldeyr shrugged. "It will serve as a deterrent."

Barrett shoved the girl behind him. "This is madness."

"And I will relish in every part of it if it gets me what I want." Faldeyr made for the door, turning to regard Barrett over his shoulder. "It's your choice. This can be quick and clean or drawn out and torturous. You have until sundown, brother."

CHAPTER THIRTY-SIX

Only a coward hid in their room.

The notion stung with its truth. Hiding from the world had its comforts rather than facing what waited for her beyond the bedroom door; Islone would make her leave after what happened last night.

Erissa squeezed her eyes against the tears, not from sorrow but anger. They spilled over, leaving a trail that ended in salt against her lips. She pressed them together, grinding her teeth against the unfairness of it. For Wilidon. For Rhazien. For herself. Her powers offered no escape.

She sat with her back to the door, perched on the side of the sunken spring. Her feet dangled in the water. Erissa wanted to submerge her entire body in such a luxury one more time. The foolish action would do nothing except taunt her.

The door swung open with a creak. Erissa sighed at the intrusion. "Rhazien, I'm not ready to face anyone."

"Which is why I came to you instead of him."

Erissa's head whipped to the side. Islone stood in the doorway. She carried a tea service and a plate piled high with food in her arms.

She chuckled as Erissa's stomach grumbled. "If I had known you refused Rhazien's offer of food this morning, I would have come sooner."

Islone walked over to the spring. She sat the tray down, leaving enough room between it and Erissa for her to sit. "You're hiding from me."

Erissa wiped at her tears. She stayed silent, a mulish set to her mouth.

"I can't blame you." Islone used her shoulder to bump against her. "Rhazien talked to us."

The blood left Erissa's face. "Then you already know who I am and what I can do." She moved to stand, tripping. She righted herself before she pitched herself into the water. "I'll leave first thing in the morning."

"None of that now. We have no desire to make you leave. Rhazien told us everything and suggested I talk to you about it. But all I want to know is if you're alright." Islone busied herself pouring tea. "I can't imagine how hard it must be to see such a fate when there's nothing you can do to change it."

Erissa tracked the movement of the older woman's hands, her chest as tight as her brow. "You're not making me leave?"

"Why would you leave?" Islone held out a clay cup. "Drink this. You've built this interaction up in your mind into something terrible, and I'm afraid you're in for a bit of a shock."

"I don't... what?" Erissa gripped the cup, trying not to drop it as Islone shoved it into her hands. She held onto the clay with a desperate strength that would have broken porcelain.

"A shock, dear. You're having a shock." Islone picked up her own cup, sipping the hot tea.

"A shock?" Erissa met Islone's calm gaze.

Islone nodded. "Take a sip of your tea. It will help your nerves."

Erissa lifted the cup to her lips. Anything to keep from shaking. The floral flavor burst over her tongue, balanced by a sweet mint, and something sharp warmed its way down her throat to settle contentedly in her stomach. She drained the cup.

"Better?" Islone leaned to pour her another cup as Erissa nodded. "Tea has a way of soothing the most ragged parts of us, and I would wager you need more soothing than others. You carry the weight of something so heavy for one so young."

Erissa sipped the next cup, savoring the taste. The tension she held onto waned, whether from the warmth of the tea or the calm presence of the woman beside, made little difference. The gentle slopes of her shoulders dropped in relief. "We traveled for quite some time while seeing no one. I had almost forgotten what I am until last night."

"What is it you think you are?"

The question made Erissa pause. Her power held no name to her knowledge, and she had never thought to ask Reeva if one existed. "No matter where I go, I will see the souls of those fated to die. I am sick of being a symbol for death."

Islone waved a hand in dismissal. "You give yourself too much power."

"And you give me too little." Erissa's gaze held firm. "It was different seeing Elder Wilidon's soul. I felt the Veil pulsing through it. Had Rhazien's arms not held fast, I'm not sure I could have resisted its call. And then what would happen? My parents feared me with such conviction they held me as a prisoner most of my life."

Fire entered Islone's eyes. "Your parents are not worth being called such. To blame a child as if magic were a sin is despicable. Had they nurtured your gifts, taught you to use them instead of fear them, you would not feel this way."

If Erissa had thought the attention in the market felt odd, it had nothing on hearing Islone come to her defense. No one had ever done such a thing. Even her uncle defended the actions of her parents. Would it have made a difference to have her powers nurtured and protected instead of feared and contained?

"I will never comprehend how a parent can harm a child and what Rhazien told us you faced at the hands of the people who were supposed to love and protect you..." Islone's voice broke, and she paused momentarily, wiping furiously at her tears.

Erissa gathered the courage to speak, whispering the words. "I thought I deserved it. For a long time, I thought I had brought it upon myself. Because it wasn't just them. Everyone turned their backs to what happened in that room."

"You deserved nothing, Erissa. Nothing you did caused anyone's death. You were a child and should have been protected, not hidden away and abused out of prejudice and fear. No one would dare treat you that way here. Croparians do not fear the blessings of the Creator." Taking the cup from Erissa's hand, Islone sat it on the tray and moved it to the side. "And make no mistake, child, the Creator blessed you. Even the gods can't give such gifts. To be touched by the Creator's hand is nothing to be ashamed of. He does not give without purpose."

"I doubt the elder's family feels the same." Erissa wanted to cry, but no tears came again to break the numbness spreading through her chest. She stood, wiping her feet on the towel beside her.

"How would you know what they feel when you've done nothing but wallow since last evening?" Islone rose, her tone gentle, but the rebuke hit Erissa where intended. "People are not the same in every city, dear. Don't hold Emberhold against us. Talk to them. They're here, waiting for you in the main room."

Erissa tightened and loosened her fists as she paced away from Islone. The numbness spread from her chest, down her arms, and into her hands. "Why would they want to talk to me?"

"There's only one way to find out, little doe."

Erissa's hands grew sweaty, the moisture beading across her lip and forehead as Rhazien entered the room. He grinned unapologetically with a lift of his shoulder. "I was listening from the other room."

"You know nothing of privacy." Erissa huffed, crossing her arms. "Have you come for your special brand of convincing?"

"No convincing. An ultimatum." Rhazien crossed his arms across his wide chest. "You can walk out of here, or I can throw you over my shoulder and carry you out."

"Either way, you're leaving this room." Islone lifted her chin. "We won't allow you to repeat the mistakes of your parents."

"Some choice." Erissa rolled her eyes. "How is this different when you're forcing me to do something I don't want to?"

"You will not wither away out of fear, Erissa, any more than I would let any of the rest of my children. When I spoke as your mother to the elders, I meant it. I might not have birthed him, but Rhazien is one of my own, and if you're his, you're mine, too." Islone walked to the open door. "What will it be, daughter? Are you coming by choice or by force?"

She wanted to be mad, to rage against them for forcing her to confront fears she would rather leave buried even though she knew they were right in doing so. But still, she wanted to upend the tray, throwing the clay tea set to the ground, shattering into pieces to match her brokenness. But she did not want to bear that brokenness anymore, not alone.

Erissa instead chose to savor how natural it felt for Islone to call her daughter. She stared between her and Rhazien. They both knew the truth and understood the consequences of what she saw, even if none of them understood the full extent of how the magic worked, they were still there. Neither tried controlling nor confining her. They were there to make her choose to live, and if she refused the choice herself, they would drag her from this room and back into the light. No one was hiding her away in fear, shame, or anger.

The time had come for her to choose to live. Erissa breathed deeply. "I'm coming out by choice."

Rhazien wrapped his arms around her waist, hugging her close as he spun them around in a circle. "That's my girl."

Erissa laughed. The last of her reservations faded against the pride in Islone and Rhazien's expressions. Whatever Wilidon's family had to say, she would bear it for the sake of their belief in her.

Rhazien put her down and placed a hand against the small of her back, leading her from the room, Islone following. "We're with you, little doe. You won't deal with this alone."

Erissa nodded, her nerves keeping her from speaking. She heard the indistinct murmur of voices the further down the hall they went. It sounded like more than one person waiting for her in the main room.

Squaring her shoulders, Erissa schooled the panic from her features and allowed Rhazien to lead her into the next room.

Nothing prepared her for how many people filled the space. Someone occupied every available pillow, and more than half of those present sat directly on the floor. The elders and those Erissa had seen speaking with Wilidon last evening were there. Wilidon remained the only one missing.

All the bravado she summoned faded upon the realization the man had died. She had not said so to Rhazien or Islone, but the smallest part held onto a ridiculous and unrealistic hope she had been wrong and they would find the man sitting whole and healthy among his family.

If she had tied another *rihpaidir*, begging the Creator for Wilidon's life, would it have lessened the ache she carried today?

Erissa pushed away from Rhazien when they reached the center of the room. Dropping to her knees, she cupped her hands over her heart and bent low until her forehead kissed the ground.

She had no way of knowing if she did the right thing, but it felt natural after the events of last night. The Croparians had humbled themselves for Erissa and Rhazien's sham of a marriage so easily. If they would do so for something as ordinary as marriage, doing the same for the death of an elder felt like offering him and his loved ones honor.

"Rise, child." A woman's voice, thick with emotion, rang out in the tense silence.

Erissa placed her palms against the floor and pushed herself back to sit on her heels. Rhazien and Islone moved to either side of her, holding their hands out to help her rise. Erissa ignored them. "I'm sorry for all you have lost. I did not intend for something like this to happen."

"Do you believe yourself responsible for Wil's passing?" An older woman leaned forward.

Like Wilidon, her back bent with age. Where his skin had the look of leather, the thinnest of papers made up hers, the pale tone standing out against the dull brown of her eyes and making her frail face appear hollow.

Erissa dropped her gaze, her lip trembling. "If I had not come, he would—"

"Still be dead. You are not the Creator." The woman's words were blunt, bordering on being unkind, as they lacked patience.

"I meant no offense," Erissa whispered. Her shoulders hunched as she curled in on herself. She wanted to hate Islone and Rhazien for letting her build hope that these people would treat her differently. She understood they held no blame for the woman's words, though the thought did little to lessen their pain.

"Mother, you're scaring the poor girl." A woman around Islone's age placed a hand on the knee of the old woman.

She wiggled her knee, slapping the hand. "Is it my fault she's made of glass?"

The younger woman crossed her arms. "It's your fault when you're blunt to the point of rudeness. We've talked about this."

"And I've told you, Cosasria, I'm not minding the delicacies of others," the old woman fired back.

Islone spread her hands out, waving away the tension as if she were soothing overcome children. "I think we've lost sight of this conversation. Might we get back to the matter at hand?"

"Always diplomatic, Islone." The old woman's tone was sharp. "It's irritating."

Islone moved to the side of the room. "But it keeps things on target, Selsula. Something Wilidon appreciated."

"That he did. What he did not appreciate is shattered glass." Selsula tipped her head, fixing her gaze on Erissa. "She is made of sterner stuff. It's time she acted like it."

Rhazien stepped in front of Erissa. "I agreed to this, expecting my wife to be treated with respect."

"Rhazien." Erissa tugged on the hem of his shirt, waiting until he turned his head to speak again. She wanted to kiss him for standing up for her, but she needed to do this for herself. "She is giving me respect. I'm acting like a child cowering against criticism, and I know that as well as she does."

"Mother could still say it nicer," huffed Cosasria.

"What would be the point of that?" Selsula leaned back against the pillowed wall. "Wilidon loved me well enough with my manner. Who cares what you lot think of it?"

Erissa pressed a hand to her mouth as she giggled, trying to cut off the sound.

Selsula eyed her once more. "I will ask again. Are you responsible for Wilidon's passing?"

"No. I know I'm not responsible." Erissa sat up straight, letting go of Rhazien to answer on her own strength. "But it still feels like it all the same.

I see them the moment death decides to claim them, and there's nothing I can do to stop it."

"You can't stop what isn't yours to interfere with." Selsula gentled her voice. "The Creator planned to take my Wil no matter what you saw. In telling him, you gave us the time to say goodbye."

"It's not enough." Frustration caught in Erissa's throat, burning against the tears she choked down.

"It will never be enough. No amount of time will be when the Creator decides to call a life's time, and the Keeper of the Veil calls the soul into the afterlife." Cosasria wiped away at her own tears, which had begun to fall. "But because of you, we could gather as a family and celebrate my father's life until the morning saw the last of his breath. He died in peace, surrounded by love, and all because of you."

"Which is why we have come." Selsula unwound her scarf, passing it to Cosasria. "He was grateful for your warning. You gave us a gift without measure in a measured amount of time. There is something Wilidon asked of the elders as a way of saying thank you."

Higcraes stood. "Wilidon wished to honor you as a Croparian, Erissa. He approached the elders with a request for you to be allowed a *maharigra*."

"*Maharigra*?" Erissa turned to Rhazien, a brow arched.

"Erissa put the needs of Wilidon over that of herself. To reveal this gift in an unknown land where she would be unsure of the reception shows the strength of her character." Higcraes inclined his head toward Erissa when she turned back to him.

"For all she knew, our lot held onto the same superstitions as the old fools down south who treat magic as a cursed word." Selsula laughed.

Erissa froze. Did they know of Faldeyr and his daughter beyond the wall? Panicked sweat coated her upper lip, and she scolded herself for jumping to the conclusion. If they knew of her, they would have known of her power as well. She reached a hand for Rhazien's. She needed comfort, and he met her halfway as if his worries matched hers.

Rhazien tugged on her hand, bringing Erissa to her feet. "You wish to make her a Croparian through the *maharigra*."

"It was Wilidon's last wish, and one the rest of us agree with, though we would shorten the *maharigra* to a single night given your relationship." A chorus of agreement backed Higcraes's words. "You have found yourself a good wife, Rhazien. It would honor us to call her ours as well."

"We will need time to discuss and be sure Erissa understands what she would be agreeing to." Rhazien held Erissa's hand in a death grip.

Erissa squeezed his hand in question. "Wilidon's last wish should be granted."

"What's there to discuss?" Selsula stiffened, her voice rising. "You would turn down such an offer?"

Rhazien opened his mouth, but Erissa stepped before him, cutting him off. "No. If this was Wilidon's last wish, I will honor it without hesitation."

"Good." Selsula's wide smile transformed her face into a younger woman. "Islone will make the preparations?" At the other woman's nod, Selsula continued. "You have one hour. The hunt begins on the noon hour."

Everyone stood, the younger generations helping, the older without another word before they filed out of the home.

When the door closed on the last person, Islone turned to the couple in a panic. "This leaves little time for you to run and hide. I'll gather food supplies. Rhazien, see to whatever things you need for your comfort."

Erissa gaped after Islone as she ran from the room. "Run and hide? Why would we do that?"

Rhazien rocked back on his heels, an amused smirk across his lips. "Because you just agreed to a marriage hunt, little doe."

CHAPTER THIRTY-SEVEN

"The Cropari tradition where couples run away?" Erissa shook her head in denial. Rhazien spoke utter nonsense. "I never agreed to that. I said I would take part in the *maharigra*."

"The *maharigra* is the marriage hunt." Rhazien bit his lip as if to stop the satisfaction from radiating across his mouth. The action did nothing for his smug golden eyes.

Erissa stood dumbfounded, her mouth opening and closing as her mind fought for what to say. She settled on slapping Rhazien's chest. "Why didn't you stop me?"

"I tried to keep you from agreeing to it." Rhazien walked in a slow, determined circle around her, his voice deepening into something husky bordering on a growl. "Someone was rather insistent, though."

"I wouldn't have had I known that's what they meant." Erissa stamped her foot in frustration. Why could no one speak plainly about what they were asking of her? Selsula and the Higcraes reminded her of Reeva, giving only enough information for her to agree to their whims without truly explaining anything. Getting angry with them changed nothing about the situation. She had agreed without asking any questions, and now she found herself facing a marriage neither of them asked for. Would Rhazien want this?

"What's done is done, little doe." Rhazien stopped behind her. He pulled her arms down from where they had crossed against her chest, hugging her. "You don't have to go through with this. We can hide at first and let them find us later."

They grew quiet as they embraced. Erissa enjoyed being held like this. It made her wish all of it was real. It felt real the longer they traveled together, but she remained unsure of Rhazien's feelings even after all that had transpired. He desired her; she could feel that through their bond, but what of love? Kisses and gifts from the townspeople were hardly a declaration, and she had yet to truly confess her own feelings. How different would their lives be if they had met in a normal way?

But did that mean she should participate in the hunt? The Croparians held tightly to their traditions. Erissa wanted to honor them. Did agreeing to the hunt honor them? Or did taking part in the hunt spit on the desert land's culture? The questions circled around her head until she thought she might go mad.

"What questions are there?" the voice asked. It purred against Erissa's mind. *"It's Rhazien. We love him, don't we?"*

When the silence felt as if it had grown unbearable, Rhazien shifted his hold and whispered, "Would it be so bad? Being married to me?"

Erissa dropped her head back against his shoulder and closed her eyes, thinking of all the ways he might convince her of how good it would be. "Rhaz—"

Islone walked into the room as she rambled, straining under the weight of the three bulging satchels she carried in her arms. "I've packed all the fresh food we have in the home. It's most likely too much, but you'll have it all the same if you decide you don't want to come out of hiding right away. Fhacia's girl was gone for a week before she returned a wife and well on her way with child. Not that we expect the same from you, although a grandchild would be most welcome. There are some intimate positions that can encourage a girl. Rhazien's warm skin tones with your lavender eyes and raven curls would be precious."

Erissa said nothing as Islone dropped the bags at their feet, her mind reeling. A child? What had she agreed to?

The voice crooned. *"How lovely would it be? To dance with her among the winds and flowers we can make? To give her all you were denied?"*

Panic clawed its way up Erissa's throat. Everyone needed to slow down. The wistful tone of Islone's words spoke to how happy she would be with her grandchildren, giving Erissa pause. Never in all her years had she imagined herself having children. She knew nothing of parenting, only the brutality of crossing one and suffering at the neglect of the other. What kind of mother would that make her? And what of her powers? A child of hers would suffer the same curse.

"Not if we love them," the voice reasoned. *"Not if we cared for them, nurtured them, and taught them how to live with their powers. We would love our child."*

Erissa mentally scoffed. She had no way of doing that, not when she knew nothing about controlling her own powers. And she understood less about children than she did about magic. She would be a terrible mother.

"Your talk of grandchildren will scare our daughter away faster than she can make one. They should have things well in hand by now without your interference." Micmus ambled into the room carrying a large sac draped over his shoulder. "Going to the spring, Rhazien? I've packed some bedding."

Erissa heard nothing Rhazien, Islone, and Micmus said after that. Her mouth still hung open from when Islone had cut her off, and Micmus had done little to ease her shock. What did everyone expect from this hunt? What did Rhazien expect?

"Little doe, I can feel your mind whirling." Rhazien stepped to her side, aligning her body to his chest. Islone and Micmus huddled together, oblivious to what Rhazien whispered as they compared what each had packed. "I would never do something that made you uncomfortable or ask something of you that you didn't want. This can be pretend."

"Can it?" It surprised Erissa when she found her voice. Lifting her head to stare into Rhazien's eyes, she asked the question that had been bothering her since they arrived the previous day. "Can any of it be pretend with the way I feel?"

Rhazien's expression turned serious, his jaw tightening until a tick developed and cords strained down his neck. He opened his mouth to answer, but whatever he planned to say disappeared as Micmus inserted himself.

"Go out the front and take the long way around. It should throw everyone off to see you walk through the city, and while you do that, I'll take the supplies down into the cavern. Take one of the lighter satchels. The elders won't be fooled if you leave here with nothing."

When Micmus held an arm out, Rhazien grabbed it at the elbow in an embrace.

"Go now." Islone pushed the bag into Rhazien's arms as he moved back. She sidestepped him to take Erissa in her arms. "Don't think about anything tonight, dear. Let things go. Enjoy what the cavern has to offer. There's time enough for everything else when you return.

CHAPTER THIRTY-EIGHT

Sweat soaked Erissa's skin as Rhazien led her around the outer wall of the city, their movements careful. It had taken them hours to make it through the city and out of its gates without being stopped by everyone they passed. Erissa longed to reach their hiding place.

She cursed every time Rhazien stopped to survey the surrounding land. Her damp clothes clung to her skin. She wanted a bath and a nap this evening spent curled in Rhazien's arms. Maybe it would not be so bad to end the hunt early and return to their room.

"Where are we going?" Erissa glanced over at him in annoyance. He bent over a group of bushes, brushing sand from around their bases.

"Somewhere only Micmus, Islone, and I know about. We can stay there until the hunt is over, or you want to be found."

Erissa's mood soured. "Hunted by madmen and hunted for marriage. I told you I was hunted from every side."

Rhazien stopped his inspection of the bushes and looked over his shoulder. "We're safe here, little doe. Let the worries fall from your mind. I won't let anything happen to you." He brushed a hand against the sweat beading atop his brow and resumed his search. "I know the entrance is around here somewhere. The sands have shifted, but it will be well worth the wait when you see where we're going."

"Why does it feel like we're walking through the Keeper's swamp?" Erissa gagged against the thick air.

It had grown increasingly humid the further they moved from the house, the air cloaking her skin in a sheen that became slimier the higher the sun rose in the sky.

Rhazien moved on to the next grouping of plants, feeling his way around their bases. "A monsoon is rolling in. We need to get into the cavern soon."

"What does that mean?"

"It means a thunderstorm is coming."

Erissa laughed, staring up at the sky clear of all clouds. The sun was brutal today, punishing anyone who stayed too long under its rays. "I think you're mistaken."

"Found it." Rhazien leaned over beneath a scraggly tree, its dark bark offset by beautiful yellow flowers that smelled of honeysuckle and smoke. Rhazien dug against the sand at the base of the tree until a smooth rock the size of a doorway appeared. He wiggled the rock back and forth until it gave way with a resounding crack that echoed through the sky. "And not a moment too soon."

Another crack rent the air, and Erissa realized the rock did not make the sound. She stepped back as lightning forked through the sky.

Great, billowing black clouds appeared on the horizon, rolling in fast toward the city. Their depths charged with lightning, the brilliant flashes startling in their violence with the sun shining opposite them. Dark shadows poured from the clouds, falling in a thick curtain to the horizon, leaving Erissa nervous as the storm pushed closer. Storms rolled in from the bay of Emberhold, but nothing like this.

"The monsoon is coming in fast. We need to hurry." Rhazien turned back to the rock. He braced his arms on either side of it and lifted. The heavy weight gave way beneath the groan of metal hinges, revealing a wide hole with a spiraling clay staircase framed by phosphorescent blue light. "Quickly, inside."

Erissa hesitated long enough for another crack to snap through the sky. The intensity of it scared her, forcing her into action. She ran to the hole and descended the steps. Rhazien grabbed their bag and followed.

He lowered the door once inside, blocking out the darkening light of day. Within minutes, the sound of raindrops pitted against the rock. "This works out better than I thought it would. The rain will hide our tracks."

Rhazien nudged Erissa along until they reached the bottom of the stairs. "We'll be safe here even if the storm should last for days, but I doubt it will. The monsoon storms are wild and fast."

"Is this safe?" Rivulets of water tunneled their way down the walls in thin strips, pooling in shallow depths before flowing down the sides. Worry consumed her as she pictured the tunnel flooding.

"Micmus made the tunnel, but the monsoon waters carved the cavern. They feed into the hot spring. I've been down here during the worst of the monsoon season, and it's never come close to flooding."

Erissa pressed a hand into a dryer spot on the wall, running her fingers along the stone. A blue light illuminated the walls, and when she pulled her hand back, the same blue glow coated her hands. "What is this?"

Rhazien ran his fingertips down the wall. "It's a spore of some kind. We can view its light in the dark, but it's invisible in the daylight." He inclined his head toward the faintly lit passage. "Let's keep going. If you thought the bath in the room was great, you're in for a surprise."

He took the lead down the narrow passageway, ducking as the overhead dipped low enough to brush his hair.

Erissa grabbed a fistful of his shirt, shuffling close behind him in the unfamiliar space. The faint light guided their steps, growing in intensity and depth, but Rhazien neither paid it attention nor needed it. He moved through the space with an effortless grace that spoke of his doing so many times before. "How did you know this place was here?"

"It's attached to the spring that feeds the baths at the house. The house is on the other side of the wall from where we entered the passageway. Micmus found the original entrance by chance when digging out the bath in their room."

Erissa groaned. "You mean we didn't have to wade through the air like that to get here?"

Rhazien laughed. "There's an entrance in the house, but we still had to come this way to avoid suspicion. If no one saw us leave the house, there would have been questions."

"We might have saved half the day by not doubling back." Erissa huffed, her mood souring her tone.

"Poor, grumpy little doe." Rhazien stopped, motioning her ahead. "The wait will be well worth it."

"I highly doubt that." Erissa stepped past, running her fingertips absentmindedly along his stomach.

"The pool is beyond that bend." Rhazien cleared his throat, motioning ahead of them. The ceiling climbed above, leading around a wide curve. "I'll be ready to accept your apology after you pick your jaw up from the floor."

Erissa rolled her eyes. "Always so arrogant, Rhazien. Is there a reason for your inflated sense of ego?"

She giggled as he reached around her, jerking her into him until her back lay flush against his front. She loved it when he did that. It made her feel a different kind of safe. Her father's whip had plagued her back more times than she could count. Rhazien's warmth radiated through the memories, slowly replacing them.

One of Rhazien's hands caged her beneath her breasts as the other moved lower, fingers spreading across her belly to press Erissa's hips back into his. "I would like to think so, little doe. I could show you." She stilled against the press of him. Her breath hitched, lodging in her throat as he rubbed his hand in lazy circles below her navel. "Would you like me to?"

Erissa thought about pulling away and denying the feel of him, but only for a moment. The other day, she had been so certain of what she wanted, but Rhazien had also spoken true, if they took this step, there would be no taking it back.

Time suspended as Rhazien's hand stopped its movements, waiting for Erissa to decide what she wanted to happen next.

As the moments dragged on, Rhazien decided for her. He placed a kiss against her shoulder. "Come, let's get into the chamber up ahead and ready things for the rest of the night. Micmus should have left the supplies by now."

Rhazien placed a hand against her back, but Erissa stopped him as he made to push her forward. She turned around, biting her lip. "What if... I wanted you to show me?"

He blinked at her hard, and Erissa remained unsure if he heard her clearly. "Rhazien?" He said nothing again, and not knowing what else to do, she turned back around, humiliation staining her cheeks.

"Erissa—" Rhazien grabbed her arm, the faintest hint of a wince in his voice.

She refused to look at him. "Let's go get settled."

"I wasn't refusing you, little doe." Rhazien walked in front of her, taking her chin between his fingers and raising her face to his. "I just didn't know if you were prepared to take things further, even for all my teasing and your response."

Erissa's tongue darted out to moisten her lip. "Then why do you tease me so?"

"Because I want you to be comfortable with me." A pink stain accentuated Rhazien's high cheekbones with the admission.

Erissa liked seeing the color. It made him more approachable. His arrogance had become endearing, but a part of her remained intimidated by him, knowing what he wanted from her. What if she gave herself to him, and he found her as lacking as everyone else had?

But this side of him differed from his usual cockiness. He looked as lost as she felt. She needed to stop approaching him as if he were like the other people who had made up her old life.

She lifted a hand to cup his face. "It wouldn't be so bad, Rhazien."

He dropped his hand in return. "What wouldn't?"

Erissa met him halfway, as he had done with her since the moment they met. Rising to her toes, she touched her lips to his in a slow, sweet kiss. At his groan, she dared to flit her tongue against his.

It surprised Erissa when he played against her gentle exploration. He did not try to tame her mouth. A leisurely kiss, it asked instead of demanded, with Erissa's tentative swipes of her tongue setting the pace. She fit her body against him, tucking her hips into his and wrapping her hands into his hair.

When she finally broke the kiss, Rhazien breathed raggedly. "What wouldn't be so bad, little doe?"

"Marriage." Erissa breathed the word against his lips, her eyes burning brightly with passion. "If it is real, it wouldn't be so bad. Being married to you. To be considered a Croparian."

Rhazien cupped her face and pushed it back from him. "You don't have to say that. Not if it's not what you want. We can hide until the storm passes, make our way back into the city, and let them find us."

Erissa touched a finger to his lips, silencing him. "You're not forcing a decision from me. You have given me so much. I didn't want to trust you even with the connection I could feel pulsing between us. But I was desperate enough to accept your help, and things changed as we traveled.

You proved yourself to be someone worth trusting. You've helped me stitch the broken pieces of myself back together with your love."

Her eyes widened with what she said, and she had never felt more stupid than at that moment. She declared his love without him saying anything of the sort. She stumbled over the words in a rush to fix her mistake. "I—at least—I thought it might be... love..." Erissa trailed off, feeling like a fool, afraid he would say something full of arrogant dismissal.

Rhazien wrapped her in his arms, cradling her close. "It is love, little doe. The gods know I have little to my name to give you beyond my love, but you have it all the same. My heart is yours alone." He touched his forehead to hers. "Tell me it's the same for you."

Erissa's heart pounded against her breast. He loved her. All the things he knew of her and her powers, and he still loved her. A warm sensation spread through her chest and outward. The radiant glow of her eyes reflected in the honeyed depths of Rhazien's.

In that moment, the full force of her feelings swept through her as she allowed herself to drop the wall she had erected after all the years she spent alone. "You have little to your name, and I have even less to mine, with nothing to give you but my heart. The beat of it is tied to your own. I'm yours, Rhazien. I love you."

"I love you too, little doe." Rhazien bridged what little distance remained between them and took Erissa's lips in a heated kiss that burned its way through her body.

The cord between them tightened with their declarations until a bond lay blanketed beneath her skin. Its strength rivaled anything that came before it. And for the first time in over a decade, Erissa knew peace.

He said he loved her. When no one else had spoken the same words since the day her life ended.

Rhazien backed her against the wall. She cared little for how the rock dug into her back as he ravaged her mouth. She feared she might snap at the pressure building within her.

She broke the kiss as Erissa fisted her hands in his hair, grumbling a protest against his lips. "Please, don't stop." It would give her too much time to think, and she only wanted to feel.

"If I don't stop now, I'll take you here against the wall, which would be a shame considering what's around the corner." He gave one of his light-hearted grins. "You're going to love the cavern. It puts the bath in our room to shame."

Erissa let him lead her around the bend. She stopped short as the cavern came into view, speechless at the sight before her.

The tunneling water joined wider strips running into a pool the deepest shade of blue. It was so dark it was almost black, the color putting the night sky to shame as its luminescent waters shimmered across the bubbling surface like it was a sea of stars.

The reflective water and walls illuminated the cavern, revealing a high ceiling covered in rock formations. They reminded Erissa of the icicles winter brought to the frame of her bedroom window, beautiful with how they, too, glowed with the azure light.

Several bags lay beside the pool, and linens lay spread out next to them over a low mattress piled high with pillows. Erissa was relieved to see the mattress. She had slept on the ground enough over the last couple of weeks to last a lifetime. They would at least pass this night in comfort.

Another tunnel lay carved into the western wall of the cavern, leading to Micmus and Islone's home if Erissa were to hazard a guess.

The air cooled as they walked further into the cavern. Steam rose from the pool, the mist looking like clouds across the night sky. Erissa could feel the warmth enticing her with its promise of comfort from the chilly air.

Rhazien drew her into the room, not stopping until they reached the pool. He pulled his shirt off, gesturing to the where a basket sat by the pool's side, filled to the brim with various pieces of soap. "Islone always thinks ahead. The spring is shallow at this end. We could bathe, wash the day away, and relax for a time."

Erissa bit her lip, her nerves building as she imagined them bathing together, sharing the same water, the same soap. Maybe they would wash each other. Her teeth dug harder into her bottom lip, feeling a blush swell against her breasts and rise all the way to her high cheekbones.

Rhazien touched a gentle hand to one cheek, tracing the splash of red down her face and the column of her throat to the high neckline of her sea-green dress. "You're adorable, little doe. A moment ago, you'd have let me take you against the wall, and now you shy away over a bath."

"It's different." Erissa fidgeted under his hand. Bathing was traditionally a shared affair. Whether it was families with a common tub or maids helping those of higher status, it was something one rarely did alone or so intimately. She had experienced the same for a time, although with her father's actions, that had changed. To think of bathing with another person—of bathing with Rhazien—was enough to leave her breath coming in small bursts. "Bathing's more intimate."

A smirk pulled at the side of his mouth. He trailed his hand from her cheek to the base of her throat. "More intimate than me buried between your legs?"

"Rhazien! You can't say things like that." Erissa would never admit how she liked it when he said such things. His words created images in her mind that left her toes curling against the soft leather of her shoes.

"Why not, little doe? It's the truth." His hand moved lower still, coming to rest between her breasts, his fingertips skimming the sides of them. "Do you want me there, riding between them?"

Erissa breathed deeply. The air smelled of rain and the crispness that followed its descent. It mixed with the scent of Rhazien, a sweet citrus woodiness, and it threatened to be her undoing as his hand curled into the fabric of her bodice. "This was much easier in the wood when you took charge. I didn't have to think about what to do."

"Is that what you want? Me to take charge?" Rhazien's hold on her dress tightened. He used it to pull Erissa closer until she lay nestled against his hips. "Do you know what sex is, little doe?"

"Yes. I told you my mother read nothing but romance stories. They would…" Erissa lifted her chin, refusing to bow to the embarrassment staining her skin. It flowed down her chest, and Erissa hoped the heat of it did not reach his hand. "I know what sex is. I also know you're older than me. You must have some level of experience, and I don't know what you want me to do."

Rhazien leaned into her and kissed the area of her neck where her pulse thrummed slow and steady, the heavy beat of it thickening her blood with desire. "I'm a little older than you think I am, little doe."

"Which means you're more experienced than I probably even realize." Erissa cringed. Did her words come out as breathy as she thought they did? "I don't want to disappoint you."

"It's not possible for you to disappoint me." Rhazien trailed kisses up her neck. When he reached her lips, he claimed them in a fiery kiss that melted her worries.

Erissa clung to him, letting him lead her through it. The feel of his lips against hers left her dazed.

He broke the kiss and tapped her nose. "If you want me to take charge, I can, but I don't know if you're ready for what that means. It wouldn't do if I frightened my little doe away before I made her mine."

"I'm not afraid of you, Rhazien." Erissa's voice definitely came out breathy that time, but she did not care. She stood on her toes, trying to capture his lips for another kiss.

Rhazien evaded her attempts, a roughish grin splitting his lips with a chuckle as she pouted in frustration. "Turn around, little doe."

He dropped his hands against her hips, his fingers gripping the soft curves of her hips as he turned her body. Rhazien ran his hands up her back. Erissa moved the length of her hair over one shoulder, allowing him better access to the row of buttons down her dress.

Rhazien unfastened the buttons, taking his time. His knuckles brushed against the slivers of skin he exposed with each one. Erissa swayed against the light contact, her skin coming alive with the teasing touches.

When half of the buttons lay undone, Rhazien pushed the folds of her dress to the side and down her shoulders, and his hands stilled. His breath escaped in a hiss, his hands resuming the path.

His hands trembled against Erissa's skin, his motions jerky as he struggled with the remaining buttons. When he unfastened the last one, Rhazien pushed the material over her shoulders and down her arms, letting the dress fall about her waist.

CHAPTER THIRTY-NINE

Erissa heard his intake of breath, how Rhazien held on to it, his hands shaking harder as they traced over her skin.

"You should have told me."

"There's nothing to tell." Erissa pulled from his hold. She reached for the sides of her dress, wanting to cover herself.

"Is that all you have to say?" Rhazien grabbed onto her shoulders, not letting her shimmy back into the fabric. He turned her to face him, his face losing all color as his eyes raked her body.

Erissa stared down at her chest, imagining what it must be like to see it for the first time.

A crisscross of long scars intersected with deep, smaller ones, the flesh tattered and puckered where it had knitted itself together unevenly in a haphazard jumble that nearly marked her entirely from her shoulders to her waist, across her torso and back.

"What am I supposed to say, Rhazien? It's nothing." Erissa wanted to convince him it meant nothing to her, and maybe it would do the same for her. She had ignored the scars for longer than she wanted to admit, forcing herself to let them go unnoticed to cope with her bleak reality. Rhazien was undoing all that with a single look, and she resented it. "They're only scars, so why does it matter if I told you?"

His mouth settled into an angry line, tension stiffening his shoulders while he breathed heavily through his nose.

Something tasting of magic pebbled over her skin the longer Rhazien remained silent. Curls of smoke floated into the air from his mouth and nostrils, the smell of burning ash freezing in her lungs.

A gold light surrounded his body, warming his smoky quartz skin with its intensity. It shimmered against the tiny hexagonal shapes appearing over every exposed inch of his neck and arms and outlined in carnelian. The red color gave way to a gleaming black as they lined up flawlessly against the lines stained over his skin. The shapes reminded her of glass.

Erissa staggered at the site in front of her. Rhazien wrapped his arm around her waist, bringing her flush against him to keep her from falling.

"You have magic?" Erissa demanded. "You're taking me to task over scars when you've been hiding your powers all this time?"

"It's not like that." Rhazien struggled to control the rising magic, twisting his neck to each side as the light burned brighter with his anger.

A frown marred her features, and Erissa crossed her arms over her bare chest, pushing her breasts together. "Then what's it like, Rhazien? Explain it to me."

"I didn't want to tell you then." Rhazien ran a hand through his air, pulling lightly on the strands when Erissa snorted.

"You made me stop in the clearing. You gave me an ultimatum for telling you the truth about Reeva. All the while, you were hiding something."

"I know it sounds bad…"

"Because it *is* bad, Rhazien." Erissa dug her nails into her arms where they still lay folded.

"There are things I would take back in this life, but hiding this from you isn't one of them." Rhazien held up a hand when Erissa tried to interrupt him. "You were terrified, running away with a man you didn't know, and finding out all this new information about who you are and grappling with how much to tell me. I didn't want to add to your burden. So I waited. I was always going to tell you. When things were safe. When you were safe."

Erissa chewed on her lip, mulling over all he said.

"I'm sorry, little doe. My only intention was to get you somewhere safe first. I was going to tell you. Hurting you is the last thing I wanted to do. I understand if you want to end the hunt. The storm should have passed by now. We can get you dressed and return." He sighed, bringing his forehead to rest against hers. The sound of it echoed through the cavern, the weight of it pressing in on them.

Erissa wanted to push him away. She wanted to pull her dress back up and leave the cavern and Rhazien's lies. But the sigh stopped her. His shoulders slumped. He closed his eyes, and Erissa's heart wrenched at the defeat rolling off him.

Erissa wanted to stay angry with him, but his sincerity burned its way through their tethered emotions, emotions that had grown stronger since they descended the clay stairs.

Her gaze traced over the differences in his skin. She had seen very little of life, and none of it compared to how Rhazien looked with his magic taking over. She laid her hands on his arms and gasped.

The shapes were exceedingly hard and glossy. Erissa expected them to feel like sandpaper, like a lizard she'd once found in her room, but they were smooth in their texture until you reached the raised middle. The spine-like ridges running down the center of each shielded shape radiated a fiery heat that made the room cold in comparison.

Rhazien flirted on the edge of being something human and something more, keeping Erissa trapped between awe and fear. "They feel so different from my..."

The scales flexed beneath her touch, the heat intensifying as Rhazien's temper rose. She doubted he heard her. He remained fixated on her scars.

"Who did this to you—no, don't answer that. I already know. Your father did this, didn't he?" His voice broke into a pained whisper. "You should have told me."

Erissa flinched at the raw emotion in Rhazien's voice.

"I forgot." She shrugged, her scars shifting with the movement. The quick crease of a frown transformed her features. Nothing good would come of Rhazien's questions. The scars were long healed. Neither one would gain anything from talking about them.

"You forgot?" Anger turned Rhazien's eyes into the darkest of amber, the color almost crimson in its depth. The smoke billowing from his mouth and nose became thicker. Whether his rage built at her, for her, or some combination of the two, little disguised the growing tempest inside of him.

"It's normal, almost?" Erissa slanted a reproachful scowl at Rhazien when his jaw slackened into disbelief. Remembering only brought back painful memories she would rather not see as snippets of what caused them flashed through her mind.

"It's been years since a new one was added. Playing the broken, compliant daughter had its perks." She struggled with how to explain her apathy to the marks. "Besides, it's easy to forget them when you're not looking at them. It's not like I had a mirror in my room."

Rhazien gaped at her, his mouth opening and closing as if struck mute.

Erissa bristled under his regard. "Don't stare at me like that. Have you looked at yourself, Rhazien?"

"You're deflecting, but you forget the tether that binds us. The stronger your emotions are, the more I can sense them and see what's going on inside that head of yours. You're hiding nothing from me." Rhazien raised his hand. It hovered over her skin like he was afraid to touch her for fear of worsening the damage.

"Either I'm not explaining this well, or you're not listening, but I don't want to talk about it. I can put the dress back on." Erissa pushed against his chest, backing away from him as his arms released their hold. "This was a mistake."

Rhazien's arm shot out as she turned from him. It gripped her arm, refusing to let her move away. "Your mistake is in making light of this. You should have told me. It's hardly fair to be angry when I can't immediately wrap my head around it."

"I never lied about what I experienced. You're angry with me for not telling you about how far it went when you didn't even ask?" She had thought to make things better and relieve some of his anger, but judging from his reaction, she had made things worse. It fired her own fury. "You have no room to talk, Rhazien. There's a burning light haloing you. You're covered in *scales,* for gods' sake, and there's *smoke* rising from your nostrils and between your lips. And you want to be angry with me for not telling you about some stupid scars?"

"Don't turn this around on me, Erissa. You want to convince me this is nothing? Your father whipped you. More than once. The bastard intentionally carved through your skin with a mistdrite-tipped whip. You don't understand the implications of this, but I do." Rhazien shouted now, the rage in his voice echoing around the cavern. "What he did... it matters. *You* matter."

Erissa stayed silent. A mistdrite-tipped whip meant nothing to her. She had a feeling that saying so would only make Rhazien's temper rise more.

Rhazien's grip tightened in the wake of her silence, but even in his anger, his hold did not bruise. Erissa had believed he would never hurt her, but with his anger overriding everything else in his nature, the truth of his actions comforted her.

After what she endured, fear always existed. It hovered below every thought, questioning the intentions of everyone around her except Rhazien.

Erissa's arm vibrated against the trembling of his hand, and she did not think it shook from rage alone. Her heart broke more for him than for herself as she reached for his feelings down the strands that tied them together.

Rhazien hurt for her, hurt against the proof laid bare before him. It hovered under his volatile emotions, threatening to break through the anger and overwhelm him with grief. He wanted to fix it. He wanted to take it away, wipe the scars from existence, purge the sins committed against her and their memories, but he was powerless to do anything.

"I don't want to fight with you. Not over this." Erissa stepped into him, pressing her scared chest against his torso and resting her head against the pounding beat of his heart. She wrapped her arms around him. "I'm sorry for not telling you. It's easier to ignore them, to forget they exist."

"I don't want to fight either." Rhazien gripped her tightly, resting his chin against the top of her head. "I've made a mess of this, but I can't say I'm sorry for it. Knowing what happened is one thing, seeing it is another. I was shocked. I can understand why it's normal, though. Having dealt with something like that for so long. It must be startling seeing other people react to it."

"I could have handled this better." Erissa nuzzled against his chest. "I do truly forget sometimes. How different things were for me."

Rhazien sighed, and the smoke receded until only a trace of ash lingered in the air. He smelled of campfires and sweet oranges, and he might as well be a fire himself. Heat poured off his skin, melting into her bones and warming the parts of her having gone cold at his show of anger.

They settled into a comfortable silence, each holding on to the other. She feared moving and breaking it, but curiosity got the better of her.

Erissa stroked her hands across his back, marveling at the differences between his skin and the scales. She trailed her fingers down a ridged line running down the length of his spine.

Rhazien shuddered under her hands. A low, rumbling growl moved through his chest. "Careful, little doe."

He stepped out of her arms, that damned smirk sitting smugly across his lips again. Erissa reached for it, tracing the smooth, devilish upturn of his mouth to his dimpled cheeks. "Or what?"

Rhazien said nothing. He placed his hands on her shoulders and pushed gently, turning her around until her back faced him. Rhazien growled again, the sound low and menacing, at odds with the gentle way he traced his way across the scars. His attention left her shuddering.

"Do they hurt?"

Erissa hesitated, not wanting to say anything to start another argument. Rhazien asked for nothing more than her honesty, and she would give it to him. "Sometimes. The surrounding skin is tight. It pulls when I move and aches with a hard day's travel."

Rhazien hummed a response. It reverberated within her, creating a languid calm. She almost missed what he said next as she basked in the feelings it provoked.

"I can ease the ache for you." Rhazien kissed her shoulder.

She fought to find her voice against the sensations threatening to pull her under their spell. "There's nothing more that can be done for them now."

"There's a way to soften them." Rhazien placed another kiss against her tender flesh. "You need only to trust me, little doe."

Erissa stifled a moan.

"Should I take that as enthusiastic consent?"

Rhazien laughed, a thick and throaty sound that had her tightening her thighs. "Would you try to *convince* me if I said no?"

He hummed once more, the feel of it engulfing her, tangling the calm inside of her until she felt nothing except for a growing desire to lose herself in his arms. "You're a little beyond convincing right now, little doe."

She shuddered again as Rhazien's hands kept moving down her back. His lips followed the light touches until his fingers lay against the buttons still holding the dress in place.

He deftly unfastened the rest of them. Erissa shimmied against the borrowed fabric, allowing it to fall and pool around her feet. She made to turn around, but his hands halted her movements as they spread across the tightened flesh.

"I want to care for them—and for you—if you'll let me."

Rhazien's assurance that the scars were changeable baffled Erissa. She understood his desire to help her. She would wish to do the same if his body held memories of such savagery.

Moving from beneath his hold, Erissa turned to face him, clad only in her leather shoes. A blush spread across her face. It traveled down her body, deepening the color of her breasts. She resisted the urge to cover herself.

Rhazien's primitive gaze raked Erissa's body, lingering over her breasts and what lay hidden between her thighs. "If I had known you wore nothing else beneath your dress, I would have removed it sooner."

"I'm not used to wearing other garments. There was no need to with only myself to entertain."

This time, Erissa expected the flash of anger that came to Rhazien's eyes at the mention of her past. She refused to let him dwell on it and refocused his attention by grabbing onto his shoulders to balance herself as she sought to remove her shoes.

Rhazien lowered himself to his knees in front of her. The quick action forced her hands to slide down and grip his arms tightly to keep from falling over, her heavy breasts swaying with the movement.

The position placed Rhazien's face in line with them. He placed kisses along the full slopes, drawing bumps along her skin while he removed each of the light shoes. He tortured her by avoiding the tightened peaks of her nipples.

Flicking his tongue out, Rhazien traced one of the worst scars, following the line of it as it went from her breast to her waist.

He circled the wet heat of his tongue along her navel. Rhazien chuckled as Erissa's back bowed, and a gasp escaped her lips. "There's no going back from this, little doe. You'll be mine, and I'll be yours."

"I'm already yours, Rhazien." Erissa reached for Rhazien.

He stood, pushing his pants until they dropped against the tops of his books in a motion that left Erissa breathless with anticipation. Rhazien removed his boots, his socks and pants following in their wake as he tossed them away.

Erissa fidgeted as the heat in her face grew and spread everywhere. She worried she might panic if she looked down at the length of him, keeping her eyes on his chest.

A hesitant question hung between them as she reached, her hand hovering over him. "I'm already yours too, little doe. You can touch me all you want."

She spread her fingers until they met the pattern stained against his skin. It lined up along the scales still present. Erissa ran her fingers along them, following the design as it outlined the ridged scales wrapping around his back. Her hand halted at what she found there.

The golden body of a dragon curled up his ribs, ending on his back, where a head stretched across the broad flesh. Smoke rose from its mouth and nostrils, framing eyes that mirrored Rhazien's. Differing shades of red, yellow, and black bled into one another, creating a back-light against the perfectly aligned scales. Wings of fire rose on either side of the dragon. The golden light built into the deepest of reds before darkening into tips of a rich black that put the night sky to shame. The wings covered the remaining room on his back, stretching over his ribs.

Erissa gasped. "It's the dragon from the house."

Seeing it on the wall had been beautiful, but seeing the dragon against Rhazien's bronzed, muscled back left her wanting to run kisses along the black lines.

She gave into the desire, pressing kisses along the raised lines, flicking her tongue out the way Rhazien had done to her. His skin tightened under her hands as his back flexed. A grumbling moan echoed through the cavern.

Rhazien abruptly turned around, catching her hands. "You're playing with fire, little doe. I would hate for this to be over before it started."

He laced their fingers together and led her down the sloped floor and into the shallows of the hot water, taking a piece of soap from the basket sitting on the edge. They waded deeper into the spring until it reached her waist.

"I've wanted to do this since my impromptu bath in the Wilds." Rhazien lathered the soap in his hands, moving to stand behind Erissa. He washed the day from her hair, his hands gentle as they massaged her scalp.

Erissa groaned. It had been a long time since someone else washed her hair, and she found it to be nothing like her memories. She leaned into the intoxicating sensation of Rhazien's touch.

She bent her knees and let him help lean her backward to rinse the soap. "I can't imagine growing tired of having you wash my hair."

With the suds gone from the dark strands, Rhazien molded himself against her back. Erissa tensed as the rigid length of him pressed into her backside. His body radiated a heat that rivaled the depths where they stood. She shivered at the differing temperatures.

He caged her with his arms, wrapping them around her front, the soap in one hand. Rhazien lathered his hand once more and lazily traced them across her shoulders and chest, avoiding the sensitive peaks begging for his attention.

"Rhazien..." Erissa lifted her chest, chasing his touch.

"Yes, little doe?"

Erissa whimpered her plea. "Please, I need you to..."

Pressing a kiss to her ear, nibbling the lobe between his words. "Need me to what? To touch you here?"

A mewling gasp left her as his fingers brushed against her nipples. His light touch explored the nubs, but Erissa needed more.

She ground her backside against the hard length of his member. The sensation of his silken skin sliding against her in the water drove her wild. She wanted something else, something stronger, unsure of how to ask for it. "Rhazien, I don't... I need..."

"What do you need, little doe? Do you need more?" Rhazien bit down on the delicate skin in the crook of Erissa's neck. She cried out in pain, the sound fading into a moan as he eased the pressure and nibbled against the marks left behind. "There are other places I'd like to sink my teeth into."

Erissa wanted to ask where, wanted to know if it would ease the ache growing inside, but words failed her as his hands moved.

Rhazien rubbed the soap against one nipple while his other hand palmed her breast. He fixed his attention on the breast he held, teasing and pinching the delicate nub until it forced her to rise to the tips of her toes.

Her ragged breathing filled the air, mixing with her moans as pleasure spread through her and slickened the pulse between her thighs at the light bite of pain.

"Is this what you needed, little doe?" Rhazien breathed the husky words against her ear. "Or is this what you need?"

With his hand still manipulating her peak, Rhazien slid the soap down her body. He washed her with infinite care, his other hand switching from breast to breast, winding her up as he stroked a path to her most intimate area.

She nearly came undone when he reached between her legs.

Rhazien pushed on her thighs, and she opened them wider, giving him greater access as he ran his hand through her folds and cleaned her with firm strokes.

Erissa closed her eyes, whimpering. Her desire built, growing the wetness between her thighs.

She cried out in protest when he pulled away from her, and Rhazien laughed darkly.

She spun around, wearing a displeased pout. "You're being a right tease, Rhazien."

"Is that so?" The air tasted of magic again as Rhazien placed a hand against her back and guided her across the pool to an outcropping jutting from the side where the ground was higher. He grabbed her hips, lifting her up and on the ledge. "Lay down, little doe."

Nerves, excitement, and curiosity warred within her as she lowered herself and rested her back in the shallow water, her legs hanging over the edge. The cooler water lapping around her sides had her nipples pebbling, raising the flesh along her limbs.

"There's something I want to do for you. Something for your scars. It will ease their tension and pain. It might seem frightening. But you will have to trust me, little doe." Something deeper echoed in Rhazien's voice, his magic coating the air. "I would never hurt you."

Erissa reached for him, her features gentle with a confident smile. "I'm not afraid of you, Rhazien. Whatever you wish to do, I trust you."

Rhazien's chest rumbled in a husky purr, and once again, it seemed he danced on the edge of being human, more light building from his skin. He tapped her leg. "Remember you said that."

Erissa stared at him blankly, unsure of what he wanted her to do or what his words meant.

Rhazien tapped her leg again. "Spread your legs. I want to see what's mine."

Her damp skin flushed with equal parts embarrassment and awareness for how he stood naked, but she did as he asked, spreading her legs wide under his relentless stare.

Erissa thought she might fall apart from the predatory way he watched her sex. It responded to his gaze, a pulse ticking from within its depths, leaving her breasts heavy with need and a desperate desire drenching her folds.

She tried distracting herself, staring in turn now that the water only came to his mid-thigh. He was beautiful, all hard angles and harsh lines across his well-built form. Her eyes traveled the brown hair that covered his chest, following the line past the markings that intersected below his navel to where it tapered until flaring out to cushion the thick length of him prominently displayed.

Staring did nothing to counter her nerves. She understood the mechanics, but the size of him left her with questions about him fitting inside her. Erissa wanted to try anyway. And she wanted to touch him. Would he be as soft and warm as her own folds or as unyielding and cold as the steel it appeared to be?

"Like what you see, little doe?" As Rhazien's voice hardened with his question, the length of his cock pulsed.

"Please, Rhazien." Erissa choked against a breathy moan, hot with the need to reach out and touch him.

"Touching me now would be my undoing." Rhazien stepped between her legs, the water splashing around them. He cupped her sex, eliciting a low moan from her. "When I lose control, I'm going to be buried here."

Heat rose from his skin where his hand cupped her, and his thighs brushed against her own. The light framing him grew out from his body, a near corporeal extension of himself, building into wings of fire that stretched from his back. The smoke returned. It eased from his nostrils, the damp scent of soot mixing with the aroma of desire.

Erissa reached for the fiery wings. Rhazien made no move to stop her, even as she hesitated. Gathering her courage, she touched the tips of her fingers to the blazing wings.

A tingling sensation spread through her body as heat rippled along her fingers. Erissa had never seen anything more stunning than this man and his magnificent display of magic. "Rhazien… you're not human, are you?"

CHAPTER FORTY

Erissa waited for Rhazien to offer a denial. She lay there vulnerably displayed to him, the question hanging between them as seconds ticked by.

"No." His brow furrowed, his eyes fading in and out with a glow that matched the fire from his wings. "There's nothing human about me, little doe."

She stared at him, surprised he had answered her so readily. She grappled with what to say next. "Why didn't you tell me?"

"I wanted to. But I wanted you to see the man first. To get to know him. Fall in love with him." Rhazien sighed, his wings drooping as his shoulders slumped. "I didn't want you to be influenced by what I am—or worse—afraid of me."

Rhazien pressed a finger against her lips when she started to speak again. "There is much we need to talk about, but it can wait for tomorrow. I promise to answer any questions you have. Let's have this one night together where all of tomorrow's problems can't touch us."

Erissa considered his request. His being more than human had been clear since their encounter with the Veil, and tonight's events only strengthened her suspicions until hearing him confirm the truth of it. But did it matter if he told her about the rest tonight or on the morrow? She loved him. Nothing would change that now.

Lifting her eyes to his, the worry in his gaze surprised Erissa. His stiff posture hinted at his fear she would turn him away. Everything between them built to this moment, and she wanted this time with him more than she had ever wanted anything else. Rhazien had given her a sense of freedom and a home in his arms, and she wanted to return the feeling.

Erissa gave him a reassuring smile as she spread her legs wider and beckoned him home into her warmth.

The joy and relief in Rhazien's smile rivaled the sun's intensity. "You still want to do this? You're sure, little doe?"

"I've never been more sure of anything." Erissa's reply was breathless with anticipation. "Do what you want with me. I'm yours."

A wolfish gleam sharpened his gaze. "You might regret saying that when you can barely walk out of this cave. I want you to feel me for days, little doe. In every step you take, in every way you move. I'm going to mark you as mine."

"The way you look at me makes me think such filthy things." Erissa clasped a hand against her mouth, unbelieving she admitted to having the same thoughts about him.

"Filthy things?" Rhazien trailed his hands up her inner thighs, stopping short of touching where she so desperately wanted him to. "Care to elaborate?"

Erissa wanted to swallow her tongue for revealing that to him. But a part of her longed to continue, to tell him all the ways she imagined them being together. Instead, she tried distracting him. "Wasn't there something you wanted to do for me?"

"There are many things I want to do for you, especially from this position." Rhazien hummed low in his throat. His fingers brushed against her folds, flicking against the bundle of nerves that throbbed with need.

He smiled devilishly as her back bowed in response. "But they will have to wait."

With a roll of his shoulders, the flaming wings spread out behind him, burning brighter. Rhazien grew their ferocity into ropes of living fire that moved down his arms. "You will feel the heat from the flames, but they won't burn you."

Rhazien left her no time to answer as the fiery coils snaked around his hands, and he placed one against her center.

"Sweet gods!" The words left Erissa with a yelp at the shock of the heat against her skin. Nothing could have prepared her for the intensity of having Rhazien's living fire cupping her most sensitive area.

"Are you with me?"

Erissa barely registered Rhazien speaking to her. She writhed beneath the heat. The sensation verged on the cusp of burning her, the heat carrying a sharp bite to it even as it tingled pleasurably on her skin. It spread from Rhazien's hand through her damp folds, and Erissa lost herself to it.

"Little doe?" Rhazien lessened the pressure of his hand.

Erissa protested, lifting her hips to claim it once more.

"Erissa?" Rhazien waited until her eyes locked onto his. "It's not too much?"

A moan broke through Erissa's lips. She panted, forcing the words out. "It feels... it's unlike anything..."

Her hips lifted once more, seeking Rhazien's hand, and he laughed. "Wait until you see what else these flames can do."

He placed his hand more fully against her, using the pressure of the heel of his palm to press into her center, teasing the opening and adding weight to the flames that left her breathless.

The flames curled around the nub at the apex of her thighs in a temptation that demanded a response. Erissa moaned as they covered the source of her pleasure, teasing it with the heat.

Rhazien turned his hand at the noise and slipped a finger into her tight channel. An ache built within her core. It grew stronger with every thrust of Rhazien's hand, leaving her panting for more.

Erissa struggled to keep her breathing even as he toyed with her. "Rhazien…"

"If you're still talking, I must be doing something wrong." Rhazien added a second finger, pumping them in and out as Erissa caught his rhythm and matched it, the full swell of her hips lifting to meet each thrust.

She choked on the moan lodged in her throat. She clenched around him, lifting her hips higher to force his touch deeper. More, she wanted more.

Tension built in her core. It grew with every pass of the flames and Rhazien's touch against her sensitive hood. He hooked his fingers inside of her and found a spot that left her biting her lip to keep from screaming her pleasure as he massaged the area in firm strokes.

Rhazien let out a deep purr. "Come for me, little doe. I want to feel you clamp down as you suck me in."

Everything weaved together, overwhelming her until her inner walls shook with the power of her release, the cavern filling with Erissa's purple light.

Erissa knew nothing but Rhazien in the moment, unsure if she even knew her own name. She lost herself in a haze of bliss and never wanted to leave its embrace.

Rhazien took one of her nipples into his mouth. He sucked the peak, biting down, and Erissa came, clenching around his fingers as she screamed.

The flame licked across her folds, their movements gently bringing everything back into focus. Erissa caught Rhazien's gaze. She started to speak, started to beg for more of him, for the hardness nestled between his legs, but Rhazien's hands drew her attention.

Scales covered the back of his hand. They stopped short of the webbing that had appeared between his fingers. The length of them grew with onyx talons protruding from their tips. Flames coated both hands, burning against a golden aura.

Words failed Erissa.

Rhazien stepped closer in the wake of her silence, and Erissa shivered when his length brushed against her thigh. "Do you trust me, little doe?"

"Yes." No hesitation weighed down Erissa's answer, but wariness darkened her eyes. She swallowed the lump in her throat. "I trust you, Rhazien."

He placed one hand against the scarring, spreading it until the talons spanned the width of her chest. The other hand moved to his cock. He took the length in hand and brought it to rest against Erissa's center. "Hold still for me."

Erissa's desire stirred again as the head of Rhazien's cock teased her opening. Her breath hitched, pressing her breasts into the sharp ends of the talons, eliciting a frustrated moan. She circled her hips, trying to draw Rhazien into her.

He only chuckled at her efforts. "Is this what you want? My cock inside of you, claiming you?"

Erissa nodded. Her blush highlighted the glow still marking her skin.

"I need to hear you say it, little doe."

"Yes, Rhazien. Yes. Take me as yours."

His eyes darkened to a deep amber, and he smiled at her.

Erissa answered his smile with a loving one of her own. She needed this and reveled at the feel of him as he rubbed his length against her slick opening, coating himself in her essence. Nothing would lie between them now.

Rhazien worked his length into her with slow strokes, carefully stretching her. His talons flexed across her chest with each shallow thrust.

The deeper he went, the tighter she became, and Erissa winced at the unfamiliar pressure.

Rhazien stilled as he noticed her reaction and withdrew until only the head of his cock remained inside. Wrapping a hand around the base, he directed his flames to spread the flickering heat across it.

"Are you insane?" Erissa propped herself on her elbows. "You can't possibly think you're putting *that* inside me when it's on fire."

A rakish quirk of his lips brought out his dimples. "That?"

Erissa twirled a hand, gesturing at his hips. "You know what I mean."

"My cock?" Rhazien leaned to kiss her belly button. He kissed up her torso and her throat until he reached her ear. "Say it for me. Tell me how much you want my cock."

He rubbed himself against Erissa in taunting circles as he pushed in slightly and withdrew, setting a slow pace that kept her far away from reaching her peak. "I can always *convince* you, little doe. Would you like that?"

Rhazien nuzzled her neck, his mouth resting against her pulse. He nipped her vein and chuckled when Erissa bit her fist to keep from screaming, his cock inching deeper with each shallow thrust.

Erissa clenched around him. "Rhazien, please."

"Say it, little doe." Rhazien sucked against her pulse.

The heat and pressure combined into a deliciously wicked sensation that eased the ache and drove Erissa wild. With each thrust, she rocked her hips against him, wanting him deeper. "I need... Rhazien... I need... your cock. Please."

Rhazien abandoned his restraint. He slid home with one smooth, powerful thrust that hit the deepest part of her desire.

Erissa screamed as she clenched around him, but not from pleasure alone. As Rhazien thrust into her, he raked his talons down Erissa's scars, opening the old wounds with shallow cuts. The fire traveled down his arms and across her chest, sinking into the open skin.

Differing sensations warred within Erissa as the pleasure of Rhazien's continued thrusts mixed with the pain his talons inflicted. The flames added another level to the sensations pulsing through her, and Erissa gave up trying to let one win over the other. She surrendered to them all, letting them blend into a brewing storm that threatened to break loose.

Her eyes opened, seeking Rhazien's. And by the gods, he made a breathtaking sight.

The fiery wings spread out behind him, the bright light mixing with her iridescent glow as his power filled her.

She heard a low mewl echoing through the cavern, and it took a moment before Erissa understood the sound came from her.

A black mist formed around her, coating her skin as it became one with the flames. Erissa could no longer tell if the fire caressed her skin or the glittering depths of the black magic. They worked in tandem, coaxing the heat along her scars in a pleasurable mix of comfort and pain as Rhazien repeatedly slammed himself to the hilt inside of her.

The combination confused her, but she pushed it to the side and surrendered entirely to the moment and Rhazien's hands on her body.

And then his flame-coated cock hit the perfect spot, the heat intensifying her arousal until the storm finally broke, and release blazed through her.

She vaguely noticed Rhazien still pumping into her as he sought his own release. His body went still with a final thrust, spilling himself deep inside her. Rhazien leaned forward, pressing his forehead between her breasts and peppering kisses along their generous swell. Her core throbbed with the aftershocks of her release. But the world still spun as the flames played against her scars.

Rhazien called back his fire. He helped Erissa sit up slowly. She shivered as the movement caused her folds to rub together.

"Look down."

She gave Rhazien a puzzled look before doing as he asked.

The scars were no longer raised. They lay flush against her skin, the puckered lines no longer angry. Erissa trailed a hand down the length of one, not fully believing her eyes. She rolled her shoulders and let out a shocked cry at finding the stiffness and pain gone.

Rhazien had remade her this night, in more ways than one.

Erissa grappled with what to say. Nothing seemed adequate, and a different emotion swelled inside her, drowning her in its intensity. Her breath came in ragged gasps, tears blurring her eyes, and she felt the fire of his magic burning from a never-ending well. It drew hers into it, the two melding into one until the royal purple glittered in the flickering flames. A permanent piece of Rhazien lodged in her very soul.

"Thank you, Rhazien." The words failed to contain the gratitude and love she had for him for sharing in the burden of her pain, choosing to remove it from her, replacing the torturous memories with one so pure nothing else compared.

She reached for him and pulled his head down to kiss him. Erissa poured all her love and gratitude into that kiss and smiled against his lips as she felt his heart warm through their bond.

He broke the kiss and picked her up as if she weighed nothing, carrying her through the water to the soft mattress awaiting them. "Come, wife. You can spend all night showing me just how grateful you are."

CHAPTER FORTY-ONE

"I would rather spend eternity chained to the Keeper himself than listen to another moment of this nonsense." Yorrith's chest heaved, his breath laboring against his rising temper. "Will the two of you cease your fighting?"

Novus agreed. He watched the Seelie King, Yorrith, argue with two of the Zorathi as they set up camp in the shelter of the surrounding forest, Novus's magic shielding him from view in the gathering shadows. Kyrenic and Imryll had done nothing but bicker since Novus had arrived.

The Zorathi twins quieted and turned as one to stare at the Seelie king. Kyrenic's fiery temperament flared to life, and the time had come to intervene. Novus let the shadows fall, motioning Nephinae to walk ahead of him.

Kyrenic advanced toward the Seelie with lethal grace. "You dare speak to us like—"

"Like the children you are?" Nephinae stepped into the clearing, Novus trailing a few steps behind, and made her way to the King's side.

A tense silence followed her words, but Kyrenic stopped advancing.

"Come now, Kyrenic. You will send poor Yorrith into hysterics if you keep it up." Nephinae patted the King's arm, honey dripping from her tone as Yorrith rolled his eyes. "We can't have a fainting King on our hands when we've no settee to offer him."

"A settee?" Yorrith arched a brow but did not move, letting the Zorathi's hand linger. "You can do better than that."

Nephinae squeezed his arm. "Perhaps I can fan Your Highness and his delicate sensibilities."

Pink stained the high cheekbones of Yorrith as Nephinae poked a leg from beneath her dress. The sides were slit clean to her hips, and she pulled at the long panel shielding her front. "Do you think the length of my dress will do the trick?"

Interesting. Novus indulged in the interplay of their conversation, allowing Yorrith a response. The Seelie did not disappoint.

"Tell me something, Zorathi." Yorrith bent forward until his gaze reached Nephinae's height.

Her eyes brightened, the white sharpening as light built through the enchanted orbs, and Yorrith smiled.

But whatever else he intended to say became overshadowed as Kyrenic swore and spat on the ground before Yorrith's feet. "Watch yourself, Seelie shite."

Yorrith cut a bored look at Kyrenic. It proved to be motivation enough for the hotheaded twin.

With a flick of his fingers, Kyrenic prepared to release his power.

Imryll dropped the bedroll she held. "Brother…"

Kyrenic paid her no mind, his fingertips and eyes glowing.

A sigh left Novus as he stepped into the shadows, prepared to use them to appear next to Kyrenic and intervene, but the Seelie King surprised him.

Hooking an arm around Nephinae's waist, Yorrith tried to twist her behind his back. The Zorathi moved faster. She used the momentum of Yorrith's action to step in front of him.

Lightening exploded from Kyrenic's fingers. It streaked through the air with an angry scream, heading toward Yorrith and Nephinae.

Wrath crackled along Nephinae's ruined skin, and a white shield grew from her body, shooting behind her and encasing Yorrith in its protective circle.

"Nephinae!" Yorrith fought against the shield as Kyrenic's power raced toward the unprotected Zorathi.

Novus halted, watching. Nephinae was more than capable of caring for herself against the likes of Kyrenic. After all, she made him.

A devilish smirk turned Nephinae's expression into something strong enough to strike fear in most creatures. It distracted Kyrenic, and his magic faltered long enough for Nephinae to strike with hers.

Kyrenic's display of magic held nothing over Nephinae's. She called to the heavens, summoning the strength of the moon overhead, the only Zorathi with power enough to pull from its well. She wrapped herself in its bright light, and it only took seconds to charge in the scarred channels marking her flesh.

With the light at its maximum, she wound it around Kyrenic, letting the white magic bleed into his ears and nostrils, taking hold of his mind as his sister screamed behind him.

"You think to attack me, young one?" Nephinae stalked toward Kyrenic, tightening her grip on the magic, the height of her power making the twins and king flinch. "Do you forget who I am? *What* I am?"

She forced Kyrenic to his knees, throwing up a hand to silence Imryll's pleas. "Let me remind you, young one, so you may remember to bow next time before I command it of you."

Imryll stepped in their direction. "Enough. He has learned his lesson."

"I doubt he has. But one more interruption and you will take his place," Novus cautioned.

The heated color left Imryll's face with Novus's warning, bringing a deathly pallor to her skin.

Nephinae held tighter, twisting her magic through his mind until she grabbed Kyrenic's lightning. She called it back to him, and it inched closer, sullen at her sharp command. "You think to turn your power against someone without provocation?"

Kyrenic stared at her with more than mutiny in his eyes. Jealousy flashed across his face as his attention snapped between the vengeful Zorathi in front of him and the Seelie King she protected behind a wall of her power.

Novus laughed to himself, studying the exchange. This day proved to be full of revelations.

"Open your mouth, young one." Nephinae tapped Kyrenic's chin.

When he refused, she pressed her nails to his temples, digging the sharp ends into his skin. Her eyes shined brighter as their depths rivaled the lightning dancing around them. She whispered to Kyrenic, words that were for him alone, and the magic-bound Zorathi opened his mouth.

"Good boy," Nephinae encouraged. She called to Kyrenic's magic again, and it came willingly, slithering through the air until the charged bolt hovered above the male's head. "You will swallow it and keep it there without uttering a sound—no matter the pain—until I permit you to release it. Do you understand?"

Kyrenic nodded, keeping his mouth wide.

Nephinae smiled, stroking her hand down his cheek. She beckoned the magic forward until it touched the Zorathi's lips and slowly entered his mouth.

The joining offered no peace. Kyrenic convulsed as the lightning inched down his throat, the smell of burning tissue filling the air. But he remained silent.

Yorrith stared at Kyrenic with horror, banging his fists on the imprisoning shield, and Novus chuckled. It had been some time since the

Seelie King visited the Court of the Frosted Moon. He should visit more often—if only for the desensitization to the methods of the Zorathi.

When the last trail of lightning disappeared into Kyrenic, Nephinae tapped his chin. "Close your mouth and do not move."

She turned, dismissing the disgraced Zorathi, and dropped the barrier around Yorrith.

A scowl darkened the King's features. "What have you done?"

Nephinae balled her fists into the layered fabric at her hips. "Is that all I get after saving your life?"

"Saving my life?" Yorrith sputtered, pointing to where Kyrenic seized against the burn of the pure light energy. "Does this look like saving my life?"

"The Zorathi have their own code of honor." Nephinae sniffed and tried to hide the action by scratching the tip of her nose. "What Kyrenic did warrants justice."

"This is justice?" Yorrith shouted.

"And this is thanks?" Nephinae's tone matched the King's raised voice. She crossed her arms. "Am I not supposed to value your life? Should I have let him strike you dead before me?"

Nephinae's questions left Yorrith standing there mute. He opened his mouth only to shut it again.

"Careful, Neph," Novus crooned. "Someone might believe you care for the King."

The white-haired Zorathi laughed, the lyrical sound catching on the wind. "You say that like it is the absolute truth. I avoided war between the courts. Why else would I intervene?"

Novus looked her up and down. Something fake rattled behind the laugh as if he hit too close to the mark. "Someone needs to consider my reputation. One of my own cavorting with the Seelie—and their King at that—reflects poorly on my authority."

Nephinae shifted from one foot to the other, and Novus's face turned hawkish, sensing an easy prey. He rarely caught the leader of the Zorathi in a weak moment.

"Cavorting? Even you go too far." She moved away from Yorrith as Imryll rushed over to her brother. "Can we return to why we are here?"

"I would like that as well." Yorrith's voice betrayed his rising temper. "But can we do something about this?"

Novus followed Yorrith's outstretched arm, a cruel smile playing about his lips as he watched Kyrenic shake against the pain of the magic burning its way through his body. "A fitting punishment for violating the Zorathi code. My own attention would not have been so lenient. Nephinae offered him mercy. Although I do have to give the Zorathi credit, a lesser Fae—a Seelie perhaps—would have succumbed already."

"The Unseelie need to move beyond such brutality," Yorrith argued.

"You forget the atrocities of the Remaking far too quickly, Yorrith," Nephinae scolded. "The Zorathi were bred in brutality. It is all we have known."

She did not react if she noticed the pain stiffening Yorrith's features. Yorrith's role in the War of the Remaking had always been a closely regarded secret, but the pain of losing his god and entire court to time magic gone wrong remained the stuff of gossip even three and a half thousand years later. Yorrith never recovered, choosing to remain alone in the Seelie's crowning city, Zaestiraen. Whatever magic he possessed, he never practiced. Even by Novus's standards, Nephinae's comment hit low to dismiss Yorrith in such a way.

"Lesser Fae never survive the Zorathi making. He bore that, and he will bear this. It is not open for discussion." Nephinae rolled her shoulders. "Kyrenic will learn no one is above our laws. Only then will he be released."

Yorrith threw his hands in the air. "Backward bastards."

A barely perceptible flinch pulled at Nephinae's features, one so small Novus nearly missed it. Interesting indeed. But fun for another night. There were more pressing matters to address. "Have you sensed the girl, Yorrith?"

The King did not answer, returning to where his belongings sat. He fiddled with the layers of his tent, expertly arranging the folds around wooden poles.

Novus took the continued silence as an answer. He pushed the sleeves of his tunic up to the elbow as a throne of shadow emerged behind him, with the simplest of thoughts directing its formation.

Its presence did not escape the notice of the older king. "Ostentatious even here?"

"Is there any other way to be?" Novus arranged himself on the shadowed throne. "Focusing on a magicked chair will not dissuade me from my purpose here."

Again, Yorrith remained silent.

"I grow impatient, *Your Highness*." Novus crossed his legs, lounging back against the pliant shadows. The Seelie King would sense the girl one way or another. "Your cooperation can be forced."

Nephinae froze at the threat, and Novus observed her from the corner of his eye.

Yorrith halted, turning to stare at Nephinae with a challenge. "You would do such a thing, Zorathi?"

No hesitation swayed Nephinae's answer. "I swore an oath at the Remaking and again at the Keeping. As did you. The girl has been promised, Yorrith. There is nothing to be done."

Yorrith drove one end of the tent pole into the ground. "I didn't know, Nephinae. Damn the gods, I didn't know. Should that not count for something?"

The Zorathi made to step toward the king, but Novus held up a hand, stopping her. "You are only dragging this out, Yorrith. It has been five days since I called in the bargain. Either you sense her voluntarily, or it will be coerced."

"She is happy, Novus." Yorrith's words shouted their pain for all they were calmly stated. "I can feel it. Wherever she has found herself, she is happy."

"Without her, we will all die. The girl included." No time remained for emotional drivel. Novus needed the girl as quickly as possible. Whatever demons the King carried, he would not entertain them. "Tell us where the girl is, or Nephinae will pull it from you."

Yorrith busied himself with the rest of the tent poles. Novus let him have a moment to weigh his options.

When the king spoke again, malice colored every word. "South. She is heading south."

"He lies." A shadow grew from the throne, weaving itself around Novus.

A scoff came from Novus. The shadow must be mistaken. Nephinae's magic always proved to be an effective motivation.

"I am beyond mistakes." The shadow slithered across his shoulders. *"The Seelie lies."*

Novus looked at the king. "Where is she, Seelie?"

"You doubt my word?" Yorrith demanded an answer.

"I believe my Lord does." Nephinae went to Yorrith then. She circled around him, clicking her tongue in disapproval. "Lying is unbecoming of your stature."

"Let us speak of your unbecoming stature, Zorathi," Yorrith returned.

The sound of Yorrith's reply grated in the background as Novus's magic spoke once more. *"You underestimate him. He would do anything to keep the girl from you. His concern for her outweighs anything else. But it is of no matter."* The shadow laughed, the sound low and gravelly. *"He is not the only one who can find her."*

Novus inclined his head, allowing the words to wash through him. No one else held a link strong enough to hear the girl's magic, and without it, there was no finding her if she did not wish to be found. Yorrith is the only way.

"Ah, but this is where you are wrong." The shadow played about his ear. *"Listen... her magic calls to you. It draws me even now. Can you not hear it?"*

Try as he might, Novus heard nothing through Nephinae and Yorrith bickering. "Nephinae..."

Nephinae stood in front of Yorrith, fists clenched. "You condescending, arrogant ass—"

"Better to be an arrogant ass," Yorrith snarled, "than the pampered princess of a feral dog."

"At least that feral dog has no fear of his own shadow." Lightning danced across Nephinae's face. "Tell me, Seelie King, how long has it been since you have used your magic? Centuries?"

Yorrith took a threatening step. "You know nothing of—"

"Silence!" Novus stood, roaring the word. He dropped the shield around his power and let it pulse through the camp in rolling waves that stilled everyone. Even Kyrenic stopped fidgeting against the punishing presence. "I give no care for how it started, only that it stops. I cannot think through your endless yapping."

Silence reigned. Novus turned from the murderous glare Nephinae directed his way. The Zorathi's anger mattered little to him. If she did not wish to be called down like a child, she should cease acting like one.

He called the magic to him, moving to sit once more upon the throne of shadows, but stopped when the magic did not respond to his summons.

It moved away from Novus toward the northeast, its attention drawn beyond the town of Freyborn. A large section of the magic shimmered with violet and crimson light. The colors twisted through the darkest parts of his shadows, where the blue deepened nearly to black until night met sunrise and sunset, the three blending together into something that defied explanation in its simple beauty.

The voice purred. *"There she is. The violet comes to life against every fiber of my being. Can you not feel her as you see her?"*

The swirling magic pulsed through the space as the colors continued to intertwine, and the girl's presence hovered against him, a tangible sensation that coated his every nerve ending. It grew and then faded in its intensity before starting the teasing dance all over again.

"Is she..." Novus laughed, the sound of it startling everyone. When had he last laughed?

"Who?" Nephinae asked. "What are you laughing at?"

"She is," the voice answered him, bringing the entwined magics to wrap around Novus. *"Do you feel her against you? Moving beneath your chest as surely as she moves beneath another?"*

The magic's assurance of the girl's actions made Novus pause. He stilled himself, and something bloomed beneath his breast when all had quieted inside of him. He smiled as the sensation moved through his body to lay parallel against his own soul.

"Ah, Veiled One. You are full of surprises." Novus sat on this throne again, studying the combined colors. Did the connected powers work both ways? He hummed low in his throat, letting the vibration grow and reach into the magics.

Novus laughed again as the vibrating strands traced along the lengths of purple. Its touch feathered out across the other magic, a languorous caress that grew the light coming from them in a shivering display. The shadowed mists followed in its wake, nipping and scratching behind its seductive touch. And Novus laughed once more as the lighter magic bowed into its ministrations.

Yorrith's voice cut through the unexpected moment. "Care to share what has your attention?"

"I'm afraid if I did, *my King*," Novus sneered, "you would expire on the spot. Or attempt a beheading. I have no patience for either."

"If you will not share, I insist you do something about this." Yorrith gestured to the Zorathi writhing on the ground. "Or do you intend to let your dog torture him for what remains of the evening?"

"Why should I intervene?" Novus enjoyed the red color suffusing the king's cheeks as he toyed with the Fae as easily as he did the combined magics. "The Zorathi can handle their own."

Yorrith did not back down. "Because you have pledged to free them from the Zorathi vow that binds them to blindly follow anything the Unseelie Lord commands. How is this freedom?"

"Oh, for the Creator's sake!" Nephinae turned to Kyrenic. She snapped her fingers, drawing the electricity from the lesser Fae. It came to her, laying along her lines of scarring until the light faded into the grooves. She waved a hand at Yorrith. "Run to him, then. He might appreciate your nursing hand."

As Kyrenic tried to protest, a choking sound escaped him, a glare landing on Nephinae.

Novus sighed, the deep sound lacking all mirth. "It appears the young one has not learned his lesson."

Nephinae ran her fingers through the length of her hair, avoiding looking toward Yorrith. "Until his throat heals, he can think of his insolent behavior with every raw swallow."

Pinching the bridge of his nose, Yorrith stalked back to his tent, ignoring them all and missing the drop in Nephinae's posture as he walked past her. Novus watched her with renewed interest. He needed to talk with the Zorathi, but it would wait another day. The girl demanded his immediate attention.

Novus beckoned his magic. It came readily, bringing the seamless blend of midnight, morning, and evening with it. Tomorrow would take them northeast and toward the girl, but for now, she demanded his attention in other, more pleasurable ways. With a feral grin, Novus seated himself on the shadowed throne and caressed the shimmering strands.

CHAPTER FORTY-TWO

Erissa never wanted to leave the seclusion of the cavern.

This evening would bring with it all the questions she needed to ask Rhazien. She had her suspicions about the source of his magic, the implications making her worry her lip.

He came up behind her, placing a hand on her hip. "Ready, little doe?"

"In a moment." Erissa reached for the last blanket and spread it across the mattress, returning it to the condition with which they found it. Her thighs tingled as she bent over, teased by the memory of last evening—and of today—spent on its soft haven.

Leaning over her, Rhazien spoke against her ear, eliciting a shiver. "Care to share what's making you color so prettily?"

Erissa tossed her hair to the side. "Not in this lifetime."

"Come now, wife. Only filthy thoughts would redden you so." He kissed behind her ear, his lips brushing against her skin as he spoke. "Tell me which of them is playing in your mind."

Erissa regarded him over her shoulder. "You're never going to let go of that, are you?"

"Not in this lifetime or the next." Rhazien gave an anticipatory smirk, humor etched in the lines of his mouth. "Unless you tell me what those thoughts are. Maybe I'll have mercy on you. Better yet, I can make them come true for you."

Erissa rolled her eyes. She turned and pushed him playfully. "Has anyone told you that you're insufferable?"

"Not today."

"I could change that for you." Erissa tapped her foot against his lower leg. "Give you a good kick while I'm at it."

Rhazien laughed. "I love seeing you like this, little doe."

Erissa tipped her head. "Like what?"

Rhazien tapped her on the nose. "Sassy. Happy. Content."

"I am happy." It surprised Erissa that she meant it. This time spent with Rhazien was precious to her. "Thank you, Rhazien."

"For what?"

"For all of this." Erissa shrugged, fidgeting with the sleeves of her dress. "It's been a long time since I had anything to be happy about, and it's all because of you."

Rhazien pulled her into his arms and kissed her. What began as a slow meeting of the lips quickly became thick with emotion. Their unhurried embrace turned into a frantic exchange of tongues and hands.

Rhazien picked Erissa up and laid her face down on the mattress. He undid the row of buttons, almost tearing a few in his haste.

When he had undone enough of them, he flipped her over, freeing her breasts.

He sank into them, taking one of the stiffening peaks into his mouth.

"Rhazien? Erissa?" Islone's voice carried down the passageway leading to the house.

Rhazien cradled his forehead between Erissa's welcoming cleavage, sighing. "The gods be damned."

"Rhazien Merrick, I heard that," Islone said, her scolding tone echoing through the cavern.

"Good. Then you can hear me when I tell you to go away."

"Rhazien!" Erissa sat up on her elbows, staring at him in reproach. "Don't talk to Islone in such a manner."

He helped Erissa stand, turning her around to do up her dress.

"Listen to your wife, Rhaz. You might be older than me, but I can still take you over my knee." Islone's voice sounded closer. "Are the two of you decent? There's something we'd like to show you."

"Older?" Erissa's jaw dropped. She blinked several times, convinced she had misheard Islone. She turned to Rhazien. "What does she mean that you're older than her?"

"The Creator be damned too." Anger laced Rhazien's words. "Of all the things you could have said, Islone, and you choose to point out our age difference?"

"Like it's my fault you haven't spilled your secret to your bride." Islone stomped around the corner, clearly annoyed with Rhazien's temper. She stopped as soon as she entered the cave, her face full of shock. With great care, her hands traced the moss and flowers now covering the walls. "How did this get here?"

"Erissa made them. Her magic takes over when she's happy." Rhazien's grin was rakish. "And I made sure to make her very happy. For hours."

Islone chuckled. "By leaving her alone? That would make any girl have a wonderful night."

Rhazien put his hands on his hips. "I'll have you know—"

Erissa ignored them as they bickered and replayed her conversation with Rhazien from the previous afternoon. She regarded him with a new consideration. "You're a little older than I think you are..."

Even for someone as uneducated in the world as she, Rhazien's craftsmanship in his wind chimes was remarkable, with fine detailing that would have taken considerable time to master. She assumed only a few years lay between them, but Islone's words, his actions yesterday, and his significant skill left her with more questions to add to the endless pile.

Rhazien cupped her elbow, leaning into her side. "Little doe, I promised to tell you the truth, and I will. Tonight."

"No, not tonight." Islone picked up the sack they brought with them. "We can drop the pretense. All Cropari knows you're here. You can come back through the house."

"And why can't I talk to my wife tonight?" Rhazien crossed his arms. He did little to disguise his irritation with Islone.

Islone swatted her hand in his direction, dropping the bag. "Will you settle already?"

"Will you get on with it already?" Rhazien grumbled, crossing his arms.

Islone cut her eyes at Rhazien, staring him down like a naughty child. Erissa tensed beside him, waiting for a verbal lashing, but one did not come.

Instead, Erissa smothered a giggle as Islone mimicked Rhazien's stance, surprised by the other woman's lack of anger. She would have regretted the choice if she had dared to speak to an elder that way in Emberhold. Then again, Islone hardly counted as the elder in this room.

"Will you get on with listening to me?" Islone grumbled at Rhazien, having fun with her mimicking role. She straightened, trying to suppress her own laughter. "Do you have any idea how childish you sound?"

"Do you have any idea what you interrupted?" Rhazien rubbed a hand against his jaw, trying to disguise the slight tilt to his lips.

"Oh, I know exactly what I interrupted, and I'm not sorry for it." Islone dropped her arms, resuming her collection of supplies. "The entire populous is waiting for you both in the market."

Rhazien groaned. "Tell me they're not throwing a festival."

Islone paused momentarily as she took the linens off the mattress and placed them in an empty basket sitting to the side. She said nothing, letting the silence lengthen.

Erissa tried not to laugh again when Rhazien threw his arms up in exasperation and paced away from them.

He turned around abruptly, his eyes narrowing. "Islone, I swear to the gods, if you helped them make a fertility blanket..."

A choking noise came from Erissa as Islone slyly regarded them. "I may have contributed some of the fabric..."

Rhazien pinched the bridge of his nose, breathing heavily.

"But the sewing was all Selsula and her brood." Islone held a hand over her heart. Her expression held not an ounce of regret.

He shook his head. "You're going to scare her away before our bed has even gone cold."

"Rhazien!" Erissa scolded.

"Do you want a fertility blanket, little doe?" He walked toward her, his steps filled with a leisurely grace and a wicked smile on his handsome face. "I'm happy to oblige the desire once we get rid of the old bat—"

A boot interrupted Rhazien as it hit him in the head. "By the gods!"

Erissa dissolved into a fit of laughter as Islone lowered her arm. She struggled to breathe, her stomach cramping with the force of her mirth.

Islone went to retrieve her boot, her stride boastful. "What were you saying, Rhaz? Something about an old bat?"

Erissa quieted her laughter. "Are you both finished? I believe people are waiting for us."

Islone picked up her boot and shoved her foot into it. "Of course, love. Let's get going." She tossed a wink at Rhazien. "Your fertility blanket awaits you. I can't wait until I have a baby Fef—"

"That's it." Rhazien picked Islone up and walked over to the side of the pool. He tossed her into the deeper end. He returned to Erissa's side, where she stood crying from laughing so hard.

Islone broke through the top of the water, coughing over the water and her own laughter.

Taking Erissa's hand in his, Rhazien led her to the passage Islone had emerged from. "We'll see you in the market, Izzy."

"Are you a Fefnirion?"

Rhazien missed a step at Erissa's question, coming close to tripping over his feet and taking her with him as they left the house and walked toward the market.

Horror gripped her features as she steadied her footing, her chest tightening. Erissa did not intend to say the question out loud. At least, not yet. She had no idea if dragons were even real, not to mention they were about to reach the market.

"You don't need to answer now. We can talk about it later." Awkwardness gripped her heart, squeezing it in the quiet that followed her accidental utterance.

She continued talking, trying to fill the space that opened between them. "The flames, the scales, the smoke, the wings, your age—how old are you anyway? Oh, and the painting on your body. It's identical to the one on the house, and your scales looked awfully similar to it as well. It can't be a mere coincidence."

Rhazien stared straight ahead, his lips pinched together.

Erissa winced, cutting him off when he opened his mouth to speak. "On second thought, there's no need to answer the question."

"The word you're looking for is a tattoo." At Erissa's bemused look, Rhazien tapped his hand against his stomach where the drawing lay. "The painting. It's called a tattoo."

"That's what you choose to say now?"

Rhazien stopped walking and turned to face her. "I know you have questions, and I want to answer them. We don't have to go to the festival. We can go back to our room and talk through this right now. You need only say so."

Erissa wanted to agree to the tempting offer. She opened her mouth, prepared to agree to forgo the festival. The words never came, though, as a bundle of children raced past her to throw themselves onto Rhazien. Micmus and Orbas trailed behind them.

A chorus of greetings and giggles came from the four children plastered to Rhazien's tall frame.

"Uncle Rhazien!" The tallest of the children wrapped her arms around Rhazien's waist, her red hair a beacon in the waning sun.

"Move over, Meired." A younger boy tossed an elbow into her side. "Uncle Rhaz, why did you leave yesterday? We missed you."

"Be patient, Towin." Micmus admonished.

"You're asking for the impossible." The girl looked identical to her brother, with the same sharp nose, bright green eyes, and dark hair.

"Shut up, Thomrynn." He threw his other elbow in her direction.

The youngest of the children hid behind Rhazien's leg, staring at Erissa through a mop of dark curls. "Who's the pretty lady?"

"That's Erissa. She's my wife." Rhazien freed himself from the other three and crouched beside the little girl. "Erissa, this one is Ysalila. Don't tell the others, but she's my favorite."

Erissa froze as each child stared at her. "Hi." She gave a little wave, feeling stupid as the older children snickered and whispered behind their hands.

"If I hear one more sound out of you three, you will head home." Islone appeared behind Meired, Towin, and Thomrynn.

Properly chastised, they dropped their hands, and each muttered a greeting.

"That's better." Islone stepped around them, taking the arm Micmus held out. "Everyone ready?"

"Your hair is soaking wet," Micmus said.

"You have Rhazien to thank for that. I didn't have time to dry it." Islone headed toward the market. "Come now. I've changed into something dry and warmer, and we're late enough."

As they grew closer, the air rang with boisterous chaos. The sounds of people singing blended with the laughter of easy conversations.

Dameknaars weaved along the path, their glowing light leading them closer to the revelry. Above them hung lines of *rihpaidirs*. The burning light made the color of the fabrics richer, their tattered ends fluttering in the light breeze flowing through the city. People lined the streets. They threw flowers as Erissa and Rhazien walked past them, calling out to the couple with good wishes and teasing comments about the *maharigra*.

When they finally reached the market, Erissa stopped, speechless at the changes.

Low tables of various shapes and sizes were spread around the market in a half circle. Rugs sat under each table with pillows spread across them. In the center sat a raised platform. It housed a table for two overflowing with food. Behind it sat a pile of gifts around the *rihpaidir* tree.

A fire sat in the middle of the crescent shape. Most of the people gathered around its warmth. Some played instruments Erissa had never seen. Others danced to the hypnotic music, stomping their feet and rolling their bodies to the fast melody.

One of the women noticed them first and called out. Everyone turned their attention to the newlyweds, cheering their union.

Erissa's eyes jumped from person to person, trying to take it all in. Never in her life had she received such a reception.

"Erissa?" Rhazien squeezed her hand, nodding his head back in the direction they had come.

With such genuine happiness, Erissa shoved away her reservations and questions. She needed to talk with Rhazien but did not have it in her to deny the generosity the Croparian people continued to give her. It had been freely offered from the moment she walked through the city gates.

So, she placed a brilliant smile on her face, allowing the infectious happiness in the air to permeate her senses, and squeezed his hand in return. "We have a celebration to attend."

The late hour wore on Erissa. Her jaw ached from smiling all evening, her feet hurt from dancing, and her chest felt tight like someone sat upon it.

She shifted from hip to hip and tried to get comfortable against the cushion beneath her.

"Erissa?" Rhazien cleared his throat.

Erissa stopped moving and focused on him, her chest tightening. "What?"

Selsula held a folded blanket out to her. "The fertility offering. I asked if you wanted to take it, child."

"Oh, I'm sorry." Erissa blinked at her for a moment, the old woman's words not registering. Her breath picked up speed, and the market closed in on her. "What did you say?"

Selsula glanced between her and Rhazien, her brow drawn. "The fertility blanket. Our people's tradition is to gift a newly wedded couple with a blanket made from blessed *rihpaidir*."

Erissa reached for the blanket. Selsula kept talking, but she struggled to hear any of it over her heartbeat. Had it always been that loud?

Rhazien rubbed a hand across her back, drawing her attention once more. "Erissa, are you feeling well?"

"Yes. No. I—" Erissa stood, his touch burning against her skin as she knocked the table and sent everything tumbling. She passed the blanket to Rhazien and reached for the turned-over items but gave up halfway as Rhazien tried to touch her again. "I think I need a moment of privacy."

Erissa bolted toward the women's tent and slipped through the flaps guarding its entrance. She found the inside empty of anyone else. Her chest heaved, trying to draw a full breath. When did she start holding it?

Forcing herself to exhale, Erissa massaged her chest. It did little to help the building ache. The thought of going back out there made her head spin, and the pain worsened. There were too many people out there, too many people who wanted too much from her on the day when she had the least to give. On the day when it all started.

She moved away from the entrance, glancing at it warily over her shoulder. There had to be another way out of the tent.

Moving to the back, Erissa felt along the fabric folds, searching for a break in the tight weaves. She found one just as she heard Rhazien calling for her.

She needed to run, to get away. She could not return to the party with all of its guests wanting her to take their gifts and accept their well wishes. It felt like a trap, and that any moment, someone would come and snatch all of it away.

Ducking out the back of the tent, Erissa took off running. Footsteps sounded behind her. She ran up the back road, diving down the first path she saw.

The pain in her chest burned unbearably with her ragged breathing. Another path came into view, begging her feet to run faster so she might disappear down the darkened road.

The footsteps pounding behind her grew closer. "Erissa!"

Hearing Rhazien's voice, she hesitated, slowing down. That moment cost her dearly. He grabbed her from behind and pulled her to a stop.

She jerked out of his arms, backing away.

He held his hands out in front of him. "What happened? Why did you run?"

Erissa put her hands over her ears, shaking her head.

He stepped closer. "I can't help if you don't tell me what's wrong, little doe."

"I don't want to feel this way."

"Feel what way?"

Erissa wrapped her arms across her stomach and whimpered. "I don't know. It's everything. The people, the noise, the gifts, the food... it's too much. They're all too nice."

Rhazien tipped his head. "Did someone do or say something to upset you?"

"You don't understand."

"Then help me."

"Everything is new, Rhazien." Erissa shook her head again, hoping it would dislodge her wayward thoughts, but it did nothing. They remained, racing through her head and straining her breathing as they grew more intrusive. "My world has completely shifted. If I didn't know my place in it before, I certainly don't know it now. And I'm supposed to be here and be happy when I didn't even know what the word meant not too long ago. It's too much. I couldn't breathe with everyone around me. Talking to me and wanting to give me things."

Erissa's eyes were wild with despair. "Do you know the last time someone gave me a real gift?" She laughed, the sound hollow and ugly. She tugged on her necklace. "It was thirteen years ago. On the day my parents left me in that room to rot. And even now, I can't find it in me to take it off."

Rhazien reached for her, his face filled with compassion. And somehow, that made things worse. She never wanted his pity.

She jerked away from the gesture, tightening her arms until her fingernails dug into the fabric and pinched her sides. "Don't touch me."

Something broke a little more inside of her at Rhazien's hurt expression. It unleashed a flood of tears. "I'm sorry. I didn't mean..."

He tried to touch her again, reaching for her hands this time. She allowed him to take them. They were bigger than hers, dwarfing her slender fingers. How did she never notice their size before now? How safely they could hold her?

Rhazien stroked his thumbs across the back of her hands. "We can leave, little doe. Let's walk back. You need to rest. Islone will make excuses, and everyone will understand. They will think we snuck off to be together."

Her eyes glazed over when she lifted her gaze to his. "I want to go home, but I don't have one."

He kissed her head, tucking her under his arm and leading her toward their borrowed room. "Shh, little doe. You have a home with me. Always with me."

CHAPTER FORTY-THREE

Erissa paced inside the bedchamber at Islone's home. Rhazien had argued with her over his return to the celebration. She had insisted, though, not wanting to disappoint everyone more than she already would by leaving. And she wanted to be alone. Clearly, the Creator's plan differed from her desires as usual.

Erissa remained calm as Reeva appeared before her, lost in her emotions fighting for dominance. She ignored Reeva and continued pacing the length of the bedroom, trying to still her tumultuous thoughts.

When Reeva remained, she glanced in the Fae's direction, noting her guarded look. Seeing the expression only fueled Erissa's ire. "What do you want?"

"You left the party rather abruptly." Reeva stepped into Erissa's path.

Erissa sidestepped Reeva, continuing to run from her thoughts as if she could outpace them in the confines of the room.

"Did something happen, child?" Reeva moved into Erissa's space once more when she refused to answer. "Talk to me."

Erissa stopped and planted her hands on her hips, her chin high as she shrugged. "Nothing happened. Everyone and everything has been great tonight."

"Then why are you angry?"

"I'm not angry."

"Maybe you were not when you first arrived. That has changed. What has stirred your ire?"

"You know, I was fine until all of you came along!" Erissa's fists balled at her side. Her chest heaved, fighting against the weight of her anger.

Reeva took a step back at the unexpected outburst. "What?"

"My life might not have been much, but it was mine, and I found a way out of that hell by myself. I did that, not Rhazien, and certainly not you. And tonight? Tonight, with everyone so kind and accepting..." Erissa trailed off, looking lost.

Reeva nodded, taking a step closer. "It was too much."

"What I went through... it's all I've known. And then Rhazien and these people show me how life can be different. It's not supposed to be like that. And every one of you wants something from me. It's one thing to know your life can be different, but it's another to experience it. It's all too much. The noise is too much. On today of all days, when it's the day that started it all."

"'Tis your naming day, is it not, child?" Reeva sucked in a breath. "That is what drives your anger."

Erissa snapped. "I was dealing with it, and then they tried to give that damned blanket. They were excited for me to have a family. To have a future here with them and all their support." Erissa clapped a hand over her mouth after shouting once more. Tears pricked her eyes as a torrent of pain ripped its way through her chest. "Today is a day like any other. It shouldn't matter."

"Is your shouting supposed to convince you or me?" Reeva clucked her tongue. Her face softened in sympathy, her gentle voice washing over Erissa. "You are anything other than fine. Surviving is not living, child, and that is all you have been doing for a long time. It is time to live."

Erissa shook her head, her voice hard. "I don't want to feel this way if that's what it means to live, to break down at kindness because it makes my skin crawl and my breath hitch. I'm angry. I'm so angry."

Reeva stepped closer. "To let the anger win is to lose yourself. You have fought so hard for that little girl to survive. Now is the time to let go of her. You did your duty to her. You *survived*, Erissa. Not because of Rhazien, myself, or anyone else here. *You* did that. And you deserve to give yourself permission to want to live. To have that future. To have it here if you so desire."

Erissa tried not to collapse under the weight of that survival. "I'm afraid."

"Of what?"

"Tonight... this is what life should have been. It's different when you don't know what you've missed. All those years of pain and for what? To escape it only to break down when people are *nice to me*?" Disgust dripped from every word Erissa spoke.

And she *was* mad. At Rhazien and his secrets, she would rather not know. At Reeva and her vague warnings, she wanted to ignore. At Islone and Micmus for treating her as parents should. At the people who came to celebrate her marriage with unbridled joy. At her parents and all their selfishness and neglect. At the gods and their feigned ignorance. And at the Creator and his so-called gift. But more than anything, she was mad at herself. She had finally found her freedom, so why did she feel anything but free? Why did it scare her to want to live?

"You need to be gentle with yourself." Reeva moved closer to her. "It is a strange thing to want to live after a lifetime of nothing but survival. Peace will only come with time."

"I was fine. I was free. I freed myself." The words were a broken whisper, and Erissa had to fight the tightness in her chest even to utter them as it cost her something dear to keep saying the same phrase out loud.

"I was fine, too. For a time. And then I was not. 'Tis the way of things. Your story mirrors my own in some ways." Reeva gave a pointed nod toward Erissa's chest. "There are some wounds that run too deep to see, child."

"I'll never be the same, never be whole. Not when my skin crawls, and my chest freezes when people are decent to me. It's like I never made it out of that room. Part of me is still trapped there, and she's never getting out."

"Erissa..." Reeva trailed off, her face full of pity and understanding, the combination pulling Erissa's darkest thoughts forward.

"I can't do this, Reeva. I'm afraid they'll hate me too. Maybe not tonight or tomorrow, but that hate will come." Erissa choked on the tears clogging her throat. Tears she refused to shed. If she started crying now, the tears would not halt.

Her parents had broken her in ways she thought were beyond repair. Then she met Rhazien, and he started helping her mold the pieces together. To lose so much a second time would be the death of her.

"I won't be able to bear it when they hate me, too. Not after this night and what they've given me. It was acceptable when it was one old man, but what happens when it's a child? What happens when it's two or three? If it's Towin, Thomrynn, or Ysalila?" Erissa's eyes were as hollow as her voice. "They will blame me, and they will hate me. Rhazien, Islone, Micmus... they will all hate me. I don't want to live with it. I've had enough hate for a lifetime."

"Oh, child. You are letting fear take hold of your heart when you need to stand fast in what these people have shown you to be true of their character.

They see you as you are and love you for it, not despite it. What more could you pray for?" Reeva's arms twitched.

Erissa flinched as if she thought Reeva might want to hug her. To be touched by anyone right now would send her hurtling over the edge, and it twisted the last drop of emotion she had left to be grateful that Reeva held a spirit's form.

"What more could I pray for?" An ugly twist shaped Erissa's mouth. "Why should I spend my time making wishes to a Creator who abandoned me long ago?"

Erissa moved to the bed. Taking the pillows, she threw them to the floor and settled herself onto them. She pulled on the edge of the blanket. Dragging it off the bed, she tucked herself under it. "I spent my childhood on my knees begging for the Creator's help while those pleas fell on deaf ears. My knees are too tired to keep praying. They will all leave me in the end. It's better to accept it now than hold on to a blind faith that doesn't exist."

Erissa said nothing more and rolled over, covering her head with the heavy quilt, hoping Reeva would take the hint and disappear.

She wanted to sleep and forget that peace had existed in her world, if only for a short time. Maybe if she slept long enough, she would forget what it felt like to be loved. It would hurt less if she did.

CHAPTER FORTY-FOUR

"You *married* her?" Reeva's shout could wake the dead with its ferocity.

Rhazien had expected Reeva's appearance. He stood in the main room for half an hour waiting for her. He knew Reeva came during the night's celebration. The hairs on the back of his neck rose through the night as if someone were watching them from the shadows. At least she had sense enough to corner him while Erissa slept.

Rhazien bristled at her anger. Reeva knew nothing of his relationship with Erissa and with secrets of her own. She had no room to take him to task for following his heart. "I love her."

"Some love." Reeva choked on a scream, lowering her voice to a more reasonable level. "You're her mate, and she doesn't know. Do you not see you are taking advantage of the bond? You didn't give her a choice, boy."

"I gave her every choice." Rhazien slashed a hand through the air with vehemence. "I told her there is a bond between us, that she is my *nayanam*. I want her to make any connections beyond that herself. After all she's been through, Erissa deserves to know her own desires, free of any influence the bond might hold over her. Telling her about it would create confusion and make her second guess herself when she's finally finding who she is. I'm not taking that from her. It will cause more harm than good."

"What you have done serves your needs alone. Do not act like it is in the girl's best interest. She is stronger than you think. She would not have survived this long if she were not. Your deceit will be what breaks her, not the truth."

"I'm trying to protect her. To let her build her own opinions, her own choices."

"There is no choice when you keep the bond from her."

Rhazien struggled to keep the anger from his words. "I haven't kept the bond from her, so why can't you see that everything I've done is to protect her and nurture that bond? I'm trying to do what's best for her."

"What's best for her? Do you think this is something to be proud of?" Reeva sneered. "Proud that you tricked a vulnerable girl into marriage? What you have done is disgusting, and I do not think pretty words will sway Erissa as you speak of protection. You have stolen her choice. You are a vile, selfish creature and will break everything you have built with this deception, deserving what comes next."

"You have hated me from the start, and it's never made any sense. Erissa had a choice. I would never force her to do something she didn't want. She married me because she wanted it as much as I did." Rhazien refused to back down at Reeva's accusations. "Out of the two of us, the one who will harm her intentionally is you."

Reeva sighed, her features falling as if the weight of creation rested on her shoulders alone. "My wish is to protect Erissa even if my actions do not align with such a desire. The Keeping denies all when it comes to free will."

Rhazien's brow furrowed. "Is there truly no way to break its hold?"

"Only the Creator can break the Keeping, and he has abandoned me to this fate for reasons I cannot fathom." Reeva swallowed, her eyes brittle with unshed tears. "Do not think I regret my decision. There is much I would change about this half-life, but the Keeping is not one of them. It is a price I would pay a hundredfold to achieve the same result."

"What is worth a price that steep?"

"The mate bonds were originally a curse created by the god Malcufyre to force the Fae to do as he commanded." Reeva lifted her gaze to Rhazien's. "Those in the Keeping War followed in his footsteps and used something they knew would force my hand into taking the Keeping."

The sorrow in her eyes was enough to break off something inside of Rhazien. "They used your child against you. That's why you agreed to the Keeping, isn't it, Reeva?"

"He remains protected to this day, and there is no breaking a bargain made in Keeping." The gleam in Reeva's eyes became one of pride as her tears dried, giving truth to her lack of regret. "I made sure that even in what is to come, he will remain untouched."

"If Erissa had been blessed with a mother who loved her as deeply as you loved your son, we wouldn't be having this conversation." It was unfathomable how Erissa's parents had sentenced her to a life of violence and neglect. Rhazien's blood boiled when he remembered her scars, and it took everything within him to control the magic of the mating bond flaring to life with his anger. "I love her. She deserves everything good and pure in this world, and I want her to have everything she's always been denied. Love, peace, a home."

"But that is not what you are doing. You are taking advantage of her. She is not mine any more than this life is, though I want her to be, even if it would damn us all." Reeva's shoulders dropped. "If I were not already bound to the Keeping, I would pledge to it once more for her sake. She is too innocent and has gone through too much to be saddled with the weight of all that happens next and your deceit. She will not come through any of this unscathed. It pains me greatly that I can do no more to protect her. You must tell her the full truth about who you are."

Rhazien studied the Fae. Her argument made no sense. Nothing malicious colored his actions, and he struggled to see how Reeva did not understand his intent. "Why are you so angry with me?"

Reeva seethed, her emotions laid bare as hatred burned in her gaze. "Because you are as selfish as the rest of your kind."

Rhazien reared back. "What?"

"I know who you are, Warden." Reeva spat the word. "The Fefnirion are selfish, vain creatures who only care for their own happiness. They abandoned their calling, giving up their powers for mortal lives, and because of them, Draven nearly succeeded in the Keeping War. They chose themselves over their vow, and you will do the same when it suits you best."

"So you're not angry with me," Rhazien reasoned, "you're angry with what I am and blame me for the actions of the other Fefnirion."

Reeva crossed her arms. "Who you are is rooted in being a Fefnirion. You will be no different from the rest of your kind. When it comes down to it, you will choose yourself as the rest of you have."

Rhazien studied Reeva, mulling over her anger. The Keeping was a living hell, and the pain she carried from it bled from her. He understood her anger. The Fefnirion might have saved everyone in both wars, but their delayed actions in the second harmed everyone, too. If he could do nothing else, at least he could put her mind at ease where Erissa was concerned.

"The mating bond for the Fefnirion differs from that of the Fae. I hold two sacred vows. One as a Warden and the other as a mate. I am promised to the earth, my soul linked with its magic. I hold fast to that magic—my life depends on the link as the only powered Fefnirion left—but I would toss the vow away without hesitation if honoring it meant dishonoring Erissa. I am as bound to her now as you are to the Keeping. I will do anything to ensure she remains happy and loved."

With her eyes half closed in contempt, displeasure radiated from Reeva. "It is hard to believe your love is pure when you have yet to remove the spelled choker she wears. She can never fully be herself so long as it graces her neck, and her true form remains hidden."

Annoyance flashed through him. Reeva did everything she could to find fault with his actions. "It's not as simple as taking it off. The spell is weakening. It's allowing her powers to come through in bursts, especially when I touch it. She barely survived her last show of power, and that was with the spell dampening it. I don't know how to take it off without killing her, but I did infuse it with part of my void when I touched it the first time. It should work to slowly counteract the magic while I look for another solution."

Reeva relaxed slightly with his reassurance. "Is the answer not the same now as it was at the Veil? You have already shared power with her."

"In different circumstances. You should know that. Magic isn't something we draw on at will. It's a living being inside us, and it calls to Erissa in a way I've never seen before." Rhazien sighed, his posture drooping. He was failing to free Erissa, and it cut him to the quick. "To break the spell's hold, I would need to leave my magic coursing through hers, using it to contain the source. No Fefnirion has done anything like it, and I don't know how to keep the void from consuming her magic. If it is bound to her soul, to harm that magic would be to kill her. I won't take that risk. She is more precious to me than that. But I promise you this: I won't stop until I find a way to free her from the spell."

"You love her? It's not merely the bond driving your emotions?" Reeva's hostility had abated from her tone, but a desperate note lingered, making Rhazien wonder what she wished his answer would be.

"It didn't take long to figure out we shared a mating bond. I knew it within hours of finding her hiding behind a splintered old cart. But love?" Rhazien grinned like a besotted man. "Did you know I make wind chimes?"

Reeva raised a brow at the odd turn of conversation. "We were discussing Erissa, not chimes."

Rhazien continued like he had not heard her. "A traveling merchant brought one with him when I was small. I obsessed over it. My father finally grew sick of my fixation and bartered a gift with it for my mother's naming year. I honed my smithing skills for years, trying to figure out how to make one from memory with the right sound. Everyone thought me mad, and they never sold, but I loved them."

"Have you considered you *are* mad?" Reeva glowered with impatience. "Is that why I must listen to this ridiculous story?"

Rhazien laughed at her irritation. "There's a point to it if you'll let me finish."

"Get on with it, boy. I grow tired of you and do not like you enough to entertain this nonsense much longer."

"The feeling is mutual." Rhazien rolled his eyes, his tone dry, but a smile still played about his mouth.

Reeva's lips twitched, but she said nothing.

Her silence only increased Rhazien's amusement. He had mercy on her and did not point out the smile she fought against. "Erissa saw my wind chimes the night she ran. She said they were like stars twinkling in the night sky. I think she had my heart that night. Seeing how her eyes lit up when she saw them and how she giggled at their music was my undoing. She saw beauty and magic in something everyone called a waste of time. I have never felt more seen."

"The girl loves you. And I can see you love her too." Reeva sighed, and with it, the anger faded as the Fae begrudgingly acknowledged everything Rhazien had said. "I am sorry. Part of me knows you did not trick her, but I have spent centuries living out the consequences of the Fefnirions' choices. I do not want Erissa to bear the same burden."

'She won't," Rhazien promised.

"It is the child's naming day. Did you know?" Reeva waited until his head whipped in her direction before speaking again. "She is grieving her memories. Don't let her grieve them alone."

Rhazien had no chance to respond. Reeva quickly faded into nothing, leaving him alone.

He walked quickly toward the room he shared with Erissa. The soft sound of the water filled the space when Rhazien entered, the damp air a respite from the dryness of the climate.

The dragon inside him rumbled at the feeling of the moisture against his skin. Rhazien wanted to transform and let his scales soak in it. He trampled the urge, his desire to find Erissa stronger than his baser needs. He needed to know how she fared. It killed a piece of him when he left her alone earlier.

The bed lay smooth in the dim light of the moon shining through the window. Erissa's form should break the lines of the bedding as she curled beneath the covers. The pillows were missing, along with one of the blankets.

Rhazien grew concerned as he looked to the spring bath and found her missing from its warmth. Had Erissa heard his conversation with Reeva and run from him? Worry threatened to steal his breath as his eyes scanned the room.

A whimper caught his attention. Relief nearly buckled his knees as his eyes fell on locks of raven hair lying in the moonlight spilling across the floor.

Rhazien walked around the bed. The pillows were strewn across the floor, hidden from view on the other side. Erissa lay curled on top of them, covered in the missing blanket. Discomfort etched across her face as she fretted against her dreams.

Rhazien bent down, gathering Erissa into his arms. She tensed for a moment and then settled against his chest. Drawing a deep breath, the lines of her face smoothed. He eased her onto the bed and reached for the blanket.

After tucking it around her, Rhazien sat on the edge of the bed. Erissa turned into his warmth, and something inside of him broke. The day held the worst of her memories, and he had not even known about it. They must have weighed on her heavily if she sought comfort in the familiarity of lying on the floor.

He sat there for hours, trailing his fingers through her hair, offering her the only comfort he could as she slumbered.

CHAPTER FORTY-FIVE

Barrett risked everything as he defied Faldeyr. He would never willingly kill the blacksmith's children, and if he wanted to avoid his brother commanding it of him, he had to move fast.

He stood in Susreene's chamber, pleading with her to trust him as he handed her daughter back into her care. "I'm sorry my brother took her, but you must come with me—now. This is my only chance to help you escape."

She grabbed her daughter, her gaze sweeping over her as she looked for any injuries through the tear stains covering her face. Finding none, she pushed her behind her and stood in front of the children as a shield. "Where is my husband?"

"In the dungeons below the stronghold." Barrett winced at the fury radiating from the woman. "If I moved him first, it would alert the guards. We have little time as it is. We have to go now."

"I don't trust you." Susreene withdrew a knife from her skirt.

"I know he's a Warden." Barrett lowered his voice. He did not want to have to use the information, especially not in front of the children. If they did not know the implications of such a title and said it to the wrong person, the results would be disastrous. "If I wanted to hurt either of you, Faldeyr would know it by now. Please, trust me. My only aim is to get all of you to safety."

Susreene's fury settled into a cautious interest. "Why would you hide who he is from your brother? A Warden is an unmeasurable prize to the humans and the Fae. There is much you could gain from the revelation."

"My actions are not my own." Shame radiated from Barrett. "They are the result of an abused Fae bargain. I have no desire to harm your family. I know it's hard to believe against my actions, but I'm risking everything to help you."

The woman stared at him for a long minute. Sweat broke out on Barrett's brow as he waited for her to decide. If she did not make one quickly, he would decide for her, and he did not want to be pushed to such actions. If he had to drag a child out of the room and down to the dungeons to get her to follow him, so be it.

"We will come on one condition." Susreene turned to her children before facing him again. "We don't leave without Tyrmar."

"We will free him as we leave, but it has to be now." Barrett smiled in relief and gestured for the women to follow him. "Don't take anything with you unless you have to. If the maids notice anything missing, they will alert their mistress."

He led the women from the room, turning down the hall toward an unguarded part of the stronghold. With Erissa gone, fewer guards remained inside, and none bothered the end of the floor where her room lay. If he wanted to get the women out and to the dungeons without seeing anyone, it would be through that room.

When they reached the room, he cautioned the child as he approached the hearth. "No matter what happens, remain silent. Your father is in rough shape but will be fine once we get you out of here."

Each of the girls nodded, and he answered them with one of his own.

Susreene remained wary of his intentions. "Why have you brought us here?"

"There is a secret passageway with one way that leads to the dungeon and another that leads to the outside. It's how Erissa escaped." Barrett revealed the hidden doorway by pulling the hearth's floor from its place.

Susreene turned to him with tears in her eyes. "You meant it. You're really helping us."

His heart squeezed painfully at her surprise. He never desired to be the villain his brother made him into. "I couldn't protect her. No matter how much I wanted to. I won't let the same happen to your children."

She studied him as she chewed on her bottom lip. "There is a way. To break the Fae bargain."

Barrett swallowed hard, tears gathering in his tired eyes. "No such magic exists."

"But it does." Susreene smiled. She reached for his arm, patting it as if soothing a small child. "Vilotta might be a right cow, but she's an honest one. Only one of Morthyra's court holds the power of the Void. And only one of the Wardens can imbue its magic and use it to break a Fae deal. I can void the magic, and Tyrmar can imbue it to nullify the consequences of the bond."

Barrett's pulse galloped as he tried to process Susreene's words. "You can break the deal? Erissa's life won't be tied to my obedience?"

Susreene nodded, her smile growing wider. "We can break the deal. With its magic gone, she will be free of your choices."

A true smile broke across Barrett's face for the first time in years as a wild hope gave way to tears. He gestured toward the passageway. "Go, we've not much time."

CHAPTER FORTY-SIX

Rhazien slipped from the back of the house, avoiding those still celebrating. There were questions he did not want to answer, like why he snuck away from his bride and their bed. He loved the people of this city, but they were nosey at best and without boundaries at worst.

He stuck to the shadows as he hurriedly made his way. What he planned would take most of the early morning hours, and he needed to be back in time for Erissa to wake.

Those who were no longer at the festivities had long since retired. He considered doing so himself, but Erissa's naming day nagged at him.

She had told him little of her time spent imprisoned, but he doubted her parents celebrated the day with her. How many times did she spend the day alone, haunted, trying to survive her father's wrath?

He might have lived in Freyborn, but Cropari traditions raised him, with his father calling the city home. Naming days were a grand affair attended by all. His family made the two-day journey on horseback to invade Micmus and Islone's home for each of the children's naming days. Those memories were some of his happiest.

He would give anything to trade them for what Erissa went through, and he had a plan to make up for those dark days. At least, he hoped it would offer her some semblance of peace to buffer the worst of the memories the day carried.

He walked for several minutes, his pace brisk to avoid the cold as much as the potential for prying eyes. One man never joined the celebrations, and Rhazien sought him.

As Rhazien came within sight of the forge, he chuckled at the sound of hammering coming from it. Light spilled from the arched doorway. The frame hung empty, the door having long been removed. A need never existed for a door to be closed, and the heat from within suffocated during the coldest nights.

Rhazien walked into the light. "Predictable as always, Thitelar."

"Evening, Rhazien. Come to steal the forge from me?" The hammering ceased as a man placed a hammer down and stepped away from the anvil, his hand held out in greeting.

Thitelar surprised people with his blacksmithing profession. Exceedingly tall and lanky, despite his height bending slightly with age, his arms were half the size of Rhazien's and half as long. The man's trousers shifted at each step as the waist slipped against his thin hips. A knotted rope barely caught the fabric against his protruding bones. Thitelar might have swung a hammer all day, but he always looked on the brink of death.

Rhazien grabbed the offered hand. "If you don't mind? My wife had her naming day. I want to make her a ring as a gift."

"Wondering what drew you away from the festivities," Thitelar chuckled. He clapped Rhazien across the back, the force of the motion nearly knocking Rhazien from his feet. "Use whatever you like. It'll be my gift to the newly wedded couple. You'll find the finer metals and stray jewels in the strongbox, as usual. I trust you remember where the key is."

Rhazien regained his footing. The old man's strength always surprised him. "Thank you, Thitelar."

"Make sure to keep everything in order." Thitelar ambled to the doorway.

Rhazien quickly called after him. "Don't leave on my account."

"Relreina will be pleased with my company this early morning hours. She's quite the thing when I stroll in half past dawn after getting carried away. You know how it is when you're working." Thitelar waved a hand over his shoulder. "Enjoy the forge, young master."

Rhazien strode about the room with purpose, taking the items he needed and making a small pile of various scraps of metal. He set to work, heating the pieces and hammering them into thin lengths.

Raising one of the strips, Rhazien carried it over to the hearth. He held the metal over the fire using a pair of tongs. He glanced around the space, ensuring no one lingered in the doorway unnoticed.

Rhazien drew a deep breath, warming it with a rumbling of his chest. Smoke rose from his nostrils and mouth as he drew on the dragon's breath inside of him. He blew a stream of fire against the metal, using the magic to burn the strip until it stained red.

Satisfied with the color, Rhazien picked up another strip, repeating the process with a different result. He changed the temperature of his fire, guiding the magic until the metal darkened the red with blue, changing the hue until a bold purple remained.

Rhazien carried the strips back to the anvil, placing them against the warm iron. He flexed his fingers, letting scales overtake the skin, a protection against the heat of the dragon's fire still heating the metal. Rhazien picked the pieces up and started braiding them.

"You should add a deep blue to the ring."

Rhazien raised his eyes. He found Reeva on his left side, perched against a cold anvil in the forge's corner. What more did she have to argue with him over? "Thought you left."

"I thought I did too, but..." Reeva looked uncomfortable. She shifted from one foot to the other and sighed, stilling her nervous movements. "You put me at ease, and I should offer you the same."

Rhazien paused his work, giving Reeva his full attention.

"I cannot tell who hunts her and why. The Keeping..." Reeva trailed off. She cleared her throat to continue. "There is another who seeks her, and when he finds her, you must let her go with him."

Rhazien threw the barely braided strips down, anger clouding out reason. His hold on his magic slipped, scales erupting further across his skin as smoke rose from his nostrils into the cold air. "I will never hand her over to another."

"Calm your bond before someone sees you." The hissed words had some effect as Rhazien tempered the glow trying to overtake his body.

"This is your idea of putting me at ease?" Rhazien grit his teeth, fighting for control.

"I realize it might not be the easiest thing to hear, but at least you will be prepared." Reeva waited to speak again until he forced the magic back. "He has no wish to walk this path. It is beyond your control and his. Bargains were made long ago in haste and anger, and with prophecy dictating events, there is little anyone can do to change what happens. He will take you too, though not in a way you will appreciate. For that, I am sorry. But he will not harm the girl. He needs her. The world needs her. Without her magic leading the way, we will not survive what comes. You need to trust him, if only for now. Trust him, and Erissa will remain safe."

"When?" Rhazien had little reason to doubt her after her warnings to Erissa proved true.

"Soon, and I pray with the speed of the Creator." Reeva stood, shaking out the folds of her dress. Not a hint of a wrinkle graced the fabric. "For if Virion finds her first..."

"That's the first time you've said it." Rhazien answered the puzzled question on her face. "Virion. You've never said his name until now."

"My tongue is unbound. You knew his name without my having told you from overhearing his men in the forest." With a lift of her shoulder, Reeva faded away, her last words lingering in the forge's heat. "Do not forget the blue. It is important and will mean much to Erissa with the passing of what comes next."

Rhazien stared at the spot where she disappeared for some time.

CHAPTER FORTY-SEVEN

Things were not going as Tiovriss planned. Cropari stood in the distance, its image wavering against the dawn-lit horizon, a mirage luring desperate travelers.

An entire night spent traveling left Tiovriss painstakingly counting the seconds, anything to distract himself from the endless whining coming from his right.

He envied Novus. The reigning Unseelie Lord had the ability to shift through the shadows of the world, traversing vast lengths in the blink of an eye. Cropari taunted Tiovriss with its unreliable distance. He longed to get there and deal with the girl.

He snapped his gaze to consider the man prattling beside him. A dirty hand clutched the reins too tightly, leaving the horse tense beneath him, but Castian paid no attention to the steed. The young girl from Gailme sat in front of him, recoiling at every twisted desire the Fae breathed against her ear.

Tiovriss ground his teeth against his rising temper.

"Keep doing that, Tio, and you will snap a tooth." Kaellam rode up on Tiovriss's other side.

It took every ounce of self-control Tiovriss possessed to keep from launching a fist into the deadpan expression, straightening Kaellam's dark features. He chose to speak instead, the words a forceful exhale against the backs of his clenched teeth. "Do you have a death wish?"

"Hardly," Kaellam snorted. "It is bad enough I must listen to Castian, so I have no intention of listening to you whimper the rest of the way through the desert lands."

A snarl left Tiovriss, and he tightened his hands in the reins, making his horse chafe against its bit. "Better a whimper than Castian's endless simpering."

Castian remained undaunted by Tiovriss's mood. "Seduction is hardly simpering."

"Seduction requires willingness." Kaellam nodded toward the young girl. "When is the last time you have known a willing bedmate, Cas?"

"Probably the last time you pronounced someone's entire name," Tiovriss grunted.

"You are hardly one to comment on willing bedmates." Castian leveled an amused grin at Kaellam, his eyes raking down the burn across the other man's face. "But then again, can you get a willing woman in your bed with that scar? Rumor has it the puckered flesh travels lower."

"The women I bed are at least women, willing or not." Kaellam stopped his horse.

"You wouldn't have a problem with the girl if you took up my offer." Castian hitched the girl tighter against his front. "There is more than enough of her to please us both."

A hollow laugh left Kaellam. "There will never be a point where I sink to your level, Cas. Nothing but madness can be found there. Ask Tiordan how that fared for him when he imprisoned his son and Novus escaped. The Unseelie lord wouldn't even spare his own father for the same crime, so he certainly won't spare someone like you who fucks—"

The girl cried, drowning out the rest of Kaellam's words, and Tiovriss resumed grinding his teeth. The two Fae accompanying him might be skilled assassins, but they always found their way into an argument.

Castian opened his mouth to respond. Whatever sat poised to leave his tongue fell off when Tiovriss snatched a handful of the girl's hair. She let out a sharp scream, surprise making the high-pitched note hysterical.

Tiovriss moved too fast for Castian, and with a hard movement, he dragged the girl from the other Fae's horse and onto his own.

The girl fought against his hold, raking her nails down the leather of his jerkin, trying to find a hold in the age-worn softness of the grimy sleeves.

No hesitation stayed his hand. With quick and vicious intent, Tiovriss drew a blade from the length of his boot and stabbed the young girl in the heart, twisting the blade and severing her binding to this world.

When her arms fell from his sleeves, the limp limbs hanging by her sides, Tiovriss loosened his hold on her hair. The girl slid from his lap, falling at the feet of the unfazed horse.

"Not another word. The two of you want to bicker? Do it over the little bitch's corpse. It's not like Castian even had her. You've done nothing but argue about his bullshit since you met me on the road." Tiovriss glared from Castian to Kaellam, his bloodied knife held at the ready daring either man to say more. He let the silence grow, gripping the blade until his pale knuckles turned ghostly before speaking. "Virion cared nothing for Alrithia's death, and if you cost him the girl again, he will feel even less for yours. I won't lose my life because the two of you can't shut up and focus."

Tiovriss returned the knife to his boot when the men remained silent. The faster they reached Cropari, the better. Virion would balk at him killing the men outright, but the girl killing the likes of them? Accidents were bound to happen, and he had no intention of sharing in the spoils of his promised reward. The Keeper willing, Castian and Kaellam were not long for the Veil.

CHAPTER FORTY-EIGHT

Rhazien slipped into the bedroom a few hours past dawn, glad to find Erissa still slept. Her gift took longer than he expected. Reworking the design to incorporate Reeva's suggestion of blue made the extra time he spent on it worth the effort. He hoped she would love the ring, the colors woven together around stones of the same hues.

Careful not to wake his sleeping bride as he crossed the room, Rhazien submerged himself into the spring and bathed the grime of yesterday from his body. He let his scales come forth in the rare moment of privacy. The warm water caressed each one, the scales soaking up the moisture while Rhazien flexed them, allowing the water to slide between the stacked layers.

His eyes traced Erissa's form on the bed. What would she make of his lizard-like tendencies? He wanted her beside him, basking in the water's warmth, but a chance always remained that the needs of his dragon scales would repulse her. He forced himself to put the thought aside and relax.

The tension faded from his body the longer he sat in the bubbling water. As good as the hot water felt against this armored skin, he wanted to be lying next to his wife.

Grabbing onto a strand of his magic, Rhazien glided it into his scales, suppressing them back beneath his skin. He dried himself off when he rose from the water. He did not bother dressing as he moved toward the bed.

Rhazien slipped beneath the covers, snuggling against Erissa's back. He slid his hands up her back to the tied laces and unraveled their bindings.

The further he loosened them, the more the garment hung from Erissa's shoulders, the front gaping.

With the laces untied, Rhazien parted the folds of the material. Anger burned within him again with the reveal of her scars, but it was tempered by how his dragon's fire had softened the rigid lines and removed the stiffness from the marks. Nothing he could do would fade them completely. If they had been born of magic, he might have voided the marks, but these were mistdrite made. No magic countered the harm done by the god-made element found within the barrier of the Mists. But he pushed such thoughts from his head.

Rhazien nudged Erissa's shoulder until she rolled onto her back. He pulled the sleeves of her dress down, trailing kisses from her collarbone down to her breasts, revealing them inch by inch. He let out a sound from the back of his throat when he wrapped his lips around her nipple, sucking and nipping the pebbling peak.

Erissa's back arched. She wiggled against the hold his lips had, murmuring nonsense. She slowly came awake.

Rhazien gave her other breast the same treatment, teasing her with the gentle strokes of his tongue. And then he raked his teeth across it, biting down.

She moaned, thrusting her chest up toward him as her eyes opened. In a choked whisper, she asked, "Rhazien?"

A deep purr vibrated through his chest. His mouth let go, and he nuzzled her breast with the shadowed growth of a beard he had yet to shave. "Good morning, wife."

Fingers threaded themselves through his hair. Erissa held his head against her, squirming under his prickly stubble. "Can you wake me up like this every morning?"

"Greedy," Rhazien murmured as he latched onto her nipple again, sucking hard. He moved a hand down to part her folds, finding her passage slick, and slid a finger into her.

Erissa cried out, tightening her hands in his hair while his finger pumped in and out of her slowly, driving every thought from her mind. Her hips lifted with need, undulating as she sought to drive his finger deeper. Withdrawing his finger to the tip, Rhazien added a second, plunging back in. She whimpered, not from pleasure alone, and twisted her hips.

Rhazien eased his hand from between her legs, and Erissa swore at the loss of him. He sat back on his heels. "Poor little doe. You're too sore for what I have planned."

"Please, don't stop."

"Who said anything about stopping?" Rhazien's laughed. His hands tugged on her dress. "Lift your hips."

Erissa moved so Rhazien had room to pull her dress down and off. He knelt between her legs. His hands were on her thighs, an arm sliding beneath each of them as he shoved them wide, tilting her hips until she lay bare before him, a feast he longed to devour.

"What are you doing?"

He leaned into her, dragging his tongue from her center to the bundle of nerves resting above it.

"Oh." The word broke on a moan, and she arched into his mouth.

Rhazien licked her again, lingering over the sensitive nub. He sucked on it, nipping it with his teeth before pulling back and running his tongue down to her center.

She drove her hips into his face, seeking more as she cried out against every pass of his tongue against her most sensitive area, luxuriating in his unhurried swipes.

Erissa's hips continued to twist, chasing her pleasure.

Rhazien savored the taste of her as he lapped at the growing wetness, plunging his tongue in and out, his fingers plucking against the nub already swollen from where his teeth had claimed it.

Her pleasure built into an ecstasy that threatened to drown her. She let out another cry that bordered on desperation as her hands tightened in his hair. Her release became tangible. It shimmered just beyond her grasp. "Rhazien, please..."

His fingers dug into her hips as he curled his tongue, holding Erissa down and open to his mouth. The shield around his power dropped as he directed flames to dance along his tongue.

Erissa went liquid beneath the fiery heat flickering against her hooded pleasure, unable to stop the writhing demand of her hips as they bucked against Rhazien's flames.

His tongue, teeth, and flames created a cascade of pleasure, pushing her over the edge. She bowed off the bed at the fire that erupted through her. It burned with the sweetest of heat, centering at the apex of her thighs before spreading out across her body until it reached her breasts. The flames worked in tandem, burning across her nipples while Rhazien played against her center, making a beacon of her flushed skin.

Rhazien watched her as she came apart. Their eyes found each other's, and neither held anything back. He would do anything to protect her. To protect this.

When her hips settled against the bed, he eased away from her swollen sex. Rhazien pressed a kiss against it, and he smiled when she shivered with a soft moan. Climbing up to the head of the bed, he gathered her into his arms until Erissa's back lay flush against his front and tucked the blanket around them.

Erissa wiggled against Rhazien's hips and sucked in a breath as he hardened against her. "Let me take care of you, Rhazien. I want to."

"Another time. If you touch me now, I'll be tempted to slide inside you, and we can't have that when you're this sore." Rhazien tightened his arm around her waist, stilling her hips with this iron grip. "Sleep, little doe, and dream of everything I intend to do to you later."

Erissa sighed when he kissed the area below her ear but settled into his arms. Rhazien stroked a hand through her hair, and it was not long until sleep claimed them.

Much later, a knock at the door roused the sleeping couple. The high noon sun filtered in through the small windows at the top of the wall.

Rhazien got up, grabbed his trousers from the floor, and stepped into them as he went to answer the summons.

Micmus stood on the other side. He aimed an amused glance at Rhazien's ruffled hair and shirtless chest. "Interrupting something, am I?"

"Not at the moment. Erissa sleeps." Rhazien's voice held a satisfied smugness.

"Oh, to be newly wed again." The older man chuckled. "Come, grab a meal with me at the tavern. There's something we need to discuss."

"Give me a moment to get dressed. I'll meet you outside."

Micmus nodded. "Be quick. And wake your bride. Islone is looking for her."

Rhazien turned back into the room. He stripped off the pants and quickly washed, tossing on fresh clothing.

Erissa woke as he pulled on his boots. "Rhazien?"

He moved to the edge of the bed, leaning down to kiss her still-swollen lips. "Sleep well, little doe?"

"Oh, yes." She stretched, rubbing her thighs together.

Rhazien laughed, squeezing her thigh. "Get dressed. Islone is looking for you. I'm going with Micmus to the tavern for the noon meal."

Erissa nodded, and he leaned in for another kiss.

"I won't be gone too long."

Micmus waited for him in the front courtyard, and the pair walked in silence to the tavern situated a short distance from the home.

The building left something to be desired by Cropari standards, with walls painted gray and holding few embellishments.

The tavern owner waved as they entered through the swinging doors. "Micmus! And Rhazien, too! Go find your corner, gentlemen. Edrora will bring your usual."

Micmus waved his thanks and seated himself at a table in the back corner. Rhazien sat across from him.

They sat in silence, waiting for their food.

As soon as their meals hit the table, Micmus got straight to the point between bites of food. "Son, did you know your wife talks to the dead?"

Rhazien choked on the lamb as he tried swallowing. Edrora hurried over and slapped him on the back repeatedly. He waved her off, his cheeks going pink.

"You knew." Micmus sat back in his chair. "When you said she could see fated souls, you failed to mention her conversing with them. I heard her last night. You too."

Rhazien stalled, picking at the food on his plate. No lies had ever separated the two men, and he hesitated at letting them stand between them now.

Micmus placed his fork down, shoving his plate to the side. "There's no doubt the girl is Fae. One only has to look at her eyes to see it. Clearly, no one has taught her how to hide the glow. But does she even know that?"

Rhazien pushed away his food. "No. I'm not sure she knows enough of the world to understand who she must be."

"You haven't told her." Micmus declared it rather than asked. Disapproval deepened his voice. "And yet, you married her anyway. I can't say the soul was wrong in anything she said to you. If anything, she let you off easy. What you're doing to Erissa is wrong."

Rhazien crumpled under the weight of Micmus's disappointment. "I thought I was doing the right thing in not telling her, allowing her to make her own decisions—come to her own conclusions—without being influenced by anything I said or the bond."

"Oh, son." Micmus shook his head. "Your intentions come from a good place, but you made the wrong choice. The pull of the bond is strong. Without her knowing it exists, you never gave her the opportunity to explore her feelings outside of it."

"There's so much she has endured. I wanted to remove part of that burden."

"Instead, you created a bigger mess. How do you think she will react when she learns you knew one lay between you?"

Rhazien winced, a frown marring his features. "Not well, especially when I also haven't told her about my being Fefnirion and half-Fae. She did ask if I was a Fefnirion, but we haven't had the opportunity to speak about it.."

Micmus sighed, resting his elbows on the table. "You must tell her the truth. About the bond, yourself, and her identity."

"I want to. I'm going to. Tonight. I was thinking of taking her to the oasis and spending the evening there. We can talk with more privacy than we have here."

"It sounds like you know what you need to do. But let me make this clear, Rhazien. You tell the girl, or I will tell her for you." Micmus picked up his fork and prepared to begin his meal again. "Now, let's get back to our fare before—"

"Micmus! Rhazien!"

Thitelar ran into the tavern, a hand held to his side while he gasped for breath.

"Thitelar?" Micmus stood and ushered the man into his vacated chair. "What has you in a hurry?"

"Men... in... the market," Thitelar wheezed. "They were... asking after... your... wife, Rhazien."

Rhazien's skin paled. He pushed away from the table, urgency in his voice. "Where are they now?"

The blacksmith gulped for air, a hand pressed to his chest. "No time... heading... for... the house..."

Rhazien did not wait for Thitelar to finish. He bolted from the tavern. He dropped the barrier around his power and used the magic of his fiery wings to add haste to his legs as he ran. Micmus followed behind.

Prayers whispered across his lips, begging the Creator to let him make it in time.

CHAPTER FORTY-NINE

The rambunctious laughter of children drowned out the growing rumbles of thunder building in the distance. The older children chased Orbas through the back of the yard. He ran around kicking a ball, smiling as he kept it away from them.

Erissa sat on a cushion near where they played. Ysalila perched on her lap. A clay pot full of yellow flowers rested beside them.

The young girl picked one from the pot, weaving it into a strip of flowers she held in her hand. Her movements were slow as she showed Erissa how to twist the stems together, adding flowers as she went until a crown of them rested in her hands. "Like this, 'Rissa."

She copied Ysalila's motions, laughing in delight as it yielded the same result.

Erissa called out to Islone, holding up her flower crown as the older woman stepped out of the house, an empty basket under her arm. "Look what I made, Islone!"

"You're doing very well, love." Islone smiled. She carried the basket to a clothing line hung between two trees. "Come help me with the linens. The rains will be here soon."

Erissa tousled Ysalila's curls. "Go play with the others."

The little girl bounced out of Erissa's lap and ran straight for Orbas and the ball. He did not see her coming. She kicked the ball from underneath him, catching him in the legs. Orbas toppled over as Ysalila stole the ball, laughing madly.

Erissa shook her head at the girl's antics as she stood and went to help Islone.

Islone nodded toward Orbas. Ysalila had tired of kicking the ball. She ran back to where he lay, pouncing on him in a flurry of curls and bouncing skirts. "That girl will be the death of him."

"He's very good with them." Erissa removed the pins from a pair of trousers, watching Orbas pick up Ysalila and swing her around in circles.

"He was the oldest of his siblings before the Wasting hit. The poor child lost everyone and hasn't spoken a word since." Islone tilted her head to the sky as monsoon clouds gathered in the distance. She held the end of a sheet out to Erissa, motioning for her to help fold it. "Micmus brought him into our home after finding him hiding in the stables."

"The Wasting is responsible for many monstrous things." Erissa picked at the ends of the sheet.

A resounding crash sounded as the outside gate split from its hinges in a display of brute force, drowned out Islone's reply. Three men entered the yard, each bigger than the last, their pointed ears marking them as Fae.

Their gazes swept the yard, landing on Erissa. They started in her direction, stopping when a child's scream filled the air. They turned as one toward it.

The shortest of the three leered at the young girls. "What fun do we have here?"

"Who are you?" Islone side-stepped toward her children, her features tightening. "What do you want?"

"Leave the children," the tallest commanded, ignoring Islone. "We're here for the Veiled One."

"Always a spoilsport, Tiovriss," the shorter Fae lamented.

"We've no time for your proclivities, Cas." The middle man unsheathed a dagger. "Let's get the girl and be gone."

Castian licked his lips. "So long as we bring the girl back alive, I see no harm in enjoying ourselves, Kaellam."

Islone's face reddened with fury. "You will never touch my children."

Erissa's eyes darted from the men to the children. What she saw threatened to break her as nothing ever had before.

Behind each child stood a faceless soul, flickering in and out of the afternoon light. Terror gripped Erissa. She wanted to turn to Islone to see if the same fate hung in the balance for the woman who was more of a mother to her than her own. But to do that might cost her any time she might buy for the children to run.

Panic spread a tingling sensation throughout Erissa's body. She tasted magic on her tongue, her desperation urging it to build.

"Take it," the inner voice hissed. *"Take it or we all die here this day."*

Erissa latched onto the power, letting the potency of it drive her actions.

A moment of silence descended, the three men standing off with one another as the monsoon gathered overhead. They failed to notice the growing light in Erissa's eyes as they argued.

Castian removed his dagger and stepped toward the girls, a hideous cackle coming out of his mouth. "If you have time to indulge in killing Virion's pet, Tiovriss, there's more than enough time for my desires."

Islone screamed, the sound fading into the thunder rolling through the clouds. She lunged for the men, faltering as a concussion rent the air, the force of the impact knocking all but Erissa to the ground.

She remained upright, her feet dangling above the ground, an arm stretched out toward the children. Her eyes flared brightly, the wind gathering around her in a cyclonic force.

"They will not go unpunished. We can be one if only you will trust me." The voice laughed, a high-pitched, girlish sound. It spread through Erissa's blood, cool and warm at the same time as it melded itself into Erissa's very soul.

Erissa breathed deeply. She let every wall she erected around herself drop on a slow exhale. Heat built within her, not unlike the heat she felt in the Wilds with Rhazien's magic coursing through her body.

"Hold onto it," the voice commanded. *"Hold the wind. We must buy them time to escape."*

With another brutal concussion, Erissa palmed the air and gathered the wind, slicing it across the ground to stand as a living barrier between the young ones and the Fae. She paid no heed to how the barrier trapped her and Islone.

Islone scrambled closer to the men on her hands and knees, pulling a dagger from her skirts with one hand while the fingernails of her other dug into the ground. She tried to fight Erissa's power to reach the men and buy the children more time to escape. "Orbas, run! Take them and run!"

Orbas boosted each of the children over the low clay wall surrounding the yard as lightning gathered overhead in the darkening clouds.

Castian bellowed, rolling over to glower at Erissa and Islone. "You'll pay for that."

"Focus," Tiovriss snapped. He unsheathed a dagger and hurled it at Erissa. It struck her arm, and the piercing of her flesh broke her concentration. The magic slipped, the wind faltering, allowing enough space for the Fae to react.

Tiovriss's face dragged into a snarl as he took another knife from his belt and flung it toward the children. It struck Orbas in the chest, and he faltered, falling to his knees after shoving the last of the younger children over the wall. Tiovriss smiled as he fell, the grin deepening with Islone's wail of despair. "Get the Veiled One."

Kaellam scrambled to his feet and reached a hand out to Tiovriss and then Castian, aiding them in standing. Wind still swirled around Erissa, growing in intensity as she drew power from the storm overhead and closed the gap in the wind. "How do we get to her with the air as fast as blades?"

"Grab the brats' mother," ordered Tiovriss. "If the girl won't come with us, we'll kill the woman."

Castian dove for Islone.

"Again," the voice commanded.

Islone had barely managed to scream when Erissa raised an arm, twisting her fingers. Air pulled itself into the wind, snatching the breath from the males' lungs. Islone scrambled away from them and toward Orbas. Her hands met the wall of wind, and she pounded her fists against it.

Each one fell to their knees. They clawed at their throats, tearing the skin apart in their search for life.

"We are far from finished," the voice goaded.

Lightning flashed through the sky overhead. Erissa lifted her face into its brilliance, and a twisted smile spread across her mouth. She lowered her eyes to the men, letting the wind carry her to stand within an arm of them.

Erissa cocked her head to the side, her magic looking through her eyes, examining them. When her eyes landed on Castian, they darkened, her smile fading as death blanketed her face like a mask. "You will die first. And painfully."

"You spoke to the vines once. You can do so again," the voice encouraged. *"Make them suffer the wrath of all that nature offers."*

She snapped her fingers, and two pieces of wind separated from the wall and bound two of the Fae in place as the swirling bands wrapped around them like a vice. She left the third alone as she thought of how to punish him.

With another snap of her fingers, thorny vines grew from the trees, rushing over to wrap around the legs of Castain, rooting him in place. Thick thorns broke through his leathers and pierced his flesh. They tore deeper into the skin, and blood gushed from the wounds. Even then, the vines tightened, squeezing against the bones with brutal force until they finally snapped.

Bone broke through the skin, shooting across the yard in minuscule pieces. The Fae let loose guttural choking sounds, unable to scream. He writhed in untold misery on the ground. Every movement added another cut from the thorns as his companions watched with twin looks of horror.

A giggle broke from the voice. It delighted in the carnage, as gleeful as a child opening a gift on their naming day.

Erissa echoed the feeling. "But it's not enough. He deserves worse."

The Fae turned purple as they suffocated, and Castian's broken bones caused him to collapse to the ground just as Rhazien and Micmus ran into the yard. Erissa watched them from the corner of her eye.

"Do not allow them to interfere," the voice ordered.

Micmus scanned the area, lingering on Erissa for only a moment. He sought Islone and ran over with one question. "The children?"

Islone let him help her stand, tears streaming down her face as she fought him. "Orbas. The dagger struck him."

Micmus shoved his wife toward the house and away from the men, diving for the other side of the yard where Orbas lay bleeding out. Erissa dropped the barrier protecting Orbas, allowing his father to reach his side before she closed the wall again.

Rhazien tried to approach Erissa, but she threw a gust of wind his way, keeping him still. He punched against the wind barrier, shouting for her attention. Erissa ignored him. She had not finished punishing the men and would not allow Rhazien to stop her, even if the voice had not already commanded it.

With a twist of her fingers, Erissa forced air back into the men's lungs. She waited, letting them fill themselves with life. She wanted them to know a moment of hope, wanted them to believe for a moment that she might show them the smallest of mercies. And then she wanted to take it away, taunting them as she had been during her thirteen years of darkness.

She turned her attention to the one called Castian, staring at him as he lay bleeding on the ground. Bone shards protruded from his hair, the brown mess a tangle of viscera. It spurred Erissa's blood lust. He had wanted to harm the girls. To defile them in ways that went against everything good in this world. And he would pay for that.

Drawing on the well of power within her, Erissa heard something calling to her.

A voice echoed through the air, different from the one inside her head with its distinctly male tone. *"My enraged sweetling. How beautiful you look in the throes of your magic. There is much I can do to guide your anger."*

She followed its call along the lines of her magic, tracing it until she met a gleaming black mist. The same mist that appeared to her in the wood and again in the cavern.

The voice inside her responded to the black mist with a low purr that raised the skin on Erissa's arms. She glanced at Rhazien. Did the call come from him? Only he had elicited such a reaction from the voice. But he stood where she left him, barricaded by the wind.

The new voice savored her anger, flattering her for it. *"Your punishment is beautiful to behold, sweetling. Fae such as these are not worth breathing the Creator's air. You can change that. Make them pay."*

Erissa smiled against the face of death she wore, moving to hover over Castian's feet. She pulled the mist forth, surrounding herself with it.

It spoke to her of utter depravity, telling her all the ways she might torture the men. *"There is much we can do. Fillet the flesh from their bones. Castrate them one by one. Remove a few toes. Torture has no limit for their crimes. And you, my sweetling, are something rare. You can make them weep."*

She liked how it talked to her. Liked how it encouraged her to punish the male who would hurt a child as he desired. It spoke to her in a way no one else had before. Erissa wanted to be everything good and wonderful in this world for Rhazien. But the black mist and its voice wanted nothing of the sort. It delved into the deepest parts of her heart, finding all the pain layered beneath Rhazien's love in the cracks it fused together. And then it set the pain free, allowing her to give justice to Islone's children and her inner child without judgment or restraint.

The mist whispered to her again. *"His hate-filled heart wants to betray the innocence of a child, and you can take it from him so that no other falls victim to his sickness."*

The voice stroked the flames of her anger, and with it, a plan emerged. Filleting the Fae would not suffice.

The wind froze around her on a howling screech. The sound ripped from the air until the broken cries of Castian were all that echoed through the silence. Erissa touched the solid mass of wind before her, removing a jagged piece, a dagger made of wind and fury. She tested the piece against the tip of her finger. It sliced through the skin with ease, drawing blood.

The black mist snarled. *"Do not hurt what is mine."*

It quieted when Erissa licked the blood from her finger, her magic sealing the wound, and the coppery taste invigorated her. She turned her vengeful eyes back to Castian.

The Fae tried wriggling away from her, hampered by the masticated flesh of his lower legs. They drug across the ground. He had barely moved more than a few inches when Erissa stepped toward him. The Fae soiled his pants, the stench filling the air.

Erissa called to the vines, encouraging them to grow until they wrapped around Castian's arms and neck. He loosed a high, keening sound at being bound as she dropped to her knees at his side with the sharp piece of wind held between her fingers.

She positioned the wind dagger over the man's heart. Her arm burned with the weight of holding it there.

The Fae's eyes pleaded with her in a way his voice failed to do, the murky brown depths haunted by the violent light in her eyes. He grunted, trying to find air for the words to beg as he struggled with the vines around his neck, letting out a pathetic noise.

The plea failed to sway her.

Erissa plunged the wind dagger into Castian's chest, taking delight in ripping it through his flesh as the mist and inner voice invigorated her efforts with their praise.

Over and over, she repeated the process, striking him in the same pattern that lay across her own chest. Blood sprayed across her dress. It soaked into the thin cotton. Erissa did not mind the sticky mess. She reveled in its heat as much as she did the screams from Castian.

With every plunge of the wind dagger, a sound ripped from his lips until the strain proved too much, and his cries ended in a hoarse hiss forced around the blood filling his mouth.

The mist drew her attention with the slowing of the Fae's breathing, and the swing of her arm stopped. It whispered further into her ear, and Erissa listened intently, the sweetest of smiles tilting her lips.

Nodding her head, she released the blade and stood.

The wind picked up speed. Someone called her name in the distance, someone familiar, someone she loved. But the black mist twined its way around her. Erissa caressed it with her fingers, giving one last nod, and reached her hand toward the tumultuous heavens.

CHAPTER FIFTY

Rhazien stared at Erissa with awe-filled horror. Her magic held him, leaving him powerless to do anything as a black mist grew around her, untouched by the vigor of the wind as it whirled once more.

Rage spent after killing the Fae, Erissa stood and looked over her shoulder at him.

The thoughts swirling through her mind gutted him to the core. His anguish flooded their bond, and it triggered a cascade of pain. Memory after memory played through her mind as a young Erissa lay trapped, held suspended by mistdrite cuffs, and severely beaten in ways that fractured more than her skin.

Her fears dominated the worst of the memories. Each one held a question of whether her punishments would go further at the hands of her father. Those fears drove her actions as she decried the foul desires of any being who would harm a child and sought vengeance, not only for the sake of Islone's children but for the little girl locked away in Emberhold's stronghold who had been powerless to save herself.

A heap of torn tissue and broken bones lay where the Fae's legs should be, and even less remained of his torso, his chest a caved-in sea of red. The other two stood behind his mutilated body, trembling with fear in their wind prisons.

The clouds churned overhead, flashes of lightning charging within them at the direction of Erissa's fingers playing through the air.

Rhazien called forth his magic, devouring the spell surrounding him. He needed to intervene and stop Erissa before things went any further. Her power, strengthened by the black mist, kept feeding the barrier, making it difficult to take down.

Tiovriss found his voice. He grit his teeth, managing to wiggle an arm free, a dagger clutched in his hand. His own feeble attempts at magic puttered along the blade. "You'll die for this, bitch." He used the last of his strength to throw the dagger, and it hit as intended, striking Erissa in the shoulder.

She staggered backward, struggling to keep her footing as the magic wore her out as fast as the blood poured around her wound. Her strength faded, and Erissa called forth the black mist to boost her power.

Rhazien snarled, fighting harder to break through the barrier. "I'll fucking kill you."

"No, you won't," Erissa spoke with an eerie calm. The world around them crackled with the barbarity of the magical lightning. "I will end their lives." Erissa lowered her arm in one swift motion, unleashing the power of the heavens on the three Fae.

Lightning struck each of them, the next strike more vicious than the last as they screamed. Their bodies flopped on the ground, the other two having fallen with the first strike as they burned beneath the charged energy. Less and less remained with each hit.

Erissa stared at the lightning, enthralled by its breathtaking brutality. Her head tipped to the side, a small, pleased smile on her face. She looked like a spirit against the violet beacon of her eyes, the image intensified by the white-hot lightning as it continued to strike the ground.

The lightning never slowed as Erissa waved a hand at Rhazien, releasing him from the last binding holding him at bay. He slowly approached her, his magic at the ready, careful not to startle her.

He tried processing what Erissa had done and her pleasure in killing the Fae. They lost her to the magic, leaving him worried about freeing her from its hold this time.

The void might be his only option. Even without having access to all of it, Rhazien's void could take her magic, but it might end her life in the process. He did not want to chance it. He had to draw her out from under the weight.

Erissa turned her head to face Rhazien when he came closer. It still tipped at an odd angle as she intensely studied him, trying to piece together who he was. Her grip on the magic remained firm, the lightning striking each Fae in the same pattern—or what she left of each Fae.

"Can you hear me, Erissa?"

He reached out to touch her, and she bared her teeth in a menacing hiss that had him pulling back. The black mist flared around her, a living entity that bent to the will of her emotions.

"That's not what you call me." Erissa snarled the words, taking a step toward him, the mist following. "I like my special name. Say it."

"Little doe," Rhazien crooned. He held his arms out for her, waiting for her to decide. "Come here, little doe. Let me hold you."

Erissa plastered herself to his chest, winding her fists into the front of his shirt. The mist blanketed them, twisting around their forms and holding them together.

Rhazien clasped her. "There, little doe. Is this what you need?"

She breathed deeply. A low, throaty thrum that made him smile as she nuzzled into his chest. "You smell like home. All sweet oranges, floral wood, and smokey fires. I love it. I love you."

The lightning continued to strike beside them. The bodies were long gone, not even a pile of ash remaining from the force of the strikes.

"I love you, little doe." Rhazien held onto her, rubbing small circles across her lower back. She wiggled against him, another thrum sounding. "It's time to let go of your hold on the lightning. The men are no more."

A feral growl broke through her lips again, her eyes cutting to where the Fae had turned to ash. The lightning intensified, its strikes coming faster. The ground cracked under the pressure. "They tried to hurt the children and Islone."

"I know, little doe. But they're gone now. You saved everyone. Islone and the children are safe." Rhazien kissed the top of her head. "*You* are safe. You need to let go."

Rhazien spread a hand through her hair and gently tugged on the strands until Erissa raised her head. He kissed her, a gentle meeting of the lips.

She raised up on her toes and wrapped her arms around his neck, stealing the breath from his lungs and replacing it with the hidden flow of air inside of her. At every exchange of their tongues, the lightning dwindled until it receded into the turbulent sky Erissa had called it down from.

Rhazien ended the kiss with a series of nibbles against her lips. Erissa's eyes still glowed with the force of power she drew from, and the mists remained. It twinkled like a starlit night sky, waving around her like it loathed the idea of parting from her side.

"Are you with me, little doe?"

Erissa nodded. "I'm tired. Will you sing me a song?"

"Of course, little doe." Rhazien sang the song of their mothers, stroking the hair from Erissa's face.

Her head drooped from the weight of the magic as she swayed to his gentle song. The monsoon finally broke, and with it, Erissa's ability to remain upright. Rhazien caught her, swinging her up into his arms. The black mist pulsed around her before fading.

The rain fell in a thick curtain, soaking through their clothes. Islone rushed to open the back door for Micmus as he carried Orbas into the house. Tears mixed with the rain coating her face, and she stared at Erissa in Rhazien's arms, the dagger still protruding from her shoulder. "Is she..."

"She'll be fine." She had to be fine. Rhazien hitched her further up his chest, gathering her head beneath his chin.

Islone followed Micmus to the other side of the house to care for Orbas. Rhazien knew not if the boy would live, but Erissa's wound lay near her heart and needed attention. He carried her to their room, murmuring prayers to the Creator for both of them.

Rhazien carefully placed her on the bed, rolling her onto her side to open the row of buttons down her back. He stripped the dress from her before grabbing fresh clothing and tending to Erissa until she wore warm clothes and her shoulder lay exposed. He covered her with a blanket, not a moment too soon, as a shiver wracked her frame.

The dagger slid from her shoulder with more ease than he thought it would, and Rhazien pressed a cloth over the wound. The bleeding picked up, but as he applied pressure, it slowed. Rhazien breathed a sigh of relief.

Thoughts of Orbas haunted him as Rhazien sat next to Erissa on the bed. He tried to leave her side but found it impossible; the bond needed her near while she lay injured.

Hours passed when a knock finally sounded on the door.

Rhazien called for them to enter the room, and Islone rushed in, Micmus not far behind.

Islone stood by the bed. "Is she alright?"

"The shoulder will need time to heal, but the bleeding has stopped." Rhazien turned to look between the couple he loved as deeply as his parents. "The children?"

Micmus opened his mouth, closed it, and swallowed hard. He took a steadying breath and began again. "All safe. Orbas got them over the wall in time."

"She saved us." Islone tucked a wet strand of hair behind her ear. "They were after her. But one bastard... the way he stared at the girls..." Islone shuddered. "Erissa put a barrier of wind between the Fae and the children, giving Orbas time to get them to safety."

"Orbas?" Rhazien's voice caught. "Is he..."

"He will pull through so long as a fever doesn't take. He's resting in our room with the other children. Thitelar and Relreina are looking after them."

Micmus guided Islone from the bedside, leaving room for Rhazien to tend to his wife. "We were already on our way back. Thitelar told us men were asking around."

"They called her the Veiled One," Islone said the words with fear-laced wonder. "And after what she did, controlling the elements of the gods, there's no doubt they were right."

"It's time then. For the prophecy to unfold." Micmus's mouth thinned into a grim line. "They must run. Draven comes for the girl."

CHAPTER FIFTY-ONE

Erissa's head pounded as she awoke, making her thoughts sluggish and her eyelids heavy. No one seemed to notice she had woken up, too preoccupied with their conversation. She cracked an eye and lay there, listening to everyone speak around her, lying still to help keep the world from spinning.

"The Veiled One. That's what the ones who attacked us in Eshirene's Wood called her." Rhazien moved away from her side. "What does it mean?"

Neither Islone nor Micmus paid any attention to Rhazien's question.

"If Erissa's the Veiled One, that makes Rhazien..." Islone looked at him, horror overtaking her normally mischievous countenance.

"The last Warden." Micmus wiped a hand against his weary face. "Rhazien is the last Warden."

"Oh, Micmus." Tears welled in Islone's eyes. "She might as well be a child for all she's lived. You saw how she acted with Rhazien just now. And Rhazien? He might be older than me, but he's still a youngling himself."

"I'm right here, Islone, and I assure you, I'm a fully grown Fefnirion." Rhazien tried to reign in his temper. "Can one of you tell me what's really going on?"

Erissa wanted to scrunch her brow at what she heard, but even that felt like too much after using her powers. She relaxed further into the bed and let the conversation wash over her as she watched them from beneath her hooded lids.

"Like you telling Erissa what's going on?" Islone's tone held a bite to it.

The question piqued Erissa's attention. She and Rhazien had yet to talk. Something always interrupted them.

Rhazien pinched the crooked bridge of his nose. "I'm going to tell her. But I can't tell her the whole truth if I don't know it. The Veiled One, the last Warden... what are you talking about?"

"It dates back to the War of the Remaking. When the god of darkness, Malcufyre, led the chaotic gods in the fight for domination. The god of stone, Belfyndar, created the mistdrite to help fight against the Fae Malcufyre created." Micmus motioned for them to all sit on the decorative cushions next to the side of the bed. "The area where the mistdrite grew changed the soil. Magic sank into the land, and the Fae who gathered the precious metals were changed by handling it."

Islone picked up where her husband had left off once the three of them found their comfort. "Those Fae became known as witches. Many among them developed additional magics. One—Berthina—developed a gift for prophecy."

"There's a prophecy about the Veiled One and her last Warden. Only a part of it was given to the Fefnirion by the Seelie King." Micmus cleared his throat and recited it:

"Beware what lies behind the patterned wall
—the forewarner of death.
For there is no way for one to stall,
—'til only bones are left.
Her violet eyes are in their thrall
—even The Veiled One cannot escape,
The destiny that dooms us all

—and the world she will reshape.
Hunted then and hunted now
—the last Warden heeds her need.
An alliance made in favored vow
—stands against a binding forged in greed..."

"An old crone in Emberhold sang part of that the first time I saw Erissa." Rhazien recounted. "It was much the same as what happened with Wilidon. Only the citizens of Emberhold didn't handle it with the same grace."

"There's more I know of it." Micmus spoke from memory again:
Her glowing eyes will see their souls,
—with whispered words, they call,
An enticement meant to make worlds whole,
—or one to forsake us all.
He will come for her with no delay,
—the true King behind the wall,
A bargain made that will betray,
—she stumbles and will fall.
Fate cannot decide her will; for her alone, it bends,
—her power will, in time recall
The ways to destroy or mend,
—or falter here, forevermore, with trouble to befall.

"The wall refers to the Mists," Islone said.

"And you've already said I'm the last Warden." Rhazien turned his head toward Erissa, and she shut her eyes, hoping he did not see them open. Her worries were for nothing as he continued speaking, his voice lowering. "Which makes sense. I'm the only actual Fefnirion left."

Fefnirion. Erissa heard it that time. He called himself a Fefnirion. Rhazien really was a dragon. Her question had not been stupid after all. The sneaky, lying lizard. What else is he hiding from her?

The voice flickered at the edges of her mind. *"Give... him... the... benefit."*

"The alliance made in favored vow... if the prophecy is talking about Erissa and me, then that line has to refer to us being married mates," Rhazien mused.

Mates? Rhazien was her mate? Erissa listened to the tread of Rhazien's boots as he stood and paced the room. The sound echoed loudly alongside her erratic pulse. He knew they were mates and said nothing this entire time. Erissa felt the revelation like a physical blow.

"Stop... being... dramatic," the voice scolded. *"He did... tell... you... nayanam... called you... nayanam."* It went quiet then, too tired to continue, and faded behind her thoughts.

Her anger faded along with it. The voice had a point. Rhazien had said they were bonded, that she was his *nayanam* more than once. If Rhazien was truly a Fefnirion, that meant the bond they shared was more than a human's soul tie—to him, Erissa must be his mate. He had told her the stories, why hadn't he just told her they were living them?

Rhazien continued thinking out loud. "And the binding made in greed must be the soul you heard, Micmus. Reeva. She's bound to the Keeping."

Erissa opened her eyes enough to see Micmus turn white.

Micmus reached for Islone's hand. "Of course, Reeva would be involved."

"How do you know Reeva?" Rhazien asked.

"All the Fefnirion know who Reeva is. She's whom they named the Keeping War after. Through her sacrifice, we could band together with the Fae and end the war, sealing Draven in the Veil." The timber of Micmus's voice turned somber. "But I'm afraid we only delayed the war instead of stopping it altogether."

We? Micmus was Fefnirion too? All this talk of war and dragons made Erissa's head spin again. What did any of this have to do with her, Rhazien, Virion, and the men he kept sending after her?

Micmus answered Erissa's unasked questions. "A Fae called Draven started the Keeping War. He wanted to continue what Malcufyre started centuries before in the Remaking and convinced one of the Unseelie courts and one of the Seelie courts to join his efforts. The Fae went to war against one another until the conflict grew to the point of needing the interference of the Fefnirion. There were so few of us after most had given up their power. We had to combine our powers with the Fae fighting against Draven, but it still wasn't enough with Draven aided by the Keeper himself. Draven's son and one of the other courts allied with Draven turned against him at the last moment, and with their powers adding to our collective, we confined Draven in a prison within the Veil."

"How does Reeva fit into this?" Rhazien asked.

"She died on the battlefield," Micmus answered, "her life stolen after the Keeping, and her blood used to open a rift in the Veil. This rift was the only way to seal Draven within the Veil. Reeva's sacrifice saved us all that day, but she bound herself to the Keeping before her death. It was the only way to save her child's life."

"Reeva's been very clear her allegiance lies elsewhere, though I don't doubt she cares for Erissa." Rhazien sighed, scratching against the stubble staining his chin. "That still leaves the true King behind the wall. I think Reeva knows what it refers to. She told me someone was coming for Erissa, and I must let her go with him.

Erissa bristled. Rhazien's secrets were piling up, as were Reeva's. How deep do the lies and half-truths run between the three of them?

Micmus took his time answering as he considered the possibilities. "Much has happened beyond the Mists since the Keeping War, and the Fefnirion have been kept from almost all knowledge of it. The Fae bow to two Kings, one Seelie, a King of the lawful, and the other the Unseelie, a King of the chaotic. Draven is technically still the Unseelie King unless the Unseelie magic has passed to another more powerful Fae on this side of the Veil. Erissa holds the key to breaking him free from his prison. I doubt the prophecy is referencing him, not when the entire thing is about the conflict that is to come against him. It can't be Virion either."

"Why not?" Rhazien tapped his foot, betraying his nerves.

"Virion is Draven's son." Micmus sighed. "Why he's helping his father after assisting in his defeat centuries ago, I don't know. But the prophecy is clear in one aspect. The reigning Fae Kings are not whom the prophecy references with this verse. The lines of the prophecy distinguish themselves from one another. This "true King" is unknown to me."

"Whoever this true King is, he must be Fae to come beyond the wall," Rhazien mused. "If Reeva is right about someone else coming for Erissa, this has to be who it is."

Islone wrung her hands. "We need to wake Erissa. She needs to know the truth of what's happening."

"No." Rhazien's reply held no hesitation.

Erissa's hands clenched beneath the covers at his automatic dismissal.

"Rhazien, you can't keep her in the dark forever." Islone's rebuke cut like a whip. "She needs to know the truth. You saw what happened in that yard. She sacrificed a part of herself in killing those men. It's a piece of her soul that will never return. We owe her the debt of truth."

Owed it to her. Erissa wanted to snort, as annoyed with Micmus and Islone as she was with Rhazien. What happened to telling her the truth because she had every right to know what affected her directly?

"What just happened is the reason we can't tell her, not right now." Rhazien moved toward the bed, and Erissa snapped her eyes closed. "She needs to recover from what she's done, and we have to leave Cropari. There isn't time to have this conversation again. I promise to tell her. Everything. But I need to get her away first."

Micmus and Islone reluctantly agreed.

"Where will you go?" Islone asked.

"You should head for Umirian. Several Fefnirion settled there after finding their mates." Micmus rubbed his brow. "The old codger down there hates magic. No one would expect Erissa to walk amongst their numbers with her eyes giving her powers away."

"To Umirian then." Rhazien nodded. "We will leave as soon as she's awake."

Erissa couldn't help the anger that still grew. The conversation she had heard should have taken place *with* her, but now she needed to wait for someone else to decide she was ready to hear it. She stirred against the heaviness of her limbs, wanting to get up to confront each of them. They would not cooperate with her. She lay there, exhausted from using her magic, unable to do anything, as the people she loved and trusted denied her a basic knowledge of the events shaping her life.

Rhazien ran his fingers through the damp strands of her hair and let loose a spellbinding hum that captivated the very heart of her being. It did little to soothe the fire raging beneath her breast, doing nothing more than blanketing the feeling against a weighty sensation of contentment. Erissa felt her eyelids soften against her anger. Her body melted into the mattress as her thoughts slowed their racing, and with one last rumbling hum, Erissa gave into the beckoning sleep of its song.

CHAPTER FIFTY-TWO

The wind whistled through the gnarled, black trees of the Crying Grove like an ensemble of wailing souls. Drurrah thought it fitting, considering its proximity to the Veil. Even more fitting when he thought of how Virion would throw a tantrum at the news he brought. The Fae often sounded like an emotional child when things did not go their way.

Speaking of the bothersome fool, he came into view as Drurrah came around a bend in the path.

Three bodies littered the ground, their eyes wide and glassy. He had bled them, and none too gently by the look of things.

Virion turned at Drurrah's approach. His eyes narrowed when the other Fae gave a shake of his head. "Something wrong?"

"I'll never understand your enjoyment of theatrics." Drurrah sniffed. "They leave such a mess."

"What do you want, Drurrah?" Barely contained contempt laced Virion's words.

Drurrah smirked, pleased to have riled him. Virion would do nothing about it. He needed Drurrah's support for the coming war. Not alienating him meant more than the satisfaction of a lost temper.

"Your plan has gone awry." Drurrah sauntered over to the chair Virion no doubt had the servants bring from the temple. He sat down, crossing his legs at the ankle. "It appears they got on the wrong side of the Veiled One."

"Tiovriss?"

"Dead, I'm afraid, as are Castian and Kaellam."

Virion swore, kicking at one of the bodies. "What happened?"

"Judging from the number of times lightning struck the ground, I'd say your girl fried them into oblivion." Drurrah sighed. "You should have known better than to send children after her in the city."

Virion swallowed hard, his eyes dark with thinly controlled anger. "Imbeciles. Putting Tiovriss in charge was my first mistake."

"One of many where the bumbling trio is concerned. Thonalan has his own agenda. Trusting his men was the height of stupidity, and the fool can never keep his mouth shut. He told me where to find them almost eagerly." Drurrah's smile was saccharine. "Even I am not as corrupt as that bastard, and I've sold out my entire court for your schemes."

"If you had not sold out Draven in the Keeping, we wouldn't be having this discussion."

Drurrah ignored the pointed remark. "Sending those fools when they had little magic to their names... what were *you* thinking? None of them stood a chance against the Veiled One's power."

"Do you have anything of use to say?" Virion finished tracing the bloodied runes across the stone slab in the center of the clearing.

The runes burned a deep green, a ghost of their essence rising into the area to create a swirling oval mass.

"I thought you might never ask." Drurrah leaned forward, steepling his arms over his thighs. "I have a plan. The girl won't stay in Cropari for long, and the King is already on his way to claim her."

"Which one?" snorted Virion. He turned to the newly formed portal, waiting patiently.

"*Both*. Although who reaches her first is anyone's guess." Drurrah let the implications of the word sink in before continuing. "This presents us with the perfect opportunity. No matter who claims the girl, they wouldn't dare believe you would be so foolish as to snatch her from them. And with a little help from the Keeping, it will be easy to lure her away."

A third voice joined them as a man materialized behind the phantom glow of the portal. "Drurrah. Nice to see you being useful for a change."

Drurrah gave an easy grin, refusing to rise to the bait. "Draven. Took you long enough."

The image in the portal sharpened until a large, muscled Fae appeared on the other side. He looked every bit the savage he had portrayed himself to be on the day they sealed him within the Veil, covered in blood with runes traced in black down his chest and arms. Long, dark hair framed a cruelly handsome face with intelligent gray eyes.

"Still testing your welcome after all these centuries?" The malice in Draven's voice was clear.

Drurrah waved it away. "Save your threats, Draven. You needed me during the war, and you need me now."

"How dare you—"

Drurrah cut Virion off. "Are we going to dance around this again, or do you want to hear my plan?"

Draven seethed but motioned for him to continue.

"As I was saying," Drurrah went on, "we need the Keeping. Where is Reeva?"

CHAPTER FIFTY-THREE

"You forced my hand, Barrett." Faldeyr crouched, careful to avoid the mud collecting beneath his brother.

Barrett disgusted him. His time spent bound in the dungeon did little to keep up one's appearance. The unkempt man's stench rivaled the pig shit in this gods' forsaken town. Orina hardly boasted the same comforts Emberhold did. No matter. He would return to Emberhold soon once they found the girl.

"Did you think Vilotta wouldn't notice the women missing? That I wouldn't question your actions? If I wanted to foil your plan and stop the blacksmith and his family from escaping, I would have, but the blacksmith served his purpose. It tested your loyalty and Vilotta's." Faldeyr laughed at the betrayal on Barrett's face. "I told you already, brother, my wife knows her place even if you do not, and that place is sitting on the throne beside me as we rule over the human realm of Kaidreth."

Barrett's jaw clenched. His hands fisted and tested the strength of his restraints. "You can't make me your faithful dog anymore. I'd rather she dies than fall into your hands."

"There are worse things than death for the girl."

The color left Barrett, his ghostly pallor standing in stark contrast to the mud on his face.

Faldeyr considered killing him now. It would not take much effort. His clothes lay in tatters, revealing welted and cut skin. Being dragged behind

Faldeyr's horse left a multitude of injuries, many appearing infected in between globs of mud. The skin under the ropes lay raw and angry from the constant chafing. Barrett's clothes hung across his frame. Faldeyr fed him enough water to keep him alive but took delight in starving him.

Faldeyr longed for the day when the executioner's axe would end his brother's pitiful life. Tricking him into the Fae bargain had been easy enough, but Barrett grew a backbone through the years. Controlling him became harder with the passage of time, especially with Vilotta's bastard on the run.

Faldeyr stood, turning a curled lip to the creature on his left. "Are you sure this time?"

Someone walked around Barrett. He fought against the ropes, binding his arms to his chest as they came into view. "Thonalan."

The Fae peered down his nose at Barrett and sneered. "Did you drag him through horse shit on his way here?"

"Not far from it." Faldeyr laughed. "My brother is in need of a lesson, but sadly, a week being drug behind my horse has done little to make him more cooperative. Or appreciative for my sparing his life."

Rage burned through Barrett's blood as he stared at the Fae. If not for Thonalan and his proposition, Erissa might have had a different fate than what Faldeyr visited upon her.

He gathered the saliva at the back of his throat and spit at Thonalan's feet. Contempt laced every word when he spoke. "Mark my words, Thonalan. I will peel the skin from your bones for your part in this."

"Humans are full of theatrics." Thonalan ignored him, turning to address Faldeyr. "It is better to kill him now."

Faldeyr shook his head. "Not until the girl returns."

"My guard followed the Fae Virion sent to Cropari. The Fae I slipped into their ranks failed. The girl had already killed them and left before the guard's arrival. She's headed south with the blacksmith." Thonalan glanced around the town, his mouth tightening. "Trilux or Theanelis would have offered more comforts. Please tell me this ramshackle town boasts an inn?"

Erissa killed someone? Barrett sagged against his bonds.

"The inn is the least of my worries." Faldeyr ground his teeth impatiently. "When will they be here?"

Thonalan sighed. "Two night's time. The river barge will stop in Gailme for the night. My men will grab her there. This will be our only chance. The Unseelie Lord is after her. His half-breed dog kicked the High Lords out of a meeting with the King to call in his bargain. If Novus gets his hands on her before we do, there will be no overthrowing Yorrith."

"And no guarantee of bringing the human realm under my rule with your support." Faldeyr crossed his arms. "Are your men up to the task?"

"I have instructed them to do what is needed." Thonalan sniffed, looking at Faldeyr down his nose. "By any means possible. So long as they do not kill the girl, nothing is off the table."

Faldeyr cackled, rubbing his hands together. "Everything will come together soon, then. We should celebrate. The inn is shit, but the ale is some of the best in all of Kaidreth. Let us toast to finally capturing the girl."

"A little ahead of yourself, brother." Barrett struggled to his feet. "Erissa might still escape your grasp."

A resounding crack ripped through the air as Faldeyr's fist met with Barrett's face. He went flying backward, falling into the mud with a splash that coated him from head to toe, adding to the dried layers.

"Take him away," Faldeyr screamed at the guards.

Barrett fought as the guards carried him to the stables behind the inn. Faldeyr's horse already occupied a stall. The guards tossed into the same one, slamming the door shut and closing the heavy metal bolt on the outside.

A plan began forming in Barrett's mind as the guards left. He rolled onto his stomach, biting his tongue against the effort of the movement. He searched the stall for anything he might use to cut through the thick ropes tied around his chest.

Thank the gods the guards were dumb enough to leave him in the same stall as his brother's horse. The stallion, used to his presence through the years, kept quiet as Barrett inched his way across the old straw along the ground.

Tears sprang when he found a nail, rusty with age, sticking out from the wooded planks of the stall. Barrett placed his bound hands over it, gritting his teeth against the pain. He needed to hurry and saw through the ropes. Nightfall would be here soon. He had two days to reach Gailme if he wanted Erissa to live.

CHAPTER FIFTY-FOUR

Erissa's heart cleaved in two as she waved farewell to Micmus and Islone from the deck of the river barge. Rhazien hovered behind her, his hands resting on her shoulders.

A part of her remained with the couple. Cropari became home in more ways than one, and Erissa would miss its people and their brightly colored world. She had needed three days of hard sleeping to recover from using her magic and one more spent on horseback to reach the barge south of the city. The time had done little to soften Erissa's ire.

Their only option had been to leave. More men would come. Not that any of them knew Erissa understood the notion. They considered her too fragile for such a realization or the conversation that should have taken place around it.

Rhazien talked to her but of nothing important. He told her more stories, regaling her with his siblings' antics. The stories were a welcome distraction from the sickness that tormented me. Her stomach pitched at every sway of the barge despite the gods' favor bringing a steady current that hastened their journey. If anything, the quick pace led to Erissa's undoing as she spent the day hanging over the railing, retching into the water below.

The second morning held few differences from the day before. Rhazien held Erissa's hair from her face once again. When she finished emptying her stomach of the stale bread she tried to keep down, she flopped across the railing, grateful for the cold air blowing in from the south.

"How long until we reach Umirian?"

"Four days. Five if the current doesn't hold." Rhazien jumped up when Erissa did the same, reaching for her hair as she retched once more. He continued when she stood and wiped her mouth. "We'll reach Gailme's port by the end of the day. We should stop for the night. Find a room and let you rest without the sway beneath you."

A protest built, but nausea built faster. Leaning over the rail once more, Erissa had to agree with Rhazien. A night off the barge had to be better than another one on it.

Evening descended by the time they veered alongside the docks of Gailme, and Erissa's temper had come in with it.

After bundling Erissa's hair into the hood of her cloak and shifting the folds to disguise the glow of her eyes, Rhazien led her through the docks and onto the main road. She kept her head lowered, avoiding catching the eye of anyone they might pass.

Rhazien cast her a concerned look Erissa ignored when she flinched against his hand when placed on her lower back. He guided her further down the road, finding the inn tucked against a large stable.

Erissa's only knowledge of an inn came from the books she read. This inn might resemble their physical description with its wooden tables and chairs with candles burning in the center, but the resemblance ended there. Unlike the rambunctious atmosphere she expected, melancholic dilapidation bled from every corner of the large main room.

All heads turned in their direction as they entered and walked to the bar. A large woman stood behind the counter, her apron stained and hair poking out of her sloppy up-style. The gray hair and wrinkles weathering the woman's face placed her age far above Islone's.

Rhazien called out to her. "Orrae, it's been a long time."

"Rhazien?" The woman removed her apron and walked around the bar. "It's been moons. The South not to your liking?"

He let go of Erissa, wrapping his arms around the woman. "We were visiting Micmus and Islone."

"We?" the woman asked. She looked at Erissa.

Rhazien wrapped an arm around Erissa's waist, a smile softening the fatigue that darkened his features. "My wife."

If the woman felt shocked at his announcement, she hid it well. Orrae reached for Erissa's hands, gathering them in her own calloused ones twisted with age. "You must be an astonishing woman, dear. All the young ladies have been after your husband for years. Every time he came to hunt with his father, I'd have to chase gaggles of them away."

Erissa fought to keep her lip from curling. Maybe she should tell these other women her husband did nothing but hand out lies covered with sweet words. The line chasing after him would surely diminish then.

At her silence, Orrae clucked her tongue. "You poor dear. You're as pale as the new moon. The barge can be rough on someone unfamiliar with the river's rolling. Let's get you into a room, and I'll bring some broth to settle your stomach."

The old woman turned toward the stairs to the bar's right. Rhazien motioned for Erissa to follow, bringing up the rear as the three of them climbed to the next floor.

"I didn't see Harduin when we walked in. Is he chasing after Harlais in the wood?" Rhazien chuckled. "The girl never stayed out of the wood for long."

Orrae missed a step, a hand shooting out to grab onto the rail to keep her from falling.

Erissa reached for the woman's arm, steadying her.

When she regained her footing, the woman turned her head, speaking over her shoulder. "Trouble came looking for them. Harduin is dead, and the girl is missing."

Tension radiated from behind her, the feeling engulfing her in Rhazien's moment of shocked grief.

"Dead?" He pulled Erissa closer to him, squeezing her hip in his hand. "How?"

"A traveler butchered him. Someone found him in the morning, dead in the common room. Harlais wasn't found with him. We searched the surrounding wood and used poles along the embankment but found nothing."

The silence in the stairwell threatened to suffocate the three of them.

"Come, let us get the two of you settled. Speaking of the dead will hardly return them from beyond the Veil." Orrae cleared her throat. "And I am tired of crying."

A somber air chilled the corridor as the trio reached the next floor. It tasted of the grief in the air, building on Erissa's ire, and the space turned colder still. She turned inward to avoid the pain and anger of Rhazien's deceit, refusing to soften at his grief. Her heavy heart pounded painfully beneath her breast. She ignored it and followed the old woman into the room furthest from the stairwell.

"Here we are." Orrae opened the door, allowing the couple to enter through it.

The small room held simple but tasteful furnishings, with a large bed dominating the center and a chair-flanked hearth on the other wall. A loan wardrobe stood between the two, and a mirror sat propped on its surface against the wall. Heavy drapery hung around a small window; the glass frosted against the chilled night air.

"Plenty of wood for the fire and a jug of water on the dresser." Orrae backed out of the room. "If you need anything else, someone will be keeping watch downstairs. You need only ask."

When Orrae quit the room, Erissa breathed deeply, shaking the tension from her shoulders as she removed her cloak. She ignored Rhazien, walking up to the bed.

"Erissa." Rhazien's hands came from behind to rest on her shoulders. "Something is bothering you, and it's more than what happened in the attack. You've been distant since we left Cropari, and I didn't push you to talk about it with how sick you were on the boat. But I can't help if you don't tell me what's wrong."

Erissa did not deny it. Offering no explanation, she ran a hand across the homespun fabric of the bedding.

The pressure on her shoulders forced her to turn and face her husband. He lifted a hand, using it to tuck a strand of hair behind her ear. "Tell me what's going on. I can feel something isn't right."

Twisting, she moved out from under his hold. "Maybe you should discuss it with Islone and Micmus. The three of you know everything already. I'm sure you can figure things out."

Erissa's waspish tone caught Rhazien by surprise. He stared at her dumbfounded, his mouth opening and closing.

"Keeper got your tongue, husband?" Erissa balled her cloak in her arms. "You had plenty to say when you thought I lay sleeping."

All the color drained from Rhazien's tanned skin, a grayish pallor overtaking him. "How much did you hear?"

"That's all you have to say?" Erissa threw the cloak at the door.

Rhazien spread his arms out. "Little doe, I can explain."

"Explain what? That you're Fefnirion? That I'm the Veiled One?" Erissa stepped closer to him, balling her hands into fists. "You wouldn't continue things in the wood until I spilled my secrets, but that didn't seem to matter in Cropari. You had few qualms about joining with me with all your own secrets between us."

His eyebrows lifted with a twitch of his lips. "Joining?"

Erissa watched him press his lips together, swallowing hard to keep the laughter from spilling out. Her eyes narrowed. "Are you laughing at me?"

Rhazien reached for her. "No, of course not, little do—"

"Don't touch me, and don't call me that." Erissa stepped back, needing space between them to say everything that weighed on her mind. "You had good intentions behind lying, but it doesn't change that you hid everything. And what's worse is you did it when you demanded honesty from me."

Her words landed like a physical blow.

"How long did you know?" Erissa demanded.

"What?"

"That we were mates. How long did you know, Rhazien?"

"From the beginning."

Erissa closed her eyes, breathing deeply to master the rage sweeping over her. "So when you talked about your mother and souls recognizing one another, you knew then. You knew what the connection meant."

"It's not how it seems, Erissa." Rhazien pleaded with her. "I did tell you. I told you what you were to me. I told you there was a bond, that you are my *nayanam*. But I didn't tell you that we were mates because I only wanted you to make the connection yourself. You've never had a chance to live in the world. The last thing I wanted to do was tie you to me with a mating bond."

Erissa mulled over his words. She knew he meant them. She felt everything down their bond—their mate bond. Rhazien believed he was making the right decision by not pushing her, and could she honestly put all the blame on him when she never questioned anything?

Rhazien sank onto one of the small chairs by the fire. "I'm sorry, little doe. I was trying to protect you, not lie to you."

All the anger left Erissa's voice at the pain in Rhazien's. "Even with your conversation with Micmus and Islone? You've lied about so much."

"I tried to do what I thought was right to protect you and keep you from dealing with more. I never lied about what I felt for you. I love you." Rhazien's voice broke on the last words. "Can't you trust that?"

She wanted to, but doubts overtook her. He wanted her to make a connection between them herself, but was that even possible? How much control did she have over her own feelings? "How can I trust anything I feel with the bond between us? How can either of us?"

"Are you saying you don't love me?"

Silence met his question. Erissa wanted to tell him no, to deny the fast beat of her heart at the thought of denying she loved him. The words would not come. Even with everything broken, her heartbeat remained tied to his. Was that her own hesitation or an effect of the bond between them? But did it matter anymore? "I'm saying I need time to know my own mind. Time to know you and for you to know me."

"What does that mean?"

"Exactly what it sounds like." Erissa sighed, sitting on the edge of the bed. "It's been less than a moon, Rhazien. Everything I've felt, everything we've done… it's the bond. We don't really know each other enough to be certain it's love."

"I do know you. I know everything I need to."

A sad laugh left her lips. "I can't trust you. I'm a world away from Emberhold but back in the same lies."

Rhazien looked as if she had slapped him. "You're comparing me to your parents?"

Erissa shook her head. "I would never think you acted like them, but you remind me of my uncle and every time he didn't tell me something for my own protection. Everything was always half-truths with him, and I don't want to have that with you. I want you to be honest with me, even when you think I will struggle to hear it."

The silence lengthened between them. Erissa did not want the distance to do the same. She left him with something that rang of hope. Because even though the anger and hurt suffocated her, and a part of her longed to hold on to that, a stronger part wanted to be with him. To believe in the love they declared.

Whether or not the bond drove this mattered little to her when Rhazien's dejection coated the air. "I don't need you to protect me, Rhazien. I've had enough of other people's protection to last me a lifetime. What I need from you is to be on equal footing. I need us to be partners."

"We are partners, Erissa."

"We don't have a partnership, Rhazien. We have a mate bond driving everything, and your failure to be open with me clouding the rest. How am I supposed to know that our feelings are real?"

"Don't say that. Don't say this isn't real."

"Why not? How can I trust a love when you've been hiding so much?"

"That's not fair, and you know it." Fire flashed in Rhazien's eyes. "If you heard my conversation with Islone and Micmus, then you know I planned on telling you the truth. But how was I supposed to do that when you were barely awake before we fled Cropari? Was I supposed to do it while you retched over the side of the barge?"

The fight went out of Erissa with those words, and she hung her head, grumbling. "That has nothing to do with making me tell you about Reeva before you'd take things further."

"You're right, it doesn't." He forced the anger from his face and walked toward her, stopping a few inches from touching her. "I'm sorry, little doe. I shouldn't have manipulated you into telling me about Reeva."

Erissa crossed her arms, not sure of what to do next. Her anger was gone, but her annoyance still simmered below the surface, and she struggled to let go of it even with Rhazien's apology. He meant the apology; the bond let her feel his sincerity, but did it also force him to apologize?

"Look at me." When she did not raise her gaze, Rhazien moved closer, taking her chin in his hand. He lifted her face, forcing her eyes to his. "It's not the bond forcing me to do anything. You've trusted me this far, so trust me in this."

She wanted to tell him she distrusted herself more than him, but she struggled with the words. Rhazien had consumed her from the moment he caught her hiding behind the cart. Everything happened so fast after that. What if she did not know her own mind, her own heart?

Rhazien dropped her chin, his arms coming to rest on her shoulders. "We're not going to solve this tonight. We have a lifetime for me to show you this love is real. Let's retire. You've been sick for days, and the rest will do us both some good. We can finish talking in the morning."

Erissa allowed him to lead her to the bed and tuck her beneath its patched quilt. As he slid in beside her and pulled her against his chest, Erissa settled her ear over his heartbeat and let the sound lull all her worries into a fretful sleep.

CHAPTER FIFTY-FIVE

For the first time since meeting Rhazien, Erissa passed a restless night. When she awoke, the dawn peeking through the window, Rhazien's name hovered on her lips.

It pained her, the doubts she lay between them. He became her entire life in a matter of weeks, and maybe there lay the problem. She lost herself in him.

Her heart vehemently disagreed. She ignored its thrumming. It did nothing but mislead her where it concerned Rhazien.

They were tangled around each other, and when she looked at his relaxed face, heavy with sleep, every missing piece of her found itself. She ached for him, for the smile ever-present in his eyes, the warmth of his body against hers, and for the world he created for them.

As if he sensed her gaze, he woke and hesitated, his mouth open and poised to speak.

Whatever he had to say, Erissa did not want to hear it. She sat up, put her shoes back on, and filled the silence. "Are you hungry?"

Disappointment dimmed Rhazien's eyes, the golden color muddying. He got up slowly. "Orrae makes a great rice porridge. It sticks to the ribs after a cold night."

The conversation dwindled into an awkward silence.

Erissa struggled with what to say next. Things had never felt like this with Rhazien. She got off the bed and took a step toward him, determined to put last night behind them. "Rhazien, I—"

Orrae saved her from answering. The woman burst into the room, the door crashing into the wall behind it. Her eyes latched onto Rhazien, and she ran over to him, grabbing his shoulders. "Run. Now. Go out the back of the inn and into the stables. Don't stop running until you reach the wood."

"What's happening?" Rhazien grabbed onto the old woman's hands.

"Fae. At the barge. Old Petlamar sent his youngest running as soon as his riverboat docked. The Fae sought passage with him from Cropari. They've been following a girl with purple eyes. Run, now."

Rhazien gave the woman a quick hug. When he stepped out of her arms, he grabbed their bags, motioning to Erissa to put on her shoes and cloak. "Thank you, Orrae. I'm sorry to bring trouble to you."

"You've no time, boy. Run." Orrae pushed him toward the door.

He held a hand out for Erissa, and she came willingly, swallowing her fear for them and replacing it with fear for whoever hunted them now.

Erissa turned to Orrae. "Thank you."

Orrae nodded, and the pair ran out the door.

Erissa followed Rhazien down the hallway. They ran past the main stairs to the other end of the hall. He turned to the left and pressed a knot on the wood paneling, revealing a servant's stairwell.

Lanterns lined the wall of the dank stairwell, providing enough light to keep someone from missing a step. Erissa thanked the Creator for this slight change from the secret passage that started this journey. She let Rhazien lead her down the steps.

The passageway ended in the stables. The horses nickered at their presence, not appreciating being startled. Rhazien moved to the closest one. He hushed its fretting, the tense mare settling at his touch.

As the other horses calmed, Rhazien motioned Erissa to stay behind him. He crept toward the stable door and opened it to peer around its side.

"It's clear." Rhazien kept his voice low. "Run straight for the wood. Don't turn back."

He pushed Erissa out of the door, and she stumbled, grabbing onto his arm. "What about you?"

"I'll be right behind you, I promise." Rhazien gave her another push. "Run, little doe."

Erissa hesitated. "Rhazien, I—"

He crushed his mouth against hers in a harsh kiss that caught her off guard.

It ended too quickly, and Erissa rested her head against his chest. "You promise to be right behind me?"

"On my life, little doe." Rhazien kissed the top of her head.

She hesitated, worried about him keeping his word. But he smiled at her, and the bond pulsed with life between them, offering reassurance. When Rhazien gave Erissa another nudge, she went this time, running for the tree line a short distance to the side of the stable.

Shouting filled the air when she crossed over into the wood. Erissa turned around, looking for Rhazien, expecting him to be right behind her. A scream logged her throat as she found him confronting a wave of Fae as they rounded the back of the inn. They circled Rhazien, offering him no escape.

Erissa begged her magic to rise within her, to help him, but nothing met her pleading. The magic stayed silent, fatigued from its use in Cropari.

The Fae tightened their formation. Rhazien's eyes glowed brightly in the early morning light, their golden depths standing out as sharply as the dawn. Erissa did not think his magic was strong enough to save him against their numbers.

She made to run to him when galloping hooves broke through the forest behind her.

Erissa turned in time to see a disheveled man launch himself from the horse. He crashed into her, the horse racing past them, and they fell to the ground.

The man turned then, taking the brunt of the fall. Erissa found herself splayed across his chest. With a shove, she pushed away from him, scrambling to her feet. She kicked him between the legs with all her might, buying herself a little time as he grunted and wrapped his arms around himself.

Her eyes flew to Rhazien and found him fighting against the Fae. He swung his axe and dagger with bloodthirsty intent, fueling the blades with his dragon's fire. But there were too many of them.

Erissa lunged for him, willing the magic to answer her, to add wind to her flight so she might reach her husband in time and save them both. But it again remained silent.

The man grabbed onto her waist and threw her over his shoulder. She fought against him, trying to find leverage to kick him again.

He shook her, nearly tossing her from his shoulder. "Stop, Erissa. We have to run. They will kill him and come for you."

Familiarity slammed into her. She struggled to believe her ears. "Uncle Barrett? What are you—?"

"We've no time for explanations." Barrett ran, jostling Erissa against his shoulder. "We have to run."

"No, we have to go back." Shock gave way to desperation, and Erissa fought against her uncle, kicking, scratching, and biting—anything to make him drop her.

"I'm not here to harm you or to return you to your father." Barret held onto her with an iron grip. "I will keep you from him if it's the last thing I do."

"Let me go. You don't understand." Erissa screamed in frustration.

"We can talk later." Barrett whistled for the horse.

"No." Erissa pummeled his back ineffectually. "We have to go back. We have to help Rhazien. They will kill him."

"Then his death will ensure your escape."

Erissa fought harder. She twisted at the hip and reached an arm around Barrett's head to drag her nails down his face. Blood welled beneath her fingernails, and Barrett howled in pain, but his hold never loosened. "I won't leave him. I won't leave my husband to die for me."

Barrett's hold slipped at her declaration, shock raising his voice. "Your what?"

"Husband. He's my husband." Erissa squirmed out of his grip, and he let her go this time. "I won't leave him."

Erissa turned and ran back toward Rhazien, her uncle on her heels. They made it to the tree line, and Erissa's blood ran cold.

Two bodies lay at Rhazien's feet. One held the handle of a dagger, the other burning beneath furious flames. Rhazien stood, his back against the stable wall, his chest heaving in the cold air, while the other four Fae closed in.

Barrett ran up beside her, panting. "Husband? Tell me you didn't say you have a husband."

Erissa grabbed her uncle's sleeve, tugging on it. "Please, we have to help him."

"He is really your husband?" Doubt hardened Barrett's features.

"We don't have time for this, Uncle." Angry, desolate tears ran down Erissa's cheeks. "Please, help him. I'll explain after."

Barrett stared at her, taking her measure, and Erissa prayed she conveyed whatever he needed to see.

"Stay here." Barrett removed her hand from his sleeve. "They are after you. If I fail to save him, take the horse and run as far away as you can. Cross the Mists if you must, but do not let your father find you."

And with those words, Barrett took off, running for Rhazien.

Erissa clung to a tree, her nerves buckling her knees. Barrett limped as he ran, drawing his sword even as he raised Erissa's doubt at his chance of success.

There had to be something more for her to do besides cowering against a tree. Her eyes flew to where the horse stood a ways behind her, an idea forming.

She approached the horse as fast as possible without startling it. It eyed her warily, and Erissa held her hand out the way Rhazien had shown her all those weeks ago in Emberhold. Tears threatened again. She shook them off, determined to hold it together and help her husband and uncle.

The horse accepted her presence, and Erissa thanked the Creator for it. She grabbed the reins and led the horse until it stood on the forest's edge.

Barrett engaged two of the Fae, his sword slicing through the air with impressive speed and precision that spoke to his experience as the head of the guard. "Run. For the gods' sake, run."

Rhazien ignored his screaming and fought off the other two, his axe and flames warring for purchase in the enemies he danced with.

A part of her wanted him to run. To turn his back on Barrett, letting every memory of Emberhold die with her uncle. But a deeper thought took root, one where both men came out of this alive.

Erissa spun on her heel and walked to the side of the horse, careful not to place herself directly behind it. It shuffled its hooves as her nerves built. She breathed deeply, raising her hand, and slammed it down with all her might on the horse's backside.

The horse reared on its hind legs, kicking them wildly through the air. Erissa waited until its hooves touched the soil once more, and then she struck the horse again in the same spot, harder this time, making a numbing pain shoot up her arm.

It proved to be enough to spur the horse into a gallop. It tore past the trees, heading straight for Barrett and Rhazien.

Erissa waited until the last minute to warn them, her shrill scream shredding the air. "Watch out."

She gained the attention of everyone, but only Rhazien and the Fae he fought reacted in time. He dove to the side as the Fae moved in the other direction, slamming into the stable wall and plastering himself against the aged wood to avoid the mad flight of the steed.

Barrett did not hold the same luck.

The horse barreled through where he fought with two of the Fae. It crashed into the pointy-eared beings in a clash of hooves and weapons, taking Barrett to the ground in a tangled heap as the tallest of the Fae fell on him.

Erissa gagged as a hoof trampled the tall Fae's head, bursting it across the ground and covering all in its path with gore. The other Fae fared no better, thrown by the impact of the horse. He slammed into one of the Fae fighting Rhazien, knocking him to the ground and impaling him against the sharp edge of a metal feeder sitting in the stable's arched entryway. The metal protruded from his neck, blood bubbling from his mouth.

Those still fighting against Rhazien used the distraction to their advantage as the horse ran off. They abandoned the men, running straight for Erissa.

She screamed again as the Fae drew closer, and Barrett sprang into action, disentangling himself from the body of the headless corpse. He found his blade in the remains, hoisting it into the air like a spear. He bellowed in defiance and drew his arm back in a steady grip.

The sword whistled through the air. The men screamed at her to run, their voices blending and ringing in Erissa's ears as her eyes locked on the Fae. Erissa tried to heed them, but her heart would not obey and abandon them for her own safety. Maybe if she stayed, maybe if she grabbed their attention, it might give Rhazien and Barrett more time.

Rhazien raced after the Fae. One of them slowed, and Erissa feared Rhazien would draw his notice. No hesitation existed when she stepped in the Fae's direction. Her feet moved without thought, gaining speed.

It surprised the Fae, his widened features morphing into an evil grin. Fear gripped Erissa's spine, but she did not slow, gathering her courage as she forced her feet to keep moving faster.

She palmed at the folds of her dress. Islone had given her a knife, sewing a pocket into the fabric to hold it. Erissa dug for it with enough desperation to rip the folds with the blade, nicking her leg. The pain of the cut spurred her on. She ran full force at the unsuspecting Fae. His soul flickered behind him, and Erissa gave a sickly smile.

When she closed in on the Fae, she threw herself against him, using the momentum to drive her knife into his throat. Blood poured from the wound over the handle of the knife and down the arm and bodice of her dress. It soaked the fabric, sending a shiver down Erissa's spine.

The man staggered against her, his weight falling forward. It proved too much for Erissa to hold with her adrenaline wearing off now that the Fae's eyes turned glassy with death. He fell against her, and her legs collapsed, taking them both to the ground with him landing on top of her, his weight falling against her wounded shoulder. The pain of the impact knocked the breath from her lungs.

"Erissa!" Rhazien's voice sounded muffled.

She kept staring into the dead eyes of the Fae. His blood still flowed over her, but it began slowing. She lay in a pool of the thick liquid, her dress ruined by the coppery mess. Her eyes flicked down to her soaked bodice. The breath the Fae knocked out of her returned with a vengeance, and her chest heaved as it tried to pull in more and more air, her shoulder burning.

"Erissa!" Rhazien's call faded into the background.

Blood rushed through her ears, and she panicked, believing it to be the blood of the Fae. It drowned her. She would never escape the sticky feel of it against her skin as it cooled.

"Little doe." Rhazien shoved the dead body off her. He knelt by her side, picking her up and cradling her to his chest.

She held onto him, looking over his shoulder at the carnage left from the attack. The other Fae lay a few feet from her, Rhazien's dagger sticking out from his chest.

"Thank the Creator." Rhazien kissed all over her face, uncaring of the blood covering it. "I don't know who that man is, but we'd both be dead without him. I'll never be able to repay his kindness."

"Barrett—it was my uncle, Barrett." Her gaze snapped to Rhazien's. "Where is he?"

She looked over Rhazien's shoulder, trying to find her uncle. Her blood ran cold when she found him lying on the ground. A soul stood behind him, sharp with its harsh blurring as it hung between life and death.

Erissa shoved Rhazien away, stumbling to her feet. He helped to steady her as her limbs trembled and refused to work. "Uncle..."

As she made to reach his side, she stopped short as more Fae poured from around the stables. She would never get to Barrett in time.

Rhazien dropped the shield around his magic, and fire built around him. He breathed through clenched teeth. "Run, little doe. Run as far as you can. I'll hold them off."

Erissa grabbed his sleeve, shaking her head. "No. I'm not running. We are in this together. If you don't make it, I don't want to."

The Fae closed in on them.

"Don't be foolish." Rhazien pushed her toward the woods. "Run, Erissa. Now."

A tear fell down Erissa's cheek. "Rhazien—"

An arrow cut her off as it flew from behind them to hit one of the advancing Fae. He dropped to the ground, leaving the rest of them stunned as they took a hard look behind Erissa and Rhazien.

The two turned, and Erissa's tears began in earnest as a second group of Fae entered the clearing through the forest. They were doomed to die this morning.

A tall male Fae with brown hair and blazing green eyes led the newest Fae. Rhazien and Erissa stepped back from him, toward the other group, and he held his hands up. "I'm here to help."

"Help with what? Our deaths?" Rhazien snorted. He grabbed Erissa's arm and moved her behind him, placing his back to the side so he would see if the other Fae advanced on them. His eyes darted between each of them.

"I am Yorrith, the Seelie King." The Fae stepped forward, addressing those at the stable. "The girl is under my protection, and she will come with me. Leave or suffer the consequences."

Those at the stable laughed, one even spitting on the ground before he spoke. "The girl is coming with us."

Erissa shivered. Everyone had turned mad. She would not leave with any of them, especially this self-proclaimed King.

"Nephinae?" The King called to the white-haired Fae next to him. "It appears they need your attention."

"Gladly." She removed her cloak and the cloth veil she wore, revealing iridescent orbs that held no irises, and several of the attacking Fae swore.

The Fae called Nephinae had deep scarring that ran along every inch of her exposed body in the cut-out dress she wore. The scaring filled with light as the Fae's eyes turned as bright as a full moon on a clear night, and her magic built.

"Charge the bitch." One attacker ran forward, knife at the ready.

Erissa saw their souls appear one by one.

Nephinae laughed, letting loose a bolt of pure white energy. It struck the advancing Fae through the heart, leaving a large hole. It splinted into smaller shards, heading for the other Fae. Only one evaded their wrath. He ducked into the stables, and the bolt struck the open door, obliterating it into small pieces.

Erissa stared dumbfounded at the dozens of bodies littering the ground. Rhazien tried to shield her from them and the Fae responsible for their deaths. "Who are you?"

"Your savior." Nephinae let go of her power, and the light faded from her scars. "A word of thanks would be appreciated." She turned to the two other similarly scarred Fae behind her. "Go get the last one. You know where to take him. He's waiting."

"Be nice, Zorathi." Yorrith never took his eyes from Erissa. "They don't know us."

"Who are you?" Rhazien demanded an answer as the other two did as their mistress told them.

Erissa had no patience for any of this. She shoved Rhazien, catching him off guard, and ran to where her uncle lay, his soul still shimmering behind them.

He looked a fright, battered and bruised, and covered in blood. Barrett reached a hand for his niece when she knelt at his side. "Erissa..."

"Hush, Uncle." Tears fell as she choked down a sob. Her eye flicked to where the soul hovered. "We'll get you help. You have to hold on."

"It's... too late." Barrett coughed, blood dribbling from his mouth. "But... worth it... to save... you. I'm... sorry. By the... gods... I'm sorry."

"It's not too late. It can't be." Erissa turned to the King. "Please, you have to help him."

"I don't hold the power to save him. None of us do, except..." The King hesitated, shifting from foot to foot.

Erissa grabbed onto the little hope that one word gave her. "Except who?"

Nephinae walked over to her. "You have the power, little one. Only you."

"But I can't... my power is drained from the last attack." Erissa's lip trembled. "He can't die."

"It's... alright." Barrett lifted a hand to cup her cheek, smearing blood across her skin. "I made... things right. I... protected you. Sorry... I... didn't... before. I made... a... bargain with Faldeyr. A... Fae deal... binding me to... his... bidding. For... you. To protect you. If... I broke his... command... the price was... your death."

He gave a shuddering breath, and his hand fell to the ground. Barrett's eyes turned to glass, and the soul behind him wavered before it faded into the early morning light.

Erissa screamed, shaking him, begging him to wake up. She called for the voice, demanding it come to her aid.

It flickered to life against her consciousness. *I am weak but not incapable. Draw on me.*

And Erissa did, using the connection as a lifeline until power flickered against her fingertips and her eyes glowed. She kept pulling on the magic, building it until she swayed in the bloodied mud.

The more she drew on the connection, the more something else tickled against her mind. She opened herself to it, and the familiar black mist appeared.

Her magic purred against it. *"He will help us."*

Erissa turned to the Fae. "There has to be a way to bring him back."

"There is no coming back from the dead, little doe." Rhazien moved to her side and placed a hand on her shoulder. "He is gone into the Veil."

"There is a way. To return his soul. To extend his life." The black mist weaved around Erissa, her magic stirring at its presence. It growled at Rhazien, turning away from him to focus on Erissa. *"You hold the power to bring him back."*

"What is he doing—" Nephinae cut off Yorrith with a hand across his mouth. She gave him a murderous glare, her eyes glowing with power.

"What blasphemy is this?" Erissa asked. The mist's words left her reeling. "There is no bringing a soul back to life." If Erissa held such power, she would have used it for the Abrahms and for Wilidon. Damn the consequences.

"Yorrith!" Nephinae shrieked, jerking her hand away from the other Fae's mouth. Her glare intensified. "You *bit* me? Are you a child?"

"Nephinae, he is telling her she can bring back the dead." The Fae thundered at her—Nephinae. "He crosses the line, even for him."

"So you bit me?" Nephinae waved her injured hand.

"Be quiet." Erissa snapped the words, drawing the shocked attention of everyone in the small clearing. "I can't think with you arguing back and forth."

"Well done, Veiled One." The mist laughed, the frosty sound sending shivers down Erissa's spine. *"Their foreplay will continue unchecked without someone taking them to task."*

Erissa had no desire to hear about the relationship dynamic between the two Fae. If a way truly existed to return a departed soul, she had to know. "Tell me what I need to know."

"It is an ancient magic from the gods, lost until the Veiled One appeared." The mists answered her thoughts, startling Erissa. *"From the sky above, the earth below, and in between the fabric of time and the boundary of the Veil, you hold the power to call a soul. The magic is a taste meant only for the divine. The one who can show you stands near. Ask the Seelie King."*

Erissa's head lifted, the back of her hand wiping blood across her tear-stained cheeks. She studied the Fae standing around her. Only one of them held the bearing of a King—Yorrith, the female called him. He stood as the tallest of the men, ocean eyes holding a compassion that Erissa did not want. But she hesitated to speak.

Even knowing a way existed to reach Barrett's soul behind the Veil, she remained undecided. Did Barrett's sacrifice matter? Would it matter if it were her father giving reasons and excuses?

Rhazien dropped to his knees beside her, lacking any regard for the blood-stained ground ruining his trousers. Erissa focused on the liquid spreading through the fabric. No amount of washing would remove it. The strangeness of it all threatened her sanity, and she questioned if the blood only came from her uncle. So much lay beneath them, cooling quickly as it thickened. How did it all come from him?

A jolt snapped through Erissa when Rhazien wrapped an arm around her shoulders, guiding her to lean against him. His touch grounded her thoughts and pulled memory after memory to the forefront of her mind, her eyes never leaving the glossy death in her uncle's gaze.

They were not memories of a happy childhood. She found her uncle's support fickle around the orders of her father. But at the same time, Barrett made sure she did not starve and risked the wrath of her father more than once to sneak food into her room. He brought books into her life and sang to her every night during those first years, stealing moments of joy for her even on her worst days. And then he attended her on those days, suturing wounds when they proved too much to handle on her own, with a comforting song that took the bite from each pass of the needle.

"Time is running out, Veiled One," the mist warned. *"Make haste with your decision."*

Tears clogged her throat. Barret should have let her die rather than honor his foolish Fae bargain. Erissa struggled to understand his reasoning. How different would his life have been if he chose himself and abandoned her to the darkness? How did she weigh this against all he allowed to happen to her?

The questions circled endlessly as the mist pulsed against her consciousness, its beats echoing the waning time.

Erissa tucked her chin into Rhazien's neck for only a moment, taking comfort in his warmth, so different from the chilled blood, and made her choice.

CHAPTER FIFTY-SIX

"How do I call a soul?"

The silence following Erissa's question screamed its discomfort.

The Seelie King said nothing. He crossed his arms over his chest, staring daggers at Rhazien touching her.

Erissa gripped her uncle's body tighter. "Please, I beg of you, tell me what I can do. I know I'm nothing to you, but he is the only true family I have. I can't lose him."

The Fae King flinched, his face holding a grief Erissa had no time to consider. She needed answers. Barrett's life teetered in the balance, and she had no patience for the emotions of others, particularly strangers.

Nephinae stepped closer to Yorrith. "Soul calling holds great danger, and there is no guarantee of success."

"But there is a chance?" Erissa would beg, if needed, for another moment with her uncle.

"The calling of souls differs from other types of magic." Yorrith's reluctance colored his tone. "Magic is sentient, with a mind and soul of its own. The magic works in tandem with the bearer of this power. Only the Veiled One can call a soul, and the magic is different. You must draw on that sentience, merging it with yours to use your power, and call the soul from the lure of the Veil and through time."

Hope taunted Erissa. Surely the magic will not help now when it allowed her uncle to die without a second thought.

"You underestimate me." The voice of her magic huffed. *"His death ensured your protection. You are always my concern, but it changes things, knowing what he willingly sacrificed when he thought it would save you. I will no more abandon him now than you will. In this, we shall work together."*

If the voice were corporal, Erissa would have kissed it. "How do I merge the two?"

"Ask the Seelie King." The mist moved as if standing to look at Rhazien. *"Caution is required. You need the Warden for this task. Only his magic will avoid the attention of the Keeper."*

Erissa turned to the king, her mind set on her course. Her uncle would live, no matter the cost. "How do I call a soul?"

"Through time magic." Yorrith rubbed a hand over his light growth of facial hair. "But it's unpredictable. Other magics have limitations, but time magic is wild. It does as it pleases. There are ways to guide it, but you need an anchor. The mists are right. If that boy is a Warden, he's your only hope to complete the spell and remain unaffected."

Rhazien rubbed her shoulder. "Little doe, I know you want to bring him back—"

She jerked from beneath his hold, turning to frown at him. "No, you don't understand. He is all the family that I have, but it's more than that. I need to know why. I don't know why he came here to save me after everything that happened. I need to know, Rhazien."

When he did not give her an answer, Erissa lost all hope. Her face crumpled, the tears of thirteen years hitting her all at once. She broke apart.

It proved to be Rhazien's undoing. He pulled her into his arms, running a hand through her hair. "All right, little doe. Don't cry. I'll be your anchor."

Erissa lifted her tear-stained face. She wanted to feel guilty for her tears changing his mind. It spoke of manipulation, but her desire to bring back her uncle left her willing to do anything to make it happen. "You will?"

"Are you going to try either way?" When she nodded her head, he smiled, love spreading down their bond. "Then we'll try together."

Yorrith cleared his throat. "You can let go of her now."

He yelped as Nephinae elbowed him. "Never mind what the Seelie says."

"He's been holding her far too long as is." Yorrith glared at Rhazien.

"And you've held women way too little." Nephinae poked a finger into the King's shoulder as he blushed and stammered. "They're clearly involved."

The black mist growled at Nephinae, slinking around her like a predator sizing its prey.

"Not you too." Nephinae held a hand to her head, massaging her temple. "You will both be the death of me."

This mist moved to pulse beside her. *Time is running out.*

Erissa shared a look with Rhazien, and he cleared his throat, drawing the attention of the Fae. "We are pressed for time. How do we call her uncle's soul?"

"I can't." The King's shoulders dropped. "I can't tell you. It is too dangerous, and she is too precious to lose to this magic."

Erissa pushed away from Rhazien to stand before the King. She fell to her knees and pressed her hands to her heart as she did in Cropari, bowing to lay her forehead into the muddied ground. "Please, I beg of you."

A tense moment followed, Erissa's pleas echoing as she repeated them, and the King caved. He reached down to help Erissa to her feet. His eyes softened at her tears. He wiped them from her face with a gentle hand. "Don't fret, little one. I will tell you."

Yorrith took her hand and led her back to the body of her uncle, Rhazien, not far behind. He crouched in the mud beside her, placing one hand on her uncle's chest and the other in Rhazien's hands. "The only way the spell will work is to power share, and there is no guarantee you can do it."

Erissa brightened with excitement, and she turned to Rhazien. "But we have. We've power shared before, right, Rhazien? When you saved me at the Veil?" She turned back to Yorrith when Rhazien nodded. "That means the spell will work, right?"

Yorrith swallowed hard. He closed his eyes and took a deep breath, leaving Erissa to question what she had said that pained the King so.

He opened his eyes, staring at Rhazien with a different curiosity than before. The hostility still lingered in his gaze, but it had a resigned quality to it, one reflected by the king's next words. "Are you mates?"

The betrayal of Rhazien's lies stiffened Erissa's spine, but she nodded. "Yes."

Another hiss came from this mist, its black deepening until no speck of light remained visible in its depth.

Erissa glanced between it and the King before turning to lift a brow at Nephinae. The Zorathi remained silent, and Erissa added the odd reactions to her list of questions that would need answering when she completed the spell.

"With the mate bond, it's possible the magic will work." Yorrith turned to Rhazien. "I am sure you were taught to shield your magic?"

"It's the first thing a Fefnirion learns." Rhazien tightened his hold on Erissa's hand. "I can drop the shield with ease and call the Void."

"The Void?" Yorrith and Nephinae spoke in unison, their tones hard. Rhazien closed his mouth.

Yorrith and Nephinae shared a long look, and then she gave him a curt nod. He squared his shoulders. "To call a soul, you must send your words through both time and the Keeper's realm. When you open yourself to the Veil, you will allow the Keeper an opportunity to reach your soul, and it is a chance he will not miss."

"I'm assuming this is where my magic comes into play," Rhazien caught on quickly. "The void will help hide her magic while the Fefnirion flames can protect her if that fails."

"Yes." Yorrith gave him a tight smile. "With Erissa wrapped within your flames, her magic will remain undetected until it's too late for the Keeper to do more than throw a tantrum."

Yorrith turned to Erissa, placing a hand on her shoulder. "Your part is harder. The magic coursing within you is its own identity. To complete the calling, you have to merge your soul with the soul of your magic. It is something you do by instinct alone. It differs with every being."

"Have you done it?" Erissa feared her ability to do as the king said. "I have no control over my magic."

"It's not about control, youngling." Nephinae came up behind her. "It is like welcoming another, deeper part of your own self. You need only be open to it, and your magic will do the rest. You're the Veiled One. Your magic is Creator given and exists outside of the abilities of the Fae. It will know what to do. You must only trust its instincts and follow it."

Erissa shivered under the weight of it all.

Her magic's comfort bled through their bond. *"Don't be afraid. It is nothing we haven't done before. At the Veil with our mate and in Cropari. We are one and the same."*

"Close your eyes and take slow, deep breaths." Yorrith tightened his hand on her shoulder. "We are all here with you. I will feed my magic into yours, and your mate will keep you from going too far. My magic won't be hidden from the Keeper, but he is used to the interference of time."

Nephinae pushed at the King's shoulder. "How can he be used to time magic with the God of Time long dead?"

"Hush, Zorathi." Yorrith cut a glare at her. "We need to concentrate."

Erissa concentrated as their touch grounded her. With Rhazien on one side and the Seelie king on the other, Erissa rolled her shoulders, relaxing the tension from them, and slowed her breathing. Even the eerily beautiful Fae standing behind her brought comfort, and the strange sensation left her reeling after a life of no support. Cropari and her panic attack hovered in the background, and she sucked in a huge gulp of air, trying to smother her growing unease.

The black mist cocooned her, wrapping over where the other men touched her. It added its own level of comfort, making her panic grow more.

It whispered calm into her being as if it sensed her unease, making her magic purr again while it settled between the mists and Rhazien. *"Open yourself, Veiled One. The magic will not harm you, and your Warden will protect you."*

Erissa focused on her breathing, calming the panic, turning to Rhazien as he tugged on her hand.

Her steady breathing came to naught when she looked at him. Gold light suffused his skin until flames danced in its radiance. It continued to grow, the flames stretching into a proud set of wings, a deep shade of gold turned crimson that darkened into back tips. Smoke curls rose as he breathed, and he flexed his wings, relaxing into the power. The stones on his ear cuffs glowed, and he leaned to give a smoke-stained kiss to her lips and pressed their foreheads together. "I won't lose you, little doe. Trust me."

And so she did. She stared into his eyes and at his beauty, feeling the two on either side of her, the mists wrapped around her, and her own magic tickling against her consciousness.

She held onto Rhazien's gaze, letting all of it flow through her until nothing remained but the press of her magic beneath her skin and the warm glow of his fire as he fed it down her arm to sit beneath the black mist, both magics cocooning her in their embrace.

As the flames engulfed her, Erissa felt her power swell, hidden from view of the world. The Fefnirion flames and void protected its mate, and for the first time since leaving Cropari, Erissa truly relaxed with a feeling of safety she had long ago forgotten.

"We are almost there." Erissa's magic nuzzled its host.

The Seelie King's magic followed. It surged into hers, boosting her natural reserves and opening time as everything stopped. Rhazien's flames were the only thing moving.

Erissa stayed in this place momentarily, staring around her as the world lay still. Even the sound of the wind and birds faded. And only when time halted did she see the souls.

All their voices rang through the ethereal plane where time did not exist, making it hard for her to concentrate on the task at hand. They called to her, though they did not sense her presence. Each voice tugged at the very core of her, making it hard to ignore their pleas, especially as her magic reveled in the melody of their combined tones.

There were dozens of them milling about, walking toward the Veil. Some moved with purpose, others more slowly, and a curious number stopped walking to turn in her direction. Their blurred faces turned this way and that, as if they noticed her magic but not her corporal form in their realm.

Those souls were the ones that made the hair stand on the backs of her arms. She needed to call her uncle's soul and quickly, but how?

"Whisper his name." Her magic kept its own voice low. *"Doing anything more than a whisper will call their attention. They can sense something is not right, and already the Keeper watches through them. And you must hurry. I cannot withstand the call of the Veil for very long. It pulls at me even now."*

The pull lingered for Erissa, too, and she struggled to concentrate. The resplendent call lit up the darkness inside of her, removing the corruption of her pain, and leaving her longing for its embrace. Erissa ground her teeth against the call and spoke her uncle's name with a sound softer than a whisper as fear began to override everything else. "Barrett Nierling."

Nothing happened.

The magic nudged her. *"Try again."*

She hardly dared to breathe, let alone get the words out, but she had to keep going. They had come this far. She would not leave him behind to die for her. "Uncle, I call to you. Come to me, Barrett Nierling."

Her whisper stirred the souls, and two broke from their ranks, standing at her side. Panic gripped her. Which soul belonged to her uncle?

The warmth of Rhazien's flame intensified, a warning that skittered down Erissa's spine. One soul held the eyes of the Keeper.

"If you pick the wrong one, it will unleash the Keeper." Her magic's warning echoed in the timeless space. *"All it will take is one touch to pull the soul into the living. Be sure you do not pick the wrong one."*

She had no way of telling the souls apart. They were the same faceless forms as always. There had to be a way to mark their differences, but the longer she stared, the harder it became. Panic lodged within her throat, choking the air from her lungs. She shoved it down, forcing herself to breathe, and tried again. "Barrett Nierling."

And again, nothing more happened. The two souls still stood there, staring at her despite their featureless countenances.

The magic pleaded with her. *"There must be something more. A way to know his soul from the other, something only he would know that you can use to call him."*

Erissa burned through her childhood memories, looking for anything she might use to distinguish her uncle from the other soul. She had to fight through the lull of the soul's song. Her memories held pain, but they offered occasional bright moments. Each of those memories centered on Barrett's actions. One memory stood out from them all, and Erissa took a chance with it.

She opened her mouth, whispering a song sung to her on many a lonely night from outside her bedroom door long after the bolt had been shut. A song that brought comfort on the worst of days when her uncle's shadow never left the light peaking from under her door.

"The stars, they linger, as morning calls,
— afraid to leave the moon.
For it binds their souls and brings them home,
—dancing to its tune."

The soul to the left turned its head at an odd angle, but the one to the right grabbed her attention. It lifted a hand, scrubbing it down its face, and Erissa knew. She kept singing, distracting the Keeper-eyed soul to her left, and slowly lifted her arm.

"The stars, they linger, as morning calls,
—softened by the early dew,
For it feeds their souls and brings them peace,
—through a sleep the sun renews."

As she sang the last word, her hand connected with the soul on the right, and the faceless visage shifted into the familiar features of her uncle. The soul on the left screamed, throwing itself at her, but Rhazien's magic reared up. It blocked the Keeper as he sought to touch Erissa. As the Fefnirion flames connected with the soul the Keeper controlled, its screams turned into something foul, and Rhazien's void-bound fire burned through its form.

Erissa did not waste the opportunity. She yanked on her uncle's soul as Yorrith and her magic worked to pull them all back, Rhazien's flames continuing to hold the Keeper at bay as he overpowered another soul.

When Yorrith's magic finally succeeded in pulling them into the present time, the four of them collapsed to the ground, the soul no longer held by Erissa.

It moved to stand over her uncle's body, and Erissa thought it had not worked, that the soul remained half-trapped in the timeless area. But it stared down at the body, a smile on its lips, and the soul lowered until it rested in its form.

"*We did it.*" Erissa's magic flickered in and out and faded into the back of her mind, exhausted by its continued use.

"*You did well, sweetling.*" The mist kissed her skin and faded into the night. But Erissa did not miss its presence, for it felt like it still hovered near, watching her.

"Quick, we must heal the body." Yorrith lunged forward, placing his hands over the wounds. "Nephinae, I would appreciate your help."

Nephinae came to a crouch on the other side of the body, mirroring the Seelie King's actions. Both their eyes glowed with magic, and within only a moment, her uncle's wounds knitted together.

All were on edge as they waited.

When Barrett stirred, Erissa burst into tears. She flung herself across his chest. He brought a hand to her hair, stroking the strands as she cried. "Hello, my star."

CHAPTER FIFTY-SEVEN

Erissa lifted her head, thanking the Creator for her magic, and encountered the night sky. "How…" She stared in wonder at the star-filled expanse above them.

"Time magic." Yorrith stood and tried to brush the mud from his clothes. He gave up with a sigh when it would not budge. "It can move you forward or backward anywhere along its route."

Nephinae walked to his side. "Judging by the moon's position and the surrounding bodies, it is the same day, only much later."

"Then we are lucky." Yorrith's voice lowered. "Many have suffered graver consequences than a day's passing."

Rhazien helped Erissa and Barrett stand. The latter wobbled, and Erissa pulled his arm over her shoulder, steadying him.

Barrett looked at the newcomers with confusion. "Who are you?"

Nephinae huffed. "Finally, someone with enough sense to ask questions."

Erissa sulked. "We haven't had time for questions."

"Would you have asked them at any point or followed blindly like a sheep?" Nephinae's waspish tone left her as she gestured to the king and then to herself with a shrug. "He is Yorrith, the King of the Seelie Fae, and I'm Nephinae, Unseelie, and leader of the Zorathi."

"Fae." Barrett paled, shoving Erissa behind him. "They can't be trusted."

"The one you would deny trust did much to ensure your soul's safe return, human." Nephinae advanced menacingly.

Yorrith shot an arm out, grabbing onto her. "Look who's not asking questions now." His retort settled the Zorathi, and he asked what she did not. "We helped save your life. Why can't we be trusted?"

"Not her. You." Barrett shuffled to the side, blocking Erissa as she tried to step around him. "You're Seelie, are you not? King of Thonalan?"

The king exchanged glances with the Nephinae. "What does Thonalan have to do with anything?"

Barrett laughed, cynicism dripping from every note. "Don't play dumb. You know as well as I that I can't speak of it or risk my niece's death. The Warden could only break the part of the Fae deal that bound my actions, but I still can't speak of it to Erissa. It was a nasty piece of magic without his full Fefnirion powers."

Bewildered stares met his words, and none were more confused than Erissa. She tugged at his shirt. "Uncle, you're not making sense. How would you know anything about the Fae and Fefnirion, and what does my death have to do with it?"

He pointed at Yorrith. Anger slashed across Barrett's brow. "You know what I'm talking about. I can't disclose anything more, or the Fae deal will see you dead, something he also knows. That is the price I paid for my foolish actions at your birth."

"Thonalan wasn't at her birth. You know that as well as I." Yorrith spread his arms wide. "How would he know anything about her or you?"

"Stop lying." Barret stepped toward the King, uncaring as the Zorathi's stance changed.

Nephinae placed herself between the two. "The Seelie has not lied in centuries. He is as honest as anyone can be, which I have often told him is dangerous given his position as acting King over all the Fae."

Barrett snarled. "And I'm supposed to take your word for it? The dog to the Unseelie bastard behind everything? The one who warmed the very Lord's bed who's trying to kill my niece?"

All the color drained from Nephinae's face, and she did nothing as Yorrith shoved her behind him, shielding her from view.

"Hold your tongue or I will remove it." Anger stormed in the Seelie King's eyes, their depths the color of the ocean of Emberhold's bay when trouble brewed on the horizon. "Draven is a depraved monster. None went to his bed willingly."

He pitched forward as Nephinae shoved him from behind. "My story is not yours to tell, Seelie." She turned to Barrett, staring him down until he swallowed in fright-hardened resolve. "I admire the lengths you are going to for her protection, but that is why we are here, too. The girl is the Veiled One. She is our only salvation from Draven's madness with the Keeper."

Yorrith straightened his robes, shooting a glare at the Zorathi. "What is this mess concerning Thonalan?"

Barrett opened his mouth, but nothing came out. He snapped it closed, his eyes cutting to Erissa. "I cannot say in front of her."

"What do you mean, Uncle?" Erissa tugged on his sleeve. Everyone kept her in the dark, and she would have no more of it. "If this concerns me then I want to know."

A sigh left the weary soldier, and Barrett turned to her, regret settling between them. "I want to tell you, but if I do, you will die. That is the cost of the magic."

Erissa dropped his arm, backing away. "Nothing has changed. Even now, after I risked everything to bring you back, you still won't tell me the truth."

"I came here, didn't I? I found a way around part of the magic, and I'm here. That should count for something." Barrett scrubbed a hand over his growth of facial hair, desperation making him sweat. "It's not that I don't want to tell you everything, Erissa. I can't. It's a Fae deal. The magic always has a price, and I agreed to a stupid one. The blacksmith was able to break part of the deal, but he did not have the power to break the entire thing."

"And I'm supposed to believe I'll die if you tell me the truth?" Erissa's voice kept rising. Her chest heaved, and she tried to fight off the rising tears. She did not want to keep crying at the omissions of others.

"The magic of Fae deals requires a price." Nephinae folded her arms across her chest. "And knowing Thonalan, I would not put it past him to add a caveat concerning your life. He would not hesitate if it meant achieving his ends."

"He has always been an ambitious Lord." Yorrith mimicked Nephinae's stance. His eyes narrowed in thought. "I consider it his greatest flaw. Thonalan would sell his own daughter if it meant he could become King, and he has been foolish enough to challenge me in the past. I'm certain this deal you speak of concerns his plans to rip my crown from my cold, dead hands."

"Nothing about your crown has anything to do with me." Erissa swayed as they all stared at her, each looking more guilty than the last. Only Rhazien looked at her normally. She understood their expression well, for those with secrets held such looks. Her soul grew weary at the thought of more being kept from her, but she did not think anyone would tell her the truth right now. And did she even want to know what they hid? With each new revelation, her life changed. Erissa wanted nothing more than to have power over what happened to her next. Their words would do nothing but cause more upheaval in her life.

Rhazien wrapped his arms around Erissa from behind, pulling her against his chest. He nuzzled into her neck, his skin still warm from his flames. "We will not sort this out tonight, little doe. One conversation isn't enough. Let's make camp for the night and revisit this tomorrow. You're beginning to shake from exhaustion."

Erissa sighed, letting her mate soothe her emotions. She loved when he held her like this. His scent washed over her, clearing the worst of her anger and frustration. She envied Rhazien's ability to calm her and gave over to the sensation of settling in his arms as everyone talked around her about making camp. Envied it and resented it all at the same time, given his lies—ones that the others were holding tightly to as well.

"We set up tents near here, and I've spelled the area." Yorrith agreed with Rhazien, and Erissa tried to concentrate on his words as tiredness swept through her. "The men can take one, the women the other, and the Zorathi twins can take the third when they return."

"We're not sleeping apart." Rhazien's tone booked no refusal.

Erissa tightened her grip on his arms. "I won't go anywhere without him by my side."

"Good luck getting them apart." Barrett laughed, moving next to them. "I died because she wouldn't run and leave him behind."

"Uncle..." Erissa paled. What must he think of her?

"Oh, my star, I didn't mean it like that." Barrett smiled at her, raising a hand to brush a strand of hair from where it fell over her eye. "I would never expect you to abandon your husband."

"What?" An unnatural shriek came from the Seelie King. He stared at Erissa in horror. "You *married* him?"

She nodded. "A week ago in Cropari."

"No..." Yorrith paced back and forth. "A week ago? I won't... you can't..." He turned to Nephinae. "Don't stand there and pretend to be stupid, Zorathi. Do something."

Nephinae pinched him, holding on even as the King yelped. "Do what exactly? Travel through time to prevent it? The only one with controlled time magic is you, Seelie."

"No one is doing anything." Erissa broke from Rhazien's arms, immediately missing his scent and warmth. "Rhazien and I are married, and we're not sleeping apart. Our relationship is none of your concern."

Yorrith tried to take a step toward her, but Nephinae held him back. "A conversation for another time, Seelie. The boy is right. There is nothing to be done tonight. We are all tired, but the girl more than most. It took great magic to call a soul. She needs to rest."

"Fine." Yorrith shook her off, turning to point a threatening finger at Rhazien. "This isn't over, Warden."

He stomped off toward the camp, leaving everyone to stare behind his retreating form. He stopped when he realized no one had followed him. "Well... is anyone coming?"

Barrett hurried after him. "Wait, Seelie. There's more we need to discuss."

The two bickered in low voices as they neared the camp. It stood far from the bodies but still close enough to see them. Erissa stared at the one she killed over her shoulder as they walked.

Without hesitation, she killed a man tonight, and she would not hold back if they found themselves under attack again. That made four. Four lives she had taken and given into the Veil. But she found no regret when she searched the deepest parts of her heart, and that worried her the most.

Rhazien's arm came around her shoulder as if he sensed her fears down the bond. "You did what you had to, little doe. Nothing more."

She nodded, too exhausted by what happened and her own thoughts to do anything else. Whatever came tomorrow, they would deal with it. Erissa wanted nothing more than to lay in her husband's arms tonight. She let him lead her toward the tent Yorrith stopped in front of and gestured them into. It sat in the middle of the camp, the largest of the three.

The King spoke through clenched teeth. "I will leave the happy couple here." He stomped away, flinging the front of another tent open and disappearing inside as Barrett and Nephinae followed.

"Come, let's go to bed." Rhazien held the tent flap open for her, gesturing her inside.

Erissa did not want to sleep. The magic had left her tired, but her mind whirled with more questions than she had answers for. As Rhazien ducked into the tent, his height brushing against the top of the fabric, Erissa found herself unreasonably angry with him. She slapped him, her hand flying before she even finished the thought, and she stared in amazement as her heart pounded and heat flooded her cheeks.

She brought her hands to her face, hiding behind them, and burst into tears. "I don't know why I did that. I'm sorry, Rhazien. There's no excuse for slapping you."

Embarrassment and shame coursed through her. She refused to look at him, even as he tugged her arms down and dropped to one knee. He kissed the backs of her hands, smothering a laugh.

She finally looked at him when his chuckle broke through. "It's not funny, Rhazien. I've never been a violent person, and in the span of a week, I've killed four people and slapped my husband."

Rhazien doubled over at that, laughing hard enough that he needed to hold his side, and Erissa lost her temper again. She shoved him, striding away to stand on the opposite side of the large tent. "It's not funny."

"C'mon, little doe. I deserved it, and we both know it." He stood and tried to control the little laughs still slipping from him. "You have been aiming for a fight since we left Cropari, so let's get it over with and move on."

"Move on?" Erissa narrowed her eyes. "You told me you'd be right behind me. You sent me running with no intention of following me. You were going to die at those stables. You promised you'd be right behind me, Rhazien. Do you know what that was? Another lie all in the name of protecting me."

Her outburst sobered him, and regret hollowed his face. "I needed to keep you safe, little doe. My only priority is you—"

Rhazien pulled a ring from his pocket, holding it up for her to see in the lamplight. "I left the night of the gathering to make this. When you woke up the next morning, I planned to give it to you and reveal everything. Reeva even helped with the design and told me it was time to come clean. You can ask her. I swear it, Erissa."

Erissa stood with her fists balled at her side, her chest heaving. She stared at the ring, taking in the entangled design of red, purple, and blue along the black band. It reminded her of his wind chimes. The stones twinkled in the lamp's light and some of Erissa's ire melted into anguish. "You can't leave me like that again."

Rhazien nodded. "I won't. I'll never leave you." He stood, moving to pull her into his arms. Rhazien gripped her chin and raised it until their eyes met. "I promise, little doe."

She did not want to soften at his touch, but she did all the same. "Why do you keep lying to me?"

"I knew you wouldn't run without me, and as for the rest? Telling someone you're a fire-breathing dragon doesn't roll off the tongue, nor does telling them you're both part of a wartime prophecy." Rhazien grimaced as he kept talking, his voice growing quiet. "I didn't want you to be afraid of me. You think yourself a monster for your magic. What would you think of me?" He rushed on when she opened her mouth to speak, not allowing her to interrupt. "The way you spoke about yourself broke me. You are everything that is good and beautiful in this world, and you can't see it. I wanted you to see me—the man, not the dragon—before fear clouded your judgment. I wanted to get you somewhere safe where we could talk, but then everything fell apart in Cropari, and it was one more thing I felt I had to wait to tell you. Don't keep doubting me, little doe. I love you."

He opened himself down their mating bond, and Erissa gasped as his emotions overwhelmed her. His words were sincere, and with his love and passion burning through her, she lost the last of her anger. She wound her arms around his neck and sighed with contentment as he dropped his forehead to hers. "You made me a ring?"

A brilliant smile lit up Rhazien's features when he pulled back. He lifted her hand in his and slid the ring onto her middle finger. "Little doe, you've had my heart since the stable loft when you turned to me with all the enthusiasm in your heart for my wind chimes. It's silly, I know. But in that moment, with your eyes full of light and wonder, you became mine. I will never leave your side. My heart is tied to yours. I've waited over a century to find you, and I would wait a hundred more for you to forgive me."

"I forgive you, Rhazien, but only on one condition." Rhazien's words filled Erissa with a happiness she never thought possible, but one thing needed settling. "Tell me how much older you are."

His golden skin paled, and Erissa smirked, enjoying having caught him off guard. "Are you sure you want to know?"

Erissa nodded. "Please tell me. I've been dying to know since Islone spilled your secret."

Panic filled his eyes, and Erissa enjoyed watching him have a moment where he remained unsure of her response. It made up for the torment his lies caused her.

He muttered something under his breath, turning his head from her.

She turned her head to the side, tapping her ear. "Louder, husband. I didn't hear that."

"One hundred and forty-three seasons."

Erissa blanched. "What?"

Rhazien finally looked at her, and her heart filled with overwhelming love at the lost look he gave her. He repeated the number. "One hundred and forty-three seasons. That's how old I am."

She said nothing, simply staring at him, letting herself enjoy a moment of torturing him. His age shocked her. He looked to be in his thirties at most, and she never would have guessed another race lived as long as the Fae. When his eyes dropped, she finally gave in, pitying the pathetic creature in front of her. "Alright, my dragon husband. So you're one hundred and forty-three. That must be fairly young for a dragon, right?"

He lifted his gaze, grumbling. "It places me around five and thirty in human years."

"Good. Now kiss me, please." She cocked an eyebrow and copied his smirk when he looked confused by her reaction. "Were you expecting something else?" She stood on her tiptoes and kissed him. They were both breathless when she pulled back. "I missed you last night. You held me in your arms, but it wasn't the same with my anger and mistrust between us. I missed this closeness."

Her whispered declaration proved to be his undoing. Rhazien devoured her mouth in a soul-melting kiss that burned down their bond as he lifted her in his arms. He placed her on the furs arranged on the rug covering the ground. "No more than I missed you."

She pulled at the laces on the front of her dress, grateful for the travel-friendly style, but she did nothing more than tangle them in her haste. Erissa groaned in frustration as the fabric moved against her breasts, her nipples already pebbling with desire.

A growl built in Rhazien's throat, a feral sound that melted Erissa's core. He leaned down and replaced her hand with his own. He ripped them with a sharp tug on the laces as she laughed. "Impatient?"

"Yes." Rhazien moaned the word, using his hands to pull the torn sides of her dress to the side, exposing her stiff peaks. He deprived her of his mouth, trailing kisses across each mound, teasing her by avoiding her nipples.

"Rhazien." Her breath hissed out of her when his tongue finally connected with a sensitive nub, and he pinched the other, adding pain to the tantalizing sensation of his mouth. She bucked against him, and he laughed, biting down until she cried out. "Careful, little doe, or everyone will hear you."

A blush spread up her breasts, and he nuzzled into them, his prickly facial hair adding to her pleasure as it teased her flesh. He gripped the ripped sides of her dress, tearing it more until it fell open to her knees. Erissa pulled her legs from it, spreading herself for Rhazien to see.

He pulled back from her chest to stare down at her sex. His hands moved to his belt, unfastening its closure, and he pushed his pants down, exposing himself. Erissa reached forward as soon as he did, placing her hand against his length and pumping it the way she had seen him doing in the cavern.

Rhazien let her play, gritting his teeth. He shuddered when a drop of liquid slipped from the tip, and she ran her thumb over it, smearing it across his head. He groaned and pushed her hands away. "Enough of that, or this will end quickly."

He tugged her a few inches closer and settled between her spread thighs, his head nudging her entrance. Erissa stared down at where his cock pressed against her. One thrust and he would claim her, and she didn't want him to be gentle. "Please, Rhaz... I need you. Don't pretend to be gentle."

He growled, pressing his head against hers. "Do you know what you're asking for, little doe?"

She wrapped her arms around him, bringing her lips to whisper in his ear. "You're a dragon, aren't you? Fuck me like one."

A bark of laughter left him, and he bit down on her breast, smiling against her when she choked on a scream. "Language, little doe. Is this one of your filthy ideas?"

His question left her blushing again. "And if it is?"

"Then filthy you shall get, my mate." Rhazien pulled away, much to her surprise. He flipped her over, pressing her stomach down into the furs. "If you want me to fuck you, I'm more than happy to."

Rhazien wrapped an arm around her waist and pulled her hips until she rested on her elbow and knees. Her blush spread further with her exposed position, but a strangled gasp left her when he lined his cock up at her entrance.

He growled again in approval, the sound a low thrum that left her skin vibrating. He pressed his hips forward until his tip pushed into her. She spread her legs wider, surprised at the depth as her body fought to stretch around him, and she gasped. "Rhazien... more. Please, I need more."

Her begging tipped him over the edge, and he slammed into her, rolling his hips so that she took him deeper than the first time.

Erissa screamed, shoving her face into the furs to muffle the sound. She trembled as he started moving with long, hard thrusts that left her breasts swaying and her nipples sliding against the rough hair of the furs, adding a new sensation that left her on the brink of breaking.

His thrusts turned harder as she trembled, and Rhazien reached forward, wrapping a hand around the back of her neck, and pulled her flush against him. Flames covered her throat as he dropped the shield around his magic. He tightened his grip as another flame-covered hand moved across her hip and rose to cup her breast. The position held her open and powerless to his rhythm as he stroked within her, dominating her from behind as the flames added another layer of sensation.

Erissa wrapped her hand around the one holding her throat and moaned, not understanding what she sought. But Rhazien did. He read her desires through the bond, tightening his grip, placing pressure on her pulse point.

The slight change left her gasping for breath as she pressed her ass back against him. He reached for her breasts with the other hand, pinching her nipple and soothing it with his flames, keeping a steady rhythm between the two that matched the pace of his thrusts.

She bowed into his hand as he pulled harder on her nipple, and Rhazien took advantage of her bowed back. Her bit into her neck, hard enough to break the skin and sucked on the tender flesh, his flames burning across the mark he left there, soothing the ache and building it all over again. His other hand moved down her body, dancing around the apex of her thighs, circling the bundle of nerves that drove her wild.

Erissa lost control, unable to stifle the sounds she made. She needed this, needed him—her mate and husband—after everything that happened today. With every thrust, the stress of the last several days disappeared until nothing remained of her but a quivering mess at his mercy.

Twisting her neck, Rhazien turned her head to the side and captured her mouth with his, swallowing her screams. She spasmed around him, her warmth grasping onto his cock with a greedy desperation as she came, and a deep groan filled her ears as he followed her over the edge, his warmth spilling within her.

He pulled out of her, and she whimpered, feeling his warmth slip between her wet thighs. She jumped when his hand pressed there again. She looked down to see him kneeling before her with a scrap of her dress folded between his hands as he cleaned her. When he moved, she had no idea. Erissa struggled to remember her own name.

When he had finished caring for them both, they lay in each other's arms, tucked beneath the furs. Tomorrow would bring with it more questions than Erissa knew what to do with, but for right now, exhaustion claimed her as she slept in her mate's arms.

CHAPTER FIFTY-EIGHT

"Of all the people to be her mate, why did it have to be the lizard?" Novus paced in front of Nephinae.

Nephinae stared at Novus's clenched jaw. She studied him as a muscle ticked against it, his teeth grinding. "Why does it matter?"

He stopped and shrugged, his black mist moving with him as he tried using it as a shield to hide his agitation. "A mate complicates things."

"I'm with the Unseelie." Yorrith crossed his arms, the sullen set it his mouth making him look childish. "Who does the boy think he is anyway, marrying the girl with no family around to give their permission?"

"Mated and married? For once, our thoughts align, Seelie." Novus snarled, his magic radiating malice. "He should be strung and quartered, another prisoner for my collection."

Yorrith nodded, his tone serious and full of anger. "I agree. It's a fitting punishment for the stupid fool."

Nephinae stared at them wide-eyed and with concern. Novus was always level-headed, and while Yorrith proved himself to be more prone to fits over the years, his judgement toward others was always sound. But today? Both were acting out of character. "Have you lost your gods' forsaken minds?" She turned to Yorrith, more shocked by his behavior than her Lords. "You want to hand the Fefnirion over to be put in Novus's collection? Really?"

"What?" Yorrith snapped at her. "The boy overstepped."

"By doing what?" Nephinae came close to shouting. The two were acting insane. "He married his *mate*, Seelie. What is so wrong with that?"

"He didn't have anyone's permission to marry her, Neph." Novus's expression turned sullen. "Damn dragons. Always in between us and everything."

"Not only are you agreeing with each other, but you are speaking blasphemy." Nephinae had enough. She expected better from both of them. Novus's behavior shocked her more than Yorrith's. The Seelie King's anger was expected, having only now found the girl after waiting so long, but Novus? Whatever drove his anger now, Nephinae would put a stop to it before he did something he would later regret. "Everyone would have died without the Fefnirion getting involved in both wars. They protected us after the Remaking, and only through their power adding to our own did we seal Draven within the Veil. We are indebted to them, and if we alienate the last of them, we alienate them all. What will we do if they abandon us to a third war?"

"They already abandoned us when they gave up their call to breed with their mates." Yorrith's voice rose. "What if she is with child, Nephinae? She is one and twenty."

"Then he will most certainly join my collection. There is a new spell I wish to try. Trapping his soul within the memories of torture is not enough. I can do more." The magic around Novus flowed into him. His voice darkened, his eyes pitch black as the Fae and magic merged into one.

"He would look good with no toes." Yorrith clapped his hands together. "It's perfect. Make him another one of your pets. The collection is too good for the likes of him."

"You go too far, Yorrith. See reason." Nephinae blinked hard, believing it might clear up this confusing conversation, but nothing changed. The two Fae stood together, trading threats about the dragon when they had other priorities. "Can we get back to the matter at hand?"

"This is important, Neph. We need to have a plan." Her Lord went to stand beside the King. "Everyone's fate hangs in the balance. I will not see my life forfeited for their relationship."

Yorrith shuffled his feet forward and clapped Novus's back. "Listen to the youngling, Zorathi. He speaks sense. We can't allow this relationship to continue. We need a plan."

"Have you been drinking again, Seelie?" Only Fae wine would explain the sudden shift in their personalities. She expected dark chaos from her Lord. But from Yorrith? The Fae's words went against everything he believed. He always talked about the consequences of time magic. Mayhap something happened back in the Veil's realm.

"I'm not drunk, Zorathi." Yorrith shifted his weight, grimacing. "The boy isn't good enough for her. She needs to see reason before he bloats that belly of hers."

"The Veiled One with child? On the edge of war?" Novus's lips pulled back, baring his teeth, and the magic growled from within him with a deep rumble. "The gods be damned. I won't spare him if it comes to that. The Keeper will have him."

Nephinae threw her hands in the air, pacing away from them. "You've both gone mad. Yorrith, you're blinded by jealousy. You can't keep the girl to yourself. She's an adult and gets to live like one. And you," she rounded on Novus, "have undergone a personality change. Where is this concern about her mate coming from? I thought the girl was someone to be used and nothing more? You sound as jealous as Yorrith."

Yorrith sputtered. "I'm not jealous. See reason—"

"You dare compare me to the *Seelie*?" Novus snapped.

She whirled around, her eyes alight with magic as she glared at the Fae, both kings in their own right, although the Seelie would hardly admit to Novus's rule for all that it remained unofficial. "Wherever you have stashed the wine, Yorrith, pour it out. And Novus, pull yourself together and act like a rational Lord.

Nephinae stormed off, heading back toward the camp. They were supposed to be discussing what happened next, not making threats over the girl's womb. Males never changed. Humans or Fae. They always stuck their noses where they did not belong.

CHAPTER FIFTY-NINE

Erissa watched Rhazien sleep.

The days after their wedding festival had not contained many peaceful moments, and she swore more lines hardened his face because of it. To see him relaxed as he slept stirred something within her heart. She had done little to care for his needs since meeting him, and everything always revolved around her. This morning would see that change.

"Touch him. Offer him what he gave to us." Her magic agreed with the desire, nudging her thoughts along. *"Our husband—our mate—will welcome our desires."*

She listened to its encouragement and trailed her fingers across Rhazien's chest and down toward his hips. He liked it when she touched him last night, and she liked it when he surprised her that morning in Cropari. Maybe he would like the same attention. Erissa gathered her courage and let her hand drop lower until she palmed his length.

It jumped in her hand, and Erissa's gaze sought Rhazien's, but his eyes remained closed, and his breath relaxed.

"Keep going," the magic urged, and Erissa's courage grew.

She wrapped her hand around the base, running it up and down with slow movements, the same way she had seen him stroke himself that night in the cavern.

When his breathing stayed even, she picked up the pace, moving her hand in a quick, steady movement until his hips squirmed against the furs beneath him.

"He wakes to our touch," the voice purred.

"That's because it's divine." Rhazien's cocky smirk flashed across his lips when he spoke, making Erissa jump. He chuckled, his breath leaving on a hiss as she tightened her hold. "Almost as divine as my scent."

Magic raced along Erissa's hands, gathering the water from the heavy moisture of the surrounding air. *"If our mate would like to tease us, I'm more than happy to return the favor."*

The magic gathered the water into Erissa's fingertips and splashed the cold droplets across Rhazien's length. He shrieked with the sharp sensation, and a giggle left Erissa as the magic preened inside of her.

"You want to play?" The heat in Rhazien's skin built beneath Erissa's hand as flames engulfed his member and dried the water from them both. "I'll fight water with fire."

"And what will you give me if I win?" Erissa bit her lip, feeling less confident now that he lay there, aware of her touch.

"What will he give us if we lose?" The voice moaned as it coated her thoughts in scandalous images.

Erissa's cheeks heated, and Rhazien laughed as if he knew where the voice had directed her attention. "Filthy thoughts, little doe?"

She said nothing and instead tugged on the thread of magic she had become more accustomed to over the passing weeks. It gathered more water and splashed it against Rhazien's flames.

He gasped as the cold overtook the heat of his dragon's fire. Even against her hand, the contrast sent shivers through her body. How much more intense did it feel against such a sensitive area?

A low moan hissed between Rhazien's teeth, and Erissa grew more confident as he continued to respond to her. "There is one thought I keep having..."

Rhazien groaned louder as her grip tightened, her hand picking up speed as she learned what he liked by mimicking the pace he set with her.

He threw his flames over his cock once more, shuddering at the contrast of heat and cold and how it felt against the soft strokes of Erissa's hand. "Tell me, little doe. Tell me what you're thinking of as you stroke me."

Erissa fought the blush that spread down her chest. Now that he expected her to voice her desire, words failed her.

"Ever the little doe, even with your hand wrapped around my cock." Rhazien laughed, his breath hitching as she squeezed his length in answer, her lips pursed. "Tell me what you've been wanting to—"

The magic took pity on her, halting Rhazien's breath for long enough to steal the words from his lungs. *"Let us see if he can still tease us without his glib tongue."*

Rhazien gripped his throat as he choked on a silent laugh. His eyes turned molten when he realized what she had done, and Erissa's thighs grew slick with the promise of his retribution.

As quick as lightning strikes the ground, Rhazien's hand shot forward, his long fingers wrapping themselves in her hair until he fisted the locks at the base of her neck. She gasped as he gave a hard tug on the mass of hair and brought her face closer to his cock.

The voice purred in response, giving the breath back to Rhazien's lungs.

He sucked in the much-needed air, using his firm grip of her hair to pull her mouth closer to him as he panted. "You haven't learned how to shield your thoughts, little doe. I know every filthy one of them. I know how much you want to taste me, how the wetness collects between your thighs at the thought of it, how swollen you must be. And now, all I can think about is how beautiful you would look with your lips wrapped around my cock."

Erissa rubbed her thighs together with a whimper.

"Is that what you want?" Rhazien rubbed the head of his cock against her lips, leaving behind a sticky saltiness. "To taste me?"

The feel of his skin fascinated her, as did the bead of moisture that gathered at the tip. Would he like it if she tasted him? She wanted to with a desperation that left her slick between her thighs, curious about how he would taste and if she would like it as much as he had.

"Yes." Emboldened, Erissa pushed the furs down to his knees. He had beautiful skin, the hard planes of his body sculpted around his tattoo, making the ink stand out against his darker coloring as a trail of hair led down between his legs. Similar hair covered his muscular thighs. She found it unfair for him to captivate her so.

She leaned forward, her hair brushing over his thighs, and took him into her mouth.

Rhazien tasted of salt and something else, something light and sweet that left her wanting more of him. It reminded her of the oranges she tasted in Cropari, and Erissa hummed low in her throat, taking him deeper as she sought more of his taste.

"By the gods." Rhazien's hips bucked, and Erissa giggled around him. His muscles clenched along his thighs, his length jumping in her mouth, and he moaned as she took that as an invitation to suck on his length. "I won't last long if you keep doing that."

She hesitated, unsure of what to keep doing, and Rhazien's hands found their way into her hair. He guided her actions, pulling her head up in down in the rhythm he liked until she caught its pattern. She sucked as she moved, treating him like a delicacy that needed savoring.

Erissa lifted her eyes and found Rhazien staring at her. His breath hitched as their gazes locked, and she rolled her tongue along his tip. Rhazien's eyes rolled to the back of his head.

If she looked anything like he did with her mouth wrapped around his heat, she very well understood why he wanted to focus his attention on her. She would never get enough of seeing him like this. Every wall crumbled between them as love and desire blended together into a living entity that rivaled the strength of the flames they used to burn the Veil.

His length tensed in her mouth, and Rhazien moaned low in his throat. He pulled at her hair, trying to get her to raise her head, but she swatted his hands away and relaxed her jaw as she sucked him faster with another roll of her tongue that proved to be his undoing.

Rhazien came down the back of her throat, the thick salty liquid filling her mouth and dribbling down her chin as she swallowed around him. Only when he shuddered beneath her, his legs relaxing on either side of her, did she lift her had with a pleased grin.

He flung a hand over his face, hiding his smile, and cracked an eye open at her. "Pleased with yourself, little doe?"

Erissa nodded and crawled into his arms as he held him open to her. "You should have let me do that sooner."

Rhazien laughed and flipped her over onto her stomach. He trailed a hand down her back, making her shiver. "Give me a moment, wife, and I shall return the favor."

Erissa stretched against his touch. "Why not return it now?"

"Little doe, this seems as good a time as any..." Rhazien's hand stilled. "There is something else I need to tell you."

Erissa sighed. "Another secret?"

He ran a hand through his hair as he stalled for time. Rhazien blew out a breath, his hand dropping to his side. "I'm half-fae, little doe."

Erissa blinked at him, waiting for him to say more.

Rhazien shifted nervously. "Did you hear me?"

"Yes." Erissa tipped her head. "Is this supposed to be some big revelation?"

Rhazien was taken aback. "What?"

"While I wish you had told me outright, I was, in fact, paying attention to those stories you told. You were very clear the Fefnirion couldn't produce more dragons with humans. I'm not stupid. That meant you had to be Fae." Erissa rolled her eyes, fighting a smile at his flustered expression. "Can you get on with returning the favor now? There are so many other things your mouth can be doing."

A deep laugh came from Rhazien. His lips tickled her lower back as he pressed kisses into the skin. "Yes, wife. Anything for you."

CHAPTER SIXTY

"Where are the men?"

Thonalan watched as Faldeyr paced across the old wooden floors of the inn in Orina. The human had yet to sit still and spoke with a grating tone as he continued blathering.

"They should be back by now with my brother and the girl."

The Seelie Lord sighed, throwing a chicken bone onto the table. Humans were always full of complaints. He wiped his mouth, buying another moment of peace before he admitted the truth. "Dead."

Faldeyr snapped his head toward the Fae. "How can they be dead?"

"Do you see them anywhere? Have they miraculously reappeared in front of us? The Zoarthi leader went to Yorrith over the girl." Thonalan sat back in his chair, scratching at a pointed ear with the tip of a long nail. "If they haven't returned, the Zorathi have either killed or captured them. If they are captured, they are not long for the Veil. Either way, the men are dead."

Spittle flew from Faldeyr's mouth. "You said your men would handle this."

"And you said yours would." Thonalan sat forward, his hand gripping the knife beside his plate. This human would only push him so far. "Who lost the girl in the first place?"

Thonalan's ears twitched as he picked up the sound of the man's teeth grinding. He smirked, the cold tilt of his lips matching the look in his eyes as he narrowed them on the pathetic human still pacing before the table. "Have you figured out how your brother broke the Fae bargain? Its magic should have bound his actions."

Faldeyr grunted. "No. Why do you think I drug him behind the horse? I'm lucky I even caught him on the road to Trilux after his horse went lame."

"Naturally, the torture failed. If your command did not compel the truth, nothing would." Thonalan leaned back again, gesturing for the old woman to bring him another plate of food.

"You're one to speak of failure after sending that many Fae. They were outnumbered and still proved incapable of handling the girl." Faldeyr sneered as he threw himself into a chair at the other end of the table. "At least my brother failed as a human. How can the Fae not handle the girl when she doesn't even know how to use her magic?"

The old woman neared with his plate of food, and Thonalan's eyes narrowed at Faldeyr. He grabbed her hand as she made to lower the plate, wrenching it backward at an odd angle until she dropped to the floor in anguish. "You forget, human. How fragile your lives are."

Thonalan twisted the hand at the wrist with a sharp jerk, a sickening crunch filling the air. The woman's screams followed. He shoved her further onto the floor, pressing his heeled boot onto the oddly angled bones as her screams intensified and she begged for his mercy, her words indistinguishable from her agony. "Perhaps you need a refresher."

Faldeyr crossed his arms. "Kill me, and you will never have the girl."

"Let me make one thing clear, Lord Faldeyr." Thonalan removed his foot from the broken wrist. The woman's blubbering grated his nerves. They were already stretched thin from the man sitting in front of him. He grew tired of this pretend patience. "Instilling you on the human throne serves my purpose. That is the only reason I agreed to this bargain. But bargains can be broken, especially when the consequences are not mine to pay."

Some of the color drained from Faldeyr's face. He said nothing, and a cruel glare cracked across Thonalan's face. "I see we understand one another."

"What do you want?" Faldeyr wiped his hands down his trousers, leaving a dark trail of sweat on the heavy cloth.

"We are missing something." Thonalan kicked the old woman until she rolled on her side. With her no longer blocking his chair, he sat, continuing to ignore her broken cries. "What are you not telling me?"

Faldeyr shrugged, and his shoulder twitched with the movement as his hands moved back and forth along the dampening fabric. "The bitch had help escaping the city. The blacksmith's son ran off with her. We caught the family. Kept the blacksmith in the dungeon for days, but he wouldn't break. Vilotta kept his brats. She was taken with the wife. Some friend from her days at court. Somewhere in all this, Barrett learned how to break the bond and helped the family escape."

"You said Vilotta knew the wife from court?" Thonalan tapped his fingers against the table. "How would she come to know a blacksmith's wife?"

"Vi said the woman was an old friend." Faldeyr scratched at his brow. "Susreene. That's the woman's name."

"By the gods, you infernal idiot," Thonalan swore. "If Susreene is involved, then so are the Fefnirion."

"The dragons?" Faldeyr snorted. "They're a myth, nothing more."

The thin line of patience Thonalan grasped snapped with the human's ignorance. The Fae roared, shoving the table hard enough that the wood splintered where he gripped it. Faldeyr let out a guttural yell as he sat pinned between the heavy table and the wall, blood spilling over the lip where it crushed his abdomen.

Thonalan let go of the table and pinched the bridge of his nose. He slowed his breathing, trying to remind himself the human had not served his full purpose. A time would come when Faldeyr would draw his last breath, but until then, Thonalan needed the man alive. A magical link connected him to the girl. One he needed to magnify to usurp the Seelie throne from Yorrith. Only the human's link would sever the magic Yorrith's blood held over the throne.

The Fae lay his hands on the table and pulled it away from the man. His movements were jerky as he fought the instinct to press it further into the cut formed just below Faldeyr's ribs.

Faldeyr coughed and groaned at the pain it caused when the table moved away. His hands cupped the deep laceration. "You could have killed me."

"And yet," Thonalan sneered, "I didn't."

Faldeyr glared but wisely held his tongue. He eyed Thonalan with wariness.

"Our spy is in position, but there's no chance of grabbing the girl with the Zorathi and Seelie King there." Thonalan stared down at the weak creature before him. The wound would need stitching, but the man would live. He walked around the table and crouched in front of him. Thonalan lay his hands over Faldeyr's and let his magic trickle into the wound. The blood stopped flowing, and the sides knitted together until nothing but a faint pink line remained between the tears in the tattered cloth of his tunic. "But there is still hope. One of the Unseelie comes to claim the girl. My spy will keep watch and let us know when his guard is down, and that is when we will strike. The girl isn't long for the Keeper, and when she is dead, the thrones will be ours."

CHAPTER SIXTY-ONE

By the time Rhazien and Erissa exited the tent, the early morning had given way to the noon hour.

He looked around, taking in the other tents. One more had joined their camp, its sides covered in gray furs. Two more Fae sat around the fire, settled near it and as far away from Erissa and Rhazien's tent as possible. The bodies from last night were nowhere to be found.

Rhazien's cheeks heated as he avoided everyone staring at the married couple. He cursed the hearing of the Fae, for he knew the Zorathi and the Seelie King had surely heard all that transpired in their seclusion, and Erissa's uncle would not be fooled by the wrinkled clothes and tangled hair that spoke of more than sleep. But what lay behind the looks of the other two?

The white-haired woman—Nephinae—stood and motioned them over to sit across from her at the fire and next to the newcomers. "I am afraid you have missed breakfast, but you are in time for the noonday meal."

Erissa smiled at the Fae. "Thank you. We didn't eat yesterday with everything that happened. My magic is grumbling about the lack of food."

The Seelie King stood too and reached for one of the empty tin plates by the fire. "Come, child. Eat your fill. You and your magic will feel better with a full stomach."

Nephinae took her seat. "A full stomach or a bloated one, Seelie?"

The King cursed, dropping the plate in the fire and spilling its contents across the flames. The food sizzled against the charred wood. "I swear by the gods, Zorathi, I'll..."

"You will what, Seelie?" Nephinae arched a brow, her lips quirking to the side. "Drop another plate of food?"

Yorrith grumped as he grabbed two sticks from the kindling pile. He used them to pinch the plate between their lengths and pulled it from the flames. His eyes cut to Nephinae, and he fought a smile. "I'll do something more resourceful than that. Bloated stomachs indeed."

The King made another plate, passing it to Erissa. "There's plenty more when you finish. Soul calling will have drained your reserves, and the food will help."

He sat after she thanked him, ignoring Rhazien where he stood beside her.

Nephinae snorted. She made to rise, but Rhazien waved her away. He gathered his own food and led Erissa to the empty log beside the new Fae with a hand on her back.

The two newcomers sat shoulder to shoulder, throwing disgusted glances their way. While of the opposite sex, they had identical appearances, their beauty hard and fierce like the desert lands. They reminded Rhazien of how the moon blocked the sun once every few years. Their skin looked infused by the yellow rays of sunlight and the tattoos by the blood orange hue of the moon. The colors layered over each other until the edges bled together, and the tattoos looked like a mirage on the desert horizon, their blue eyes taking the place of the shimmering waves of a taunting oasis and their long brown locks appearing like the twisting forms of trees offering shelter. But their faces did not hold any of the desert's warmth as the two Fae stared at Rhazien and Erissa with open hostility.

Erissa must have noticed the animosity coming from the pair. She tensed beside him, leaning into his touch. Rhazien rubbed his hand in small circles on her lower back, pushing comfort through their bond.

The male gave a cruel smile as Erissa shifted away from him. "I don't bite. Can't say the same for the one who sent me to find you. I would run if I were you. Nothing good awaits you if you stay. I will see to it."

Erissa shuddered, and Rhazien felt his dragon rising at the threat to its mate. But the Seelie King bet him to action.

Yorrith stiffened. The air grew still around them as time stopped. The wind no longer rustled, and the many clouds overhead halted their pace alongside it. "Keep your mouth shut, Kyrenic, or I will shut it for you."

"Don't be goaded into losing control, Seelie." Nephinae picked at the food on her plate. Boredom dripped from her tone as she peered at the King with disappointment. "You are not some youngling fresh into their magic."

The King looked ready to rip the head from Kyrenic's body but settled with the Zorathi's rebuke. "Fine. But deal with your dog before I do."

"Seelie shite." Kyrenic stood. Power built along his tattoos. "You dare call me a dog?"

"Enough, Kyrenic." Nephinae's gaze snapped to his, malice pouring through the white eyes as they glowed with the force of the power she fed into them. "Need I remind you of the last time you proved incapable of minding your manners?"

Kyrenic's face turned murderous, but he said nothing more as he swallowed, raising a hand to rub at his throat.

The clearing settled into an awkward silence as the twin Fae and Seelie king glared at one another.

Rhazien turned back to his food when nothing more happened. He held onto Erissa's hand as he ate, balancing his plate on his knee while he used soft slices of bread to scoop the food. He found it hard to let go of her. The events of yesterday still lingered in his mind. They had come too close to losing each other, and the thought of not touching her now left his pulse racing.

Yorrith finally broke the silence as Erissa finished her last bite. His smile reached his eyes as he watched her indulge herself in the hearty stew. "Better?"

"Yes, much better." Erissa answered his smile with one of her own. "Is my uncle resting?"

Yorrith nodded. "He's feeling fine this morning. A night's rest and a full stomach do wonders for the constitution."

Nephinae adjusted the folds of the thin fabric of her dress, revealing the skin of her upper thighs to the heat of the fire. "Men are lucky they only have to worry about filling their stomachs and not someone bloating them, right, Seelie?"

The King's attention snapped to her. He stared down his nose at the Fae, his gaze tracing along the flesh she exposed. "Quiet, Zorathi. No one needs to hear your prattling, and for the gods' sake, cover your damned legs. It's cold outside."

"You were the one speaking of bloated stomachs last night, Seelie." Nephinae pulled the hem of her dress higher. "Besides, the cold is hardly felt."

"Speak for yourself." Erissa's teeth chattered when she spoke. She hugged her cloak tighter against her frame. "I miss Cropari's heat."

"Here, little doe. I can help with that." Rhazien had no more reason to hide his magic from her. He dropped his shield, letting the heat build along his skin as he pulled her onto his lap. "My fire can warm us both."

Erissa settled into the warmth. "I don't know whether to be grateful I will never again have to pass a freezing night with you around or angry you let us suffer in Eshirene's Wood when we ran away that first night.

"Both." Rhazien kissed her temple, a chuckle in his voice. "I would be angry with me too, but remember how the wood was wet, little doe?"

Erissa's mouth hung open with shock, and she twisted to his shoulder while he laughed. "You sneaky dragon. You lit the fire with your magic."

He shrugged, pulling her back into his arms. "I wasn't about to let you freeze through the night."

"Have you made a habit of lying to your mate, Fefnirion?" Anger hardened Yorrith's tone.

"We are hardly ones to comment on the actions guiding a mating bond, Seelie." Nephinae stood and moved to sit beside the other Fae. "Let the children have their peace."

Whatever lay behind Nephinae's words silenced the King. He folded his arms across his chest and directed all his ire into staring at the fire. If the Fae had been half Fefnirion, the heat from his disturbed gaze would have been enough to drive them all a great distance from the flames.

Silence strangled the clearing once more.

Erissa used her fingers to comb through the tangles in her hair as she basked in the warmth of the flames in front of her and Rhazien's fire behind. She gave up after a few moments, her shoulders slumping.

"Let me help." Rhazien replaced her hands with his own, untangling the knots in the mass of black curls. With that done, he pulled the leather strap holding his hair in place from the back of his head. His rich brown hair had grown longer as it fell in around his shoulders. He tucked the sides behind his ears, the gold cuffs glinting in the weak sunlight as he tied Erissa's hair back from her face.

Nephinae leaned toward him, catching his attention. "Who designed the cuffs on your ears?"

Something brittle sat behind Nephinae's gaze when Rhazien looked at her. "I did."

"They remind me of someone." Nephinae studied them, tracing her eyes across the wings of the dragon and the glittering stones that made them come alive. "I had a friend among the Unseelie. One who was there with me in the war of the Remaking before the Creator intervened. She loved to paint and mixed sand with different plants to create her colors. Your cuffs look like the dragon she often painted in the last days of the war."

Rhazien hardly dared to breathe. His hands stilled in Erissa's hair, and he struggled to swallow around the lump of panic in his throat. He swore the Zorathi's smile darkened as if she got the reaction she wanted. But she said no more, and silence filled the clearing again.

Erissa broke the silence. "We shouldn't stay here for long. Rhazien and I must travel to Umirian."

The Seelie King addressed Erissa. "Your uncle sleeps now but should be ready to travel by tomorrow morning."

"We're to stay here the rest of the day?" Erissa's head turned to where the bodies of the Fae who attacked them had once laid.

Her sadness trickled down the bond, and Rhazien wrapped his arms around her. "Only until the morning, little doe. We can leave as soon as your uncle can travel."

"Stay with us." Nephinae offered.

"And go where?" Erissa drew a finger across his arm, tracing patterns in the hair covering it. "I remain hunted on every side. Where can we possibly go with you and not put you in danger?"

"I've been thinking about where to go since we left Cropari." Rhazien hesitated, not wanting to upset his mate with what he needed to say next.

She would not want to hear it. "We need answers, and your uncle can't give them to us. Whatever vow he took keeps him from telling us the truth. But if you were to go back and confront your parents, we could get those answers." He looked between Nephiane and Yorrith. "I would like to ask the two of you to escort us. Yesterday was the second time we've been attacked on the road."

Erissa pushed herself from his lap, turning to glare at him. "You want me to go back? After everything I did to leave?"

"What do you mean, after all you did to leave?" Yorrith stood as well, moving closer to the couple.

She waved him off. "It's nothing. My parents..." Erissa shrugged, refusing to say anything more.

Rhazien did not dare go to her, letting her have the space she needed as she grappled with the flashes of memory pulsing down their bond. It reminded him of the day they left Emberhold when the horse spooked her thoughts. The same ones came to him now as they did on that day. His fists balled at his sides. "I wouldn't ask you to go back if I thought you wouldn't be protected. I was hiding my identity to protect more than you when we fled, but I know if we tell my father, he'll stand beside us."

"Your father isn't there anymore."

Everyone turned toward the voice, and Barrett colored at the attention. He stood leaning against one of the tent poles. His knees trembled slightly as he pushed away from its support. "Faldeyr had me capture your family. Your father is a little worse for wear after time spent in the dungeons, but your mother and sisters escaped with him unharmed."

The blood rushed through Rhazien's ears, his vision turning black as smoke poured from him and his scales became visible. "You did what?"

"I captured your family and put your father through a week of torture." Barrett shrugged as he stumbled onto a log by the fire. "The Warden can hold his own."

"By the gods." Rhazien struggled to maintain control as his dragon instincts fought for dominance. "You're not long for the Keeper."

"Rhazien, wait." Erissa threw herself into his arms.

"He tortured my father. Captured my mother and sisters. And I helped to bring him back from the Veil." Only Erissa's intervention kept Rhazien from pouncing on the weakened man by the fire. Oh, how he longed to rip his claws into the man's chest.

"Rhazien Merrick, you will do no such thing." Erissa shoved him hard enough that it helped him regain his senses. "He wasn't in control of his actions. If I have to remember that, you need to remember it too."

Her words sobered his temper. The smoke faded, the scales slipping back beneath his skin. Rhazien stood before her once again in his human form. "They're children, little doe."

"Your sisters remain unharmed." Barrett accepted a bowl of food from Yorrith with a smile. "Your father helped me break part of the Fae bond, and I helped your family escape through the same tunnels Erissa used. My actions are now my own, but the binding on my silence proved more potent than his magic could handle."

Nephinae leaned forward, a hard edge to her voice. "There is no breaking a Fae bargain."

Barrett talked around mouthfuls of stew. "The Warden had a way. He called it a voiding and bled my hand with a black blade."

"Avoiding?" The color left Nephinae's face, leaving her as white as her hair and the snow that fell around them in the frigid air. "Are you sure that is what he called it?"

"Yes, I'm sure." Barrett turned his attention to his meal, avoiding any more questions from the Zorathi.

Nephinae stared between him and Rhazien, her eyes flicking to Rhazien's cuffs once more as understanding passed over her. "You are Fae."

Rhazien nodded, his voice resigned at the implications of the admission that his parents were the rumored pair who acted against the Creator. "My mother is Fae."

"And your father, a Warden?" Nephinae asked, her gaze hardening. "You are half-Fae, half-Fefnirion?"

Rhazien rested his hand on Erissa's lower back, needing the comfort of touching her. "Yes, I am Fefnirion born, not made."

"By the Creator," Yorrith yelped, "you will draw his wrath upon us."

Nephinae stared at Rhazien for a moment before she rolled her shoulders and forced the tension from them. She looked to the heavens, a frown turning down the corners of her mouth. "Only time will tell. Let us pray it does not."

A sense of foreboding built within Rhazien's chest. Her look spoke of trouble as surely as the weather did. They would be buried in snow come nightfall, but something in the Zorathi's warning spoke of another storm brewing. But at least with the four Fae surrounding them, Erissa would sleep safely this night. He needed to convince her to travel back to Emberhold. They would always be on the run until they confronted her parents, and she learned the truth about who she was.

The fire flickered under the dampness of the snowfall, and the sound of chattering teeth broke through Rhazien's thoughts. He found its source in Erissa and guided her closer to the fire.

Yorrith chuckled as Rhazien fed magic into the petering flames. "A Fefnirion always came in handy on days like these during the Keeping War.

The Wilds are quite cold come the harvesting moons, and many a dragon kept our campfires warm as we rested."

The King pulled a kettle from a sack lying near the fire, filling it with water from a flask. "Come, children, and let me tell you a story about one of these times while we put the kettle on."

Nephinae tossed her hair over her shoulder. "No one wishes to listen to your stories, Seelie."

The Fae threw the flask at her head, letting out a bark of laughter as she caught it. "Watch yourself, Zorathi. Can't have you going soft in your reflexes."

She rolled her eyes. "My reflexes have nothing to do with your long-winded ramblings."

Yorrith placed a hand against his chest as if wounded. "I'll have you know…"

Rhazien left them to their bickering as he pulled Erissa into his lap and wrapped her in his magic's warmth. He needed to plan out their next conversation and his reasons for returning to her home. For she would not want to travel back to Emberhold.

CHAPTER SIXTY-TWO

Reeva walked through the Crying Grove, trepidation slowing her steps as she neared the Temple of Souls. What awaited her in the depths of the marble structure would only bring her pain, but she held no power to change the course of what happened this night.

She climbed the white steps. The tapping of her bare feet should echo alongside the painful beating of her heart, but she had long grown used to the silence of her passing. What she would not give to hear her light tread or the rustling of her clothing as her body moved. Even her breathing remained without sound to accompany the rise and fall of her chest.

The silence gave way to the sound of irate voices as she crested the opulent staircase.

Virion sat sprawled across a richly furnished dais, the burgundy throne standing out like blood against the holy room's white marble and gold accents. But maybe blood did stain its fabric, for the man sitting upon the throne had an astounding quantity of it saturating his clothes.

He leaned to the side, glaring at the Fae standing next to him. "If we had killed the humans in the grove, we wouldn't be dealing with this mess."

Reeva's mouth thinned at seeing Drurrah. Nothing good would come from his involvement. He had no honor and switched sides during the war to suit his own needs despite the consequences of his actions.

The Lord of the Court of the Hunter's Moon pointed at his shoes where the blood soaked the expensive fabric. "If you had not killed them in such a savage manner, my shoes would still be pristine. Come now, Virion, there was no need to bludgeon the weaklings when a slit throat would have bled them far more easily."

Of course, he pointed to his shoes, not the bodies littering the ground. Reeva never understood how so many of the Fae held such indifference to the lives of others after all the gods had put them through. But maybe there lay the problem. Maybe something inside each of them broke with the war of the Remaking. Reeva lost her life to the Keeping in the war that came next, but Drurrah lost a child to Malcufyre's schemes. She almost pitied him.

She lost the feeling as he kicked at one of the corpses.

Drurrah's lip curled. "You owe me a pair of shoes, Virion."

The portal born of blood magic materialized as Reeva neared the gruesome mess, and Draven's voice rang out in the chamber. "Must you call me in the middle of your spats? I am tempted to sew your tongues together on the day I break free of this prison."

"Your son needs a lesson in manners, Draven." Drurrah leaned against an armrest on the throne, much to Virion's annoyance.

The other Fae sulked, tucking his chin as he crossed his arms. "No one asked you to be here."

"Enough." Draven pressed his hands to the portal wall. "Where is my dear?"

"I am here." Reeva shivered, shuffling to stand closer to the portal despite her desire to run. She had been summoned, and she remained powerless to do anything but heed the command.

Draven smiled, the wide spread of his mouth looking unnatural, as if he rarely practiced turning his lips up at the corners. "My love."

The endearment left her wanting to vomit. She forced a smile on her face instead as everyone turned to her. "You have need of me, my Lord?"

"You have been watching the girl?" Draven trailed his hands down the portal in the shape of Reeva's silhouette.

"Yes." Reeva loathed, admitting she followed his order. A storm brewed on the horizon, and she dreaded thinking of what the twisted Fae had planned for Erissa. "Yorrith and Nephinae were sent to collect her. They arrived in time to thwart Thonalan's plan, and she travels with them now."

"Good work, my love." Draven's voice dripped with too much honey to be sincere. He turned to Drurrah, dropping the pretense. "You are sure you have swayed the Fae to help us?"

Drurrah nodded. "So long as Reeva lures the girl from the camp, my man can grab her."

"This is a fool's errand." Virion slapped his hand against his thigh. "They will be expecting us to take her."

A laugh burst from Drurrah as he raised a brow at Virion. "Expect us? Novus is too blinded by his own reputation to believe anyone would dare cross him. And that is what we will use to our advantage."

"And no one knows of Reeva's relationship with the girl." Virion rubbed at his chin.

Guilt sat heavily on her shoulders. She wanted to sag against it, unwilling to admit that others knew of her involvement with the girl and face punishment for it. Reeva stood straighter while trying to wipe the guilt from her emotions. Draven might not have the power to know her thoughts, but her emotions remained his with the bond in place, and he would stop at nothing to dig through the mask of indifference she tried to maintain.

Draven turned his head at an angle, studying her. "Is that true, Reeva?"

After hundreds of years, she still did not know how to break the compulsion to answer his questions. The Keeping pulled a confession from deep within her. Reeva found herself answering him before a conscious thought had even occurred. "No, the boy—Rhazien—knows of my existence."

As quickly as the unnatural smile appeared on Draven's face, a more sinister one replaced it. "You have disobeyed the intent of my orders, Reeva."

She said nothing in her defense. It would not change what happened next, and Reeva held no regret over exposing her identity and purpose to Erissa or Rhazien. At least the girl stood a fighting chance, knowing that deceit lay behind Reeva's actions, even if it did not account for her intentions.

Draven shook his head, his cruel smile intensifying. "Let your man know that Reeva will come soon, and when she does, we will grab the girl. He is to wait until then."

"Why not grab her today?" Virion stood and moved from the throne to stand at the portal's edge.

"Because Reeva has a lesson to learn." Draven's eyes never left Reeva as he answered the other male's question.

If Reeva were still alive, maybe she would have cried at the thought of a punishment. But she no longer held a spark of life, and her tears had dried long ago when the Keeping remained fresh in her mind. Even Draven's touch—the only thing in this world her trapped soul allowed her to feel—no longer inspired tear-stained sorrow. It left a hollow ache, one that had begun to fill once she met Erissa.

Life would never be hers. But if Reeva's punishment gave the girl another day of peace before Reeva betrayed her, she would gladly submit to the mad Fae. It bought the girl one more day; maybe it would be enough to turn the tide of what came next.

CHAPTER SIXTY-THREE

Novus's arms lay crossed against his chest; his head dipped low as Nephinae stepped into the small clearing not far from the camp. "You were quite chatty with the girl's mate earlier."

The Zorathi stopped short of reaching him, her breath misting in the air as she huffed. What did he hope to gain by following them so closely? They had the girl, and Nephinae made sure the conversation earlier in the day had focused on Erissa's return to Emberhold as her Lord wanted. Why did he harp so much about the damned mate? "She is married, Novus, with a mate bond that is fully formed. What would you have me do, ignore him outright and give them a reason not to trust me?"

He turned, his brows drawn and his voice full of venom as his power darkened his silver eyes. "I would have you draw a wedge between them. Nothing can come of this bond."

"I know why Yorrith balks at their bond, but there's no reason for you to be against it." Nephinae mimicked his stance. Let her King be agitated. She might bend the knee, but she would never bow. He knew more than anyone she would fall to her knees for no one after all his father had done. "You know better than I how mate bonds make for effective weapons in war. We can use her marriage to our advantage."

Novus's black mist bled from his skin, spreading through the air to cover him like a cloak of midnight and stars. "She likes you."

"And I, her." Nephinae's stance softened, her eyes tilting at the corners. "She is a kind girl, although a little lost after all she has been through. I am afraid she will not make it through the confrontation to come, and we will have to leverage whatever we can to provoke her magic."

"You would betray her trust?"

Novus's voice carried a hint of surprise, and Nephinae struggled to smother the hurt that came with it. His questioning of her now bothered her more than being near Yorrith for such a prolonged period. "I will do what I must—what you command of me. I serve the Unseelie throne, not the girl. What matters is the outcome of the war, not one misguided child."

"*You* would *betray her*," the mists hissed, the magic rising like heckles along Novus's form. "*We will see her unharmed, or the world will burn alongside the Keeper.*"

It gave one more hiss, and Nephinae swore its depths glared at her where it pulsed against her Lord's form, growing into blades that towered over his height. The magic was as bonded to Nephinae as it was to Novus. She had earned that bond in sweat and blood. Its animosity over using Erissa left her stunned. "You like the girl."

"I spent enough time in the dungeons awaiting the days of prophecy." Novus cleared his throat, exerting his control over the mists and drawing it back to him. He shifted his weight from one side to the other. "I am simply here keeping track of what the bargain with Yorrith dictates as mine. Nothing more."

Her eyes widened. Novus never fidgeted. Ever. And especially not for a woman. "The prophecy calls for three magics..."

"Neph..."

Realization flooded Nephinae as color deepened the hue of Novus's cheeks. He never could hide his emotions from her. "You *like* her. The magic has already staked its claim."

"Neph..."

"That is why you are still here." Everything made sense. Novus never strayed from court too long, not with Drurrah working to undermine his rule. He stayed for the girl. "You are drawn to her. It is only natural. She is your magical equal in a way no other can ever be."

"Neph..."

"Novus, I understand. She is beautiful, even in her human form, and kind to a fault. She reminds me of your mother. But the girl is mated and married." Nephinae stepped toward him, her gaze hard. "Separating the two of them would weaken her magic. She would be useless when Draven breaks free. Even if—"

"Will you be quiet?" The mists spread across the ground, its tendrils threatening the Zorathi as they rolled in angry waves from their master. Novus massaged his temples and spoke slowly as if speaking to a child. "There are no feelings. She is a pawn, nothing more. I have no plan to sever her bond or her marriage. The time quickly approaches when the two will be separated, and I will do what is needed to ensure she is ready for what comes next. Even if it means manipulating her feelings for the lizard to gain her cooperation."

Nephinae's heart wrenched. For all his age, Novus was immature in the ways of love. Pain spoke behind the anger, and while others might not hear it, Nephinae did. "Novus..."

"Enough!" Anger blackened the mists, and the starlight faded, leaving a mass of darkness that swallowed the surrounding light. "Let her fuck her mate for now. She will bend to my will in the end once his life is on the line."

Nephinae threw her hands up, tired of the back and forth between her and everyone in the camp. "Why are you so angry?"

The depths of the mist glittered with the intensity of night's wrath. "Because she is my mate! She is my mate, and I cannot have her."

Shock slammed into Nephinae as Novus stood, fists balled, his chest heaving as wild despair morphed his features. She stepped toward him, her heart fracturing for him. "Novus…"

"I am meant to be impartial to them. I'm not supposed to care about either…" He stepped back, holding up a hand, his voice strained as it threatened to break. "Nothing can come of this, Neph. She is a pawn. She has to be."

Nephinae stopped. She dropped her head, letting it hang between her shoulders. "Our lives would be much simpler if we were mates."

"But much less interesting." Novus forced a smile and tried to steer the conversation away from himself. "It is not too late for you. You know that."

Nephinae didn't appreciate the shift in conversation, especially because she knew exactly what the Unseelie was trying to suggest, but she allowed the change for now, giving Novus time to collect himself. If she pushed too hard now, he would run. She rubbed the middle of her forehead, her eyes closed, and humored him. "Yorrith hates me."

"Only you believe that to be true."

Nephinae knew Novus watched for the small catch in her breath. The slight tell would go unnoticed by anyone else but not him. When it came to reading one another, he and Nephinae were equals. He knew her as well as she knew him, better even after all his years of watching from his shadows.

Novus continued when she refused to answer his comment. "Everyone else has eyes that see and ears that hear. The Seelie King follows you like a starving animal begging for the smallest scraps. You need but snap your fingers, and he will bow at your feet for the remainder of his days. And yet you choose to torture yourself by watching him carry on without you."

"And what about you?" Nephinae countered. "Are you not jealous of Erissa and her husband?"

Novus mulled over her question, his body rigid. "In more ways than I care to admit."

Nephinae grabbed his hands, her heart hurting as he visibly suppressed a flinch. "Do you want her for yourself?"

He tolerated her touch, leaving his shadows to step closer to her. But he avoided her question. "If only you would give this much truth to your love life instead of mine." He placed his hand over hers, adding warmth to her freezing skin, and swallowed. "Yorrith is many things I do not like, but he is kindness personified. Do not let your past ruin everything you can build for your future."

"And what of your future?" She pulled back, crossing her arms to stare over the lake and its high mountains. "Don't think I didn't notice how you evaded answering."

"There is nothing to answer." Novus spun on his heel and walked back into the shadows, pulling the mist around him. "She will never choose me, and her dragon will never let her."

"Do you want her to claim you?" His reluctance to answer her question encouraged Nephinae to not back down. "We have never placed walls between us, Novus. Do not start now."

He rubbed his temples. "She already has claimed me. The mate bond is nearly fully formed."

Her mouth fell open. "How is that possible without the mate hunt?"

"I was with them during their hunt." Although Novus never shied away from telling Nephinae anything in the past, a pink hue darkened his skin. He sighed. "They call me through the bond when they are intimate."

Nephinae's earlier shock had nothing on how her jaw hit the floor. "And you answer this call?" At his brief nod, she let out a nervous crack of laughter. "You're having sex with them in the shadows of your magic?"

"Do not give me that look, Nephinae." Novus placed his arm behind his back, rocking on his heels. "Resisting the call of one's mate is nigh impossible."

"But you are doing this without their knowledge. In moments thought to be private—and the Fefnirion—are you touching her with your shadows... no, do not answer that." Nephinae spoke, her thoughts frazzled and scattered as they flooded their mind. But with the last one, she shuddered. "There are things even I do not need to know."

"She is not as innocent as she appears." A smirk twitched on his lips.

Nephinae tugged at the sides of her dress until the fabric frayed. The smirk and flippant tone did as little to hide his nerves as her fidgeting did. "Tell them the truth, Novus. Do not keep them in the dark about the mate bond or the prophecy. That is why you are acting this way, is it not?"

"There is nothing to tell." Novus shrugged, his voice hardening. "And you will breathe not a word of the prophecy to anyone or the bond to anyone. Our roles are clearly defined, and mine is to die in the culmination of this renewed war."

Nephinae met his proclamation with a pained wince. "Do not remind me of that gods' damned prophecy. Berthina is wrong, Novus. She has to be. I will not let you die."

"And I will not allow Draven to release the Keeper from the Veil and damn us all. I did not save the Unseelie from the rule of one tyrant to fall under the rule of another." His temper wore thin. "We have been over this Nephinae. Berthina and the others are searching for an alternative, but unless prophecy changes, my fate is decided."

"Is this why you're playing games with Erissa and Rhazien?"

"I am not playing games with either of them."

Nephinae threw her hands in the air. "Then what do you call it when you are letting them summon you while they are having sex? You are crossing a line that you cannot go back over."

Novus twisted his neck from side to side in a rare moment of weakness. "This is all I will have of her. My fate is bound, and doing this to them is cruel. But I cannot find it in myself to stay away from them with being this close to fully bonded."

Nephinae grabbed his arm. "If you let them get to know you and know the truth, what prophecy puts at stake..."

He met the intensity of her stare and dropped the facade he presented to everyone else. "I envy what they have with each other and am too selfish to let go of the chance of having whatever small piece of it I can. Whatever may come of the prophecy, I want to know more than my father's hatred and the violence following my mother's death before I make them hate me."

"Novus, you can have more than that now." Nephinae cupped his cheeks and pressed their foreheads together. "Your people love you—maybe not some of the court—you did recently remove a courtier's toes. But those outside the court's politics see the value of your actions. It is you who protects and cares for us, and it is you who delivered the Unseelie from your father's rule." She tapped her fingers against his cheek in a mock slap. "And you forget about me. We have made a family. Erissa is open-hearted and generous with her affections. She could grow to love you if you let her, and so long as she is happy and treated well, Rhazien will come around once he learns the truth of the Fefnirion mate bonds. Nothing is stopping you from having the love you want."

"They deserve more." Novus found only a whisper for the words as he pulled from Nephinae's embrace. "They deserve so much more than to be tied to a dying man as broken as I. It is why I am so angry. I can give neither of them what they need, and she will never come to love me as she does her dragon."

Her throat clogged with tears, the liquid overflowing and running down her cheeks. She wanted more for him than the half-life he sentenced himself to. "What about what you deserve, Novus? Do your needs not matter?"

His steps did not falter as Nephinae called out to him, nor as his shadows whimpered at her words. The black mist circled around Novus, covering his form as it blurred, becoming one with the surrounding air. The light returned to the clearing, the stars twinkling overhead.

Nephinae wiped furiously at her tears and waited for the mist to fully fade into the night before turning and confronting the cluster of trees downwind. "Been standing there long, Seelie?"

"The brat makes it ridiculously difficult to eavesdrop." Yorrith shuffled from behind the largest of the trees without a hint of apology softening his features. "Does he always spell the area like that?"

"No." Nephinae flipped her length of white hair over her shoulder and ignored the way her pulse jumped at the sight of the Fae. "The spell is my doing. We cannot have noisy Kings overhearing things best revealed later."

Yorrith leaned a shoulder against the tree, crossing one ankle over the other. "What is there to hide at this point?"

A snort left Nephinae's lips. "You would be surprised. The Creator must surely have a sick sense of humor with all that is unfolding."

Yorrith matched her snort, nodding his head toward where Novus had stood. "Says the one following the Unseelie. That requires its own sense of humor to understand."

The amusement drained from Nephinae's eyes. Every conversation between the two dissolved into the same squabble. "That is a matter of opinion."

"You truly believe living under Novus's rule will unite the Fae kingdoms?" No animosity curled Yorrith's words. Instead, a simple curiosity brightened his features.

"He is a righteous and just Lord who calmed the animosities following his father's crimes." A shiver forced its way across her skin, and Nephinae prayed the King mistook its origin as her being cold. "There are few worthy of my praise and none as deserving as my Lord."

"By vanquishing Tiordan's madness with his own." Yorrith unfastened his cloak, moving to stand near the Zorathi. He held the cloak out, waiting for her to take it. "There is no righteousness in the brutality of his reign."

"How would you know? You abandoned the courts during the Keeping and did not see the damage left behind. No, you remained cloistered in Zaestiraen, clinging to your throne as the world burned." Contempt curled Nephinae's lips, her eyes dancing with lightning in their moonstone depths. "Novus is the one who rescued us all from the Keeping's ruin and his father's rule. Not you."

"Clinging to my throne?" Yorrith laughed, the sound as brittle as the frigid air around them. He swung the cloak around Nephinae's shoulders. "I fought alongside the Unseelie during the Keeping War."

She tried to push the cloak away. "It was not enough, Yorrith. Not when you hold time within your hands."

"The consequences were too dangerous to involve time magic." Yorrith paid little attention to her ire. He stepped forward until his chest grazed hers, forcibly draping his cloak across Nephinae's shoulders. "You blame me at every turn for not doing enough in the war, endlessly accusing me of abandoning our people. But you forget, Zorathi, my court perished at the hand of time magic during the Remaking. A mistake so grave that even our god lost himself."

"You still should have tried. Reeva paid the price for your inaction. And the Frosted Moon Court paid for her death with Tiordan's actions. He lost his mate, and we all suffered the consequences for centuries." The fight left Nephinae, her shoulders drooping as her head tipped forward, the thick white hair swinging to cover one side of her face. She wrapped her arms around her waist, the words escaping as a strangled whisper. "I paid. And paid. Until the pain of the Remaking faded into the distance."

"I am sorry for Reeva's sacrifice and all that it cost. At that moment, the risk was too great for the soul of one when stacked against the many—when stacked against yours." Yorrith reached to tuck the hair behind Nephinae's ear. He did not speak until her eyes met his, an unreadable emotion swimming in the stormy ocean of his gaze. "You were not worth the risk, Nephinae. I would damn Reeva again before I let your soul scatter through time."

"You speak nonsense." Nephinae stepped back, shaking off his touch.

"I speak what you would deny." Yorrith reached to touch her again, his hand halting mid-air as lightning crackled against her skin. "Was I to let you die in her place? I had a choice. To save her or to save you."

Nephinae labored for breath, her chest heaving. "You chose wrong. My life held no more weight than another."

"To you, not to me." Yorrith let his hand fall. "But I would not damn you again to what came after Reeva's death. If a chance existed to take it all back... Tiordan would have died with his mate."

"Even knowing what happened, you won't admit you should have used your magic." Nephinae moved closer and pushed the Seelie King with all her strength. "You alone held the power to stop it all. Reeva's death bled Kaidreth from the moment her blood stained the Veil's hallowed soil. But only one court suffered the monstrosities of her severed mating bond."

Yorrith accepted her ire with compassion. "You see only what you want. Many suffered beyond the Frosted Moon's court. But many more would have suffered if I did as you desired."

"What would you know of suffering, *King*?" Nephinae sneered, the lightning intensifying, her hair rising in the surrounding air. "What would you know of the bond's corruption once it consumed Tiordan? You are as culpable as him, but at least he was driven to his actions. You have no excuse for your feigned ignorance of what happened at his hand."

Sorrow caught in the back of Yorrith's throat, his words thick with it. "You're right. I do not understand the mate bond. But then, who carries fault for that? I'm not the one who rejected my mate."

His words slapped Nephinae, leaving a wound the size of his hand on the deepest parts of her heart. She lowered her head, unable to meet his accusing gaze.

"What of your ignorance in this?" Yorrith chuckled, the raspy sound dark, hollow, and devoid of humor. "My soul maintains its tether with my mate. The mate who did not want me. And I bore her burden from the throne I clung to. Even now, I bear it. Every night, her plight after the Keeping haunts me. It's the reason for the wine."

He drank because of her? Because of what Tiordan put her court through—put *her* through—before Novus took power? Nephinae wasn't sure she wanted to believe it, but perhaps Novus had spoken true—perhaps it wasn't too late for her, perhaps Yorrith did not hate her despite her rejection. Or was there something more at play here than lingering feelings?

Shock slammed into her, stealing her breath. Nephinae's eyes snapped to his. "You... you never accepted the rejection?"

"No." Yorrith stepped closer, smiling as Nephinae held her breath. But the king only pulled the sides of his cloak around her and bound the clasp at her neck. His hands brushed against her throat, and they both shivered. The smile left his face. "I felt the pain of it all, believing my mate had chosen another. The bond doesn't distinguish intent. I had no way of knowing the truth of things when we heard nothing more than whispers coming from the snowy mountains surrounding Niwyth."

"You foolish King. *Why?*" If his words had felt like a blow before, they held nothing on the pain coursing through her now. Nephinae worked her throat, swallowing the whine that choked her. "Why would you put yourself through that night after night?"

"I told you long ago, Nephinae. You see only what you want, and you hear even less. The mate bond is something precious. It is not to be thrown away lightly." Yorrith removed his hands, tucking one under each arm as he walked away from Nephinae and back toward the camp.

"You think it was easy to reject you?" She balled her fists. "Nothing about it came easy."

Yorrith stopped when she did not follow, looking at her over his shoulder. "Come, Zorathi. We will solve nothing tonight, and you are cold. Let us save this discussion for another time. It has been centuries already. Another day won't matter, and there are too many around who may hear our words."

Nephinae forced her legs to follow. All of tomorrow's problems awaited them both, while the past haunted them from either end. She had grown tired of it all. But Yorrith spoke the truth. Nothing would change this night.

Eshirene's Wood

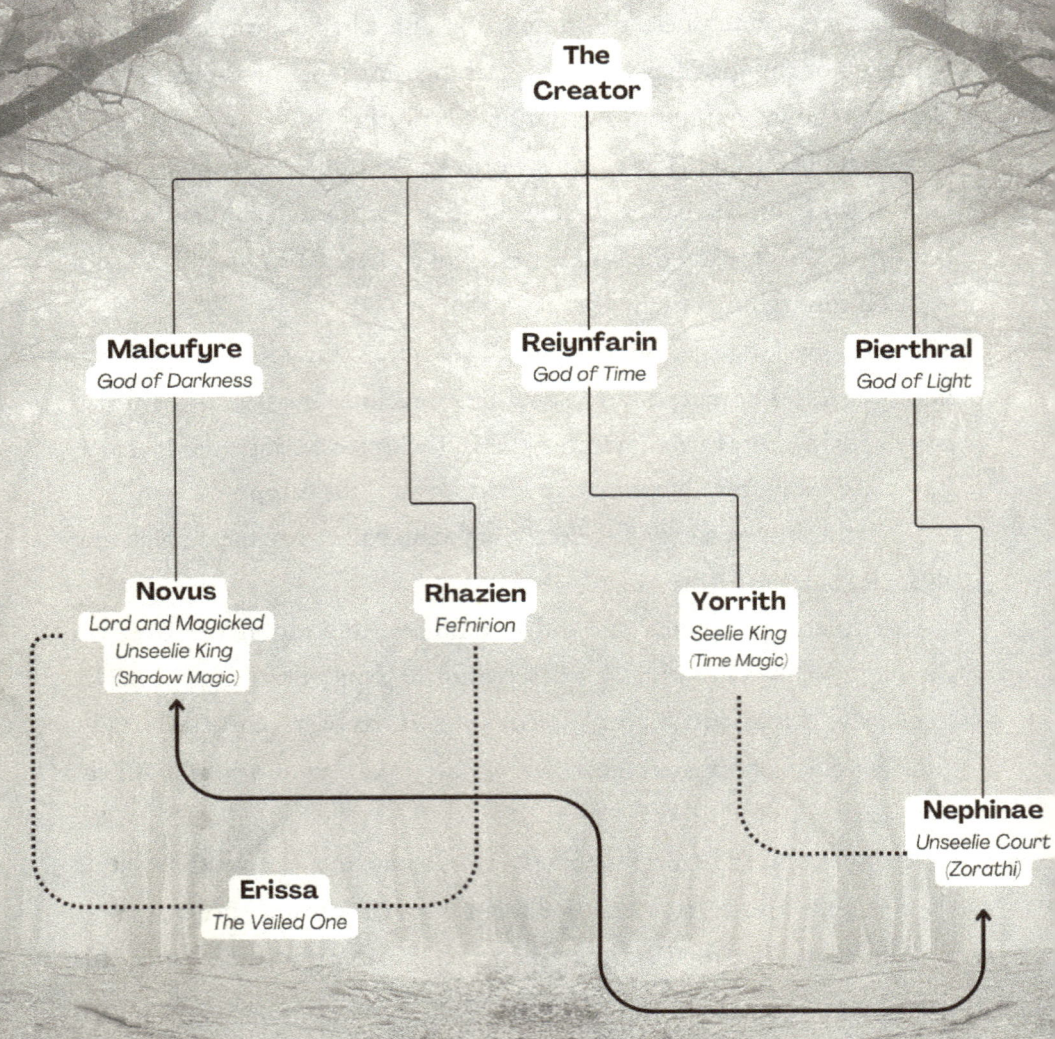

CHAPTER SIXTY-FOUR

"Would you like to hear a story?" Yorrith held a steaming mug out for Erissa.

She sat around the campfire with the Fae and Rhazien, basking in the fire's warmth after a long day of traveling in the bitterly cold wind. The night air held the promise of more snow, and she welcomed the hot tea.

They had passed the last two evenings around the fire after spending their days traveling south, distancing themselves from the Fae who hunted Erissa. The unlikely group settled into a routine as they moved further away from Gailme. Tension lay thick between the Seelie and Unseelie, and fear chased the very beat of her heart, but Erissa relaxed in the company of Yorrith and Nephinae. The Fae king kept her mind busy with stories from his youth while the Zorathi needled him at every turn. Their antics left Erissa laughing more often than not.

Erissa craned her neck to the side, peering behind the tents. "Are we not waiting for Nephinae?"

"It will be a while before she returns." Yorrith scooped snow from the ground and added it to the iron kettle he used to brew Erissa's tea.

"Where is she always running off to?" Rhazien pulled his own kettle from his pack. The king all but ignored him most of the time, and neither one of them understood why. "Between her and the twins, one of them is always gone."

When Yorrith did not answer Rhazien, Erissa tugged on the sleeve of his cloak. "Are we bothering them? Is that why they keep leaving?"

"Not at all, little one." The King offered her a kind smile, placing his hand over hers. "The Zorathi serve the Unseelie Court. While I'm the Fae king, I only hold both kingdoms because the crowned Unseelie king—Draven—remains locked within the Veil. So long as he lives, no one may claim the throne. It is how the magic works, despite the powers of the King already claiming another Lord. But while Draven is technically the King, each lesser court has its own Lord, and the Zorathi serve the Lord of the Court of the Frosted Moon. When he calls, they are bound to answer his summons. And he calls often."

Erissa wanted to know more about the Fae after spending so much time traveling with Yorrith and Nephinae. "What separates the Seelie from the Unseelie? I know how the courts came to be after the Remaking, but I don't understand how they're different. "

Yorrith crouched by the fire, stacking embers on the lid of the kettle to heat the water faster. He reached for Erissa's now empty mug, pouring another cup of tea for her now that the kettle had boiled once more. "With balance restored after the war, the Creator offered the Fae a choice to remain as they were or find peace in the afterlife. Banishing the gods weakened the Keeping bonds, allowing the Fae to keep their powers and regain their free will. He separated the Fae of the Seelie and Unseelie into courts, with each one having two lesser courts. The most powerful among them were crowned as Kings, with a Lord ruling over each lesser court. The Seelie contains the Court of the Flowering Sun with the power of the stone and the Court of the Thundering Sun with the power of air. And the Unseelie have the Court of the Hunter's Moon with their power of water, and the Court of the Frosted Moon with the power of darkness and shadow."

"But what separates them?" Erissa leaned forward, careful not to spill the steaming tea.

"Magic," Yorrith answered. "Stone and air sustain life—the stones giving us the stability of home and structure, while air breathes life into everything it touches. But water and shadows are where life ends."

Erissa scrunched her nose. "That doesn't make any sense. Stone can crush as it gives way, and air can be cut off."

"Clever girl." The Seelie King chuckled as Erissa beamed under the compliment. "What you say is true, but stone cannot crush, and air cannot suffocate without the aid of another element or person. Water and darkness act of their own accord. They conceal much in the depths and kill quickly without aid. It is the magic which sets us apart."

Erissa wrapped her hands around the hot mug, savoring the heat against her chilled palms as the steam heated her face. "Do all Fae have magic?"

Rhazien answered this time as he busied himself with his own drink. "All Fae have magic, but the depth of the power varies. Only the strongest of those in each court rule."

"Yes, all Fae do have magic." Yorrith glared daggers at Rhazien's interruption. "But not all their magic is elemental. During the War of the Remaking, the God of Stone created a divine metal called mistdrite to fight against Malcufyre's army. The mistdrite turned all those who mined its resource into witches, offering uncommon gifts like prophecy, crystals, and lunar and solar energies. The Zorathi were made from these witches by Malcufyre with the help of the God of light. He used the sun and moon cycles as he fed the flesh of the goddess of the void to a Fae and created the first Zorathi—Nephinae—and placed her in charge of creating the others. No other Zorathi holds the same level of power as she."

Erissa stared in the direction Nephinae had disappeared earlier. She did not think the Fae would like the turn of her thoughts. To be remade three times in one war only to have to pervert other witches and turn them into a lesser version of herself must have been unimaginable torture. She pitied the beautiful Zorathi.

Curiosity left her with many questions, but she asked the most pressing one that left her with endless doubts. "Are there other humans with magic?"

Yorrith startled, the cloth dropping from his hands as he went to pour himself another tea. He yelped as his fingers touched the hot iron.

"Serves you right, Seelie." Nephinae materialized behind him in a blinding flash of light. "The least you could have done was hold the kettle until I returned."

Curses left the King's mouth, but he let the Zorathi raise his hand and heal the burn across his fingers. "You've been gone for quite some time. My schedule doesn't revolve around the whims of the Frosted Moon's Lord.

"And a court doesn't run itself, lest you forget after all this time of cloistering yourself at Zaestiraen's palace." With the King's burns healed, Nephinae crouched beside him, tending to the fire and adding more snow to melt within the kettle. "What are we discussing?"

"The Fae." Erissa tried to hide how fascinated she found the history of the creatures. "The King burned himself when I asked about humans having any powers."

Nephinae arched a brow, staring between Yorrith and Erissa. The King shrugged with a panicked expression, and Nephinae snorted. "Don't start conversations you cannot finish, Seelie."

Yorrith stared at her, and Erissa squirmed under his regard. Something hovered behind his expression, something that pained him. "How much do you know about the Fae since you know nothing of their magic?"

She worried her bottom lip until she broke the tender flesh. "Rhazien's told me a little of the wars and the mate bonds, but outside of what he's told me, I know very little of the world."

His pained look intensified. "You have never been taught the magic of the Fae."

This moment felt all too much like the one in the woods before Rhazien drew his map in the dirt. The King stated instead of asking, and Erissa did not like it one bit. "No. There was little opportunity to learn about Fae magic."

The King sat back as if she had slapped him, his eyes wide and mouth hanging open. "And you think humans have magic?"

Erissa grimaced, nodding her head. Why did everyone act like magical humans did not exist? She more than proved that they did.

The Zorathi turned to Erissa. "I have never met a human with magic nor heard of one, and I have lived a long time. It would not have escaped my notice if such a creature existed."

Erissa's nose wrinkled. "You must be mistaken. I can't be the only human to ever have magic."

But Nephinae did not back down. Her voice hardened. "There have been no humans with witnessed magic."

"Nephinae..." Yorrith placed a hand on her shoulder and squeezed, his nails digging into the fabric.

"The child should know the truth of things." Nephinae shrugged, dislodging his hand.

"The truth of things?" Erissa's brow wrinkled as she looked between Rhazien, the King, and the Zorathi. "Does that mean there are humans with magic?"

The Zorathi leaned forward, her eyes glowing with something that spoke of resolve rather than malice, and it sent a shiver down Erissa's spine as she spoke again. "I am saying what they are neglecting to tell you—"

"Nephinae!" Yorrith lept to his feet and grabbed her arm. "Can you help me with something? Over there?" He pointed to the twin's tent.

Nephinae's power built along the grooves in her skin until it glowed with a ferocity that forced Erissa to look away. Yorrith yelped once more, and as the light faded as quickly as it came, Erissa turned around to find the Seelie King with yet another burn on his hand as the angry Zorathi challenged him. "I will not be silenced. You have been dancing around the girl with stories for days. You are as bad at revealing the truth as you are withholding your drink."

"Don't be ridiculous, Zorathi." Yorrith swallowed, flicking his tongue across his bottom lip before biting it.

Anger built beneath Erissa's chest. "What's going on?"

"There is something you must know, and I will not be the one to tell you." Nephinae shoved Yorrith in front of Erissa. "The Seelie has something he needs to say to you."

Erissa stared between them, her hands on her hips. "What now?"

Yorrith's shoulders slouched as he shoved his hands in his pockets and mumbled something lost to the cold breeze that picked up.

Nephinae shoved his back. "No one heard that, Seelie. Speak louder."

A shallow sigh left Yorrith, but he straightened his shoulders to their full height and moved closer to Erissa, his gaze wary. "You are Fae, Erissa."

Another wild bark of laughter broke from Erissa, her sanity slipping out with it. "I'm not Fae. My parents are human."

"That isn't entirely true." The Seelie's eyes gentled as he refuted her denial. "Faldeyr is not your father, little one. I am."

Erissa spiraled. Of all the truths that had been revealed to her—of all the mate bonds and Fae fows and unleased magic—this one was the one she refused to accept.

"No," she said.

"This is hardly the way I wished to tell you, but it's true, Erissa." Yorrith's gaze pleaded with her to understand. "You heard Nephinae. Humans don't have magic."

The soothing tone Yorrith used set Erissa's teeth on edge. "Why should I believe that?"

Nephinae crossed her arms. "Why would he lie?"

"I wouldn't," Yorrith insisted. "I'm your father. I've been looking for you all this time."

Erissa shook her head. They had all gone mad. "You can't be my father. How would that even happen?"

"Your mother was desperate for a child." Yorrith's hand lifted like he wanted to touch her, and Erissa flinched. The King pulled back, his features haggard. "Faldeyr is infertile. They traveled beyond the Mists to ask for my help, but no magic can cure his issue. Vilotta begged me to do whatever I could, so we... *conceived*... you."

Erissa staggered backward as her breathing hitched, and even Nephinae flinched at the King's words. She tried to draw in a full breath, but it did not work. She gasped, desperate to choke anything down into her burning lungs. Faldeyr was not her father. He had practically told her. He said he never should have gone along with her mother's scheme. Is that what lay behind his hatred?

Erissa searched for Rhazien, desperate for something she knew to be real, for someone to tell her this was all fake. But the expression she found on his face held concern and worry, not shock.

"You knew?" Erissa demanded.

"Not this, not about your father," Rhazien said, "but I suspected you were Fae. Your magic proved you must be."

Erissa shook her head. They had all gone mad. "You can't be my father." She challenged, turning back to Yorrith. "How would that even happen?"

She kept backing up until she hit Rhazien. His arms wrapped around her, pulling her tight against his front, his palms flat across her chest. "Breathe, little doe. Breathe for me."

Erissa shook her head. The breath would not come.

Rhazien tried again. He breathed deeply behind her, and he held her tighter, letting her feel the movement of his chest. "Breathe with me."

His words finally broke through, and Erissa dragged air into her starving lungs.

"That's it," Rhazien encouraged. "Keep breathing."

And she did, in and out repeatedly until her chest stopped burning and the world stopped spinning. Erissa folded her arms across Rhazien's, unwilling to relinquish the lifeline he offered. She stared at Yorrith, taking in his sharp features. She favored her mother and struggled to find a piece of her in his face. Something in Erissa wanted to believe him, that the madman who carved her skin did not sire her, but where was Yorrith all this time while her mother allowed her husband to abuse her?

Yorrith shoved his hands in his pockets, his face heavy with uncertainty. "Vilotta was supposed to send you to me after your sixteenth naming, but you disappeared when you were seven. The wasting had hit and cost the lives of many. Your mother told me you died."

Erissa sucked in another breath as the panic loomed, trying to gain another foothold. "Why would she do that?"

Yorrith gave a slight shake of his head. "I don't know. The story never sat well with me, but when I tried to look for you through our magic, I couldn't find any trace of you. I gave up hope and believed you dead until Nephinae told me you lived. I've tracked you since that day. It was no happenstance we found you as the Fae attacked. I was searching for you."

A low whine broke from Erissa's lips. Yorrith was here, standing in front of her, saying he wanted her. "You searched for me?"

"Of course I did. I wanted you from the moment your mother asked me to be your sire." Yorrith stepped closer, and this time, Erissa did not move away. He slowly reached for her hand, and his pained expression relaxed when she allowed him to take it. "I went to the ends of Kaidreth trying to find you. Even when I thought you were dead, I didn't stop trying to find where your mother laid you to rest."

Tears gathered in Erissa's lashes and overflowed. Her hold on her father's hand tightened. "Why would my mother keep us apart?"

Yorrith shrugged. "That I don't understand any more than you do."

Rhazien's arms squeezed her, and Erissa jumped, having forgotten he was there. His breath stirred the hair around her ear as he spoke. "We need to return to Emberhold and confront your mother."

"I can't go back there." Erissa pressed her fingers into her chest, digging for the rigged lines she forgot were no longer there as panic slammed into her. But all that remained were flat, discolored scars and the memories of how she earned each one. "Not even for this."

"We would protect you, child." Nephinae watched the movement of Erissa's hand, seeing more than Erissa wanted to reveal to the Fae she barely knew. "No one can stand against the Fae King, the Zorathi, and a Fefnirion. You will be safe in whatever would come of it. We would not leave you."

"They're her parents, Nephinae. Of course, she is safe with them." Yorrith scoffed. "They might be angry she ran away, but that will subside when she returns and confronts them."

Nephinae pushed at his shoulder. "You remain unable to see what is in front of you, Seelie."

Erissa hunched her shoulders, wrapping her arms across her waist. "I can't."

"Remember Wilidon and Selsula, little doe. You are made of sterner stuff than you give yourself credit for." Rhazien took her hand, tightening his hold when she tried to pull away from him, her lip curled in disgust. "I would fight to the death for your freedom. It wouldn't be the first time and might not be the last, but you will never walk through those gates and be alone again."

He spread his fingers against her, fusing their hands and warming something inside her.

Rhazien tried again. "You will never find answers unless you return."

Erissa looked at Barrett, silently begging him to be the voice of reason. But he only nodded, a smile lightening his eyes and making him appear younger. "Things will be different this time, my star. Rhazien's father made sure of it when he broke part of the bond with a voided blade. I will protect you."

Erissa's face turned to stone.

Yorrith looked between all of them, concern, tightening his features. "What protection would she need against her own parents?"

"Not everyone is kind in this world, Seelie." Nephinae glared at Rhazien's hand. She reached for Erissa's other one, drawing it into her own and tugging on her arm until Rhazien reluctantly let her go. The Zorathi pulled her away from the men and toward the fire left for the horses.

Erissa's gratitude for the Zorathi grew as she steered her out of their hearing. She needed a moment to gather herself. Already, she felt the fear and panic that plagued her the night of her wedding feast in Cropari.

As they approached the animals, the fire nearest them provided more warmth than it should have for how low it burned. Rhazien must have added his dragon's fire to the flames, keeping it fed so the horses would not grow too cold through the night.

Erissa stood before it, the hood of her cloak pushed back as snow fell. It never reached the ground, the fire's warmth dissolving it overhead. She wanted to snuff it out and scream at its remains. But she did nothing of the sort. She turned into its warmth and allowed the flickering light to burn the ends of her memories.

She appreciated how Nephinae stood beside her without talking. Her chest ached where she had rubbed it, but the sting faded as time allowed her breath to fall even.

When her heavy breathing stilled, Nephinae faced her. "There is more to your reasons for running than the prophecy and those who chase you."

"It isn't something I will speak of." Erissa wished the snow would land on her heated cheeks. Maybe then, the memories would fade.

"And what of your mate? Do you wish to speak of him?"

The Zorathi's question came out of nowhere. "Why do you want to talk about Rhazien?"

"To know where you stand." Nephinae sat by the fire's edge and patted the spot next to her. "You are not required to accept the bond."

"Rhazien's the only one who's real. The rest of the world? It might as well be behind the Veil for all the good it's done me." Erissa dug her boot into the ground, wishing to dislodge the worst of her memories as easily as the dirt. "Everyone has entered my life like a dream, and most of them lingered like nightmares, and now, I have a new father to contend with when the last one caused nothing but harm."

Nephinae turned from her, staring into the flames. "And this boy, is he a dream or a nightmare?"

"Neither." Erissa shrugged, a small smile lighting up her face. "He is the sun, rising each day and banishing the shadows of the night before."

"Do you love him?" The words came with a hint of mockery as Nephinae turned to regard her.

Erissa stood and moved closer to the fire's warmth. "Yes, I do."

"Does it matter?" Nephinae questioned. "Knowing there is a magical bond between you?"

"I thought it did." Erissa gathered her cloak tighter about her frame. "And I was wrong. Rhazien has shown me who he is, and I love him for it, not for the bond."

"Bonds are a precious gift. To be blessed before the gods is not to be taken lightly." Nephinae's voice became bleak. "It's a blessing fewer see with each passing year. And one some of us have been foolish enough to reject."

"The gods have been absent from my life for a long time." Erissa's voice turned as brittle as the night air. "Why should I care about their blessings? What matters is I love Rhazien for his heart and character. He has loved me unconditionally, and I would always choose him, bond or no bond. The gods and their blessing mean nothing."

Nephinae moved to stand beside her and warmed her hands by the flames. "There are worse things the gods have allowed to happen than giving you a mate, especially one you love this much."

Erissa fixed Nephinae with an unfriendly stare. "The gods have given me nothing but a life of pain, no matter how many hours I spent on my knees. But, apparently, I was praying for the wrong things. I should have been praying for a different father. That prayer, they would have answered."

"Prayers are not always answered with affirmation." Nephinae pulled her hand back and turned it over to trace the design woven into the flesh. "There are worse things the gods can do than make you wait for the dragon and the Seelie. Be glad they ignored your prayers instead of giving you a life that hated you."

"Who says they didn't give me a life that hated me?" Erissa gathered her sleeve in her hand, pulling the fabric back to expose the scarring on her wrists. "You know nothing of what life has given me."

"I know the gods protected you from life as much as they denied you a place within it."

Erissa winced. "And I bear every mark of that protection."

Nephinae reached for Erissa's hand. When she made no protest against her taking it, Nephinae held Erissa's fingers against the grooves of the markings in the Zorathi's skin and traced them along the indentations, letting her feel the way her skin had been tunneled through to make them. "We all bear the marks of gods. You have been given something few can claim. More than you can even realize at this moment. Don't be so foolish as to throw any of it away because of your doubts."

Erissa stared at Nephinae in confusion. "I'm not throwing away anything. I choose Rhazien."

Nephinae watched her carefully. "And if he were not the only choice?"

"I thought you brought me over here to talk about Yorrith, not question me about my husband." Erissa pulled her hand free and stood, intending to retire to her tent, and tossed the words over her shoulder. "I would still choose Rhazien."

"Do not be so sure of that." Nephinae stood, walking away from the camp, her cryptic words lying between them.

What the Zorathi said made no sense. Erissa's choice was made, and she would not take it back. Rhazien was her mate, the one she chose. Erissa walked back to the tent and entered it, crawling beneath the pile of furs.

Yorrith's revelation dominated her thoughts. She had a father. One who said he wanted her, and her mother and Faldeyr had kept her from him. Maybe Rhazien was right. Maybe she needed to go back to Emberhold. No one here held any answers, and Erissa wanted to know why. It would not change anything. She held no love for her parents and no desire to ever see them again, but she had to know what she was, who she was, and she would only get those answers if she returned.

As she lay there waiting for Rhazien, Erissa wished Reeva would appear so she could talk to her about Yorrith. She had grown used to her presence on nights like these when her world stopped making sense.

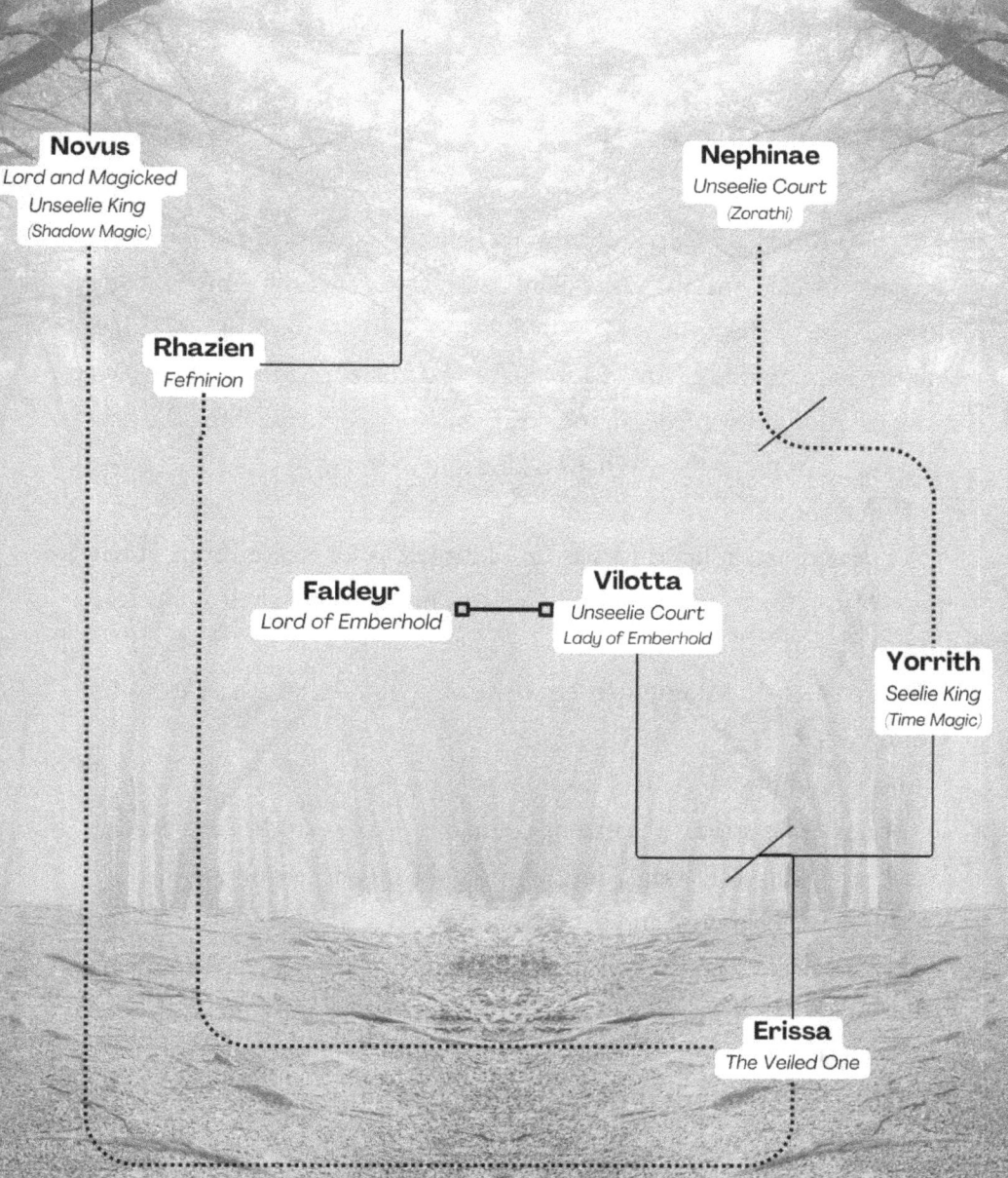

CHAPTER SIXTY-FIVE

Erissa tossed and turned for hours beneath the furs, finding no rest on the cold ground as the wind barreled through the camp and cut through the fabric of the tent walls. She missed Rhazien's heat beside her and the sound of his steady breathing, but he still tended the horses.

As the moon rose higher in the sky, Erissa considered grabbing the furs and going out to the fire. "What's taking him so long?"

"Who? Your dragon?"

A scream froze in her throat as Erissa turned to see Reeva sitting at her side. "Must you keep doing that? Can you not enter through a doorway instead?"

Reeva laughed, folding her legs beneath her. "There is no fun to be found in that."

Erissa scrambled onto her knees. "Where have you been?"

"I can hardly appear in present company." Reeva studied her hands, avoiding looking at Erissa. "The Zorathi and I are not on good terms."

"You know Nephinae and the others?"

Surprise raised Erissa's voice, and Reeva hushed her with a frantic wave of her hands. "Lower your words. The Fae have impeccable hearing. If they were to hear me over the wind's howling..."

Erissa tipped her head to the side, studying the Fae. Her eyes were wide with fear, her chest heaving with it as well. "You're afraid of them knowing you're here."

Reeva made a small noise, clearing her throat. She lowered her hands into her lap. "They cannot know."

"And you're here for a reason." Again, Erissa did not ask it as a question.

"My bond has kept me away until now." Reeva flicked her eyes to Erissa's but quickly lowered them again. "There is something I need to show you."

Unease raised the hair on the back of Erissa's neck. Reeva did not act like herself this night. "What is it?"

"I cannot tell you." Reeva's voice came out as a strangled whisper, like the words were pulled from somewhere deep inside her. Somewhere where they wished to remain. "I must show you. It is beyond the clearing behind the horses where the river is."

Erissa hesitated, something warning her away from Reeva's request.

The Fae answered her fears as if following her line of thinking. "Please..."

But what she pleaded for, Reeva never said. She stopped talking, and Erissa thought she might cry if she were still alive to shed tears. She heard herself answering those tears before she second-guessed herself. "All right. Show me the way."

Reeva became more tense. She nodded with a solemnness that chilled Erissa deeper than the evening's weather. "Follow me."

The Fae disappeared through the back of the tent, and Erissa followed, lifting the flap of fabric and slipping underneath its wall. Reeva waited for her on the other side. She made her way across the frost-covered ground, past the horses, and down to the river's edge, Erissa close behind her.

Erissa hugged her waist, more from worry than protection from the cold. "Reeva, why are we here?"

The Fae collapsed to the ground, kneeling at the water's edge. She turned her head, speaking over her shoulder as dry sobs shuddered through her thin frame. "I am sorry, child."

Something rustled behind Erissa. She turned around, tilting her head up to stare at what caused the noise, and her blood ran cold.

CHAPTER SIXTY-SIX

The fire burned hot, a pot of stone soup simmering by the time the camp came alive the next morning. Rhazien poured the soup into bowls, offering one to Nephinae and Yorrith as they came from their tents.

Barrett arrived last, his eyes flicking to the tent behind Rhazien. "I thought you were retiring after taking care of the horses?"

Rhazien grunted, handing him a steaming bowl. "One of the horses came up lame. It took hours to save the leg, and I ended up falling asleep against a tree as I watched her for a while to make sure an infection didn't set. She should be fine after some rest, but no one will be riding her."

"I'm surprised Erissa didn't sleep next to you." Barrett rubbed a hand down his face, wiping the sleep from it. "Is she still in the tent?"

Rhazien ladled a bowl for himself. "She's still sleeping. When I checked on her last night, she was speaking with someone, so I gave her privacy."

Yorrith and Nephinae exchanged worried looks. The king leaned forward. "None of us talked to her after she retired."

Rhazien took a handful of snow and used it to clean the bowl as he weighed how much he should reveal. He sighed. "There is a soul that comes to Erissa. Her name is R—"

"Reeva." Yorrith and Nephinae stood as they answered in unison.

The King grabbed onto Nephinae's arms hard enough to rip the fabric of her sleeves. Panic made his voice shake. "If she's come for the girl while we are with her, then..."

"Virion has her." Malice overtook Nephinae's voice, and the power of her magic built along the tunnels of scars. The sunlight dimmed as she drew from its source. "We have been betrayed. It is the only way she could have bypassed the protection spells."

Rhazien and Barrett stood. Erissa's uncle ran for the tent, but Rhazien's feet remained rooted in place, fear making his knees weak. "What are you talking about?"

"How long has Reeva been appearing to the girl?" Nephinae's gravelly voice echoed with magic.

"Since the night we left Emberhold," Rhazien swore. "She said she had other motives—someone else controlling her actions. Is Virion the one who holds her in Keeping?"

Barrett ran back to the fire, his face bled of all color. "She's gone."

Nephinae shook off the King's hold. "No, it is worse than that. Draven holds her Keeping, and it is he who plots against you. If he has lured the girl to him, we are out of time. He will open the portal soon."

"Zorathi... Nephinae... By the gods." Tears clogged Yorrith's throat as he reached for her. "I can't lose her again. We have to get there in time. She is all I have."

This time, Nephinae turned into his touch. She lifted a hand to cup his cheek, her voice soft but full of steel. "I will bring her back, Yorrith. I will bring your daughter home."

Imryll emerged from her tent alone, and all eyes snapped to her as she called out a greeting.

Nephinae growled low in her throat, the power pulsing along her scars. "Where is Kyrenic?"

The other Zorathi looked at Nephinae in confusion. "With our Lord, remember?"

THE DAUGHTER OF THE VEIL

Nephinae moved with astonishing speed. She flung her arm toward the Fae, and the light of her magic cracked like a whip, wrapping around Imryll's neck. It yanked her to the ground and dragged her until she rested at her maker's feet. "Do not lie to me."

Imryll clawed at the magic. Her nails broke against it, leaving them ragged and bleeding as she struggled to breathe. Nephinae lessened the lightning grip enough to allow her room to speak. "I'm not lying. Kyrenic came back to the tent last night and said he had been summoned. He left shortly after and hasn't returned."

If Nephinae believed her, she did not say. She bound Imryll in thick chains made of the white light and shoved her into Barrett's arms. "Tie her to a tree. And be quick about it. The strands are cool to the touch, and she cannot break her maker's magic. Our time is running out."

The old soldier did as commanded, shoving the other Zorathi toward the closest tree.

Panic called at Rhazien's chest. "Why would Kyrenic take Erissa? How would he know Reeva?"

"You stupid boy." Nephinae rounded on him, magic dancing across her eyes like lightning. "One bound to the Keeping can never be trusted. They have no free will and will always bend to the desires of their oath tender."

"There is no time for blame." Yorrith wiped at the tears running down his cheeks. He cleared his throat and swallowed his grief. "We must leave for the Veil. If we do not hurry..."

The King turned a sickly color, and Rhazien's panic became a living being as it tried to dig itself from beneath his breast. "They will kill her, won't they?"

The clearing fell silent.

"Do you know where they've taken her?" Rhazien dropped the shield around his power and called forth his scales. A great span of fiery wings erupted from his back, bathing the clearing in their bright heat.

Nephinae reigned in her magic as Rhazien's form changed before them. "To the Temple of Souls. It guards the entrance to the Veil, and it is where they will use Erissa to open the portal."

"Tomorrow is the full moon." Ragged breaths punctured Yorrith's words. "They will bleed her before we can get there."

"Then we have no time to lose." Great curls of smoke left Rhazien's mouth with each word he uttered, his voice deepening into a raspy growl. Golden light glittered along the edges of the red scales as his limbs morphed to accommodate their size until his dragon form stood taller than the trees. His voice rattled down to their thick roots as the entire camp quaked at the rumble of his words. "I will get us there by sundown tomorrow or so help me—the gods will feel my wrath."

CHAPTER SIXTY-SEVEN

The weight of something sharp and frigid wrapped around Erissa's wrists.

Cold slithered into her heart, and Erissa's deepest fear took root. The sensation pulled her from slumber and into a waking hell as her eyes sprang open. Erissa tried to move in the suffocating darkness as something from its depths bit into her skin. Resistance met her every attempt to stand as heavy weights anchored her tired limbs.

Sweat beaded along her upper lip. Only one thing bound its victim with such passion. Terror snaked its way down Erissa's spine, a keening, broken noise leaving her as her eyes adjusted to the darkness and she looked down.

Shackles circled her wrists, connected to a thick link of chain bolted to the floor. It allowed little movement as she pulled against its weight. The blue metal burned against her skin with a cold sensation that rivaled winter's kiss. A faint glow came from the cuffs and chain.

She held her breath, shaking her head violently until her ears rang as she sought to wake herself up. It had to be a dream. No, not a dream. A nightmare. One that followed her even as she forced her eyes wide open to make sure she did not still slumber behind their closed lids.

Erissa flinched as salt touched her tongue through her parted lips. Did the tears come only now, or did they trace down her cheeks in jagged lines long before she opened her eyes? Either way, the salt stung against her cracked and bleeding mouth where the blow that knocked her out had landed.

Her tongue traced the outline of a large lump from the inside of her cheek. She swept her tongue across her teeth and slouched against the chains as she glided its tip against each one, checking for any that were cracked or missing. She breathed a sigh of relief at finding them all intact. But no such relief existed for her memories.

Try as she might, Erissa remembered nothing beyond Reeva's appearance in her tent. But someone had struck her. That much she knew from the familiar throb in the swelling her tongue prodded, though she held no knowledge of who perpetrated the violence.

She stared around the room, straining to see anything beyond where the faint glow from a single torch lightened the surrounding shadows. Her heartbeat picked up its tempo, the sweat along her brow returning, for she knew with certainty that wherever she lay bound, it was not within the walls of Emberhold. The stone keep boasted nothing like the cold marble floor beneath her. She tugged on the chains, trying to cast the blue light into the darkness. Maybe if its light reached beyond the torch, she might find something that would give away her location.

"Ah, you're awake."

Erissa stilled as a male voice floated from the shadows. When she answered, her voice sounded shrill and loud to her ears. "Who's there?"

She peered into the darkness, and the harder she looked, the more it seemed like something lurked in its depth. Footsteps cracked across the marble floor as whoever spoke moved closer.

Erissa pulled against the chains with futile effort. "Stay away from me."

"I'm afraid I can't do that." The footsteps moved closer until a male Fae walked into the weak light of the torch. "After all, I have gone to astonishing lengths to bring you here."

The Fae's voice slid off the tongue like rancid oil. For all the male appeared handsome, his lips held a cruelty that did little to soften his harsh hazel eyes. Long black hair tucked behind his ears highlighted the lean angles of his high cheekbones and the high slants of his ears.

Erissa studied him. Something remained familiar about the Fae's features. "Do I know you?"

"No, but you should. After all, I have been sending my men after you for nearly a month now." The Fae moved closer, crouching in front of her. He ran a finger along the blue links of the chain. "But I know you, Erissa Nierling."

The sound of her name curdling across his tongue killed her remaining curiosity. She moved as far away as the chain allowed. "Virion." Erissa shuddered as he gave a slight, condescending nod. "What do you want from me?"

"To bleed you." He said the words like he was requesting dinner from a maid with a bored tone that dismissed the gravity of their implication.

Erissa's face blanched under his stare. "You mean to kill me?"

"Oh, no, darling. Killing you would do nothing for my plans. I will bleed you, but I will not kill you." The Fae laughed as his demeanor continued to be at odds with the violence he threatened upon her. "Why would I seek to kill my flesh and blood—my very own niece—when she can be of greater use to my plans?"

One word echoed in Erissa's mind, and she forgot about the threat of danger as it lingered before everything else the Fae said. "Niece? I'm not your niece."

"Oh, but you are, Erissa darling."

It hit her then why the Fae looked so familiar. The dark hair, the high cheekbones, and the disdainful tip to his nose were all attributes Erissa's mother carried. "You're Vilotta's brother."

"Very clever." Virion leaned forward. He reached out a hand, taking a strand of her hair between his fingers and rubbing the soft tresses. He smiled. "Once your blood brings my father back into this world, I will make you mine. We will bend all of Kaidreth at the knee with your power."

Erissa gave a choked laugh, eyes narrowing and anger racing through her cheeks. "You're insane. I will never marry you. I'm married to my mate, and he will come for me."

Virion's smile widened with victory as Erissa's breath caught, and he tugged on the strand of hair. "I care not for this mate of yours. He will assume you have run away. After all, is that not what you do when things are too much for you? You ran from Emberhold. You ran to Cropari and again to Gailme. Now, you will have run from your husband."

"He will never think that. Rhazien will come for me." Erissa tried to raise her arm to slap the Fae's hand from her hair, but the chains held firm, allowing no room for her to raise her arm that high. The force of her actions did nothing more than throw her off balance and into the arms of her uncle.

Virion's hand gripped more of her hair, pulling her head back until she leaned against him, trapped by his arm as it snaked around her shoulders. "You are a pretty thing. It will be no hardship to stake my claim."

"I'm your niece." Erissa shuddered as his gaze dropped to her lips. It lingered there before lowering to her breasts, and she wished she had thought to grab her cloak before following Reeva. At least its layers would offer some sort of protection from his lecherousness.

"And?" Virion lifted a brow. "What does our relation have to do with anything?"

"You're sick." Erissa fought against his hold.

"I'm practical. We can unseal Draven from the Veil with your power and overthrow his reign before he even suspects a thing. He is all that stops me from claiming the Unseelie throne. It will never be mine until he draws his last breath. That is how the magic works. You will help me kill him." Virion raised his other hand and traced his finger down Erissa's cheek. "And when my father rots in the ground like he deserves, you will help build my dynasty. I will be unstoppable with your power adding to my own."

Erissa jerked her head away from his touch. He reached for her again, and she turned her head at the last minute, biting into his flesh between his thumb and finger with as much force as possible, holding tight even as he tried to shake his hand from her mouth. She buried her teeth until she tasted blood, refusing to let go. The metallic taste of copper spread across her tongue. The Fae screamed, shoving her with all his might.

She fell back onto the floor with a loud thump that echoed throughout the room, a chunk of flesh clenched between her teeth. She glared at him with wild eyes. Erissa ignored the pain blooming in her hip where it slammed into the floor and spit the mangled, torn tissue on the pristine marble at his feet, where it landed with a splat. Blood and spit dribbled down her chin, tracing a cold, wet path. Loathing sat thick in her throat as she used her sleeve to wipe away the mess. "I will kill myself before I let you touch me again."

Virion swore, rising to his feet. "You had best be glad you are of more use to me alive, girl. Few have shown me such disrespect and lived."

"You will never get the chance to do anything to me." Erissa moved to a crouch, ready to defend herself again if necessary. She cocked her head to the side, half-mad from fear and driven by anger at herself for the way her voice wobbled. "For my mate comes for me, and when he does, nothing will stop me from ripping out your soul."

"If he comes, I will kill him too." Virion turned on his heel, pulling a handkerchief from a pocket and pressing it to the bleeding wound. The dark swallowed his form as he headed for the door, his footsteps the only sound breaking up Erissa's ragged breathing.

Her shoulders dropped at the slamming of a door, the footsteps sounding further and further away.

"I am sorry for tricking you."

Erissa whipped her head to the side, finding Reeva standing next to her. She should have been surprised, but only anger remained churning in the pit of her stomach. Acid coated the back of her tongue, mixing with the metallic blood, and Erissa breathed heavily through her nose to try and dispel the rancid taste. It did nothing to displace it.

Reeva cleared her throat when Erissa did not respond. "Are you well, child?"

"Am I well?" Erissa laughed, the sound turning into a sob as the taste lingered. It brought with it the promise of violence, the promise of more days spent bent beneath the will of a violent man, and something inside Erissa snapped. Her shoulders heaved with her tears, and all the anger left her as despair smothered her heart. "There's no point in fighting anymore."

"Come, child." Reeva lowered herself to her knees and sat back on her heels. Pity softened her tired face. "Do not let your heart falter."

"Why not?" Erissa's voice raised as she cried harder. She rubbed at her nose, sure that she looked a fright with snot mixing with the blood smeared across her chin. "My heart has seen more than its share of pain, Reeva. First, my parents and uncle, now it's you." Her voice lowered in a sound scarcely above a whisper. "You betrayed me, and I don't know if I'm stupid for believing you never would or stupid for following you when I knew something was wrong."

Reeva's gaze dropped to Erissa's hands where they pulled against the chains. "I betrayed you against my will, and I will stop at nothing to see it made right."

"Virion will bleed me before that time ever comes." Erissa tucked her knees to her chest and placed her head into the grimy fabric of her skirts. It seemed like hours passed as her tears dried. Reeva said nothing, giving Erissa her grief. "I will let him, Reeva. I will do nothing, and that madman will spill my blood. It's useless to believe that anything else will happen. Rhazien has no hope of knowing where I am or getting to me in time. He will burn this world looking for me and never know what happened. The Creator's plan has made itself known, and I've grown tired of fighting."

"So you will give up and sulk to your death?" Disappointment replaced Reeva's pity, and the Fae spirit's eyes glistened with the ghost of tears she would never again shed.

"I'm not giving up, Reeva. I'm accepting what I should have the first time my father locked me in chains." Erissa uncurled her arms from her legs. The chains clanked as she shook her wrists in front of Reeva's face. "Metal is my past, present, and future. It is my gift as surely as death is."

"You speak of nonsense, child." Reeva moved to sit back on her heels and leaned into Erissa's face. "What happened to the girl that ripped the flesh from Virion's hand? Even bound in mistdrite chains with their magic dampening your own, you fought without the aid of your magic and took a piece of him with you."

Erissa laughed, the sound morphing into a broken cry as she choked down her tears. "She remembered the pain that binds her. The cool kiss of metal against my skin is the only thing I've been able to rely on for most of my life. I will welcome its bite in death. At least its pain will be familiar to me, and I will not die alone."

"You will give up? After everything you have found?"

Erissa shook her head. "None of that matters now."

"It does matter, child." Reeva's hands twitched where they lay against the tops of her thighs. She gripped them hard enough that bruises would form if she were still alive. "It has to matter."

"Why? Every single one of you has lied to me from the very beginning. And now Virion—*the man claiming to be my uncle*—desires to force his bastards on me." Erissa gagged and swore the taste of his blood thickened in the back of her mouth. "I would rather die, Reeva."

Reeva's eyes rose into her hairline, shock wiping the plea from her face. "Virion wants to do *what*?"

Erissa became lost. Her deepest fears took root, growing until she was forced to give a voice to them, a voice she had always denied. "Do you know what it's like, Reeva? To spend your childhood waiting for your parent to cross that last line? My father beat me. Starved me. Isolated me until I thought I would grow mad from being lost in the silence of my own company day after day, week after week. He chained me to the gods' damn wall.

"Every night, I awoke with him stripping the clothes from my body. He would stand there, staring at me, his horsewhip dangling by his side." She wanted to cry, to vent the pain that left her panicked in Cropari when Selsula tried to hand her the fertility blanket. For what hope of being a parent did she have with her grim childhood? "There is no safety for a woman—*a child*—as they lie chained to the floor, naked, as their father stares at them. The thought of how far he would go haunted me. Did he stare at the fresh wounds? The thick scaring? At what my nakedness revealed beneath them? I waited every night for the day when he would drop the whip and reach for the buckle of his pants instead."

Reeva's hands twitched again, and she swore.

The foul words brought a hesitant smile to Erissa's lips. No one had sworn on her behalf in those moments, and she found it strange to hear it now. "I don't think it even matters that it never happened. Not when his eyes still haunt me." Erissa shivered. "Nephinae told me there were worse things the gods could give me rather than their inattentiveness, and she was right. My father might not have touched me, but Virion has no such control. He wants me willingly, but it won't matter in the end. By sundown tomorrow, he will bleed me, rape me, and imprison me with his child as my new chain. It will be a death born of a living hell—if the bleeding doesn't kill me first."

"Erissa—"

But she cut the Fae off. "Please, Reeva, my soul has grown tired, and I want nothing more than a moment of peace today." Erissa lay down against the hard floor, curling in on herself as she tried to keep the chains from brushing against the rest of her skin. "Please, let me have this peace before it all ends tomorrow."

And so that was what Reeva gave her. The Fae sat beside her long after the night had faded into the next morning, singing her songs long forgotten to the world of humans.

Exhaustion claimed Erissa as the first rays of sun peaked through the iron bars of a window on the far side of the room. But Erissa did not care to look at her surroundings. Her heart lay weary, and she let sleep claim her fears as surely as Virion would claim her life.

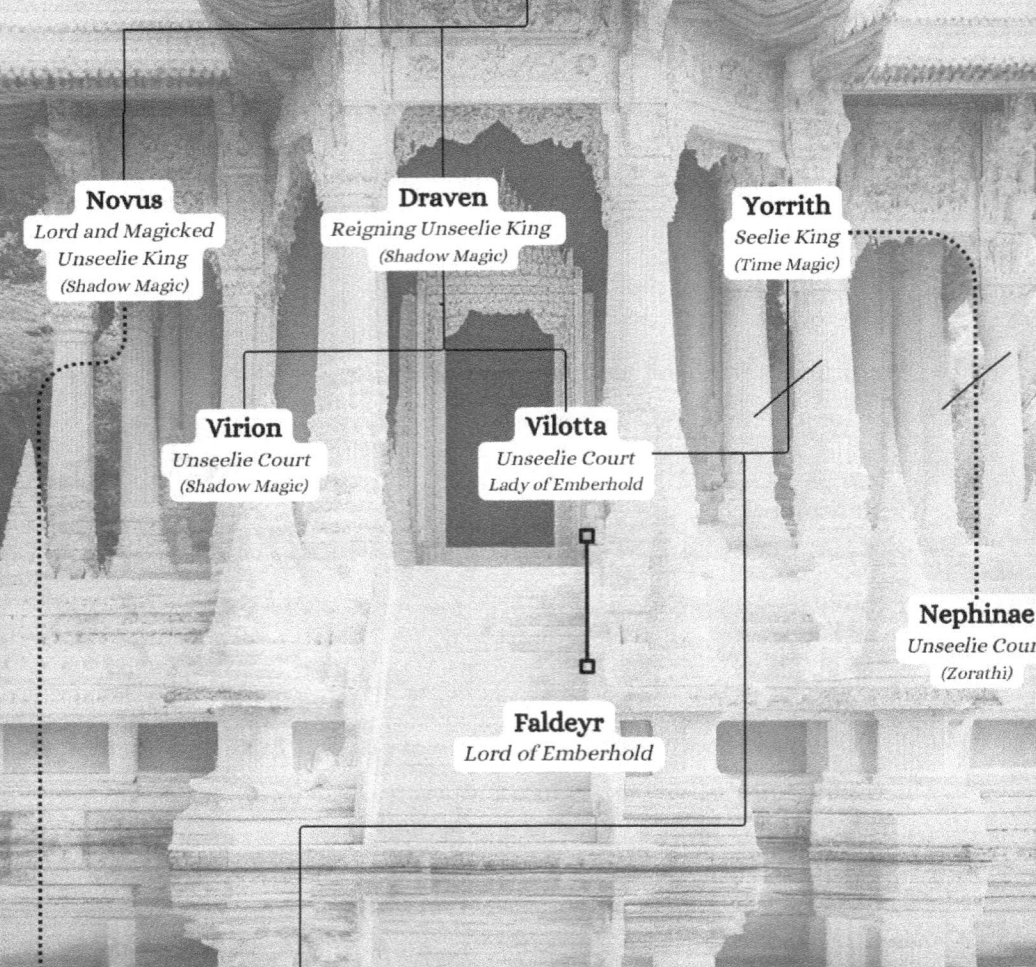

CHAPTER SIXTY-EIGHT

A battered heart and an empty stomach were the only things that greeted Erissa when she awoke. The waning afternoon light filtered into the room. It cast a glare off the white marble floors and illuminated an empty chamber that had seen better days despite its opulence.

Warm air flowed in through the open window. It ruffled Erissa's hair as the breeze stirred against her face, a stark contrast to the cold of winter she left behind in the woods and the chill in the air last night. That meant she had to be somewhere north of the Wilds or the desert lands, but where? And did it even matter at this point? She would never leave this place unchained. Whether dead at Virion's hand or imprisoned by it, her future began and ended in this room.

Erissa stirred against the floor, adjusting the heavy weight of the chain. The minutes dragged by as the sun shifted its position in the sky. With each passing hour, she grew more despondent.

She missed Reeva, the voice of her magic, Rhazien, and the new relationship she was building with Barrett. She even missed the Seelie King with his stories and the eerily beautiful Zorathi with her sharp tongue. Erissa had grown used to their company as they traveled. What she would not give to hear one of them in the oppressive silence.

As the sun finally set, the tears left with it, and Erissa shifted until she sat on her heels with her knees pressed to the marble. She resolved herself to what came next and waited patiently for the footsteps she knew would soon echo toward her prison.

She did not have to wait long. Confident steps clipped across the hard floor, each one mirroring the fast beat of her heart until they stopped before the chamber's door.

Erissa stood as the doorknob rattled, staggering under the weight of the chains. But she did not give up, refusing to meet the one who came for her on her knees.

Her stomach dipped as Virion approached her.

An eager grin greeted her as he strode into the room. He snapped his fingers, and the chains creaked as they unlocked themselves at the magical command and transferred to his outstretched hand. "The time has come. Let us not delay. The moon is almost at its peak."

Erissa's lack of response did not seem to matter as Virion turned on his heel and all but ran from the room in his excitement, dragging her along so that she struggled not to stumble with every weighted step.

The Fae led her further into the cold stone building. He guided Erissa through a maze of rooms until they reached a long, cavernous room that led to a wide, open doorway outlined by the ghostly light of the Veil. Fae soldiers lined the walls of the chamber; their masked faces shadowed and indistinguishable from one another. They stood at attention with weapons poised.

Erissa's blood froze. Her guess had not been off at all. The Temple of Souls sat north of the Wilds, guarding the entrance to the Veil. Its name haunted children's stories, telling of vraiths that came from its depths to steal away children who left their beds at night. It had once held a guardian—the God of Time—but he had long been dead, with no one to take his place.

"It's a stunning sight, is it not?" Virion bounced on his heels like a small child. He pulled out a small knife. "We will use your blood to open a portal into its depths. Draven is waiting on the other side."

Fire crept its way into Erissa's heart at the ghostly wall before her, igniting something she thought lay dormant. "I will not dig my own grave for you." Victims had graves, and Erissa would no longer be a willing victim. She was tired of digging, tired of dirt staining her nails. Their tips, once whole, lay cracked and bleeding. She would not give in easily to the deranged Fae in front of her. She would put down the dirt and reach for a thorn.

Virion snatched her wrist, pressing the knife's handle into her palm. "The Veil requires a willing sacrifice. It is the price of the magic and one you will pay, grave or no grave."

Erissa fought him, twisting like a woman possessed. "I will not pay it."

"Then I will hand you to the Keeper, girl." Virion shook her, snapping her head back with the force of his motion.

But Erissa did not give in. She punched and kicked, fighting against the resistance of the chains binding her, refusing to give in to the insistent pressure of the knife's handle. "The Keeper will not haunt me. I would rather play whore to him and his vraiths than you who stand before me."

A slap rang in the air, and Erissa's head twisted from the blow that landed across her face. Virion loomed over her. He held her palm in one hand, pressing the knife into the skin with the other until blood welled at its pressure. "You will behave and do as I ask, or the consequences will be dire."

Erissa laughed, the sound wild and unhinged against panicked eyes. "And what more can you do to me that you have not already threatened by making me yours against my will?"

"Oh, I will make you suffer. That is a surety." Virion dug the blade in deeper, leering as Erissa winced. "But you are not the one who will pay the price." He turned Erissa, making her face the Veil, and something seized inside of her at the sight of Reeva flanked by two vraiths.

Their rotten, shredded forms hovered behind the ghastly green barrier, their long claws holding Reeva by the arms. Her flesh lay torn where the hold cut into her skin, the wounds bloodless.

Erissa flinched as Virion's breath puffed against the side of her face. "She will pay the price. She is untouchable in the land of the living but as vulnerable as any within the Veil. More so since she will never pass into the next life." Virion's lips brushed against Erissa's ear, and she jerked in his hold, trying to break from his grip. The Fae held firm, a chuckle in his voice. "Can you stand it? Being the one who dooms her to an eternity of pain and suffering beyond what she has already endured at the hands of the madman who holds her binding?"

Erissa stared at Reeva. The Fae said nothing. She stood with her head raised high, sorrow and remorse wrinkling her features. Her lips pressed together until they formed a white line. Yes, Reeva betrayed her, but she warned her all this time that it would come to this. She even tried to tell her the truth about Rhazien before Erissa cut her off. But Erissa saw herself mirrored in Reeva, both left without a choice and chained to the desires of another.

"And if I take the knife?" Erissa did not pretend there was a decision to be made. "What will happen to her then?"

"She will still suffer. She is bound to Draven, after all." Virion loosened his hold. "And she was quite the naughty thing when she revealed herself to your lover."

Erissa jerked her head to stare at him. "What will happen to her?"

"I cannot say, but I know it will not be as worse as what it can be." Virion shrugged. "The touch of the vraiths is excruciating, to say nothing of Draven's desires."

"I want a Fae bargain that binds any of the vraiths from harming her." Erissa shuddered as she placed her hand over Virion's where it held the knife. She pulled it from his sweaty palm. "If I cut myself... if I give my blood to the Veil willingly... none can touch her."

Reeva's lips fought to open, the grips of the vraiths tightening. Erissa's heart hardened at what her words meant.

"A bargain is struck." Virion pressed his thumb into the tip of the knife until a drop of blood welled against the tip. He brought his hand to Erissa's mouth, spread the blood across her lips, and gestured for Erissa to repeat the gesture.

Her hand shook as she did, and when she smeared her own blood against Virion's lips, magic danced across the surface of her own.

Reeva sagged between the vraiths.

Virion pushed Erissa until she stood in front of the Veil. One of the Fae soldiers met them there with a tray holding candles, bones, and several jars of black sand. Virion reached for the items and placed the candles and bones in a circle around them. He took the sand next, sprinkling it across the floor in an intricate pattern of runes.

With everything set, the soldier backed away, and Virion turned to Erissa. "You must trace the runes with your blood."

Erissa blanched as she breathed deeply and drew the knife across her wrist. Blood welled at the pressure, and she grit her teeth against the pain.

"Cover the sand completely." Virion stepped out of the circle.

Erissa did as instructed, being careful to keep the blood from spilling over the sides of the runes. Her stomach churned as the metallic smell turned sour, as it sizzled when it mixed with the sand. A cloudy green light appeared at the edge of the circle closest to the Veil, its depths growing the more blood Erissa dropped onto the runes. The bones rose from their positions, creating the circular opening of a portal.

When she finally connected the lines of blood-soaked sand, her shoulders dropped, and she turned to look at Virion.

He had moved to stand on the other side of the room where two chairs and a small table stood. A triumphant smile twisted his mouth to the side, a dimple appearing in the corner. He reached for a decanter of wine and poured himself a glass. "Now, we wait for the spell to—"

A crash cut him off as something slammed into the temple with enough force to shatter the windows and rattle the floor.

Erissa screamed, covering her head with her hands as glass rained down around her. Her head popped up as someone screamed her name.

A hole had been torn into the roof of the temple, and a gigantic red and gold dragon with wings of black-tipped fire poised above the damage. The Seelie King, Zorathi, and her uncle perched on its back.

Erissa stood speechless as she stared at what must be Rhazien's dragon form. Something sparked to life inside of her, blooming into a wildfire that warmed the depths of her soul and burned against the chains. He had come for her. They had all come for her. Erissa smiled, staring up at her saviors with unbridled joy.

Rhazien climbed through the hole he created, his talons digging into the marble for purchase as he climbed down the wall. Yorrith and the others jumped from his back as his feet hit the floor, and Rhazien's form vanished into that of a human once more.

"Erissa!" Rhazien's eyes sought hers, relief feeling them as he found her by the Veil. The look quickly turned to rage, and fire engulfed his form at seeing the blood trailing down her arm.

Rhazien turned for Virion, stalking toward him as his magic grew into a blazing force that touched Erissa with its heat, even from a distance.

Yorrith and Nephinae left him to Virion as they turned to confront the Fae soldiers.

The air crackled with lightning that sped through the air with the aid of time magic. "I thought it was too dangerous to use time magic, Seelie?" Nephinae struck with her lightning, electrifying the Fae who had reached them. They collapsed to the ground, the light continuing to sizzle against their armor as it burned into their skin. Their screams echoed through the chamber.

"Quiet, Zorathi. More are coming." Yorrith turned to look at Erissa over his shoulder before turning back to the soldiers overtaking them. "I will not make the same mistake twice."

Nephinae smiled, and the light of her magic growing. "Then let us stop this before it begins."

They charged the soldiers, and Erissa screamed a warning that went unheeded as the Zorathi tore through the soldiers that threatened the lives of all.

Erissa searched the fray for Barrett. She found him among the Fae. He dodged the fighting, working his way toward Erissa as Rhazien stalked Virion.

Her eyes snapped to her husband as he called out to her. "Little doe, stay there." Rhazien spared her no look as his gaze honed in on his prey. But he did not see the one who snuck from the corner of the room.

Kyrenic moved with the shadows, using them to hide his movements. But his white blonde hair shone like a beacon, and Erissa screamed. "Rhazien, behind you!"

It was enough of a distraction. Rhazien turned at her call, a snarl coming from his dragon soul. Virion used the opportunity to lunge. He knocked Rhazien to his knees as Kyrenic ran forward, his knife raised.

Erissa screamed again, this time in an agonizing cry.

Rhazien grabbed the axe from his belt, bringing it up to parry Kyrenic's blow and knocking the younger Zorathi off balance. Rhazien snapped his eyes to Erissa's. They were filled with a desperate rage as he realized his mistake in leaving himself open to Virion as the Fae unleashed a knife from his belt.

Erissa watched her husband's face harden. He turned to face her and dropped the shield around his magic, pushing his power out toward her. "We've no time. Stop the portal."

Rhazien's power washed over her, freeing her own magic to rise to the surface.

The voice screamed inside her head. *"Hurry. We've no time if we are to save him."*

Erissa knew what he wanted her to do, what choice he was giving her with his power adding to her own. But the choice was never there, not with his life on the line.

Erissa's eyes snapped to the portal. She gave it only a second of consideration before turning her back to the growing green haze of magic.

She would never reach Rhazien in time. Virion held the knife above his heart, ready to plunge it into the depths of Rhazien's chest at any moment. His soul flickered in and out at his side, oddly quiet, as if it waited for whatever decision it knew Erissa would make.

CHAPTER SIXTY-NINE

Death stared back at Rhazien.

His heart slammed into his chest as he waited for the dagger to plunge into it, but he found it impossible to look away from his wife and the mask that had slipped over her features. He did not fear death. He feared losing her in this life and the next, for if the Veil opened and Draven claimed her, their souls would never find one another again.

The Seelie King screamed her name as the portal grew behind her, and he added his magic to the growing chaos as the King moved through the seconds with ease, but he remained in the middle between Erissa and Rhazien, and he would not reach either of them in time.

Erissa's face filled with malice as she locked eyes with Virion, but the Fae only smirked at her with a shake of his head. "It is too late."

Rhazien called out to her between the spaces in time, "The portal, little doe. Stop the portal."

She stepped away from the Veil and the doorway her magic created.

Rhazien tried again, his desperation growing. "Close the portal, Erissa."

"I can't." Her magic's voice blended with her own, and Erissa's eyes grew like fire-lit amethyst stones until the glow swallowed her irises. "I will not lose you, Rhazien. I will damn the world to the Keeper and his plans before I see you die. Our hearts are one. If you die here, I will perish along with you."

Virion laughed, the cackle echoing against the quiet of stilled time. "You will never reach him." The Fae's arm swung.

"I don't need to reach him." Erissa raised her arms, and time bent to her will. It stopped altogether around the rest of the fighting, removing its distraction. The soldiers stopped fighting, frozen in place with Nephinae and Barrett paused mid-fight. Even the Seelie King lay trapped in its hold despite his command over the same magic. Erissa smiled, and something that spoke of madness reflected in her face. "All I need is you."

Magic exploded from Erissa's chest, pulling her soul from her form, a gossamer copy that hovered in front of her as Erissa drew on Rhazien's void to sustain it. It tipped its head to the side, staring at Virion with curious eyes.

Erissa's magic stayed Virion's arm. It remained high in the air, poised over Rhazien's heart. Virion's face twisted into a snarl as he fought the magic's hold. "What blasphemy is this?"

"Isn't this what you wanted? Me at my most vulnerable? That's what you told me after you had me chained to the floor like an animal." The soul pouted as it moved forward with measured steps. "Nothing is more vulnerable than a severed soul, and yet, it will not be my blood that stains any more of the ground this night, nor my mate's."

Virion's lip curled. "I will bleed you until nothing remains."

"You will never get the chance." Erissa laughed, a dark, unearthly sound as magic tainted her voice. "Death is my gift, and it is one I plan to share this night. It is my birthright. One that you have killed to obtain, and I shall give it to you without hesitation."

"Don't do this, Erissa." Rhazien would beg for the bastard Fae's life before he watched Erissa lose a piece of herself with this act. "He isn't worth it."

"But you are." The projected soul met his gaze. "Nothing in this world is more precious to me than you."

Rhazien swallowed the lump of emotion that sat heavy in the back of his throat. None of the past shadowed Erissa's love as the purest part of her merged with her magic and offered the simple truth. Her intent flowed through their bond and would have dropped Rhazien to his knees had magic not held him firmly in place. "Little doe, please..."

Her eyes flicked back to Virion. "He tried to take you from me. He tried to take everything and will keep trying if he lives. I cannot allow it."

Erissa raised her arm again and snapped her fingers once more. Time kept the soldiers frozen, but Virion fell to the ground as she removed the magic from him. He scampered backward on his hands, dragging himself away from the girl. She extended the same courtesy for the family that had come for her with another snap of her fingers.

Rhazien kept his balance against the force of magic in the air, turning to Erissa and taking a step toward her.

Yorrith and Barret swayed against the loss of the magic binding them in place. They ran to Erissa's body. The Seelie King grabbed Barrett from behind as they both made it to her side. "Don't touch her." The King dragged the man away as he fought against the King's hold. "To touch her is death."

"What has she done?" The words came out in a choked sob, and Barrett sagged in the King's arms as Nephinae stepped away from the soldiers who stood frozen by Erissa's time magic.

The Zorathi's chest heaved as she stepped over the frozen soldiers, lightning dancing along the blades of the daggers she held in each hand. Blood covered her pale blue dress and smeared across her skin, her face pale as she regarded Erissa. "She is death."

"Erissa?" Rhazien tried to get through to her again. "Don't do this."

Virion tried to stand, but Erissa's soul moved faster. Within seconds, it stood in front of him, arms outstretched and alight with magic as thorny vines broke through the ground. The sharp thorns dug into Virion's skin and stopped the Fae's retreat. The madness deepened across her face. "You will die now."

Erissa's soul bent at the waist, reaching her hand into Virion's chest. It sank through his clothing and flesh as the Fae howled from pain. Pleasure glittered in the smile Erissa gave him.

Rhazien's blood curdled.

"I told you, I will not dig my grave, and my mate's death would surely be mine as well, for I will never live without him." With those words, Erissa's smile widened, and she jerked her hand back, pulling Virion's soul from his body.

The Fae's body crumpled, the knife clattering to the ground beside it. A faceless blur stood in front of Erissa. She gripped its throat between her fingers. No chanting left its mouth; the lips open in a frozen scream.

"Let him go, child." Nephinae stepped toward her. "Let him find punishment within the afterlife."

"No," Erissa tipped her head to the other side, studying the shivering soul. "He will not know peace." Her grip tightened, choking the soul until it burst into a cloud of gray ash. It fell to the floor in a dusty heap next to its fallen body.

The room sat heavy with the horror of the others as they stared at what Erissa had done. Behind them pulsed the growing portal into the Veil as Reeva fought against the hold of the vraiths.

Erissa turned her death gaze to them, and they screamed, throwing their hands up to cover what remained of their faces.

The vraiths fled from Erissa's gaze, leaving Reeva behind and her lips unsealed with the loss of their touch. "Run. Recall your magic, boy, and run. There's no stopping the portal now, and Draven comes. You must run."

"Listen to her." Yorrith let go of Barrett and moved to pick up Erissa's body. He carried it with infinite care and placed it in Rhazien's arms.

Rhazien stared at the body of his mate. It looked like she did nothing more than sleep, but her soul lingered in the air as it considered its body with the same eerie curiosity. He worried it would be too late, that Erissa was too far gone. Rhazien tightened his arms. "Little doe, it's time to come home."

He pulled his shield around him, drawing his void back into its resting place. As it left Erissa's body, the soul's form grew weaker, more transparent, until nothing remained but a memory of what the young woman had done as she slumbered in his arms. Time moved forward, sound returning to the world around them as the soldiers stirred.

Rhazien passed his wife to the Seelie King and transformed once more into his dragon form. He lowered himself to the ground, allowing the King to climb onto him, and waited for Barrett and Nephinae. The latter had already begun to climb his side when a pained shout came from Barrett.

Rhazien turned his head toward the sound and loosed a great roar that shook the temple.

Kyrenic stood behind Barret, a knife pressed into his throat and another into his belly. "Come and claim him, Fefnirion shite."

"Leave me." Barrett's eyes hardened as he struggled against the blades. He winced as blood welled around the tip of the blade, digging into his throat. "Get her to safety."

Indecision halted the spread of Rhazien's wings. He shook his head, taking a step toward Barrett, and the portal widened, the bones groaning at the force of magic.

"Leave me!" Barrett screamed, shoving against the traitorous Zorathi.

"Kyrenic, I will kill you for this." Spit flew from Nephinae's mouth. She tried to jump from Rhazien's leg, but the Seelie king dragged her onto the dragon's back.

"Go. There's no time." Yorrith wrestled her against Rhazien's scales. "We have to leave before it's too late."

Rhazien spread his wings with reluctance. One of the hip bones making up the portal cracked under the pressure of the growing spell, and he beat his wings against the air, lifting them from the temple floor. As he soared higher in the sky, Barrett became nothing but a pinprick against the expanse of blood-flecked marble, and he prayed Erissa would forgive him for his sins.

CHAPTER SEVENTY

"Rhazien Merrick, you mean to tell me we could have *flown* instead of wading through that gods' forsaken swamp?" Erissa slid from his back along with everyone else, standing in front of her husband's dragon form where it had landed before the gates of Emberhold's keep. She had awoken halfway through their flight from the temple. "Why keep something like this from me?"

"There wasn't a natural way to bring it into the conversation." Rhazien's wings pulsed with a bright, burning light as the deep rumble of his voice shook the stones of Emberhold's keep. "What was I supposed to do, blurt it out mid-kiss and ask if you wanted to ride me?"

"Does not seem you had to ask for such a thing, Fefnirion." Nephinae wiggled her eyebrows at the pair. "We know well enough how often your bride rides you."

"Nephinae, watch your tongue." The King stared at her in shock, his hands fisted at his side. "Must you be so crude?"

"Why, Seelie?" Nephinae gave him a playful smile. Her lips quirked at the corners, and her eyes were bright with humor. "Are you not the one who complained the other night about the thinness of the tent fabric?"

Rhazien's smokey laugh wrapped around Erissa as she turned scarlet, wishing the ground would open where it quaked and swallow her whole. She ignored the quip, flipping her hair over her shoulder, and spoke as if she had not heard it. "Not at all, husband. I certainly didn't expect you to say anything, not even when I told you I'm a poor man's substitute for the reaper."

His limbs shrunk, the scales fading, and Rhazien returned to his human form, standing naked in front of them and completely unashamed. He rubbed a hand across the back of his neck as a grimace twisted his features. "I thought bringing it up would pile onto an already difficult conversation for you."

Erissa rolled her eyes. "You're right. I didn't offer any natural way to bring it up." She looked around at their group, soaking in the faces of those who had come for her, and a frown settled across her brow. "Where is my uncle?"

Silence met her question as everyone looked at each other instead of her.

She turned to her mate. "Where is my uncle, Rhazien?"

"We left him behind, little doe." He grabbed onto her arms as her knees threatened to buckle, and she swayed.

"Kyrenic grabbed him as we climbed onto your husband." Yorrith's voice held great sorrow.

Panic clawed its way through Erissa's chest. "We have to go back."

"We can't go back." Nephinae's words were gentle but booked no refusal. "The portal is open, and Draven will escape. You heard Reeva. Whatever happens to your uncle now, we cannot prevent it. He is at the mercy of Draven."

Erissa looked between Rhazien, Nephinae, and Yorrith. Their faces carried the same hard resolve tempered by sorrow. "I can't leave him."

"There's nothing more we can do, Erissa." Yorrith placed a hand on her shoulder. "I am sorry."

Rhazien looked around the square, a brow rising in question. "Where are all the guards?"

"What?" Erissa stared around them. No guards were visible, the gates having been left open and unmanned. Would they not have come running at a dragon landing before the keep?

"It's too quiet." Rhazien stepped closer to Erissa.

"I'm afraid the silence is my doing." Yorrith tucked his hands behind his back, rocking on his heels as he cut nervous eyes at Erissa. "My army arrived ahead of us, it seems. I had hoped to beat them here. It would have made the next part far easier on you, little one, especially with the loss of your uncle."

A sense of foreboding rippled along Erissa's spine. "What do you mean?"

"Nephinae." Yorrith nodded in the Zorathi's direction.

Indecision crept along Nephinae's face, but she swallowed, brushing her hands down the front of her dress, the emotion fading from her face as her power built in the tunnels along her skin. White light shot from the depth of the scars, braiding into thick ropes that shot across the square to strike Rhazien in the chest.

Erissa screamed, throwing herself toward him, but the Seelie King grabbed onto her arms and dragged her away from him and toward the keep. Her magic tried to rise within her, but it quickly petered out, exhausted from the fight with Virion.

She fought against him, scratching, kicking, and biting as she sought to free herself and run to her husband's aid. But Erissa's efforts were futile. Yorrith allowed his time magic to seep into his hands where they held onto her arms, and time sped up around them as Nephinae overcame Rhazien with her magic.

Erissa stared in horror as the Zorathi and her husband sped around her as she sat trapped in between time with the Seelie King who had betrayed them all. The Zorathi held the Fefnirion axe, using its power to bolster her own and keep Rhazien pinned to the ground beneath the onslaught of pure light magic.

The wooden double doors to the keep burst open. Fae soldiers poured from their depths to surround Rhazien as he lay crushed beneath the light of Nephinae's magic funneling through the Fefnirion void.

Erissa stood powerless, unable to even scream as she sat between the seconds of time as it sped up for everyone around her and the Seelie King. Yorrith gripped her arms hard enough to bruise as she kept fighting against him, and he grunted as she elbowed him in the side, but the action had no impact on his grip.

Imryll broke from the ranks of the soldiers, and with the help of Nephinae, they bound Rhazien's wrists in black-rimmed light, Nephinae's magic pulling the void from the blade to add to her power.

Time slowed as Rhazien still fought against them, but he did not hold the power to break through the activated magic of the void. It sucked his strength and vitality, leaving him pale and swaying as he knelt in the mud filling the square.

Yorrith finally loosened his grip, and Erissa turned around in his arms to deliver a stinging blow across his face. The Fae King bore it stoically, a muscle ticking in his jaw. Erissa pushed against him. "You bastard. What have you done to him?"

The Seelie King's mouth settled into a grim line. "What I must. There are things you don't understand." He tightened his hold once more and forced her toward the keep.

Imryll grabbed Rhazien with the help of another Zorathi, and they half-carried the subdued dragon as they trailed behind the King. Nephinae followed them at the rear, magic crackling along her skin as she maintained her hold on Rhazien's magic.

"This was your plan all along." Erissa spat at the King. "You never wanted to help us."

The King sighed, and Erissa did not understand the heartbreak that darkened his features. "I do what I must to ensure your safety. I no more want what will come next than you do. But a deal was made before your birth, and it is a deal I must honor on your life."

He gave her no time to answer. Yorrith dragged Erissa through the open doors and down the hallway to the right into a cavernous receiving room lined with Fae and human soldiers, though the latter stood away from their Fae counterparts.

Erissa fought Yorrith every step of the way, kicking and scratching as she tried to break free from his hold. But nothing worked. His strength kept her overpowered as he forced her forward.

She craned her neck over her shoulder, looking for Rhazien. He still lay half-suspended by Imyrll's arms as they followed behind her and the King. "What are you going to do to him?"

Yorrith's gaze flicked to hers, the sorrowful eyes full of worry as he considered the dragon's fate. "I was instructed to bring you both here. What happens next is out of my control."

The King brought her to a halt near the front of the room where a raised dais sat flanked by two throne-like chairs. Her parents flanked the chairs, and Erissa went rigid as she caught the stricken gaze of her mother.

"Erissa, darling." Vilotta stood, but she did not run to her daughter. Instead, she turned to regard her husband as she rang her hands.

Revulsion churned Erissa's stomach as she thought of Virion and his use of the endearment, and she set her mouth, refusing to give an inch as she ignored the guilt blooming within her breast. "Mother."

But Vilotta ignored how Erissa said her name. Her face blanched as Vilotta stared at the Fae standing at Erissa's side. Her hands shook, and she smoothed them down the front of her dress as her eyes flicked between her husband and the King. "Yorrith, what are you doing here?"

Bile coated Erissa's tongue as her gaze whipped around to the Seelie King. "How can you ask him that? He's my father, as you well know."

Yorrith's eyes held a burning hatred as he stared at her mother. "I warned you I would return, Vilotta."

"She isn't yours to take!" Vilotta's panicked voice echoed shrilly in the silence. "Please, Yorrith. Don't take her."

"You dare to defy the gods once more? After all you've done?" Yorrith dropped Erissa's arms and advanced on her mother, two of the Fae soldiers taking his place. "She became mine the second our bargain was struck, Vi. A child for your immortality that I would come for on her sixteenth year. My seed that grew within you. The seed you and your human husband begged for. After everything that happened, I gave myself to you—*my* child. And then you betrayed our bargain, hiding her behind these walls. Hiding her behind a witch's spells. You didn't teach her anything about who I am, who *you* are, or who she is, denying her birthright."

Erissa pushed against the hands holding her, straining to get free. "How could you do this, Mother? You locked me in that room for thirteen years to hide that I'm Fae?"

The room went quiet as a red haze enveloped the King. He approached the raised platform with measured steps, his words laced with fury. "Locked in a room?" The soldiers drew their weapons, readying themselves as the King bellowed. "You kept my child locked in a room for over a decade?"

A soldier stepped in front of Vilotta. "Do not think to threaten our Lady."

"Oslion, don't be foolish...." Vilotta stepped from behind him, placing an imploring hand on his arm.

"I would listen to her, human." The man leaning against the door casually straightened, his words cutting like ice across the room. "He might hesitate to harm her for the sake of an old love, but I won't."

CHAPTER SEVENTY-ONE

His voice curled down Erissa's spine, the coldness of it pooling low in her belly. He advanced into the room with a leisurely pace that conflicted with the quick intelligence of his gaze. She stared in fascination as those in the King's army backed away from his approach, their fists tightening around their weapons. The hands that held her let go when he came closer. Even the King took a step back, holding his tongue. The man smirked, a cruel tilt of his lips.

He didn't stop until he had moved a step beyond the King. "Come now, Yorrith. I grow tired of the delay. If you can't hurry things along, then I certainly will."

"Do not push me, Novus." Yorrith seethed but made no move.

Novus turned, lifting his shoulder in silent acquiescence. "Continue, your *Highness*."

Erissa observed the power play with interest; her stare transfixed on the man. *Novus*. She tested the name in her mind while taking in the tall, well-built Fae.

His face held the same youthful elegance as the other Fae in the room, the proud, harsh angles framing firm lips and a pointed, narrow nose. A shadow traced along his lantern jaw, his features framed by obsidian hair, the color so dark that blue highlighted its strands.

Erissa's breath caught as she reached his eyes. They glowed like hers, but instead of violet, she encountered slate-colored depths. The frostiness encasing his irises rendered them almost white as they shimmered like falling snow, reminding her of something.

He was breathtakingly handsome with his dark, icy appearance. Unlike the others, he carried no weapon, but he did not need one. Erissa sensed the power rolling off of him. The metallic taste of it touched her. As with his appearance, it reminded her of something—something tickling at the back of her mind—but she was lost in placing the familiarity. *Who is this Fae that can overstep a King and strike fear in his army?*

Faldeyr moved closer to his wife, taking her hand in a death grip. He dug his nails into her skin and snarled. "Quiet, woman. You will get us killed with this foolishness. There are other ways to get the bitch."

Vilotta shook him off. Her features were crestfallen as she beseeched the King. "One more year. Give us one more year, I beg you. We'll send her a year from the next snow moon."

"You had your year," Yorrith said, "Five of them when you refused to honor our bargain." Vilotta cried, sobs wracking her slender frame. Her knees buckled beneath the weight of her sorrow. Yorrith's eyes softened momentarily, his gaze unreadable before turning to steel. "She will leave today. The bargain decrees it. No witch spells can save her this time."

Vilotta turned to her husband. She crawled up his legs, bringing her hands to fists in his tunic. "Berthina! We must find her. It's the only way, our only hope."

Novus laughed, the rich brutality of it rippling across Erissa's skin. "Your Fae witch won't save your daughter. Isn't that right, Berthina?"

The Fae guard parted as one of their own brought forth an old woman.

Novus shoved her to the ground. Her hands shot forward to break her fall, her cloak exposing her forearms.

Vilotta's face paled. Seeing the tattoos on the withered hands, she lost all hope. "Berthina! What have they done to you?" She stared in horror at the old woman's face.

Once smooth, young, and beautiful, half of it lay in ruins of webbed scarring and the other in wrinkles. Her milky eyes locked on Novus as the witch stayed silent and rose from the ground.

Novus circled her in slow, measured steps. "Did you think we wouldn't know who cast the spells?" He stopped and trailed a finger down the destroyed flesh. Berthina cringed against the touch.

"Punishment for helping your betrayal," Yorrith spat at the woman sprawled across the floor. "We drained her youth, but she wouldn't betray you even then. I would have allowed him to do worse if I'd known my daughter was still alive. I thought she helped you hide her body, not her life."

"So you turned her over to him?" Vilotta flung an accusatory hand at Novus. "You would place her life in his merciless hands?"

"Come now, *Vi*. Did your actions leave your old lover with any other choice?" Novus's cold eyes snapped to Vilotta. "I sent her here once it healed. Your friend turned spy. A dead daughter was all too convenient, but even Berthina did not find a way to break her own spell—not when a bargain dictated the rules. No, we had to wait for the girl to do that herself. It took a little longer than I expected, but it allowed my little pet plenty of time to feed us information. It's amazing how loyalties change after a little torture. But that was not her only use. She never lost the Sight. Not even after I took hers. Do you want to know what she sang as I carved her pretty face?" He breathed against Berthina's ear, relishing how she trembled. "Berthina, pet, sing for me."

Berthina lifted her head, careful not to dislodge the fingers against her skin, and sang.

"Beware what lies behind the patterned wall
—the forewarner of death.
For there is no way for one to stall,
—'til only bones are left.
Her violet eyes are in their thrall
—even she cannot escape,
The destiny that dooms us all
—and the world she will reshape.
Hunted then and hunted now
—the last Warden heeds her need.
An alliance made in favored vow
—stands against a binding forged in greed."

Berthina ended the note, glancing nervously at Novus.

"Don't stop, witch. Sing a little more. Let them hear the prophecy. Let them understand." Novus licked the woman's cheek, smiling at the taste of her tears.

Her eyes flicked to Erissa. The words came louder this time.

"Her glowing eyes will see their souls,
—with whispered words they call,
An enticement meant to make worlds whole,
—or one to forsake us all.
He will come for her with no delay,
—the true king behind the wall,
A bargain made that will betray,
—she stumbles and will fall.
Fate cannot decide her will; for her alone, it bends
—her power will, in time, recall
The ways to destroy or mend
—or falter here, forevermore, with trouble to befall.

Life and Death, Sun and Moon
—twice blessed before the gods.
Three magics come that must—"

"Enough. We have to keep some mystery." Novus released the poor woman, turning to Erissa. "You are destined to be our salvation or our doom. But either way, sweetling, you are mine."

Fear echoed in the room as the witch quieted.

Vilotta once again tried to plead for her daughter, her desperation filling the air. "You can't do this. You can't take her from me."

"She is mine!" Darkness sprang from Novus and exploded around the room, devouring the light. The people gathered cried out in fear as a wave of endless dark forced everyone but Erissa and Rhazien to their knees, even the Zorathi. Several people begged for mercy, their terror permeating the air. Novus sniffed in disdain as they debased themselves before his temper. "Sniveling, weak things."

"Novus," Yorrith warned.

Novus addressed the King once more. "The Veiled One will be given as promised, Yorrith, or there will be war again."

Vilotta fought against the invisible bonds holding her. "Yorrith, no… you would give your daughter to him? You know who he is—*what* he is capable of, surpassing even his father, Tiordan, in his savagery—and you would throw her to him like a sick sacrifice?"

"Do you think I wanted to find her only to lose her? I have no choice, Vi. She is the Veiled One. This agreement was made centuries ago, and I do not have the power to break it. No one does. You know this." The King turned sorrow-filled eyes to Erissa, noting his features framed with her mother's raven hair. "The amethyst eyes mark her as surely as her powers do. A child born of both Fae royal lines—of day and night, sun and moon, Earth and

Time. A child of the Veil promised to Novus after the war. You know what she is. She must go to him. It is the only way to win the coming war."

Erissa's temper finally snapped. "I'm standing right here. You will not keep talking about me like I am yours to order. I'm not going anywhere. With any of you."

The darkness moved and gathered where Erissa stood, twisting itself around her, an undulating entity that caressed her skin. She quivered at its feel, the feel of him, for Novus was the darkness. His power. His fury. And something else. Something forbidden, something familiar. It moved like a second pulse ticking beneath her breast, an unbreakable connection. She tasted his anger like it were her own. And he was furious.

Novus stalked over to her, a predator considering his prey.

Erissa braced herself against the gripping magnitude of his power as he approached. The weight of it held her in its fury, its scent intensifying. The intoxicating blend of bergamot mixed with a tinge of cypress in an icy blend that forced its way around her senses like a familiar anchor, one she had always known.

Dismissing the guards on either side with a flick of his hand, Novus built his powers until the darkness spread overhead, wrapping the pair and shielding them from the rest of the room.

"You act as if you had a choice, Veiled One." His hand reached for her black tresses, wrapping several around his fingers until it forced her to move closer to him. "Much better."

Erissa held her tongue but refused to remain subservient to those around her. Her hand flew, striking Novus across the face with all her strength.

Novus brought his free hand to his cheek, running his fingers along the heated mark. His smirk returned, undaunted by her actions. He continued to wind the hair around his fingers until she stood with her chest brushing against his.

A sound of surprise left her mouth when he leaned into her. He brushed a feather-light kiss against her lips as she fought him. But with the scent and power of him wrapped around her, she swayed into him as he stepped away.

Inhaling deeply, the glow of his eyes sharpened, rendering them the color of the most frigid ocean before a storm. "I can smell him on you."

Color suffused her cheeks with his words. She was grateful for the darkness shielding them from prying eyes and ears. "That's none of your concern, or does your other cheek need a reminder?"

"Everything about you is my concern, including your relationship with him."

Erissa was kept from arguing with him further as the darkness faded, leaving them visible to the rest of the room. Rhazien called her name, trying in vain to fight the hold Imryll had on him and failing with his power drained. He might as well be human with his magic, unable to be called.

Yorrith snarled, his eyes locked on the hand wound into his daughter's hair. "Novus—"

Erissa cried out as the hand tightened, forcing her head back and exposing the choker she had worn for most of her life. She shivered as he trailed a finger across the pendant, the cool tips of the others brushing her heated skin.

"Clever, Vilotta. Clever. Your work, I assume. Berthina mentioned nothing about transmogrifying and suppression spells, did you pet?" Novus's eyes snapped to the witch.

Berthina shrunk away from him. She was quick to answer, her voice desperate with trepidation. "No! I swear it, I had no knowledge of another spell."

"It is of no consequence. The spells are weak." Novus's hand wrapped around Erissa's throat, digging the pendant into her skin, his words quiet as if they were for her alone. "I felt you all this time, flickering against my consciousness, even when there was no breaking through the spells on the choker binding you."

Erissa strained against his hand. "What spells?"

"Let me show you, Veiled One." Novus let go of her hair and ripped the choker from her throat. He threw it to the ground, grinding it beneath his boot and breaking the stone. Breaking the remaining magic.

CHAPTER SEVENTY-TWO

The pain of the stone's magic receding hit Erissa like a waterfall of pure ice. The cold burned its way through every inch of her, consuming even the breath from her lungs. She collapsed to the ground, trying to scream, to breathe, but neither happened. Every muscle in her body locked with the agony tearing through her.

Power unending exploded around the room from where Erissa lay, pushing her back to the floor with a force that came close to breaking her ribs while the glass of the windows shattered against the pressure. The door splintered where it had been struck by the wave of magic. Huge chunks of wood ripped from the grain, allowing those in the courtyard to witness the destruction taking place inside.

Erissa turned her head, catching sight of Rhazien as he fought harder against the Zorathi holding him, almost breaking free as she came apart before his very eyes. She reached a shaking hand toward him as her screams filled the air while a deep violet light burned along her skin.

Erissa's throat became raw, tasting of blood. She choked on the magic spilling from the deepest parts of her. Her convulsing body lifted from the ground with the force of the onslaught. Her muscles twisted against the brutal movement of the magic beneath her skin as the fatigued tissue knotted until Erissa struggled not to pass out from the pain of it all.

Through the brutal onslaught, she sought Rhazien. She managed a single word in between her convulsing muscles. "Please..."

Novus dove for her, pinning her body beneath him as the pure magic continued to pour from her. He flung out his own magic, a smokey mist of shadows, twisting it over Erissa's magic as he fought to subdue it before it killed them all.

The black of night entwined itself around the strands of purple light, the colors mixing until it was impossible to tell them apart. Novus panted with the effort of containing her, sending more and more of his dark tendrils to collide with her lighter ones. He attempted to press his power into her, but she halted him with an invisible force.

"You have to stop fighting me, Veiled One. Let my magic in." Novus framed her face with one hand. He pinched down hard where his fingers held her chin, giving a firm shake as he fought to break through the pain racing through her. "You have to let me in."

The abrupt motion startled her. Erissa's attention shifted to Novus's eyes, focusing on the frigid depths as she stopped fighting him and ground her teeth against the pain.

"That's it, Veiled One. Let me in." Novus pressed his power forward again, overtaking the purple light as Erissa forced herself to relax within his arms.

It blanketed her skin, slipping under it like shadows shifting across moonlit sand. The pain started to recede, leaving Erissa's true form behind.

Her eyes glowed brighter, ringed in the power Novus had pressed beneath her skin. It shifted around her irises as it continued to calm her magic. Tousled onyx hair shimmered around blush freckled cheeks framed by skin kissed by the moon itself. Her lips were fuller and richer in color, her features more angular, and the tips of her ears now tapered into soft points.

Erissa's gaze locked on Novus, uncaring of how different she felt. Emotion whirled behind her eyes as he stared at Novus, his presence the only thing keeping them grounded against her power's seductive pull. "I can hear them. All of them. Calling out to me."

"*Daughter of the Veil. Daughter of the Veil. Daughter of the Veil.*"

"*You must come. You must come. You must come.*"

"*Find us. Find us. Find us.*"

"*Guide us. Guide us. Guide us.*"

"*Help us. Help us. Helps us.*"

"*Free us. Free us. Free us.*"

"*He wakes. He wakes. He wakes.*"

"Can't you hear them?" Erissa's gaze grew frantic, the voices echoing as they continued to call with words for her alone.

"Quiet, Veiled One. All is well." Novus pushed a little more magic into her, using his darkness to create a barrier between her and the full breadth of her power.

Erissa gasped. His magic coaxed hers, the sound of its words comforting in the way it whispered to hers, calming its desire for freedom until the voices quieted and her power lay still beneath his.

The surrounding Fae witnessed the power exchange with growing incredulity, whispers breaking out amongst their ranks as they focused on what was taking place between Novus and Erissa.

Rhazien stared at them in horror. "How can she..."

Only Vilotta was foolish enough to approach them, abandoning her position on the platform and running down the steps by the stunned King. "No, it can't be! Yorrith!" The words tumbled out on a half-choked sob. "The gods be damned. We must do something. She can't...."

"It is blasphemy to deny what the gods decree, Vilotta." The angry words were at odds with the resigned expression Yorrith held. He reached for Vilotta, dragging her backward and away from where their daughter lay. "I cannot undo this any more than I can undo who—*what*—she is."

Vilotta sank to the floor before him, the tears consuming her. "All our planning. After everything we've done, none of it matters."

Faldeyr snatched Vilotta against him, shaking her hard enough to snap her teeth as he dragged her away from the king. "Shut your mouth, or I will shut it for you."

Erissa stared after the pair, her eyes filled with pain until a hand cupped her cheek and ensnared her attention.

"That was an impressive show of power, Veiled One." An indulgent smile spread across Novus's features, with his countenance almost proud as he stared at her for a long moment.

Erissa felt connected to him in a way she did not understand, connected in a way that mirrored her relationship with Rhazien. His magic brushed against hers in gentle passes that beguiled, the wintry feeling not unwelcome against the burning pain lingering along her skin.

"Come now. We've wasted enough time with your foolishness." This time, no bite hardened his words as he helped her stand. "The change suits you, even if your powers do not."

Erissa fidgeted against the backhanded compliment, focusing instead on the destruction her power had wrought around the room. She caught sight of herself in the glass shards littering the floor.

The last of her heart broke as she took in the changes to her appearance, pieces she feared would never mend. She ignored the glowing skin and pointed ears, focusing on her eyes. They were different, surrounded by black whirls that glittered almost as much as her hair, but all she cared for was the pain within them.

Memories flooded her consciousness, memories of a little girl with royally glowing eyes who frolicked with her powers like they were the dearest of friends. Each memory furthered that feeling of pain, showing Erissa what had been taken from her, the happy child at odds with the echoes of the crying young woman left alone and beaten in chains for so long.

Erissa buried the pain, tucking it into the furthermost corners of herself. She stared between her parents and Yorrith. No, not her parents. Her mother and Faldeyr. Yorrith stared at her with an aching tenderness while Vilotta and Faldeyr only looked at each other. Even now, her mother would not spare her a second of consideration.

The anger inside of her faded into a hollow ache. "How could you do this to me?"

Novus stepped closer to her side as the first tear fell. Erissa had an odd comfort in his nearness. Like she wasn't alone in the chaos of tonight's revelations. Her mind returned to Rhazien. She wished they were still in their willow tree, warm from the cold and away from all of this.

Novus snorted beside her, and Erissa cast him a curious glance before her attention returned to her mother.

"We had no choice." Vilotta's voice begged for understanding she did not deserve as she finally lowered herself to acknowledge the daughter she neglected. "We did everything to protect you."

Faldeyr stayed quiet, his lip curling with disdain at the changes in her appearance. The sneer remained overlooked by all except for two pairs of eyes; one set cold and gray and filled with death and the other golden and brimming with fury.

"A prison is still a prison, Mother, no matter how you justify your actions or Faldeyr's. And to make things worse, you gave me two prisons—locking me in that room and within that body." Erissa's softly spoken words cut as sharply as any blade. "Everything you did—it was for yourself, not for me. I know that now."

She ignored Vilotta and Faldeyr, turning away from them to address Yorrith. "And you're no better. Handing me over without protest after lying to me all this time. You're my father. Why won't you fight for me?"

"It is not as simple as that. There are things you don't understand, things beyond anyone's control." Yorrith pleaded with her, his eyes shining with unshed tears.

"You weren't coming to claim me as a daughter." The words soured Erissa's mouth. "Why come at all when you were always going to hand me over without a fight?"

Yorrith flinched with her words. He stepped in her direction, ready to fall to his knees in front of her, begging for her understanding. For her acceptance. But Erissa backed away from his pleading eyes and into Novus's arms. A feral growl came from behind her, its sound vibrating through her chest. Darkness curled around her once again, forcing Yorrith to a halt. He was nothing more than a shell of a man to Erissa for all he was a King as the daughter he had sought for years turned her face from him.

"Erissa," her mother called, "step away from him and come to me. This is where you belong, not with any of them."

Anger fueled her, the fury radiating through the intensity of her eyes. "You have no right. You left me there to rot, knowing what Fath—Faldeyr—was doing to me."

Vilotta refused to be persuaded by her words. "Do you have any idea what this cost us? What we've sacrificed for—."

Erissa's hand cut through the air, silencing her mother. "Do not speak to me of sacrifices when my life was the one forfeited. All those years, and you did nothing more than stand idly by while your husband beat a child for the sin of existing."

Erissa held back a sob, noting everyone in the room who had failed to protect her. The weight of their inaction threatened to drown her.

"Vi, tell me this isn't true?" Yorrith's voice broke. "I beg of you... tell me you didn't..."

Vilotta's eyes grew wide with panic. "I... I..."

"Enough." The single word from Novus booked no argument as the room fell silent. The authority, strengthened by magic, forced itself on everyone but Erissa and Rhazien, who continued to jerk against the voided manacles draining his strength.

Erissa tried to draw on her magic and force it to the surface to help her mate, but it remained out of her touch beneath the black shadows coursing through her. "Let him go." Erissa dropped to her knees at Novus's feet. "Please, I'll do whatever you want, but let him go."

"You would come with me voluntarily if I released him?" Novus placed a finger beneath her chin, making her meet his gaze.

Her jaw tightened, fighting to repress a shiver at the contact. Her reaction was as undeniable as the connection between them. "Yes," she breathed the word as if a prayer. "Please, let him go."

Novus studied her for a moment. His hand twitched at his side as she kept begging until he finally had enough. "He goes to the dungeons, and you will come with me."

"You may take me now, but you'll never keep us apart." Erissa smiled at Novus with utter confidence, speaking loudly enough to ensure Rhazien heard her. She knew him. He loved her as much as she loved him. "He will never abandon me to you. He will come for me as he always has. No matter where you take me, no matter where you imprison him, he will break free. Rhazien will stop at nothing to find me, and when he does..." Erissa shrugged.

Novus dropped his hand and laughed. The change in his appearance startled Erissa. The smile accompanying it made him younger and devastatingly handsome as the harsh angles of his face softened. He flicked his hand at the Zorathi holding Rhazien.

"Don't take him." Erissa tried to run after Rhazien, but they dragged him across the room while he continued to fight. Novus wrapped her in shadows, binding her from moving, but still, she did not stop. She had to reach him. "Please…"

The Fae guards standing at the door sprang into action as the ones leading Rhazien approached. As they tried to open the damaged door that led into the inner courtyard, it fell from its hinges. The thud of it hitting the floor echoed in the room, and Erissa flinched against the sound, finally staring at Rhazien's back as it retreated into the courtyard.

"How naïve you are, sweetling." Novus invaded her personal space, leaning into her, his lips brushing her ear. "What makes you think he will ever see the light of day again? A dungeon cell is all that awaits him, and trust me, as someone who has resided there… If I did not break out of its depths, there will be little your lover can do to escape its walls."

Novus left her no time to respond. The shadows faded as his long fingers wrapped around her arm with enough strength that it forced her to go with him. "I have grown tired of this." Sweeping his other hand before him in a gesture of mock servitude, Novus lowered his head toward Yorrith. "Until next time, *King*."

Novus pushed Erissa before him as he steered her to the door. She held her head high, refusing to show any more weakness in front of all the people who had hurt her. Erissa clung to the parts of herself that Rhazien helped her rebuild, telling herself she would not break even as Novus forced her to bend to his will. She would not break.

"Oh, but I can break you, Veiled One."

Novus's whispered words ripped through her prideful moment. "How did you know…?"

His lips tilted to the right. "Time enough for that revelation."

Novus did not falter at the broken door on the ground. He stepped over it, pulling Erissa with him.

Erissa froze as they reached the end of the stone pathway. He knelt in the mud, his hands restrained by Imryll and someone she didn't recognize standing at either side. Nephinae stood beside them, watching Erissa intently. Erissa's breath left her in one agonizing exhale as she cataloged the injuries inflicted upon him.

Every exposed area of golden skin lay covered in fresh wounds and blood. His eyes were ringed in red, the skin beginning to swell and blacken. His bottom lip was split and colored, with the blood still dripping from his nose. The homespun shirt lay in tatters around his shoulders, blood marring his torso in long strips that spoke of prolonged violence.

Erissa jerked against Novus's grip, desperate to break free from his hold and reach Rhazien. She stared at the two Fae she had come to consider friends, her gaze lingering on Nephinae's hardened stare. "What have you done to him?"

Novus's fingers tightened again, hard enough to leave bruising against her porcelain skin. "A cell in my dungeon awaits him, but that might change. Tell me, little Veiled One. Can you see his soul?"

Erissa ignored the pain in her arm, raising her gaze to meet the cold silver eyes of the monster beside her. "He's done nothing to warrant such a beating."

"Then he should not have fought the Zorathi." Novus gestured toward Rhazien with a flippant hand. "I am still awaiting your answer; can you see his soul?"

"No, which answers my questions about your intentions." Her shoulders dropped in relief. "If Rhazien's fate were sealed, I would be the first to know."

"Fate can be quite fickle, dear. It would make me happy to kill him. More than you know." Novus circled behind her.

Moving his hand, he trailed his fingers down her spine with the barest hint of a touch. She did not need to have him in front of her to see the savage smile curling against his lips.

Novus's hand stilled at the base of her spine. "Would it make you happy to see me end his life? Something tells me it wouldn't."

Then she saw it, the faintest flicker behind Rhazien's shoulder. She understood at that moment how Novus held his life in the palm of his hand. He spoke no idle threat but a promise of what would come if she made the wrong decision. "You continue to act as if my actions were my own when we both know they're not."

"Ah, but my little Veiled One. There is always a choice."

She was keenly aware of the men on either side of her—of Rhazien and Novus drawing her in drastically different directions—but she had no choice in which man she had to follow with Novus's threat hanging in the air.

"Then I choose Rhazien. Again. Always him." Closing her eyes, Erissa breathed deeply against the pain of the choice Novus forced her to make. She had been a captive before, and returning to that status churned her stomach. In the end, it didn't matter. She would gladly be one again with Rhazien's life on the line.

Even in this moment, she marveled at the magic that waltzed through the air as the breeze brought the scent of the night. The pungent smoke of oak fires mixed with the fragrance of the flowers—a standing testament of her powers against the still-warm stones of the manor walls.

She wanted to feel the comfort in the scent of the smoke. It had been a steady companion from within her room's hearth and again from the fires as she had traveled with Rhazien. She wanted to smile at the little moments of peace she had wrung from it when chained to those very stones, the peace she had created running away with Rhazien. But all the scent left was the collapse of her dreams as the warmed spice scent that was uniquely Rhazien fought against the smoke, the flowers on the walls, and the sharp coolness of Novus.

She shook off Novus's hold and stepped forward, waiting for him to reach out and stop her. When he did nothing, she kept walking until she reached Rhazien. In all her imaginings, she had never allowed herself to think of a moment without him—never believing they would one day be separated.

Rhazien struggled against the punishing grip of the Zorathi as they forced him to continue kneeling. His eyes traced over her changed features, still her in most ways, but sharper and gleaming with a subtle light that pierced the darkness. "Erissa, don't do this. My life is not worth going with him."

"Yes, it is, Rhazien. Your life will always be more precious than my own. I love you." Erissa dropped to her knees before him, uncaring of the mud. She brought her hands to his face, trying to summon her magic again through her fingertips the way Yorrith had shown her in the forest.

The small trickle of power surprised her as Novus's magic parted and allowed it to flow through her hand. The wounds knitted together, his nose straightened, and some of the tension left his frame as the angry lacerations across his body healed.

She cupped Rhazien's face. "Find me. No matter where he takes me, find me."

"I will." He leaned to press his forehead against hers, both of them clinging to an impossible sense of hope. "I'll find a way, little doe. I love you." Rhazien twisted his head, pressing a desperate, consuming kiss to Erissa's lips.

She wanted to cry at the feel of his lips, cry at the goodbye it symbolized. She gripped Rhazien's shoulders, her nails digging into his skin, trying to hold on to him. Glittering, black darkness swirled around her. It lifted her away from Rhazien and into the arms of the dark Fae Lord behind her.

Erissa's attention stayed fixed on Rhazien until the moment the dark magic blocked his stricken face from her sight, and she vanished.

CHAPTER SEVENTY-THREE

The opaque barrier of the portal rippled as it darkened with blood magic. The motion grew more violent with the barrier crashing against the bone-carved frame circling it. Cracking noises rent the air, the bones snapping underneath the fury of the magic.

Draven threw an arm into the air, protecting his face as bone shards flew in his direction. The jagged edges caught against the skin of his arm and ripped it open. No blood spurted from the wound as Draven hung between life and death in the depths of the Veil. It had been a millennium since pledging his bond to the Keeper, but the magic held firm. It bound him body and soul to the corrupt god lording over the afterlife. Draven was eager to do his bidding.

Footsteps echoed through the barrier as the magic continued to build, slowly shredding through the fabric of the world to create a hole between the living world and the Veil. The sound of their leisurely pace was broken only by the distinct echo of something wet dripping onto the floor.

Draven stiffened, his arms falling at spotting Drurrah, a bloodied sack hanging from one hand. Thick, congealed drops of blood soaked through the bag, leaving a tacky trail across the floor as Drurrah came closer to the portal. "You were not asked for today."

"Maybe not, but I'm all you have, I'm afraid." Drurrah moved to sit in the grand chair before the hearth. He crossed one ankle over the other, resting the bloodied bag against the curved arm cushion, heedless of how it ruined the fabric. "We need to renegotiate my involvement."

Laughter roared, bouncing against the weakening barrier. The maniacal sound halted as Draven's eyes narrowed to slits. "You think you hold power here?"

"Oh, I should think so. More than you, at least."

Draven choked on his fury. "Watch your tongue."

"Or what?" Draven waved his hand at the barrier. "You'll beat your firsts against the wall like a common animal. The barrier holds for now, and you will hear me out."

"It already weakens. I will not linger for much longer." Draven stared down at the blood still coating his skin, the warmth and stickiness long gone from its streaks. He brought his arm back to his face, inhaling the metallic scent he still remembered even after centuries of being locked in this prison. He drew his tongue along its path, the phantom taste driving him wild with blood lust, its own special kind of punishment as it remained unwashed and with the inability to add to it trapped as he was within the Veil. "Do you think I will forget such a slight after all that happened in the war? Lest you forget, you are part of the reason I am in this predicament."

"You'll get over it. It's been thousands of years, Draven. Time to move on from the past. We have a situation at hand, or I would not be in these gods-forsaken ruins."

The arrogance of Drurrah's reply created a beast in Draven. His eyes darkened into a glowing, bottomless pit of death, his breathing growing ragged as rage overtook him. Draven spat the words through gritted teach, "Enlighten me."

"There's been a change of plans." Drurrah uncrossed his legs, leaning to place the sack on the ground. He withdrew a severed head by its hair.

Blood, thick with death, continued dripping from the tattered flesh as if it had only just been severed. Drurrah threw the head to land at the base of the portal. It made a sickening squelch as it hit the floor.

Draven leered in disgust at the sight of his son's head. "What is the meaning of this?"

"Virion was overconfident in striking against the Veiled One unaided." Drurrah picked at the dry blood against his clothing, sighing at the stains that would never leave. "We underestimated your granddaughter, Draven. Erissa is more tenacious than I would have given her credit for."

"Interesting. And I have her to thank for this... development?"

"Could you not see what was happening through the portal?"

"The spell took time to weaken the barrier enough to see through. This magic is more complicated than other forms of blood spells, even now, we must wait."

"I have no patience for how long this is taking," Drurrah sighed. "The girl has no control over her powers, but her magic is impressive. You should have borne witness to how your son was wrapped in her thorny vines before the girl ripped the soul from him."

"How is this even possible?"

"Her lover's life was threatened. It proved to be great motivation." Drurrah's eyes cut to Draven's holding his gaze. "The boy's a Fefnirion half-breed. It was his void magic that led to your son's downfall."

Draven's lip curled as he stared at the head once more. "To be slain this easily—Virion is no son of mine."

"It was one thing to be up against the girl, but a Fefnirion as well? The odds are not in our favor."

"It seems the Creator has had a hand in things if there's a new Fefnirion." Draven's brow line rose. "All our planning and for naught. But no matter. Even the Creator cannot stop what happens next."

"I wouldn't be too sure of that." Drurrah leaned back and crossed his legs once more. "She's blessed before the gods. Not once, but twice. Each is a balance between life and death. One the sun, her half-breed Fefnirion. And the other, the moon, steeped in shadows."

"Shadows?" Draven pressed a hand against the large crack that was widening across the portal. He pushed against it, hoping the crack would give way and allow him to pass through. "You are certain of this?"

"Without a doubt." Drurrah inspected his nails. "Seems you're not the only one who's grown impatient in the thousand years since the war. He called in his bargain for her tonight."

"Novus." The name rolled off Draven's tongue like a curse.

"He power-shared with her in front of a room full of Fae and humans." Drurrah stood and moved to stand before the portal, uncaring of the blood soaking into his shoes with every step. "With Yorrith there as witness."

"So, he's claimed her. The prophecy and it's Veiled One with a Fefnirion thrown in for fun." Draven smiled, a predatory gleam in his eye that silenced Drurrah in its madness. "Oh, Reeva darling."

The beautiful Fae's soul appeared beside him, reluctance visible in her stiff posture and wary gaze. She bowed her head. "Yes, Lord?"

"I have a task for you." Draven's smile widened, morphing into something that delighted in cruelty as the portal into the Veil opened on a thundering crack. Draven stepped through the portal and into the realm. "You're going home."

About the author

Brittany Johnston is a college professor by day and a writer by night, crafting dark fantasy romances filled with plot, spice, and everything morally gray. Her stories take readers on a journey through flawed, captivating characters, weaving in magic and unexpected, darker elements. Through her writing, she explores the complexity of human nature, believing that the morally gray areas of life reveal the most fascinating aspects of humanity, herself included.

Currently pursuing a doctorate in English Literature, Brittany advocates for the power readers find in exploring lived experiences through darker themes and the acceptance of a broader, more nuanced understanding of love in literature. When not writing, Brittany can be found living along the North Carolina coast with her daughters and one incredibly spoiled pittie, enjoying game nights, watching K-dramas, and reading all hours of the night.

Printed in the USA
CPSIA information can be obtained
at www.ICGtesting.com
LVHW090051051224
798141LV00008B/42